Emma Cooper is a former teaching assistant, who lives in Shropshire with her partner and four children. She spends her spare time writing novels, drinking wine and watching box-sets with her partner of twenty-four years, who still makes her smile every day.

Emma has always want[illegible]ce child-hood, she's been inv[illegible]e being her imaginary friend '[illegible]w gets to use this imaginatio[illegible]ions.

Praise for [illegible] Cooper's novels:

'Beautifully observed, tender and genuinely funny'
Josie Silver

'Funny, original storytelling, an emotional rollercoaster packed with twists and turns that tugged at all my heartstrings'
Holly Miller

'Fans of authors Jojo Moyes and Lucy Dillon will love this touching read'
Hello

'A profoundly affecting, beautifully written story packed with heart and hope'
Miranda Dickinson

'An evocative, warm and character-driven read that is truly memorable'
Woman & Home

'A gorgeous heart-breaking rollercoaster of a love story that made me laugh and cry in equal measures'
Fiona Harper

'Quirky, clever, and original, this will break your heart, but put it back together again'
Katie Fforde

'This is a very special book indeed: funny, powerful, heart-wrenching and so poignant'
Jo Thomas

'A heartwarming, charming novel which had me falling in love and desperate to be part of their happy ending'
Olivia Beirne

Also by Emma Cooper:

The Songs of Us
The First Time I Saw You

EMMA COOPER

If I Could Say Goodbye

First published in 2020 by Headline Review
An imprint of HEADLINE PUBLISHING GROUP

1

Cataloguing in Publication Data is available from the British Library

ISBN 978 1 4722 6504 3

Typeset in 12.25/13.5pt Garamond MT Std by Jouve (UK), Milton Keynes

Printed and bound in Great Britain by Clays Ltd, Elcograf S.p.A.

Headline's policy is to use papers that are natural, renewable and recyclable
products and made from wood grown in well-managed forests and other
controlled sources. The logging and manufacturing processes are expected
to conform to the environmental regulations of the country of origin.

HEADLINE PUBLISHING GROUP
An Hachette UK Company
Carmelite House
50 Victoria Embankment
London EC4Y 0DZ

www.headline.co.uk
www.hachette.co.uk

For Jackie . . . who had to say goodbye.

Prologue

Jennifer

I always knew that I was different from the rest of my family.

They're all tall, blonde, waif-like. Mum doesn't walk . . . she glides. She is the type of woman that you would presume had been to finishing school, except for when she watches the football, when her true roots tend to fly from her mouth in a flurry of expletives. Even Dad has this elfin king look about him: gentle, elegant, commanding; it often feels that time slows down when you're around him, his words are always precise and measured, words that should be savoured. And then I came along. Their adopted daughter. I am short, dark, I don't glide, I'm heavy footed; my words don't need to be savoured, they generally tend to skitter and slide across the room like a puppy on a polished floor.

I know this description might make it sound as if I felt that I didn't belong, and that's not the case. I have always felt like I belonged to the Hargreaves; what I'm trying to say, is that when I look back on those early days of my childhood, the days where it was just the three of us, my memories don't quite feel . . . whole; those memories always feel like they are missing something, like I wasn't fully alive. I suppose my memories only feel whole from the day my sister was born, when my life truly began.

My younger sister is enigmatic and beautiful but also

quirky and lovable. She is the perfect mix of both Mr and Mrs Hargreaves.

Kerry is the name I gave her. Mr and Mrs Hargreaves – or Brian and Judith to their friends – wanted to call her Beth, but I had insisted, and for the first week of her life, she bore two names: one from her father and the mother who had given birth to her, and one from me. Kerry suited her much better: there is a perfect balance to her name, the beginning and ending lean against each other, just as she has always leant towards me. If you take the first part away from the second, there is no whole, just two parts that don't make sense when they stand apart. That was the first compromise I forced on my parents, the first step in our new dynamic as a foursome, right from the beginning . . . Kerry was more mine than she was theirs.

Kerry is one of those people who other people want to be. She's tall, beautiful but unusually so, like a model but more like one of the models where they make the headlines because they have an odd-shaped nose or really wide-apart eyes. Her blonde hair turned to grey when she was fifteen – there is no explanation why, no massive shock or trauma, it was as if her body just decided that she is different from the rest of us, that she should stand out. Kerry has always cut her fringe herself – poker straight – and has always worn the rest in a plait.

If Kerry were asked to describe me, she would say that Jennifer Jones is happy with her life. She would say that I'm happily married to Edward, the awkwardly handsome other half of me – the jam in my doughnut, as Kerry would put it. Jennifer is happy, she would say, with the way her children have turned out, a perfect pair – one of each, Oscar, five and Hailey, eight – who are both well behaved, polite and intelligent.

She would go on to say that I'm pretty. I'm not. I mean I'm not unattractive, I guess, but I have a gap between my two front teeth that I can roll a twenty-pence piece between, my hair is dark and heavy but whenever I have it cut into a bob, I always look like a Lego figure, and since turning thirty, I have this ring of chub around my waist that never seems to go no matter how many times I try to cut down my calorie intake.

'What are you thinking about?' Kerry's voice, soft and hoarse all at once – like she has the beginnings of a sore throat – interrupts my thoughts as she pulls up the handbrake in front of the carpark barrier and retrieves the parking ticket through the open window.

'Hmmm?' I question as she closes the window, cutting off the icy December wind, and rounds the car into the only free space, turning off the engine.

'You're looking off into space.' I drain the last of my coffee and return the cup to the holder.

'I was thinking about my fat roll.'

She laughs and shakes her head. 'You don't have a fat roll, you have a home-cooked, too many nights in front of the telly with my sexy husband, and not enough sex with my sexy husband to burn off my home cooking . . . softness.'

'How do you know how much sex I'm having?'

Her eyebrows raise as if asking her this question is ridiculous. 'I always know how much sex you're having . . . you get a flush.'

'I do not.'

'Ask Ed. Honestly, Jen, you should make more of him.' She winks and I stick my tongue out at her.

Kerry and Ed always had a flirtatious relationship; to those on the outside, I'd imagine it bordered on inappropriate. When we were at a wedding once, Ed and Kerry had been dancing to 'Mustang Sally'. We'd all had a lot to drink; it was one of those weddings that starts at the crack of dawn and doesn't end until the early hours. The drinks had been so expensive that we had nipped out to a local supermarket in our finery and returned with bags of wine hidden in our handbags. By 'Mustang Sally' time, we were all tottering around a two-day hangover. Ed and Kerry's moves were like something out of *Dirty Dancing* and I had sat in the corner watching them. Lucy – the bride – had leant in and with prosecco-soaked lips asked me if I was worried. I looked over to where Kerry was now leaning her body back while their hips rotated, Ed holding on to her waist, her hands on his, while her back arched and her hair fanned out behind her.

'No.'

'No?' Lucy arched her eyebrow at me, pointing to the dance floor with a lipstick-kissed glass. 'They're practically having sex right in front of you.'

Ed pulled Kerry up, both laughing as she looped her arms back around his neck.

'Ed's not her type,' I had countered.

Kerry clicks the central locking; I pull the collars of my coat up against the wind, as we begin walking into town; trust Kerry to go shopping two weeks before Christmas. I look up at the elephant-grey sky and wonder if we might be in for a white Christmas for once. Shrewsbury always looks beautiful in the snow: it's like the set of a Dickens adaptation, except with a shopping centre sandwiched between the Tudor buildings along with various high street shops.

'You're going to have to stop saying things like that once you're officially engaged, you know,' I say, bringing my focus to the job in hand. 'Nessa might not like you constantly flirting with my husband.'

'Nessa has watched me flirting with your husband since we met. Where did you say the new jeweller's is?'

The day Nessa first saw Kerry, she had been showing off on the ice. Kerry used to be a figure skater and competed nationally until she decided it wasn't the career she wanted. The first time they had met, Kerry and Ed had taken the kids on the ice; Nessa had thought they were a couple until, well, until Kerry met Nessa's eye over Ed's shoulder.

This brings us to the point of our trip. Kerry is going to propose to Nessa and I'm here to help choose the ring. Kerry's face holds still for a moment, her hand resting on my arm. There is an emerald ring on her thumb that catches the last of the sun before it disappears behind a cloud.

'What if she says no?'

I burst out laughing but check myself, because hidden in the confident poise, that is as much part of my sister as her blue eye colour, is a shimmer of vulnerability. I reach over and squeeze her hand.

'She won't. And then you can experience married life and I can get on your case for not having sex often enough.'

'Not going to happen.' She winks at me.

'No . . . I don't suppose it will.'

We continue walking, Kerry's red boots expressing our progress with firm, determined thuds.

'Being married shouldn't hold you back, Jen,' she adds.

'It doesn't.' I keep looking forward, even though from the corner of my eye I can feel her scrutinising my face. 'I mean, sure I'd like to be a bit more adventurous sometimes, but I like my life, Kerry. I'm not you.'

'I know that, but when was the last time you, oh I don't know . . . went on a roller coaster?'

'Last month.'

'I mean a real one, Jen, not the bloody pirate ship at the safari park with Hailey.'

'What's that got to do with anything?' I rummage in my pocket and unwrap a chewing gum, offer one to Kerry which she declines.

'You used to love them!' she exclaims as if me not going

to Alton Towers is the biggest regret anyone in the history of mankind has ever had.

'I still do, but me and Ed—'

'You and Ed need to stop putting You and Ed on hold.'

'We don't.' I flick my hair over my shoulder. 'We had a quickie last week while the kids were downstairs,' I say triumphantly and stop again to begin searching in my bag for my umbrella. 'Have you got a brolly?' I peer up at the swollen grey clouds which are hanging heavily above the high street.

'This is what I mean! It doesn't matter if you don't have a brolly, Jen . . . what's the worst thing that can happen? You'll get wet and your mascara will run.'

'I'm not wearing mascara.'

She shrugs her shoulders and gestures to the sky as if proving her point. It starts to drizzle; the rain runs in neat little droplets off Kerry's red coat, while it seeps into my beige mac. We continue across the zebra crossing while I pull out my phone and wake the screen to reveal Google maps. 'I think the new jeweller's is down one of the side roads,' I say. Kerry's boots continue to make their progress as I stop and check the screen. 'Hold on, Kerry . . . I think it's—'

And those are the last words my sister ever hears.

Chapter One

Jennifer

If a person could see me now, sitting on my fashionably grey sofa watching the latest blockbuster, they might be a little jealous. My home is tidy, perfectly finished, each room an exact replica of a page in the Next Directory. In the kitchen, the coffee machine gleams while my perfectly ironed tea-towels sit neatly in organised drawers.

But what they wouldn't know is that Jennifer Jones's sister died in front of her three months ago, and Jennifer Jones has just realised that, for those three months, she hasn't been living.

Not really.

I know I'm alive, but I haven't really been *living*. Being alive and actually living life are two very different things. I'm not explaining myself very well; I'll try and do better.

When you lose someone – when your life is turned upside down and you're left broken – grief clings to every part of your being: you can't see properly, you can't breathe, you can't speak, you can't eat, you can't sleep . . . you're living, but at the same time, you're not alive.

But the thing about realising you haven't actually been living life properly, is that when the fog of grief begins to lift, it makes you look at the world differently. And it makes you appreciate every little detail.

Take my husband. He is currently picking his nose. His index finger is reaching out from the freckly hand that held mine while I pushed our children out into the world, up into the nostril of the nose that I have kissed the end of, its sharp tip red and cold from the snowball fight we had in the small garden of our first home, and yet, even though he is now examining the findings of his excavation . . . my loins are on fire.

I think I can honestly say that I have never been aroused by the sight of my husband picking his nose, but aroused I am.

'Do you fancy an early night?' I ask him. He squints in response to my question, his right cheek rising and his head tilting as he no doubt mulls over my proposition. I can almost hear his inner dialogue: Why is she after an early night? Is she just tired? Why is she licking her lips like that? And why is she unbuttoning her blouse? 'In fact . . . why don't we have an early night here?' I say, my voice husky, a voice that belongs to a younger me, a thinner, less wrinkly, stretch-mark-free me.

'The kids,' he replies, swallowing hard as I take his bogey-free hand and pull it towards my hundred-wash-grey Marks & Spencer bra.

'The kids are asleep,' I reply, unzipping his flies and straddling him.

The next morning, I stare at the calendar, at the empty boxes that March has to offer – most days a blank space with a number hovering in its corner. I'm not really thinking about the calendar though, I'm thinking about Kerry. About the way that, three months ago, the electrical synapses in her brain misfired. I'm imagining a tumble of veins intricately woven in between the grooves of my sister's brain, I'm picturing the little arc of blue electricity as they ignited with

each thought, how perfectly they were working while my sister listened to me talking about the location of a new jeweller's. How they were sending messages to her body to make her walk, just in front of me, across the zebra crossing as the rain poured and I stopped to look at the location on my phone. How one of those little blue sparks flashed red, a smoky bronzed spark that reacted to the oncoming car, that rusty spark that made her push me out of the way of the car instead of saving herself.

I can still taste the mint from the chewing gum I had in my mouth, hear the conversation we had, feel the drizzle that was soaking into my clothes as I walked across the road. The image of Kerry flying through the air hits me: her body flying backwards, feet and arms in front of her as though she was just trying to touch her toes, blue eyes staring straight ahead: red coat, red boots and the screech of brakes. I let that image go as I exhale; the next breath in comes with the image of her hands. I can't remember making the decision to stop walking, I was too busy looking at Google maps, but I remember the feel of her hands and the pressure – like a punch – against my ribcage. I remember seeing them splayed against my chest. Her nails were painted silver and she was wearing a thumb ring – the one with the large fake emerald that wasn't on her hand when she arrived at the hospital; I spent hours the night of her death trying to find it amongst the debris lying beside the road: I never did.

I breathe out again.

In the past three months, I have managed to carry on, a zombie walking through life but not living it. Some people are consumed by anger, when they lose a loved one; that's where Ed focused his grief, anger towards the elderly driver of the car with the broken windscreen wiper, but I don't think I had room for anger; grief stripped me of feeling anything at all. A numbing pain had settled inside my body when I watched Kerry's coffin shining from inside a hearse. Looking back, I suppose I should have been grateful for grief's anaesthetic during those first few months because once the anaesthetic began to wear off the pain of Kerry's death suddenly exploded like pins and needles. Her loss consumed me for weeks. At first the pain was visceral, and I cried as it clawed at me, as it scratched and kicked: grief had its grip around my throat and had begun to squeeze. Some days when I woke, its grip was so tight that I didn't think I could breathe, felt that it would suffocate me, that my death certificate would read 'Cause of death: suffocated by grief'.

As time passed, grief's grip became a little looser, and the next day looser still; slowly but surely leaving me alive, leaving me with this gift: life. This gift is like a glass vase; its purpose is to be filled with beautiful things; it holds the sun's rays and splits it into a million different colours, a rainbow of possibility and directions. But if you don't hold it carefully enough, if it slides from your grasp, it will be shattered and lost: you will never be able to repair it.

This is where you find me, a woman who is somehow still alive, whose sister left her with the gift of life; I can't waste it.

I chew the inside of my bottom lip as I stare blankly at the calendar. There are a few appointments dotted about: there's a hair colour on the tenth.

Hmmm. I had better bring that forward. My roots have needed a bit of TLC for a few months, I've got to stop putting things off . . . also, I suppose my life could end before that and I don't want to have my roots showing in the chapel of rest. I pull out the notebook from my stationery drawer and begin a 'To Do' list.

When Kerry died, nothing was ready. She had no life insurance, no will, we had no idea how she wanted her funeral, why would we? She was only twenty-five. She and Nessa were just starting their life together.

Nessa stayed until the afternoon of the funeral and that was it. She didn't even say goodbye; took her daughter out of school, and just up and left. I never got to ask her about an engagement ring that was shining on Kerry's finger as the curtains drew around the coffin: a ring she must have chosen alone and slipped onto Kerry's finger in the chapel of rest . . . I think of that moment of vulnerability that Kerry had shown, the worry that Nessa might say no. Clearly, she wouldn't have.

I click the button of my pen.

To Do:

- Check life insurance
- ~~Write epitaph~~
- Make hairdressing appointment
- Write epitaph?

'Get a grip, Jen,' Kerry says. She is sitting on the kitchen counter, taking a bite out of an apple. I'm not crazy; I know she isn't really here. I keep replaying old memories, like this one: this is a conversation we had when I had been Googling brain cancer after I'd found a tiny bald patch left over after a spot on my scalp. 'Get a grip, Jen,' she'd said; she was sitting on my kitchen counter and eating an apple. My subconscious also tends to embellish these memories, replacing parts of the conversation that I can no longer recall exactly by giving Kerry lines from films that I know she hasn't even seen.

'When you die, you will be an old woman in a warm bed.' My subconscious is not very imaginative and keeps giving Kerry misquotes from films I have watched a million times. That little beauty is from *Titanic.*

Oscar appears at the kitchen door. The blue of his eyes is bluer than I have ever imagined before. You will have to bear with me for a moment as I try to find the right words. Once you realise how precious life is, the world changes. As though for your entire life, you have never really understood just how magnificent the world really is. But the magnificent world pales in comparison to the beauty of the ones you love.

So, you see, this is why I'm having a hard time conveying to you the blue of my son's eyes. I'm not talking about the hue or tone of the colour itself, rather the innocence held within them. A crystal blue that's pure; a pure blue that the toxins of the world have yet to tamper with. The whites of Oscar's eyes have only a hint of the red veins that will map their way across them as life as an adult takes hold: late nights, too much caffeine or wine or take-away food. I find myself kneeling before him, my hand stroking his cheek as I try to count the tiny veins that have already begun to break the surface: a worry about a new teacher perhaps? The day Liam Butters pinched him during assembly? Small worries that will be forgotten by adulthood, but enough to break the perfect surface. How have I missed this? He rubs them, the blues disappearing behind skin so pale and perfect – tiny veins fluttering behind blemish-free hands, hands that still hold on to Santa Claus's promises and cup his ears as he listens out for the thump, thump of the Easter Bunny's paws.

'Why are you crying, Mummy?' I didn't realise I was; the heels of my hand wipe away the stray tears. 'Do you have a ear egg?' he asks, three determinedly separate words.

'Yes, sweetie.' I stand, wipe my hands on the legs of my jeans and take a deep breath. 'Mummy has an earache.'

'You need some medicine from Dr Fow, Fow—'

'Dr Faulkner, dummy,' Hailey corrects as she walks into the room, yawning. She pulls up a chair towards the kitchen table, pushing the frame of her purple glasses up towards the bridge of her nose as she reaches for a box of cereal.

I have always thought my children are beautiful, but I now appreciate that 'beautiful' isn't spectacular enough; it doesn't sing when you say it. Hailey pushes her purple framed glasses and tucks her blonde hair behind her ears, ears that she has been teased about at school because they stick out a little further than The Norm, ears that I now see protrude just the right amount. If they were tucked closer in, you might not be able to see the small birthmark in the shape of an 'h' behind her left ear, the 'h' that made us choose the name Hailey rather than the Emily we had already decided on.

Oscar clambers onto the seat next to his sister as I fill his bowl with Cheerios, adding milk and sugar before turning and beginning to make sandwiches for their lunchboxes.

'Can we play Tumbling Monkeys?' he asks through a mouthful of milk.

'Mummy is busy,' Hailey sighs. The butter knife clatters against the counter.

Mummy is busy.

How often have I said that? How often have I missed moments to play with my children because I'm putting the washing out or making the dinner or reading a magazine about celebrities that I will never meet? Why should I care if they have split up when I could be playing with my children, holding them, making them laugh?

I hesitate, looking at the little Tupperware boxes waiting to be filled with nuts and seeds and dried fruit, looking at the pile of salad leaves, cucumber and ham. Is this more important than Tumbling Monkeys? I push the salad to one side, open the cupboard and reach for the chocolate spread, smearing it quickly over the bread and cutting it into uneven triangles. I wrap them in clingfilm, add crisps and an apple into their lunchboxes and turn towards them. Oscar has milk dribbling from his chin and Hailey is scooping out the raisins in her granola. Her systematic approach to eating has driven me to distraction before, but now . . . why shouldn't she eat things in a certain order?

I clap my hands together.

'We can play a quick game before school if you get dressed as soon as you've finished your breakfast . . . what do you think?'

'Yessss!' He shovels in his food, milk splurging out of the corners of his mouth.

'But what if we're late for school?' Hailey asks, anxiety creasing a path between her eyebrows.

'We won't be late . . . I promise.'

But we are.

I'm going to have to organise my precious time better than this.

Chapter Two

Ed

I was eighteen the first time I saw Jen. It was for a minute, max. I was on the train and a bloke was getting off with a bike. The noise of the handlebars had clattered against the doorway, bringing my attention away from the other side of the carriage where I had been studying a man's tattoo that ran along his throat, it was either a fox or an angry cat. Once the man and bike had landed on the platform, there she was. Her mouth was slightly open – like she was about to say something – and her tongue was resting in front of the slight gap between her two front teeth: her Madonna look, she calls it. Her hair was wet from the rain pouring down and her mascara was smudged beneath her eyes. But then the doors closed and that was that . . . it was three years until I saw her again.

During that time, she became a myth, a vision that I had built up in my head: The Perfect Woman. She became the star in 'The Woman I'm Going to Marry' story that I would regale over drinks in the student union bar. My mates used to get sick of hearing about the girl in the blue dress and, even though I'd never tell Jen this, I didn't believe for one minute that I would ever actually marry her. I didn't think I would be lucky enough.

I came out of uni with a broken nose (a result of falling

over a kerb while running down one of Nottingham's high streets in a pair of gold Speedos), a mediocre degree in marketing and a questionable penchant for army jackets. I moved into a small flat above a bookie's in town, let my dark blond hair grow into a tangle of curls and spent the next year trying and failing to find a job that I was good at. And then, on an unremarkable day, three remarkable things happened.

Remarkable thing number one: I went into a florist's.

I had never been in a florist's before, but it was Mum's fiftieth birthday and I felt that the usual box of Dairy Milk wouldn't cut it. I remember hovering by the door and thinking how pleased she would be to have an actual bunch of proper flowers for a change.

Remarkable thing number two: I hit a woman with a door.

You see, such was my excitement about finally settling on a present for Mum, I had opened the door into the shop – complete with tinkling bell – with more gumption than a trip to the florist's really warranted, so as the bell tinkled, it was immediately followed with a thud as the door connected with Jen's forehead. She was wearing a pair of dark blue denim dungarees and had been trying to do up one of the buckles. I remember her dungarees had tiny stars on them. That was my opening line: 'Well at least we can both see stars.' This brings me nicely to:

Remarkable thing number three: even after that line, the girl let me take her home.

The florist had guided Jen to a chair while I, flustered, ran into the Co-op across the road, garbling something about concussion, grabbed a bag of frozen peas and, inexplicably, a Toblerone. Even after that debacle, by some miracle, the girl from my story let me walk her home.

The reason I'm explaining all of this is because I never thought I'd have that gap in my life again, a life without Jen in it, but the past three months have felt like that. Like I have been waiting to see the love of my life again. And now, I think she's coming back to me. I mean, don't get me wrong, anyone can see that she has been here the whole time, still smiling at the kids when they did something funny, still functioning and keeping the house in this perfect state that has always seemed so important to her, but it's felt like she's been missing, all the same.

It was a shock to me when we first moved in together – just eighteen months after I hit her with the door – how a woman who grew up in a house filled with mismatched furniture and cupboards overflowing with board games seemed to want to create a home that looked like it was from a magazine spread. I tried to help at first, but my suggestions were always met with a look of alarm, a pull at the corner of her mouth. In the beginning, we tried to decorate as a team. She put up a shelf, I hung a mirror, both of us smiling as we created the beginnings of our home. That was until the bookshelf I had assembled collapsed, the picture I had hung remained slanted, no matter how many times I tried to straighten it, and the lamp blew the electrics out after I had replaced a fuse. The final nail in my decorating coffin was when the curtain pole bracket came away from the wall, and the curtain slid into a pool of material on the floor.

But whereas Jen is happiest with a duster in one hand and a hammer in the other, I am happiest outside. Gardening is something she hates with a passion. She would try to convince me that she liked it as much as I did, but after the first few months of living together, I swear she developed a permanent crease between her eyebrows from the look of scorn she would throw at the weeds and overgrown borders.

Life slipped into a routine of sorts; the inside of the house was pretty much Jen's domain, the outside mine.

*

I watch as Jennifer hums while making something involving mince. This is the first time she's cooked in months; cooking is another thing that she loves. I can cook, don't get me wrong – I mean, full disclosure, I did once burn a boiled egg, but that was before the Jamie Oliver cookbook – but I don't love it, not like Jen did. Does. Like Jen does. I smile as she hums along to the radio that is on for the first time in weeks; it's like she can finally see that our life will carry on without Kerry. She had me worried.

I'm sniffing the air appreciatively, hoping for shepherd's pie. Although we don't ever have lamb mince, so it's not really shep—

She is talking to me.

'Hmmmm?' I question, raising my eyebrows.

'What shall we watch later?' she asks, opening the oven door and turning her head away to avoid the blast of heat.

I didn't think I would ever get her back but here she is, a tiny piece of her at least. One of the hardest parts of watching and helping your wife grieve is when you're grieving yourself.

I loved Kerry. Everyone loved Kerry: she was beautiful . . . hauntingly beautiful, inside and out. When I say this, it's important you understand that I wasn't in love with her – I belonged to Jen the first day I saw her – but Kerry? Kerry was ethereal: pale skin, blue eyes that were . . . almost glacial.

The in-laws always said that Kerry was their miracle; maybe that's why she always seemed like she didn't belong on this earth. But I often think about that, I mean, if you've been told that your whole life, it would make you act differently, wouldn't it? Even though Jen was adopted, they never treated her any differently, but I often wondered what kind of effect that had on my wife. Hearing that your sister is a miracle . . . then what does that make you?

I mean, if it was my family, right, it wouldn't have meant much. Mum and Dad divorced when I was twelve, it wasn't as much a shock as a relief. My childhood always felt like a bit of an inconvenience to them, as though they'd come home from work one day and a baby had been placed in their care. Like a stray dog found on the streets: look after this little thing, will you? Just until it's old enough to look after itself? I moved in with Mum, Dad rang or visited once a week until I hit my mid-teens and after that, I just kind of got on with my life, while it ran parallel to theirs. They send birthday cards, they visit once in a blue moon, but my family was never how Jen's is. Or was. No actually, it still is: even though we've lost Kerry, my in-laws – Brian and Judith – still have a roast on a Sunday, still play board games with the kids, they still ring if they have a big day at school to wish them luck. I think that's why Jen has never wanted to track down her 'real' parents; she didn't need them. I feel more a part of their family than I ever did my own . . . and Kerry was . . . God I miss her.

'Ed? What shall we watch?'

This is the first time in a long time that Jen has shown any interest in our life. Sure, she has answered our questions, robotically ironing everything – even my pants, which saddens me; it's not a productive use of her time. I've tried to approach the subject of pant-ironing; I wish she'd take that time to do something for herself instead, like taking a long bath or reading a book, but, it seems, pant-ironing is a thing. A thing that helps her control yet another slot of time that she has to bear without Kerry. But asking a simple question that involves any amount of pleasure for herself is . . . new.

I hesitate before answering her. You see, the thing is, with living with someone who is still grieving, you have to avoid 'issues'. Take this question, for example: it's a minefield. I've got to be careful with my choice. No sisters and no car crashes. I'm starting to panic because she has her hands on her hips now, a sure sign she is becoming impatient . . . or eager? It could be eagerness. Pick something. Something funny? Maybe she's not really ready for comedy just yet. I'm taking too long; I just want my wife back, I don't want to lose this little glimpse of her. *Guardians of the Galaxy.* Genius . . . and she fancies that Pratt that's in it. Anything to keep her with me and not for her eyes to go blank and unfocused. With us but not really with us.

She looks at me and I worry that she knows what I'm thinking, but then something about her shifts. It's a split second, a second that nobody else would take any notice of, but it is like the haze has lifted and for the first time in a long time, I can see my wife again.

Chapter Three

Jennifer

'Are you having an affair?' Ed asks from the tangle of white sheets as I search the bedroom for my knickers. I laugh.

'Don't be ridiculous,' I reply, finding them flirting between Ed's boxers and a black sock on the floor. He rakes his fingers through his dark blond hair, short at the back, curls on top.

'Because I've Googled—'

'Googled?'

'Yes, I Googled: why your wife has started shagging you every chance she gets and why she has suddenly started wearing new underwear.' He shuffles up the bed and props a pillow behind his head as he watches me; the glassy haze that glossed over the brown eyes that drank me in just moments ago, now bright and alert – deep in the grasp of post-coital satisfaction.

'Don't you like my new underwear?' I ask, pulling on my red knickers and standing in front of him with my hands on my hips, my nipples, which at one time would face my husband straight in the face, now starting to cast themselves apologetically towards the floor.

'I LOVE your new underwear, your new underwear is my favourite, but—'

I fasten my matching bra and sit on the edge of the bed,

beginning to pull on my jeans. 'But what?' I glance at him over my shoulder.

'Well, the last time you wore matching undies was on our honeymoon so . . . why now?'

I reach for my hair bobble which has somehow found its way onto the doorknob and twist my heavy dark brown hair into a knot. 'Well, I'm heading towards my forties and . . . isn't that supposed to be when a woman reaches her sexual peak?'

'Women have a sexual peak? Men are always peaking.' He smirks, the right side of his mouth always a fraction higher than the rest of his lips. I'd forgotten about that. How could I have forgotten the part of him that I first found attractive? That and the way he appeared to saunter through life with ease, seemingly startled to find himself the main character in his own life.

I crawl across the mattress on all fours and kiss the right side of his lips, running my tongue over their familiar shape.

He pulls away from me. 'You're not dying, are you?'

'What? No! Of course not, why? Do I look ill?'

'That was the next thing on the Google list.'

Illness.

We're all going to die someday, and this is something that keeps playing on my mind. I know it's morbid, but I can't stop thinking about how it might happen.

I have been replaying the possible scenes over and in minute detail. The most obvious – and most likely – accident to cause my death would be by car crash, as I am, quite honestly, a terrible driver. When I picture myself on The Day of My Death, I see myself wearing a green top, as apparently green is blood-red's complementary colour, at least that is what it said in *Bella*. Ideally, my nails and lips will be painted in matching red too: I may be dead, but I want to look my best. My hair shall be held back from my head in either a ponytail or a chignon – if time has allowed – so that the paramedics have no trouble finding that I have no pulse behind my ear, and I shall wear the pearl studs in my ears that Ed bought me for our wedding.

The Imaginable Death of Jennifer Jones – #1

Death by Car Crash

Jennifer Jones's red nails hold tightly to the steering wheel as they try to swerve the car out of the way: the dog came from nowhere. Through the windscreen, the road, the shops, the faces of the families out for a day-trip all revolve: a kaleidoscope of colour and life blurring as the glass shatters. The car flips over and rolls two times. It stops moving: the sound of screeching metal is silenced. Her body is hanging upside-down by the seat belt, a small trickle of blood escaping the corner of her mouth, and the only sound other than the gentle tocking of the indicator will be the sirens in the distance.

Illness hasn't really occurred to me. I scramble from the bed and face my bedroom mirror; leaning forward I begin to examine myself. I pull the skin back from around my eyes, open my mouth, turn my head this way and that, but nothing seems amiss. The laughter lines around my eyes remain happy, the bags beneath them are not holding any excess weight; my blue eyes certainly don't hold the same innocence as Oscar's and with what I've just been up to with Ed neither should they, but is there something hidden? I whip off my bra and begin feeling around.

'You were not joking about your sexual peak!' Ed says, throwing the covers back.

'Shut up. I need you to feel my boobs.'

'Yes, Ma'am,' he says reaching for the discarded sailor hat and putting it onto his dirty-blond-coloured hair.

I frown at him. 'Not now, Ed. Feel. My boobs.'

'OK, OK, but you're going to have to clue me in a bit, Jen, is this like, *Fifty Shades*? Do I need a safe word, because, I'm all up for a bit of—'

I reach for his hand and he grabs my right breast. 'Can you feel anything?'

He glances down at the tent that is emerging between himself and the bed sheets. I laugh but then straighten my face. 'I mean in my boob, is there a lump?'

Ed pulls himself into a sitting position, his eyes narrowing, his expression changing into something more serious. 'No . . . shall I check the other one?'

I breathe a small breath of relief as I turn myself towards the left so he can continue examining.

'Nope. All clear. What is this about, Jen?'

'Nothing . . . I'm just being silly that's all.'

He lies down and I rest my head on his chest, listening to the reassuring thump, thump of his heart beating. *How would he cope without me here?* The image of me hanging upside down emerges behind my eyes: the trickle of blood escaping my red lips . . . *what if he finds me?* Ed pushes his way into the scene, calling my name, reaching in through the broken window, blood on his white shirt, panic across his face. I close my eyes and push the image away.

'Do you remember the first day we met?' I ask, my fingers circling the dark blond hairs on his chest.

'I remember the first day I saw you.'

'Tell me again.'

I know I've heard this story a million times, but I love hearing him.

He looks down and shifts his position, so I am lying in the crook of his arm. 'I saw you on the train platform. It was just a split second. The doors opened and a bloke with a bike got off. You were waiting on the platform.'

'I had a vile blue dress on.'

'That's not what I said. I said I didn't know how someone could look so beautiful in such a hideous dress.'

'I don't remember that part,' I say, my eyes filling with tears and goose bumps running across my arm like a swarm of ants. Another memory to cherish.

The sound of the key in the door startles us and we both bolt out of bed.

'Nuts!' I say, trying to reattach my bra.

'We're home!' Dad shouts from downstairs.

'Mummy!' Oscar's voice clambers up the stairs, his elephant-like step stampeding behind. Ed kicks his feet into his tangled jeans, leaning back on the bed in a flurry of denim and tanned torso.

'Just a minute!' we shout in unison.

'Oscar?' Dad's voice booms from the landing as the door flies open.

'Mummy and Daddy?' He clenches his fists by his side 'Why are you in bed?'

I do an over-exaggerated stretch and yawn, leaning my head backwards. I try to reply but in my exaggerated stretch I have leant back just enough for my hair to become snagged on my bra clasp. And so my red-lace-encased bosoms are now more vertical than they have been for the last ten years.

'We were just having a little snooze, now go downstairs with Grandpa while—'

This is the position I am in as my dad crosses the threshold to my bedroom.

'Brian!' Ed exclaims.

'Sorry! Sorry!' is Dad's awkward reply as I twist and turn, trying to untangle myself. Oscar jumps onto the bed and reaches for the sailor hat.

'Aye, aye, captain!' he shouts, putting the hat onto his curls.

'Good grief!' Dad replies.

'Dad, could you take Oscar downstairs, please?' I ask, addressing the ceiling as Ed lets out a yelp under his breath which coincides with the sound of his zip closing.

I tear a piece of my hair away from the clasp and my chin lowers just enough for me to witness Dad shielding his eyes.

'Oscar? Come downstairs with Grandpa—'

'What's this?' Oscar reaches for a 'toy' that has revealed itself from between the sheets.

'Noo!' I screech as Ed limps over and takes the offending item out of Oscar's reach.

Dad marches over to him, picks him up and takes a perplexed five-year-old down the stairs, the door closing behind him. Ed and I look at each other and burst out laughing.

'Help me get this untangled, will you?' I ask. He stands behind me, his fingers working intricately as he pulls the rest of my hair free. We stand opposite the mirror, his arms folding around my waist, my head leaning back against his chest.

'I meant it, you know . . .' he says to our reflection as he kisses my shoulder. 'You are beautiful.'

'You're not bad yourself,' I smile back, the mirror framing this moment in time.

Chapter Four

Jennifer

I select the photo icon on my phone, taking time to make sure I can get the letters engraved on her black granite headstone to fit into the shot along with the daffodils that are just starting to bloom. They are arranged alongside the plastic sunflowers – Kerry's favourite – which remain in the glass urn. I hope using fake flowers is OK; Kerry always had fake flowers around her house, she could never keep anything alive . . . including herself.

I get myself back into position and tap the screen. The fake shutter sound sends a flock of pigeons scattering on their way.

'*You did not just do that?!*' Kerry exclaims as she drains the last of her coffee from the Starbucks travel cup that I bought her for her birthday. This memory is from when I had taken the time to arrange a bunch of flowers for Mum and Dad's anniversary picnic and been so proud that I had posted a photo of them on Facebook. Kerry had been appalled by my actions. She had grabbed her phone from her ripped-jeaned pocket and insisted we pull funny faces: me cross-eyed and cheeks puffed out, her gurning with her tongue sticking out to post immediately in case people thought I had actually turned into our mother.

What? I reply defensively. When I say reply, I mean in my

head. I'm not talking out loud to a memory of my sister . . . that would just be weird. I think the flowers look nice. Just because it's a grave, doesn't mean it can't look nice.

'I detest the word "nice".'

Colourful.

'Hmmm, better . . . how about resplended?'

Resplended isn't even a word, it's resplendent.

My phone alarm begins to chime a tune that verges on an Argentine tango. 'Pants!' I gather my trowel and plastic bag filled with weeds. This is the third time this week that I've not noticed the time and almost been late for picking up the kids.

I make it to the playground just as Oscar's class is being released. His face lights up as he spots me, navy-blue book bag swinging in his hand as he storms across the tarmac and into my open arms. Within moments, my arms are full of him, his smell erupting from beneath the faint trace of the inside of the classroom. Before I have untangled the PE bag from Oscar's shoulder, his mouth is releasing a flurry of information about the new class pet – a stick insect imaginatively called 'Sticky' – and how he got nine out of ten in his spelling test, which is OK because the only word he got wrong was 'spaghetti' and Daddy says that it isn't even an English word and Daddy says my teacher is stupid. Time will soon steal these runaway sentences; it will replace them with grunts and shrugging shoulders.

Oscar continues talking, and I make the appropriate noises of congratulatory praise, while extracting the half-folded newsletter from the handles of his bookbag, the residual smell of cheap soap clinging to the material, but I'm distracted. As Oscar continues with his stream of information about the school day, I'm looking at the woman standing towards the back of the playground.

She's thinner, her hair is longer, but it's her. Nessa: Kerry's Nessa.

They were such an unusual couple.

Kerry's looks turned heads no matter where she went, but you could pass Nessa in the street without a second glance; you could sit opposite her on a train every day and not notice that she was the woman who'd been sitting in the same place the day before. She is opposite to Kerry in every way: dark hair, dark eyes, olive skin, quiet voice, unassuming stature . . . alive. But when they were together, Nessa became someone different. You would notice the couple sitting opposite you on the train; you would notice the chemistry between them; it fizzed and flowed and ignited the light behind her eyes.

Her daughter, Erica, is slipping her hand inside hers. Erica is a tiny little thing, her long, brown hair is plaited neatly and rests on the back of the army-green coat that is a size too big for her, and they are walking away.

'Nessa!' I shout. She reacts by slowing her pace just a fraction, but then continues walking. My heart is pounding and my breath catches. Hailey is skipping towards me. Her shoes are on the wrong feet and her hair has escaped the clutches of one of her pigtail bobbles.

'Mummy?' She sticks her finger up her nose – a trait she has inherited from her father.

'Hello, lovely,' I reply, landing a hasty kiss on the top of her head. I crane my neck to avoid the heads and umbrellas that are blooming up into the drizzle.

'She doesn't want to talk to you,' Kerry whispers, unwrapping a fruit salad sweet from its wrapper, just as she had when we actually had this conversation last year. I had arrived unannounced at their flat and Nessa had been working late. *'Ness is in one of her moods, look, she's scratching the back of her head. She always scratches the back of her head when she is in a grump.'* I can smell the artificially sweetened candy, even though I haven't had any for months.

'Mummy?' Hailey asks as I try to hurry them along. Erica has let go of Nessa's hand and is running ahead of her.

'Hmmm?'

'Why are we walking so fast?'

'I thought I saw your Aunty Kerry's friend, Nessa. Oscar, has Erica come back to school?'

'Yes, and she lost golden time because she didn't finish her work. Mummy?' Oscar asks, his feet skipping along to keep up with my strides.

'Yes, poppet?' I ask as Nessa disappears through the gates.

'Did you know your skirt is stuck in your knickers? They are blue and spotty.'

I release the hem of my skirt, walk through the gates, and scan the street, looking over my shoulder. Kerry is in between the school gates, dancing and 'Singing in the Rain', twirling her ladybug-style umbrella while exclaiming how wonderful a feeling it is to be happy again. She jumps up and kicks her heels together. *'She'll talk to you when she's ready!'*

My memory replaces 'he's ready' with 'she's ready' because in reality the day Kerry was dancing in the rain was after Ed and I had our first fight. 'He'll talk to you when he's ready,' she'd said . . . and he did.

'Mummy?' Oscar's voice is becoming more urgent. 'You're hurting my arm!' I look down to where my hand is gripping my son, pulling him along.

I blink.

Mascara is stinging my eyes. 'Sorry, I—' Taking my hand away from him, I glance towards the road, where I can see Nessa looking in the opposite direction. 'Nessa!' I shout again, spotting her about to cross the road. She turns to glance at me over her shoulder, but the moment my voice leaves my mouth I try to pull it back, retrieve it like an excited dog on a lead, because behind her, Erica is running into the road.

Air holds tight in my lungs; the sound of the car horn and the squeal of brakes taking me away to the day that Kerry died. Kerry stops singing and instead, I see her as I do so often in my dreams, flying backwards, feet and arms in front, blue eyes, red coat, red boots and the scream of horns.

A sob is clutched in my throat; I bite down on my lip and force myself to swallow it; inside my ears I can hear the rhythmic beat of my heart, becoming louder as it quickens its pace, forcing the blood around my body, battling to get oxygen to my organs so I stay standing, stay breathing, stay alive.

Brakes are applied, expletives are launched out of the driver's window; Nessa catches them and slings them back.

'Can we go now?' Hailey's voice claps, waking me from my thoughts.

I look down at my children. They have gone from dry to saturated in what feels like seconds.

'Mummy? Can we go now?' Hailey repeats. Her voice is questioning, unsure and wary.

'Yes.' I clear my throat. 'Let's go.'

The kitchen is warm, clean and the task of making a simple cup of coffee should be reassuring, but I've just sent my cup flying off the counter.

In a flurry of activity, Ed and I begin grabbing dishcloths and pulling kitchen cleaning products away from their uniformed line inside the cupboard; tea towels are shaken free of the neat creases applied on a Sunday afternoon.

'Shit!' I shout as I crouch down, spraying the tiles with something that claims it smells of lemons but instead smells of something clinical and toxic.

Ed flinches as the word is expelled from my mouth.

'What?' I ask him; it's not as if I've never sworn before.

'Mummy?' Hailey interrupts from the kitchen, where

Oscar has folded into a fit of giggles. 'That language is unacceptable.'

I didn't even realise they were in the room.

I stand, throw the dishcloth into the sink and put my hands on my hips. 'Why?' I question.

Oscar's shoulders sink into his tiny torso as he looks at me and then back at Hailey, like he is watching something on TV from behind a cushion.

Hailey's eyebrows pull together and her nose wrinkles. 'Because that's what you've always said,' she complains. '"Bad language is unacceptable because there are so many other beautiful words in the English language that could be used."'

Oscar joins in and they both mimic me: 'Swearing is lazy.'

'Well . . . I've changed my mind.'

Ed raises his eyebrows and turns his head away from me in the same way as he does when I snap at him irrationally when I have PMT.

'Swearing does serve a purpose . . . it feels good. The words feel sharp in your mouth, like when you eat something spicy or sour. Try it.'

Ed's head turns towards me, a look of guarded amusement crossing his face as he leans his body against the kitchen counter.

Oscar giggles, covers his mouth with his hand and squeaks out the word: 'Poo-head.'

Hailey chews the inside of her mouth.

'Go on, Hailey,' I reassure; she looks towards her dad for permission.

He shrugs his consent, exhaling through his lips with a 'pfft'.

Her lips press together as she takes a deep breath. 'Shit,' she says quietly, her eyes widening with shock.

Ed sniggers from behind his hand.

'Butt-hole!' explodes from Oscar's mouth, who has now taken himself off the chair and is rolling around on the floor laughing.

'Crap!' shouts Hailey, 'Crap! Crap! Crap! Your turn, Mummy.'

'Hmmm . . .' I grin at Ed, whose eyebrows have shot up into his hairline. 'OK.' I nod to myself. 'But it is such a bad word that I will have to whisper it.'

Ed's Adam's apple bobs up and down; his face takes on a look of panic. 'Er . . . Jen?'

I ignore his concerns, the kids becoming still before I beckon them over. I crouch down so I am at their eye-level. 'OK. If I tell you this word, you must absolutely promise not to use it.'

Their heads bob up and down, eyes wide, mouths agape, teeth – white and pure – visible in anticipation.

Glancing over at Ed's worried face, I lick my top lip and look back at my beautiful kids. 'Promise?' They nod again. 'Cross your hearts and hope to die?' They nod again, Oscar's brown curls bouncing up and down.

'OK, the word is . . .' I pause for dramatic effect, the house holds its breath in anticipation, the boiler finishes its cycle, the kettle emits a quiet final puff of steam. 'Vladivostok.'

Hailey nods knowingly at the word she is sure she has heard through the closed lounge door amidst gun fire and action heroes. Behind me, Ed chokes back a laugh. 'Now, off you go. You can watch one more episode of *Tom and Jerry* then it's bath time.' They scurry out of the kitchen into the hall, whispering and giggling to each other.

Ed takes my hand, pulling me up. I loop my arms around his neck and grin.

'Vladivostok?' He questions, tucking his hands into the waistband of my jeans.

'I think it's a small town in Russia.'

He leans his forehead against mine, amusement folding into something else. 'Jen . . . is everything OK?'

I kiss his nose. 'Yes, why?'

'It's just that you seem a bit—'

'What?'

'Distracted.'

'I'm fine.' I pause. 'I saw Nessa yesterday. She's back, it seems. Erica was at school.'

'How was she?'

'I don't know . . . she avoided us.'

'I wonder how long she's been back. Shall we give her a call?'

I shake my head, remembering Kerry's words. 'Let's give her time. It will be hard for her.'

'Dad! Oscar won't give me the controller!'

Ed smiles. 'You're right.' He kisses me. 'I'm coming!' he replies, giving me a smile that doesn't quite reach his eyes, and then follows the sounds of battle coming from the lounge.

Chapter Five

Ed

Can I just take a minute to say my wife is incredible? I mean it. I've always pretty much thought that she's perfect anyway – see my earlier confessions about The Woman I'm Going to Marry story, but to lose your sister the way that she did and then come out the other side the way she has . . . well. It's pretty incredible, right? I mean, she's really starting to come back to us, she even let the kids swear! She wouldn't even let me say fart in front of them before.

And then there is the sex thing. I love the sex thing. It's a bit out of character for her to want it quite so much, but I'm not complaining about the sex thing . . . not really, but. No. I'm not complaining about it, that would just be stupid.

I'll shut up now, I think.

Chapter Six

Jennifer

I roll onto my front and reach for my cup of tea, blowing over the rim.

'What time are your parents picking up the kids?' Ed whispers. It is one of those rare occasions when I have been able to make a cup of tea without the kids being up.

'Nine.' I blow steam from the top of my cup and take a sip.

'Shall we go to the garden centre?'

'Mmmm,' I answer noncommittally.

'We can have a teacake in the café,' he encourages.

I roll my eyes.

'What? Teacake is my favourite.'

'It's just that—'

'What?'

'Well it's hardly making the most of our free time, is it? A teacake at the garden centre.'

'OK. So where do you want to go? Next?'

'Not Next.' I put my tea onto the bedside table and roll over.

'Let's go to a theme park,' I say.

He laughs. 'Sure.'

'I'm not joking.'

'And after that we can go skiing in the Alps?'

'Why do you always do that? Take my suggestions and make them sound stupid.'

'It is stupid. You're thirty, not thirteen.'

'Neither am I ninety.' I shuffle up the bed. 'Come on . . . when do we ever do anything spontaneous?'

'Well, there was shagging in the cupboard under the stairs last week.'

'I'm not talking about sex stuff, and don't remind me about that . . . I've still got a bruise from the door handle. We never go anywhere exciting, Ed. Remember when we first got together? We went to Spain without a place to stay, just a cheap ticket that we bought that morning, and by the evening we were eating churros on the beach, drinking cheap wine and talking and making love until the sun rose.'

'We were young then—'

'We're young now!' I get out of bed and stand nakedly in front of him. 'Look at me!' I stretch to the right, to the left; I squat up and down a couple of times while Ed sits up smirking. 'I'm not old, Ed,' I say finally, trying not to sound out of breath. I crawl back onto the bed while Ed flops onto his back. 'Come on. Let's go ride roller coasters until we feel sick.'

He throws his arm over his face. 'OK, OK . . .' is his muffled reply.

I climb on top of him and shower his face with kisses.

I am upside down; the world around me and me in it are fighting the rules of gravity. Momentarily, the sun breaks through the clouds, my hair is hanging from its roots and we – the passengers of this roller coaster – are all holding our breath, waiting for the moment that we know will come in the next few seconds, when we will hurtle almost vertically into the darkness below.

My life is in the hands of a machine and the myriad of people who check the nuts and bolts. I think of the responsibility of those who do the safety checks. I picture a man called . . . Trevor, who after a row with his wife (disgruntled because she has lovingly packed his lunchbox every day that week for a week without a word of thanks), spent the evening trying not to become more and more frustrated by her one word answers. Let's say the argument with his wife bothered him more than he was letting on and so he didn't get a wink of sleep. As a result, poor Trevor's head is pounding while he does the safety checks. Let's say Trevor stops mid-check to swallow a couple of paracetamol and misses the one bolt that has been working itself loose over the previous day's joyriding.

The Imaginable Death of Jennifer Jones – #2

Death by Roller Coaster

The bolt finally twists its last rotation. It falls with a faint clatter inside the mechanism that holds the over-the-shoulder harness in place while the snake of carriages slithers over the tracks. It enters its final trip, one last systematic stop to enthral its prey as they hang upside down, waiting for the final descent into darkness: passengers with hair falling like wisteria. For Jennifer Jones, time slows down as the rubber-coated arms open, releasing her body. Her upper torso leaves the constraints of the carriage, legs following, and then she's flying, her arms opened as if to embrace the ground rushing towards her. For the others still strapped into their seats, the horror they see is but a split second, a flash of limbs, a green top, a black ponytail followed by the scream escaping their mouths.

I blink.

My fear bleeds into the atmosphere and I scream. I can't stop thinking about the bolt unscrewing as I hurtle at eighty-five miles per hour. Fear grips me: my hands grasp onto their bar so tightly that I can already feel the aching in my knuckles, already feel anxiety creeping through my veins, stealing saliva.

I pull the man called Trevor back into my thoughts. I replay the scene so he doesn't have that argument with his wife; instead, he gives her an unexpected bunch of flowers to thank her for the little things she does for him every day. He makes cups of tea for himself and his wife, suggesting they open the posh chocolate biscuits, and then they have an early night. So when he wakes up bright and early, smiles as he picks up his lunchbox, kisses his wife and heads to work, he is extra vigilant when checking the nuts and bolts; he knows how important his job is.

I close my eyes, the pressure in the air pushing my hair backwards until the machine stops and I'm suspended – upside down – trapped in that adrenaline-filled static that shoots through our veins before plummeting into the darkness once again. I'm filled with adrenaline; it has awoken every single nerve ending in my body: the thrill of the roller coaster has made me feel alive.

I turn my head against the forces of gravity towards Ed, certain that he will be feeling some of the endorphin-filled high that I am experiencing, but his eyes are screwed tightly shut; his face is pale, not flushed with euphoria. I slow my breathing and watch his head jolting to the left and right, a sheen of sweat along his brow. Amongst the ponchos and images of My Imaginary Death comes a memory – it's distant, a conversation we had on one of our first dates.

'What are you most afraid of?' I'd asked, reaching for a piece of pizza as we sat on plastic seats, Italian music playing, trying to kid our brains into thinking this was genuine Italian fare.

'Theme park rides.'

'Really?' I'd replied. 'I love them.'

'I suppose it's because you have to trust so many people to do their jobs right.'

'Ah . . . so you have trust issues.' I grinned and bit into the dough.

Why hadn't I considered that?

I release my grip on the bar, push my hand against the force of gravity and clasp my fingers over Ed's. His thumb finds mine, rubbing it rhythmically.

'It's almost over,' I say to Ed above the screams and the air filling our ears and mouths . . .'It's almost over.'

Chapter Seven

Jennifer

When I was a child, grown-ups would tell me that I was just like my mother. I can see why: we both have thick hair that hangs straight and heavy against our shoulder blades, even though mine is dark and hers is light, and as I pass her the milk, I think about how our mannerisms are similar: we hold our backs straight, we laugh at the same things. But as a child I could never understand why people thought we were alike. My nose lifts at the end, hers is hook-like. My eyes are almond shaped, blue and wide apart, whereas hers are round, hooded and green.

When I found out I was adopted, I felt something change. Perhaps change isn't quite the right word: it felt as though something had clicked . . . like the way you get used to a door that never quite shuts properly, and no matter how much pressure you apply, no matter how many times you have tried the handle, it just never closes. But once I knew the truth, the door inside nestled against its frame, without fanfare or ceremony, just gently clicking as it fell into place.

While I begin the crossword, I worry that my children will have that feeling if I die before them, that inside they will always feel as though the door is ajar, that for my children, it will never click into place; I'll be gone.

'Jennifer?' Mum's voice interrupts my thoughts. 'Are you OK?'

'Yes, why?'

I look down at the crossword, my handwriting is capitalised, each letter formed with a determined point, the pressure behind the ink like a scar; three-dimensional shapes with depth to each indentation: one across reads 'FUCK'; seven across shouts 'BASTARD'; the 'd' descending into nine down reads 'DICKLESS'. It doesn't stop there either. From 'DICKLESS' the word 'SHIT' is scribed and from that 'TITS' is made. Mum has interrupted as my hand has begun to write 'CUN—'. I click the tip of the pen.

'I saw Nessa the other day.'

'Yes . . . I heard she was back.'

'Has she been in touch?'

'No. I'm not expecting her to be either. I'm sure she would want to—'

'What? Move on?'

'No. Yes. I just mean it will be awkward for her, and us, if she were to visit. What on earth would we say to one another?'

'I suppose so. It just feels weird, you know, that she will be close by but not close by, if you know what I mean. It'll be odd for the kids too, they got used to spending a lot of time together.'

I close the crossword page and begin drawing a pair of glasses on the front-page picture of a portly MP.

'Do you wish it was me?' I ask Mum. The words leave their confinement; they bound from my lips hitting Mum's face, marking it with two angry red blotches. She tastes the bitterness behind them and pulls her mouth into a knot.

'We are not having this conversation,' she replies, taking the pen from my fingers and scraping the newspaper across the table.

'I understand if you do,' I continue. Mum slams the pen

down, making the sugar cubes inside their bowl jump up, momentarily suspended mid-air in shock before descending back into sweet chaos.

'I loved you both equally.' Her voice is steady: a statement, not a clause. 'I would be mourning you in the same way.'

'I'm sorry.' I place my hand on her shoulder; her head nods in response. But the subject tugs me.

'If you could have your time with her again . . . would you do anything different?'

'No. I treasured every moment of my time with her from the day she was born. I was never supposed to have her in the first place, so any time I got was a gift. You can't let life slip through your fingers, Jennifer.'

'I'm not, I'm—'

The door slams on my sentence.

'Jen?'

'I'm in the kitchen!' I reply and turn to flick the kettle back on.

'Right!' Ed's voice announces. 'I've got half an hour before I have to get back to work, so brace yourself, wife of mine.' His voice becomes muffled, a sound that I'm guessing is stifled from somewhere beneath his clothing. 'I'm about to make your dreams come true.'

Realisation dawns as I halt my tea-making activities. 'Ed—' I try to intervene, but it's pointless because Ed is naked. Naked except for one of those cardboard cut-out celebrity masks.

'No!' shrieks my mother while I begin to laugh, a deep vibration that tickles and steals my breath and bends me over. Channing Tatum's two-dimensional smiling face is pushed backwards, the elasticated thread securing it, so that the mask now rests on the crown of Ed's head. His mouth is open wide, his eyes are bulging and a flush of embarrassment floods his cheeks.

'Judith?' he questions, covering his family jewels with the cardboard mask of my chosen alter-ego: Kylie Minogue.

'Edward, I was just going, I'll just, um, grab my bag.' She shields her eyes, but even in my incapacitated state, I can tell that she is taking in what I have long since neglected to appreciate: his broad shoulders, the smattering of blond hair that trails across his chest, leading down towards Ms Minogue's grinning face. 'I'll see myself out,' she continues, chewing her bottom lip. Ed reverses his bare behind, his bum cheeks quivering white globes beneath his tan line.

I follow Mum out through the kitchen and into the hall towards the door, her hand hesitates on the door frame as she leans in and kisses me on the cheek.

'Don't let me keep you from your afternoon delight,' she smirks as I close the door behind her. I hesitate past the doorway to the lounge, where Kerry is sitting on the sofa eating ice cream out of a tub. She scrapes the bottom with a blue plastic spoon that is identical to the ones we used to get at the cinema. Her lips pull the ice cream from the spoon, which she then points at me as she talks.

'*I never really got the attraction with Kylie.*' She taps her front tooth with the blue plastic, a replica of the day we went to see *The Notebook*. '*Rachel McAdams on the other hand . . .*' She winks at me in the same way as she had years ago. I'd been swooning over Ryan Gosling. '*He's not really my type,*' she had said. '*Rachel McAdams on the other hand . . .*' It was the first time she had openly talked about being gay; she would have been about fifteen, I think.

Channing walks towards me. 'Has your mother gone?'

'Yes.'

'Good, now come here, I've only got twenty minutes left.'

I look back to the sofa, where Kerry's image has been replaced by the crushed velvet cushions which are so big that we can't actually sit on the sofa with them on. I throw them onto the floor and pull my dress from my shoulders, leaving it pooling around my ankles as I lower myself onto the cushions. Channing struts towards me but I reach for him, throwing his startled face across the room.

'I don't want him . . . I want you,' I say, wrapping my legs around my husband's waist.

Chapter Eight

Ed

I know I wasn't going to complain about the sex thing and I want to slap myself in the face right now, but. I'm going to complain about the sex thing.

Like the other day. I thought, as Jen was making an effort in that department, then so should I, and I know she fancies that Tatum Channing – or is it Channing Tatum? I always get it the wrong way around – anyway, I like to think of myself as a sensitive lover, I've always tried hard to make Jen enjoy our sex life. And she has never once complained. Not. Once. But now she has me doing this and that . . . Ed move your head, up a bit . . . that's it. And then there are these orgasms that she keeps having and they're loud. I like that they're loud, it lets me know that she is enjoying it, but. And she keeps grabbing me. My boy. All the time, like even when we're having dinner. There I was tucking into my bangers and mash watching *Eggheads* and the next minute she'd taken hold of my boy and, well, my bangers got cold.

I can't believe I'm complaining about the sex.

Chapter Nine

Jennifer

My eyelids flutter open, guilt shaking off the remnants of my broken dreams. It is already light, even though I know from the beginnings of the dawn chorus that it is not much after five.

The sounds of my house engulf me: a warm blanket of the familiar. Oscar's snores, more like a man in his fifties after a night at the pub, Ed's breath escaping in rhythmic murmurs, the cars heading along the motorway, carrying its passengers towards a new day. I take a breath, assessing how bad it is this morning. The image of Kerry flying through the air is the first taste: red coat, red boots, brakes squealing. I push out that image with a long, measured breath, but as I inhale, the image of her hands grabs me: strong hands that used to grasp her partners' when she competed in national figure-skating championships. I breathe out again.

I brace myself for what comes next, because it always comes: The Montage. The Montage filled with Kerry's achievements, her body jumping and swirling across the ice, first as a four-year-old then, year after year, the outfits changing as she grows, as her jumps become higher and more elaborate, the film rolling as it pans to her at school, always surrounded by popular friends, always laughing. Then to her first dates with Nessa, their beautiful faces smiling at each other with hidden secrets, their love pure, exciting: solid. The four of us together on the beach, sunburnt shoulders, lukewarm wine, sandy toes, Erica and Oscar making sandcastles together, Hailey hunting for shells.

And then, as it always does, The Montage rewinds, the crystal clear high definition of Kerry's life switching to a grainy camcorder recording: me on the sidelines watching her skate, clapping and cheering as the medals were placed around her neck; making excuses not to join her bunch of school friends because I knew they just tolerated me. But then . . . there is Ed, he reaches his hand towards me and I step out of the grainy picture into the real world.

My feet take me into the bathroom, my reflection beckoning me towards the mirror. I take in the first hint of a tan, the splatter of freckles over the bridge of my nose; the blue of my eyes have life behind them for the first time in months; there is a sheen to my skin that has been smothered beneath grief and is only now starting to breathe.

I turn my head towards the bedroom, where I can hear Ed mumbling in his sleep. I replay our frantic lovemaking last night, thinking of all the things that I can do to make it better for him, to make it even more exciting.

Then I have an idea.

'What? I thought it would be helpful,' I reply, but Ed looks really mad. He's not the type of man who gets mad. But, all the same . . . he is mad. I start to feel the seeds of doubt about my notes on how to improve our sex life.

'You thought that by giving me a manual of do's and don'ts when we are at it I would be pleased?'

'But I thought that—'

He storms out of the bedroom and onto the landing, slamming the door behind him.

I scurry off the bed and follow Ed as he charges down the stairs.

'What is going on, Jen?' He throws the notebook onto the desk by the front door and runs his fingers through his hair.

'Nothing is going on.' I step towards him, reaching for his hand, pulling him towards me. Reluctantly, he follows, but when I guide his hand towards my bra he snatches it back.

'Nothing going on, Jen? Really?!'

'What? Just because I want my husband means there is something going on?'

'It's not that and you know it.'

'I don't understand why you're upset. You're always moaning that our sex life has taken a nose-dive since the kids were born.'

'This isn't just about the sex. I know how difficult it's been . . . losing Kerry.'

'Me wanting to have sex – good sex – is nothing to do with my dead sister!'

Kerry raises her eyebrows at me from over Ed's shoulder. I ignore her.

'If anything about Kerry's death has taught me anything, it's to make the most out of the life we've got. And life is too short for—'

'For what? Bad sex?'

'I'm not saying the sex was bad before—'

'No, you'd rather give me a list of Improvements.' He reaches over, picking up the notepad and waving it above his head, making the glass teardrops of the fake chandelier murmur gently against each other, with voices that chime. Ed scratches the back of his head. 'I'm going to pick up the kids.'

'Ed—'

But my voice is swallowed by the slam of the door, the whisper of the chandelier gossiping in aghast tones at Ed's dramatic exit.

The Imaginable Death of Jennifer Jones – #3

Death by Chandelier

Jennifer Jones stands beneath the chandelier that catches the sunlight inside its delicate hands. She is tucking her green T-shirt into her jeans when a small sound niggling her senses draws her eyes up. Above the light fitting is the attic, filled with cobwebs and Christmas decorations, baby clothes and school books . . . and a mouse. The mouse twitches his whiskers as he gnaws his teeth against the leads. He likes that he has to scratch away at the surface beneath his feet before he can get to the next level. Down and down he goes, each day revealing a new challenge, a different texture, a different lead . . . this is the last of the maze, the only one he hasn't got through. He knows he is close. The mouse stops for a moment, lifts his nose as an unfamiliar smell floats up through the new crack he has made. It smells like food: warm and inviting. Perhaps if he works even harder at this wire, he will be able to explore where the smell is coming from.

The gentle tapping sound stops, and is instead replaced with a groan, a screech. The teardrops of glass sway to one side; they panic, clattering against each other in disarray: we're sorry, they say, we can't help it. Plaster begins to fall like rain and she blinks back the chalky dust. Jennifer knows she should move, but the family of glass tears are falling, saturating her skin with tiny cuts, rivulets of blood coursing across the woman's skin, flooding the carpet.

I blink.

I'm being ridiculous: ours is only a small chandelier, the most damage it would do would be to give a nasty bump on my head.

I pick up the notebook and re-read my notes. Perhaps I was a little too direct with my suggestions.

'You went about that in completely the wrong way,' Kerry begins, peeling an orange.

Like you're the expert?

She ignores my remark. *'Nobody likes to be told they are doing something wrong.'*

I didn't tell him he was doing it wrong, just that it would be better if he . . . Never mind.

'You should have told him what he does that's right. What you like.'

I like that it makes me feel, makes me feel . . .

Kerry begins to put on her best Aretha Franklin voice and sings, '. . . *like a nat-ur-al womaaaan.'*

I laugh. I'd almost forgotten that she loved Aretha Franklin. How could I have forgotten that? The way that she would throw her head back and belt out the chorus while she was cooking, or driving.

'Sorry,' she says, popping a segment into her mouth. *'Carry on . . . it makes you feel?'*

Alive.

'Lucky you,' she retorts as tears sting my eyes.

Chapter Ten

Ed

What person likes to be told that they're doing something wrong in the sack? And how the smeg was I supposed to know that she doesn't like it when I kiss her ears? That it sounds – and feels (let's not forget that!) – like an eel slithering around in her ear drum. Well for your information, Jen, I don't like it when you, when you . . . OK. So I can't really complain about her in the bedroom . . . especially lately when she's become so, um, flexible, but I can complain about her complaining. Can't I?

Yes. In fact, that is what I am going to do right now. She's in the bath, the kids are asleep, so now is as good a time as any. I take a deep breath and open the door, but as the door swings open, I don't see my wife lying in the bubbles, a glass of wine by her side and a book in her hands. I see her sitting up, knees hugged between her arms as she sobs.

I sit on the end of the bath. I try to rub the top of her arms, but it feels like I'm tapping an old friend who has had some bad news. She needs more than that. I step into the bath behind her, fully clothed, my jeans sticking to my skin, the water rising until it is almost overflowing. I gather her towards me, wrapping my soaking, clothed arms around her. She lets out the tiniest hint of laughter and then the sobs take over her body.

Chapter Eleven

Jennifer

I open the door to let Mum in, but she is hiding behind a tower of brown cardboard boxes.

'Hello?' I greet her, taking one of the boxes and leading the way into the lounge. 'Are you moving in?' I throw over my shoulder as I place the box on the table. She lowers hers with an 'oof!' then turns to hug me.

'I thought it was time.'

'Time for what?'

'Time to go through these. Let's open a bottle of wine first, shall we? I think we'll need it.'

My stomach cramps as I realise what is in the boxes . . . Kerry's notebooks.

Throughout our childhood, Kerry had a pen in one hand and a notebook in the other. Kerry was never happy until she had excelled; she was always pushing herself to do more, to work harder, to get the perfect outcome.

I've drained half of my glass before I reach for one of the books. The cover is purple.

'She had this one for Christmas, it was in her stocking,' I say. My fingers run over the indentations made with her pen: '*Kerry Hargreaves 2002*'. 'She was wearing her lilac fleecy pyjamas and had a big gap in the middle of her bottom row of teeth.'

'How do you remember that?'

'She liked that she had a gap in her teeth like me.'

'Oh goodness, I'd forgotten that, she'd been furious when her new tooth grew . . . do you remember her trying to pull it back out? She'd tied string around it and the door handle.'

I open the first page; the writing blurs and I take a second to wipe my eyes, take another sip of wine and a deep breath.

'The best cartweel.'

Mum points to Kerry's misspelt word and chuckles.

'This was when she was going through her gymnastic phase,' Mum explains.

1. Starting positions - scores out of ten.
    Feet together - 4/10 I fell on my bum five times AND Jen is moody and wont cartweel today.
    Feet apart. 5/10 my legs hurt and Jen laughed and said I looked like a frog.

'I don't remember this,' I say, my finger sliding down the page to the 'cartweel' that scored the highest.

The Best Cartweel 10/10
    Starting position - legs apart (Jen said to point toes like a 'balrina'
    Top tip.*
    Legs strate
    Jen clapped loudest and is not grumpy so it must be the best of cartweels.

I top up Mum's glass and glance through the window where I imagine Kerry demonstrating her best ten-out-of-ten

* Top tip is circled in a pink highlighter

cartwheel. She's wearing a white sundress; if I was closer, I would be able to see sand on her feet . . . this was the May bank holiday last year. We were on the beach at Barmouth.

We continue drinking as we go through her best handstand: *against the wall; lasted 30 seconds. Only one scraped knee.* By the time we get to the 'crab position', Mum and I have drained the bottle. I suggest putting Kerry's scores to the test in that way where ideas like this make perfect sense after a bottle of wine, when without it, they'd sound ludicrous.

Ed, Hailey and Dad arrive in the garden. It's one of those freakishly warm days in April where you are kidded into packing your boots away, only to have to get them back out again the following day. As I am handstanding against the kitchen wall, Mum is counting and giggling; my face feels like it is turning puce. Dad stands next to Mum, their faces upside down from my vantage point.

'Are you drunk?' Dad asks, his voice slightly alarmed.

'I am!' she replies as my arms begin to jitter.

Oscar runs into the garden. 'Mummy, I can see your pants again!'

'Good Lord above!' Dad responds.

The alcohol and blood rushing to my head is starting to make me feel queasy. 'Mum? Can you help me down?'

But Mum is laughing hard and Dad has turned his upside-down head away from my very visible underwear. I try to remember which ones I'm wearing and with a moment of panic I remember that I hadn't had time to put a washing load on. The 'pants' in question are Ed's *Star Wars* boxer shorts, and so right now, there will be a – no doubt confused-looking – Chewbacca staring out from beneath my dress.

'Ed!' I shout, 'I'm stuck!'

'Stuck? What are you—'

I feel his warm hands around my ankles as he rights my position, a mischievous grin on his face. I hold on to the top of his arms as he begins laughing, nuzzling into my hair. 'Star Wars? That wasn't on your list of do's and don'ts. I don't suppose you've got a Princess Leia outfit hidden upstairs, have you?'

I bury my face in his chest and start laughing.

'I could peel off a few princess layers . . .' he carries on.

'Oh, shut up.'

'Do you want to feel my lightsaber?'

I hit him on the arm and straighten myself.

'What are all of these books?' Oscar asks, sitting at the table next to Hailey. Her head is already buried deep within the pages.

'They're your Aunty Kerry's notebooks.'

Dad has sat down in an exasperated state on one of the garden chairs and is wiping his forehead with a hanky. The glimpse of my underwear, again, has obviously taken its toll.

'Well, when I was a little girl like you—'

'I'm not a girl!' Oscar holds his nose and waves his hand in front of it like he's just smelt something bad.

'Oh, you know what I mean, silly. When I was little . . .' I raise my eyes and Oscar nods, confirming that this is a better description, '. . . your Aunty Kerry used to have lots of notebooks like these and she would do the most amazing things and write them down. I thought we could do some of her crazy things.'

He leans over Hailey's arm to read the contents.

'Skipping Songs that get the biggest number of jumps.

1. Down in the valley = Me – 15 Jen – 16
2. Cinderella = Me 21 (it was actually 22 but Jen says it didn't count because I got my foot stuck on the rope but it doesn't matter because Jen only got 19 so there)

‘What’s “Down in the valley”?’ Hailey asks, pushing her glasses up her nose and turning to me.

‘It’s a song you sing when you skip . . . don’t you do them at school?’

‘We’re not allowed to play with skipping ropes after Chloe almost choked Jamil with it.’

‘Oh. Well, I suppose with health and safety and all of that . . .’ My voice trails off.

Ed’s mouth opens and closes as though he’s about to add his views on health and safety but thinks better of it.

‘It goes . . .’ I continue:

> ‘Down in the valley,
> Where the green grass grows . . .’

Kerry joins in, as does Ed:

> ‘There sat Janey,
> Sweet as a rose.
> Along came . . .’

‘Johnny? Or was it Jimmy?’ Mum questions as she goes into the house.

‘Johnny,’ Ed clarifies:

> ‘And kissed her on the cheek.
> How many kisses did she get this week?’

‘. . . And then you start counting with each jump . . . One, two, three, four, five . . .’

‘Can we do the skipping song? Can I go and get my rope?’

‘Yes! That sounds like great fun!’ Mum announces, returning to the garden with another bottle of wine and two more glasses.

The afternoon passes in a haze of laughter as we work our way through the wine and skipping songs. Even Dad has a go, but sadly only manages to get three kisses from Johnny; Ed on the other hand is all kissed out. I look around the garden from behind my sunglasses, watching them all giggling and laughing, the flush to Oscar's cheeks and the way his tongue pokes out as he concentrates; the beam of pride as Hailey gets better with each try and the memory of my sister, watching it all from the tyre swing that hangs from the old apple tree at the bottom of the garden.

Today has been a good day.

Chapter Twelve

Jennifer

I have walked past these pop-up events that are held in the centre square of town many times. At Christmas, the main square is made into an ice rink; Kerry was part of the opening ceremony once. Today, it's a roller-boot park. There is a flat surface as well as ramps and rails for the more experienced skater, one of whom – a man dressed like a teenager, his thinning hair somehow holding on to a man bun – is making a very pleasing grinding sound. Toddlers and mothers are hanging on to the sides: laughter and tears, encouragement and worry. Just past the hangers-on are the speeders, the roller-booted elite, their boots from a specialist shop brought with them. In the middle are a few teenagers, half-way from childhood to adulthood, unsure if they should look like they're enjoying it or look indifferent. A little girl with her brow furrowed in concentration has just let go of her mother's hands and is moving forward on her wheels, the mother's face a picture of pride.

My feet continue to walk past, but then hesitate. Why am I hesitating? I'm on my way to a café, it has the most delicious wares in the window, and I promised myself that I'd have one.

'*Jen!*' Kerry shouts at me from within the rink, as she did so many times when I had been sat in the stalls doing my homework while she practised: spinning on one leg, her body blurring as the momentum of her spin took hold, her arms outstretched. She pulls herself into a stop, her face flushed, her eyes wide and her black AC/DC top skimming the top of her pierced belly button. '*You don't need that! You need this! Come on . . . you know you want to!*' She skates backwards, her legs crossing over each other seamlessly.

The teenage boy looks at me as I hesitate and scour the prices board.

'Thinking of bringing your kids?' he asks. 'Only, we've got an area sectioned off for kids with a foam party running at four till five. The little'uns love it.'

'Um . . . actually, no, I was thinking that I might have a go. By myself.'

His face changes into an expression that could be interpreted in a variety of ways. It's the type of expression that shows the thoughts behind his stubbly chin. The first that comes to mind is 'It's your funeral' . . . funny in the circumstances.

'Hurry up, Jen!' Kerry shouts.

'How much?' I ask.

The boy takes my money and directs me towards the wooden booth where I am to hire my boots. I ask for a size three and a half from the bored-looking teenaged girl, who gives me a size four. I'm about to raise the issue but she has already returned her focus to her phone screen.

I lace up the boots and try to move. My knees bend and I feel my body form itself into a squatting position. Kerry's memory zooms past me in a blur, her leg balanced out straight behind her. I try to pull myself up and begin to push my feet forward in little shuffling movements as I begin to gather some pace. I feel a grin creep its way between the creases of concentration and fear that have formed around my mouth.

It takes me a while, but I manage to do a lap, my balance improving with my confidence. I continue to circuit the rink, managing to take my eyes away from the ground as my speed picks up with my mood. My breath is becoming laboured but it's a good feeling, I can feel the endorphins popping around my body; I let out a little 'whoop' as I pass the teenage admission boy for the third time, giving him a smug smile. You see? I can do this, my face tries to express. But behind the teenager, and across the street, is my sister's fiancée. Is she her fiancée? Was she?

Nessa's skin is grey, and her hair is limp. She is pacing up and down repeatedly; the air around her pulses. Nessa's phone is gripped by white knuckles, her mouth moving quickly, as angry words push and shove each other, spitting out sentences and sucking in responses.

The glory I was feeling is becoming bruised as I find myself rollering (skating?) towards her, and the barrier between us. She stops speaking. Her eyes meet mine and for a split second I feel like the pain she feels is hammering against my head, clawing at my skin.

She looks away from me hesitantly.

'Nessa!' I shout, which is quickly followed with an 'ooof!' as I avoid a speeding toddler and crash into the barrier. I catch my breath and shout at her again. She glances back over her shoulder and continues to talk into the phone, her feet taking her away from me. Beneath me is a bolt holding a gate in place. I turn my head as slowly and inconspicuously as I can towards the teenager, who is looking in the other direction. My fingers slide the bolt across; I cough loudly to cover up the squeak coming from inside my palm and continue to slide the bolt back. I step out of the rink and begin to take tentative steps on my stoppers towards Nessa.

'Hey! Woman!' the teenager shouts. 'You can't leave the enclosed area with your boots on!'

I look back towards Nessa and speed up my tippy-toed, stopper-steps, towards her, whilst mouthing a sorry gesture over my shoulder at the teenager and pointing towards Nessa by way of explanation. But in my attempts to appease the boy, my wheels have somehow tilted backwards from their stoppers, and I begin to make haste.

The path beneath me, I notice, is made of recently laid smooth tarmac and has a distinct 'downhill' feel to it.

'Oh nuts.' I try to slow my momentum, while simultaneously calling Nessa's name. She has stopped walking and is staring at me with wide eyes as I career past perplexed shoppers, my arms gesturing wildly in strange semi-circles à la the Karate Kid: wax-off, wax-off, wax-off. Behind me, I can hear that the teenager has given chase.

'Neeeesssaaaaa!' My eyes widen, an expression of 'help!' and 'look out!' all in one. I crash into her arms, knocking her body backwards. We both land with a thud, on Wilko's doorstep.

'Are you OK?' I ask as she removes herself from my tangled limbs. The teenager has come to an abrupt stop and is removing the boots from my feet.

'Oi!' An outraged woman pulling along a material shopping bag has begun hitting him on the head with her handbag. 'You.' Thwack. 'Thieving.' Thwack. 'Little.' Thwack. 'So and so!'

The teenager releases my feet and tries to protect his head. I untangle the laces, pull the boots free and give them to the boy with an apology as Nessa brushes herself down. The woman stops her assault, registers what is going on in front of her and gives me a look of contempt usually saved for dog poo offenders.

The teenager and lady retreat and I'm left in my socks, which are odd, I notice, one red and one blue.

My arms envelop Nessa in a hug, but her back remains rigid, wire arms hanging limply by her sides.

'Come and have some cake,' my eager voice says, laying out the word cake like a travelling salesman: cake is the answer, it can fix you, the voice implies, you cannot carry on living your life without it. I gesture to the café behind me. She twists her neck from side to side, both of us ignoring the cracks and snaps of her ligaments.

'I don't like cake.'

Kerry is standing beside her, skates swinging from the laces looped over her fingers, while her other hand slips into Nessa's, her head leaning against her shoulder. *'Ask her for help, she never could turn down a lost cause.'* Kerry's smile is sad.

'A coffee? Tea?'

Nessa passes the phone between nervous hands and looks over her shoulder; for a moment I wonder if she can see Kerry too, but she's looking through Kerry's face, as though she is looking for an excuse not to follow me. Kerry steps back from Nessa and I replace her hand by linking my arm through Nessa's. She is covered in grey, in darkness; her body seems to be weighted, each movement hampered by something hidden, something dark. She detaches herself from my arm.

'I don't think this is a good idea.' Nessa steps backwards from me. 'I don't think I can just—'

The teenager returns to our side and drops my Converse at my feet without saying a word.

'Thank you and sorry—' I begin, but he has already turned back and is returning to his duties.

'Just one coffee?' I ask Nessa again. She gives me a short nod and follows me in, sitting herself at a table while I go to the counter and order two drinks.

'Get her a chocolate-chip cookie, she can't resist a cookie.'

I return to the table. Nessa is tapping it repeatedly.

'I've never been in here before,' I tell her, trying to force a conversation across the table along with her cookie.

'Me neither.' The conversation slides back towards me.

'Seriously? That's what you're going with? Do you come here often?' Kerry snorts from the seat opposite me, next to Nessa, spraying bits of chocolate muffin all over her blue-and-white-striped shirt: the shirt we had her cremated in.

'Where are you staying? Back at the flat?'

Nessa's skin pales as she breaks the cookie in half. 'No. I've left the flat. I'm renting a house. I put K—' . . . the name Kerry seems too hard for her to say and she gulps it back down, 'her things into storage. I'll take them to your mum and dad's when—'

'The dust settles?' I hear myself saying. The image of Kerry's ashes seems to float between us, like motes dancing in the sunlight, before gravity pulls them down and they crash from the air, landing like a mound of dirt.

She nods.

'How's Erica?'

'She's OK. I don't think she understands that Kerry is not . . . not . . . coming back. She was used to her staying over and then not being there for a few days. Even though I've tried to explain, she keeps forgetting and will ask if Kerry's coming over. It takes everything in me not to scream at her, you know?'

I nod my head, even though I don't know. Kerry's death has had the opposite effect on me; I can't bear it when I'm not with the kids. They are the ones who brought me back when I didn't think I would ever shake off the grief.

'Where did you go, Ness? After the funeral.'

'Dad's.'

'Scotland?'

She nods. 'I just needed to be away. From here, from you and Ed and the kids and Kerry's ghost, I guess.'

'Well, that's rude.' Kerry crosses her arms and wears a mock annoyed expression.

'Are you sleeping?' I find myself asking.

Nessa shakes her head, confirming the negative, her eyes meeting mine, a thousand nightmares and night sweats shared between us with one look.

'Are you still thinking about getting a job?' Nessa changes the subject. Before Kerry died, I had been looking into going back to work since Oscar had started school.

I shake my head, remembering how I had tried to fill in applications. 'I tried to, but when Kerry . . . when she died and I, well, I . . . it's a long story.' I dismiss my months of crippling grief with a waft of my hand. 'Are you managing to—' Work, breathe? Live? My mouth opens and closes, chewing on empty words: 'Work?'

'Not yet. I've written a few reviews but not submitted them yet, I think they may well be a bit crap.'

'The films or the reviews?' I ask, trying to make light of the idea that not being immersed in her job as a film critic for the local paper is normal behaviour for her, when we both know that her job is as much part of her as Kerry was.

Nessa drains her coffee and wipes the cookie crumbs from her jeans; they are expensive, ripped in all the right places, faded with expensive dye. Kerry had loved the way Nessa dressed. '*Dress messily, see the dress, dress beautifully, see the woman.*' I ignore Kerry as she manages to misquote both Coco Chanel and *Working Girl* in one go.

The vibration of Nessa's phone and the face of Erica flashing up from the screen attract our attention. Across Erica's smiling face are the words 'Erica's School'. Nessa's body folds, her shoulders slump as she reaches for the handset.

'Hello?'

I try to look like I'm not listening, which is hard when your dead sister is leaning her head towards your companion's phone.

'It doesn't sound good,' she whispers.

Why are you whispering? She can't hear you.

'OK. I'll come and fetch her.' She hangs up the phone. 'I have to go, Erica is acting up. She didn't settle in the school in Glasgow and now she's bitten another kid. Thanks for the—'

We both look down to where my phone has begun to ring: the words 'Kids' School' are flashing.

'Mrs Jones? Hello, it's Highbrook School here. I'm afraid Oscar has had a bit of a tricky afternoon and one of the other children has bitten him. Would you be able to pop in?'

Chapter Thirteen

Jennifer

I slam the door to my car, our vehicles inches apart. Mine is filled with family detritus: Hailey's sun hat discarded on the floor; Oscar's car seat; Ed's sunglasses; a crumpled-up parking ticket from a daytrip out. As Nessa steps out of her own, I consider this. Is the interior of her car filled with parts of her life with Kerry? A thirst creeps through me, an urgent need to yank open the door, to run my fingers over the passenger seat where Kerry sat, to open the glove compartment and find a lipstick, a dog-eared novel, a sweet wrapper. I try to quench the thirst with a well-meaning smile in Nessa's direction; I pull my eyes away from where, just inches away from me, is new evidence of my sister, new discoveries to explore, treasures to uncover.

As I walk by Nessa's side, the wind winds its way around her; it grabs hold of her scent and slides it towards me: soap, fabric softener, and Nessa. The smell caresses me, strokes my skin with memories of lazy summer nights in the garden, the four of us playing cards, drinking wine. I've never noticed Nessa's smell before; Kerry always wore the same perfume that she'd had since she was fourteen. For weeks she had saved her pocket money, frequented perfume shops, spraying them on her wrists, testing them out. Did they fit? Were they her? It lasted months, Kerry's quest for the perfect scent, and when she found it, she was never unfaithful, never cheated on it or flirted with another brand. It was a heavy scent, she only needed a small spray, but it followed her everywhere she went. When she started seeing Nessa, I thought that the perfume had changed a little, become fresher, less intense, but as I walk beside my sister's fiancée, I understand . . . Kerry's smell had changed, because part of it was Nessa.

I hover behind her, breathing her in, as she pushes the buzzer. I keep my distance; I try to concentrate on the creases on her white blouse, each line veering off: a map of her movements for the day.

'What are you doing?' Nessa's voice startles me and I realise that my nose is pressed towards her armpit.

Kerry bursts out laughing. *'Are you smelling my girlfriend?'*

'Sorry, there was a bee . . .' I begin flapping my hand about, clashing against the fabric of her shirt, chasing away the imaginary bumbler. Nessa frowns at me and side-steps away, firing a glance over her shoulder at me as the buzzer sounds and the click of the doors allows us access. Our feet tread along the corridor towards the reception office. The glass pane slides open.

Nessa clears her throat. 'Hi, I'm Erica Noble's mum. Vanessa Hill.'

It's strange to think that Nessa was once married to a man, once part of a couple other than 'Kerry and Nessa'.

'Ah yes . . . Mrs Hill?'

'Miss,' Nessa corrects.

'If you can sign in. Mrs Park will be with you shortly.' The receptionist indicates the waiting chairs with a sharp nod of her head.

I step forward. 'Hello, I'm Mrs Jones? I had a phone call about my son, Oscar?'

'Ah yes . . . poor little mite.' She glances towards Nessa

with a look of disapproval. 'He was very upset. I'll take you through. We thought it best to call as the skin has been broken.' She lavishes me with small talk, casting another cold stare at Nessa as we walk past.

I'm led into a small room decorated with stick-on stencils of inspiring words meant to encourage and enlighten young minds: Dr Seuss is the philosopher to whom they seem to subscribe. In the corner, sat on a school chair disguised with a soft blue throw, is my boy. Beneath his eyes and along the tops of his cheekbones are tinged red; it's almost as though he has been punched. I have seen my son cry, I've often been the cause of such tears when I've had to have a stern word about his bedtime when all he wants to do is play on his tablet, but I have never seen these angry crescents before and that stirs something in me. A rage that begins at my toes, making them curl: spreading like fire. I rush to his side, gathering him in my arms; he begins to cry again.

'I didn't do anything wrong, Mummy, I didn't do anything wrong,' he repeats, his voice hiccupping. I look to the teaching assistant sitting beside him as she begins to explain.

'Oscar tried to give Erica some of his chocolate bar.'

'Her tummy was rumbling, Mummy, I heard it. I thought my chocolate bar would help stop her tummy from rumbling.'

I look into his eyes, red and sore. I think about the new little red veins that will scar the surface of the whites of his eyes.

'It's OK, Oscar,' I soothe, kissing his head. 'It's OK.'

'She said she didn't want my stinking chocolate. And then she bit me, Mummy, bit me hard, look!' He stretches out his arm and pulls off the wet blue paper towel.

Beneath, is a purple bruise and a track of small incisions where her teeth have penetrated my gorgeous boy's skin.

Anger and compassion fight amongst themselves as the emotions flood through me.

When I found out I was going to be a parent, I thought about all of the wonderful things that were going to happen: I thought about the little booties, the soft blankets, the strange sterilisers and the tiny hand prints captured in plaster to be framed and put in pride of place on the mantelpiece.

What I never expected was this kind of pain. This overwhelming feeling of disapproval that can pounce on me unchecked. That feeling that bites before my brain has had time to justify my reactions, before I can rationalise that the child who has hurt mine, might not have meant to hurt them, that maybe my child did something first, that maybe, just maybe, it's not worth making a 'fuss' over.

Oscar's warm, sticky arms circle my neck and pull me in. 'I was trying to be kind, Mummy.' He leans closer to my ear, his warm breath making the hairs on my arms rise. 'And now my heart hurts.'

I swallow down the lump in my throat. 'It's OK. Mummy will fix that heart right away.'

Oscar is crying as I try to put on his coat the next morning.

'I don't want to go to school, Mummy.' He pulls his arm free and wipes his snot on the sleeve of his jumper.

Ed interjects.

'If that little bugger—' Ed corrects himself: 'If Erica gives you any more trouble, you punch her right in the nose, OK?'

'Ed! I'm not sure that is the best advice,' I murmur as I manipulate Oscar's arms into his coat.

'She's always been spoilt, Jen, she needs bringing down a peg or two. Nessa always gave in too easily, even when Kerry tried to tell her—'

'Yeah, well Kerry's not here, is she?' I snap. 'Cut Nessa some slack, we need to support her, not make things worse.'

'I have a tummy egg.' Oscar pleads, his lip wobbling and his eyes filling.

Hailey appears, coat on, the blue bows at the bottom of her plaits swinging. 'Can we go now?'

The walk to school goes better than I expected: Oscar is easily distracted by Hailey playing the Guess Which Disney Character I Am game.

'Do you have black hair?' Oscar asks.

'Yes.'

'Are you a baddie or a goodie?'

The questions continue, but as we near the school, it is me who is becoming anxious, it is me that is tightening my grip on his small hand. I kiss Hailey goodbye as she goes to the upper school playground, leaving Oscar and me watching the school doors with trepidation. They are opened by the smiles of the teachers and are flooded with small, eager feet in shiny shoes and swinging lunchboxes, the faces of superheroes and unicorns battling for the spotlight, but Oscar isn't moving. I crouch down and wipe away a stray tear with my thumb, but my thumb can't go with him through those doors; my warm arm won't be wrapped around his body, there to comfort him.

'Please don't make me go.' The words explode from his mouth: they are urgent, desperate, their meaning indisputable.

He catches a glance from a girl in his class whose steps hesitate; the swing of her pink lunchbox changes trajectory, the arc of movement slowing. Oscar inhales a deep breath, trying to stop himself from crying, trying to be a brave soldier, but a tear drops from his lashes. I watch it fall down his perfectly pure skin, over the curve of his cheek, tainting it with a track that shouldn't be there. The swinging lunchbox gathers momentum and passes us by.

'Please don't make me go.'

I don't want to make him go.

So I don't.

Chapter Fourteen

Ed

I'm not a complainer. OK, so I know I've only just been complaining about the sex stuff so I'm kind of contradicting myself, aren't I? But do you know how scary it is to have the school on the phone telling you that your children aren't there? How scary it is when you then can't get hold of your wife?

I can understand why she did it, I mean, don't get me wrong, I don't like my little lad looking so upset, but the fact of the matter is, well, that's life, isn't it? You get knocked down and then you get back up again . . . well, Kerry didn't, but you know what I mean. Life isn't easy, is it? Oscar needs to ignore the crap it throws at him, or learn how to deal with it at least. You don't run away to the river and feed him ice cream, and if you do, you don't just take him and his sister out of school without at least phoning in with a sicky.

This little episode has worried me for a few reasons.

1) Jennifer does things by the rules. She makes cakes for the school fair, she sews name badges into school uniforms, she keeps receipts in alphabetical and date order . . . 'just in case'. So why has she decided to not just break a small rule but a big whopping one?

2) She never makes a fuss. Once we went out and she ordered a steak sandwich where the meat was so tough, she was chewing the same piece for about five minutes before she spat it out. When the waiter came over and asked how the meal was, I was all for sending the plate back, but Jen, well she smiled and said it was beautiful. Telling the school when they finally got hold of her that her kids needed a day out, is making quite a big frigging fuss.

I spent three hours thinking my family were hurt, or dead or abducted, but do you know what was the most worrying about it? It was almost like, deep down, I was expecting it. That deep down I know that something is wrong with Jen.

Do you know how I found out that my family weren't dead? Instagram. Thanks to Instagram I have now made an excuse about a 'family emergency' and am currently exceeding the speed limit and on my way to Muddy Creek.

Which brings me to concern number three:

3) She didn't even care if people could see that she had blatantly taken the kids out of school. There they were, smiling on a grass bank, eating ice cream.

An hour later, and I am parking the car next to the small café overlooking the stream. It's where we always brought them when they were little: toilets, café, tadpoles, all within parking distance.

Jennifer is drawing a picture in the mud with a stick; Oscar looks like he is scouring the river edge for hidden treasure, his school trousers rolled up to his knees; while Hailey's plaits hang upside down as she handstands on the grass verge in the background, her school skirt somewhere around her shoulders. I sit and watch them inside the heat of the car, with the hum and soft vibration of the engine.

I was angry when I drove here. Angry at Jen. But watching them now . . . I'm thinking that maybe she has got it right. Maybe it's the rest of us that have got it wrong. Laughter catches at the back of my throat as Oscar chases Jen around with something either dead or very much alive; her hair is tangling around her, her cheeks are red as she runs towards a startled-looking Hailey who shrieks and hops along the stepping stones across the stream.

I open the boot, retrieve the football which had been rolling about in there for weeks, and lock the car; my suit and work shoes carrying me unsteadily to my family. Oscar stops his assault on the girls when he spots me.

'Daddy!' His bare feet and rolled-up school trousers run through the grass towards me; I pick him up with my free arm, spinning him around before replacing his feet back onto the grass, mud seeping between his toes. 'Mummy said I didn't have to go to school today so we came to Muddy Creek instead and look, I found a frog.' The frog in question is not as impressed by my visit as my son and is hanging limply from his grasp . . . I'm sure it's just rolled its eyes before giving me a resigned 'gribbit'. Hailey approaches me; her smile is uneasy and in opposition to her legs, which are skipping. Jen is smiling at me from the water's edge, her arms outstretched, opening up the scene like a page from a picture book: the sun breaking through the clouds, the small waterfall behind her catching the light and expelling rainbows, her expression saying, look at this . . . isn't it wonderful?

'Hello, Daddy. Are you cross? Mummy fetched me from class.'

'No, how could I be cross when you're all having such a lovely time?' I kiss the top of her head as Jen walks towards me. She is chewing the corner of her mouth, waiting for me to react to her actions. Oscar turns to Hailey, raising the frog and chasing her away; her squeals are half outrage and half horror. Jen stands in front of me, tucking her hands into her back pockets and rocking on her feet.

'Hello.'

Hello? I raise my eyebrows in disbelief.

'I'm waiting for you to tell me off.' She runs a finger along the top of her lip, a nervous tic that I'm not even sure she knows she has. Her eyebrows question me.

There are a hundred angry words hidden in my mouth: I want to tell her that two hours ago I thought she was hurt, two hours ago I thought I might have lost my family, that they could be dead. I smile at Jen; relief sags her shoulders as I pull her towards me and kiss her: two hours ago, this kiss wouldn't have felt this good. Seeing my kids wouldn't have felt this good. Life wasn't this good.

She wraps her arms around my neck and sinks into me.

'Ugh! Gross!' Hailey exclaims.

Oscar has turned his back and is running his own arms up and down, making kissing noises. 'Mummy and Daddy sitting in a tree, K-I-S-S-I-N-G.'

The warm spring sun stays out, my jacket and tie are discarded, my trousers are rolled up, and we spend the next few hours trying to catch frogs, eating chips from cones while our feet dangle into the cool water.

I'm lying on my back; Jen's head is heavy against my arm. The kids are climbing the oak tree next to us and apart from an elderly couple walking their dog, we have the place to ourselves.

'What would you be doing if you were at work?' Jen asks, her voice thick with relaxation.

I look at my watch. 'I'd be pretending to listen to my boss talking about the best ways to market hand sanitiser.'

'Hailey? What do you do at school at half past two?' Jen sits up, waiting for an answer.

'Ugh. Assembly with Reverend Coates.' She giggles and swings herself down from a branch.

'Oscar, no higher OK?' Jen shouts, turning onto her front and propping her head up on her hand. She leans in a kiss on the top of my nose. 'I'm sorry I worried you.'

I look into her eyes. A flippant retort about how she can make it up to me is on the tip of my tongue, but I somehow can't seem to say it. The panic I felt this morning still smarts.

'Don't do it again,' I say.

She nods her head. Just one short movement.

'Muuuuummmmmy!' We're both on our feet, rushing to the base of the tree. 'I'm stuck!'

'I'll get him,' Hailey announces.

'No!' Jen and I say.

'I'll go.' I look down at my bare feet and back at the gnarly bark.

Jen puts her hand on mine. 'I'll go, you'll ruin your work trousers. Oscar, just stay there, sweetie, I'll just put my trainers on.'

I stand at the base of the tree and look up to where Oscar is perched, his face grey with worry. 'Jen—'

I'm about to tell her it's higher than she thinks but she is already running towards me, her eyes bright, her hair being pulled into a ponytail. Jen tips her head back, and nods towards a heavy branch to the right and begins to climb. Hailey slips her hand into mine as we both watch, our necks stretched, and our heads bent backwards. Jen is moving quickly from branch to branch, giving words of comfort to Oscar as she goes. It takes only a few minutes until she is level with him, her feet in a stepping position, her right hand firmly gripping an opposite branch.

'Shuffle your bum towards me, Oscar, that's right.'

'I'm scared,' he shouts back, looking down at us.

'There's no need to be scared,' she laughs. 'Look, I'm right here. Mummy won't let anything happen to you.' Oscar begins to move, his body getting closer until his arms are clutched around her neck like a monkey. Jen climbs down like that until she can manoeuvre him onto a lower branch, his thin legs finding their footing until he is safely on the ground.

Jen is sitting on a low branch, her legs dangling down either side, her hair swinging forward as she claps.

It all happens so quickly: the crack, her claps stopping, her body, the branch plummeting, my movement. All of it must have lasted only a few seconds but somehow, I managed to catch her, she is in my arms, her head thrown back in laughter, my knees collapsing beneath the impact and her weight being held by my arms.

'Edward Jones! You are my hero!' She laughs.

The breath is knocked from my lungs and sweat is running down my back.

'Did you see that?!' Oscar is pulling at Hailey's hand. 'Daddy is like Superman!'

Oscar and Jen are euphoric. But, in Hailey's eyes, above the smile that she is wearing, I see the worry I felt at the beginning of the day reflected back at me.

We need to talk.

Chapter Fifteen

Jennifer

I wish all Saturdays could be like this. I love the smell of cut grass, the hum of bees, the—

'Jen? Are you listening to me? You need to tell me what's going on.'

I roll onto my front and reach for the glass of Diet Coke next to the rug. I smile as I lift it because there is a ring of daisies around the base . . . it looks like an Instagram post.

'Ed, you're like a dog with a bone. Nothing is going on. Can we not just enjoy the peace and quiet? How often do we just get to relax in the garden without Hailey asking to play a game or Oscar asking for food?'

The ice clatters against the side of the glass as I take a few sips; I feel the cool liquid descending inside my body towards my stomach. I replace the glass neatly into the circle of daisies and roll onto my back. 'This is why I asked Mum to have the kids . . . so we can talk.'

'About what? You've said your piece about me taking the kids out without telling you, I've apologised for that even though I don't think it's that big a deal.'

I pull down my sunglasses from my head and close my eyes.

'The Nash twins' parents are always taking their kids

out of school. The only difference is that I was honest and didn't lie and tell them the kids were sick. Next time I'll lie, OK?'

'It's not just that.' He leans up on his elbow and lifts up my sunglasses; his eyes are searching mine, a crease of worry pulling his eyebrows together. 'Talk to me, Jen.'

Kerry is sitting up on the corner of the rug by my feet; she is pulling down the straps on her top and rubbing sun cream in. I manoeuvre my foot so that it connects with her shin.

I don't feel anything because she isn't there.

'I don't know what you want me to say,' I reply to Ed, pulling my sunglasses back onto my nose. 'I miss her, that's all,' I say.

'I know you do. I miss her too. But—'

I kiss his lips and pull him towards me.

'Jen—' he murmurs as I push myself against him. 'Jen!' He untangles himself and moves his body back, running his fingers through his hair agitatedly.

I sit up. 'What?!'

'You can't keep doing this.'

'Doing what? Kiss my husband? Find him attractive?'

'No! Yes! No.'

'Well which one is it? Yes or no?'

'Both. You need to tell me what is going on with you. You've changed, you're like a different person.'

'Well of course I'm a different person! I watched my sister die in front of me. This time last year, Ed . . . do you know what we were doing? It's the third of May.' His eyebrows furrow, the date not ringing a bell with him. 'This time last year, we went to that festival in the park, the one with all the tribute artists.' His eyes seem to clear as the memory hits him. 'Kerry pretended to be pregnant and hid all our booze in her bump under the maternity dress.' He smiles at the memory, but I don't.

'Yeah, that was a fun day . . . what I can remember of it. I fell in some bushes, didn't I?'

'You did. Nessa had to pull you out while me and Kerry pushed our way to the front of "Take This" and tried to grab fake fat Gary Barlow's hand even though we found out after that he was in his fifties and was a plumber.'

'Good times.' Ed laughs.

And here is the problem. He can talk about this without ice creeping through his veins, without his breath feeling heavy in his lungs. He doesn't get it; he doesn't get what Nessa and I are going through. He is able to remember this and laugh and smile. He hasn't been glancing at his watch every few minutes and thinking about where he was on that day. I know that right now, as I'm having these thoughts, we were making our way to see Mick Astley, that Kerry's festival wellies were rubbing the back of the heels that—

'Oh for fuck's sake. Can you hear yourself? Get over it already. Seriously, Jen, you're thinking about my blisters. Can you hear how pathetic that sounds?'

'I miss her so much, Ed.' I hide my face further into his T-shirt on the verge of tears, but my tears turn to laughter because I'm remembering that while Mick Astley was never gonna give us up, Kerry had farted and was wafting her hand in front of her face and looking at the woman next to her dressed in a 'Frankie Says Relax' T-shirt with disgust, when in fact, it was Kerry who had dealt a silent but violent.

I retell the story to Ed. It feels good to be talking about her.

I sit up on my knees and wipe my face with the back of my hand. 'Let's go somewhere, Ed. We've got the day to ourselves, thanks to global warming it's as warm as the Med . . . let's pack a picnic and go somewhere.'

Ed shields his eyes from the sun. 'Where?'

'I've got an idea.'

My feet slip into my flip-flops as I go through the kitchen and into the bleakness of the garage. My hand slides across the wall until I find the light switch, casting artificial orange light onto the toolboxes and old board games until I find what I am looking for. I flick the switch back off, the board games and toolboxes once again hidden in darkness.

The AA *Map of the British Isles* drops onto the grass. Ed reaches for it with an unsure smile. 'I didn't know we still had this.'

I kneel behind him and cover his eyes with my hands. 'Do you remember when we used to do this?' I whisper into his ear, passing a drawing pin into his palm. My eyes follow the line of goose bumps crawling up his arm as he twists his head away.

'Argh, you know it gives me goose bumps when you talk in my ear.'

'Yeah but you like it really.' I pull the end of his earlobe with my teeth.

He grabs my hands from his eyes and pulls me onto his lap, kissing me on the mouth.

'Ow!' I shift as the drawing pin digs into my hip. 'You're supposed to stick that in the map, not me!'

'So I've been doing it wrong all these years? I'm not supposed to stick it in you?'

'Ha ha, very funny.' I reach for the map. 'Choose a number.'

'Sixty-nine.'

I roll my eyes. 'That wasn't predictable at all. Pick another.'

He chooses twenty-five, and I open the page showing part of Wales and return to my position behind him, once more covering his eyes as he plunges the drawing pin. I scurry to his side and scrutinise where the pin has landed. Pembrokeshire fills the page.

'Ooh. We've never been there, have we?' I ask.

'No, but—'

'What?' I tilt my head and smile at him. 'Come on . . . let's have an adventure. We've got the whole of Saturday to ourselves.' I scour the map and point to a coastal town, which I Google. 'Look, there are some beautiful beaches. We could go skinny dipping.' I wink.

'Jen?'

I turn to him. 'Look, it only takes a couple of hours,' I say, ignoring the doubt pulling at the corner of his mouth.

He puts his forehead against mine; unspoken words hang between us, lingering with our breath. 'Do you know where my swimming shorts are?' he asks defeatedly, and I grin.

'In the swimwear drawer,' I say, standing up and grabbing his hands.

'We have a swimwear drawer?'

'Who doesn't have a swimwear drawer?'

'I love you.'

'I know.'

Chapter Sixteen

Jennifer

I'm happy. This is the thought that mixes with trees, the hills, the breeze coming into the car through the open window that my arm is leaning out of. My reflection in the wing mirror is that of a young woman who is happy. Everything about her tells me this, like the laughter in her eyes as her handsome husband tells her a joke; it radiates from them as she watches in awe the hills that rise and fall around the road that is leading them to their destination. The car in front slows our progress; a small grey head only just visible through the back window suggests the driver is nearing a century old.

Ed swears under his breath; he hits the brakes again as we meander around a bend in the road. We clear the turn and Ed changes gear, the growl of the engine shouting its frustration as we pass. My reflection is laughing and shifting position until the reflection is no longer smiling back at me; instead, my head is leaning out of the window, the air pushing my hair back with the speed of the car, catching my breath as I 'woo-hooo!' out of the window. The elderly driver looks at me with a mixture of surprise and annoyance. Before I know it, my hand is erecting my middle finger up at her. I don't know who is more surprised, the elderly lady or me.

'Jen!' Ed's hand has grabbed my other arm as we pass the bonnet of the car and slide into pole position. I'm breathless, my reflection confirming this with a flush to my cheeks, with the rapid rise and fall to my chest. Laughter rumbles from within my stomach, the wind snatches it, my laughter cascading over the hills along the doors of the car, laughter filling the gaps of the trees and rising into the sky. I take a sideways glance at Ed, his anger dissipating with the snorts and gasps that have taken control of me. 'It's not funny,' he snaps, although I can see the beginnings of a smile in the way he is tugging at his bottom lip with his teeth. His eyes dart towards me as I wipe a tear away from my face. The muscles in my stomach are hurting, and the sounds from my earlier laughter are now just gasps and grunts. Ed's eyes are trying to remain stern, but his mouth – his beautiful mouth – is curving, his hand rubbing the beginnings of stubble until finally he begins to laugh too. 'You're outrageous . . . do you know that? You could have given the poor woman a heart attack.'

We continue travelling, both of us singing badly to the radio, until the signal begins to break up. The car slows as we approach a roundabout. I reach over as Ed turns the wheel, resting my hand on his thigh while he looks at the screen of the sat nav.

When we were first together, we always used to travel in this position. My hand behind the gear stick, resting on his leg. I look down at my hand: it looks comfortable, there is no tension in the muscles, their weight is leaving an indentation in Ed's beige shorts, beneath the fabric the soft hairs along his thigh are bending in submission. The indicator tocks and clicks back into place. Ed's now free hand covers mine, his thumb running over my skin. I stare at our hands. They fit. Would my hand fit inside another man's in the same way?

Would his hold another woman's with the same ease, each digit perfectly sliding into place?

If something happened to me, if I got hit by a car when I was crossing the road, would he ever find another woman's hand to fit? I stare at his fingers, the creases of skin that cover the blood pulsing in his veins. I pull his hand towards my mouth. I begin to kiss it, as a need to taste his skin – to devour this part of him – takes over me. His attention is taken from the road ahead and he glances in my direction, his eyebrow raised as I open my mouth and run my tongue along the length of his index finger.

'Pull over,' I instruct.

'But we're not far away—' He meets my eyes, the hunger in them unmistakable. 'Jen, we can't just—'

'Ed.' Tears have formed in my eyes and as I blink one falls along the curve of my cheek. I guide his left hand downwards towards the hem of my dress. His knuckles are gripping the steering wheel and he's caught between checking the mirrors and taking furtive glances to where I'm guiding his free hand. 'Please, Ed, pull over.'

He checks his mirrors again, indicates and takes us up a narrow side road and manoeuvres the car so it is parked behind an old tractor. I have unbuckled my seat belt before the engine has stopped, my mouth finding his, as his hand finds its place. He leans towards me, stroking my face with his other hand.

My climax is insistent and urgent, my eyes flashing open. Ed's eyes are scanning my face, an expression somewhere between understanding and concern. He takes my hand and brings it to his lips; his kisses are firm against my knuckles, as though he is trying to leave a mark. Then he grins. A great big face-splitting grin that splinters his skin into amusement and life. He kisses the end of my nose, slides back into his seat and starts the engine.

The car eases towards the main road, but our progress comes to an abrupt halt as the car we had unashamedly overtaken flies past, the grey-haired driver flicking a triumphant V in our direction.

Chapter Seventeen

Jennifer

I lean my back against Ed's chest, resting my arms on his knees as we watch the bunch of teenagers jumping off the rocks. Cliffs peer over the pool like toddlers fishing for tadpoles, each one pushing ahead, eager to get the best view. The water is an azure blue; the result of the minerals left from the mine. The mine that now fills the lives of the people who live here with joy, rather than the pain that would have beset the workers.

The beach towel beneath me ruffles as I reach forward and grab a strawberry, take a bite and then pass it over my shoulder for Ed to eat the rest. He's been quiet since we arrived. If Kerry were here, she would have been standing next to us, her hand – flat and steady – shielding her eyes from the sun as they track the descent of one of the cliff divers.

Lovers' Leap is a ledge that juts out just that bit more eagerly than the rest. It seems to be that 'the lovers' kiss each other before jumping off either side of the shelf that overhangs the blue depths below. The drop is only that of a few metres, about five I'd say, but then again, Ed is always telling me that my spatial awareness is a constant source of confusion to him.

'*You should totally do that*,' Kerry says, turning her face towards me.

'Do what?' Ed asks, jolting me, tethering me back into a world where Kerry isn't standing in front of me but is six feet below the ground. I must have been thinking out loud. 'That?' His arm points as a couple are enthusiastically enjoying the lovers' kiss before the leap. I link my fingers through his hand and pull his arm back towards me, enveloping myself into his embrace, as he kisses the top of my head. My heart hammers in my chest as I try to ignore the fact that once again, Kerry's words have escaped from my mouth. I swallow hard, the taste of strawberries burning the back of my throat. The lovers have taken their respective positions, facing away from each other as they count down from five, then leap, both descending quickly – the boy with his legs apart and frog-like, the girl holding her nose while her legs run beneath her. The splash of water swallows their squeals, then expels them through the surface. They swim towards each other, blinking the water from their eyelashes and smoothing back hair until they are once again in each other's arms.

'Let's do it,' I say, bringing myself onto my knees and facing Ed.

'Yeah, right.' He rolls his eyes and leans back, tucking his hands behind his head.

I stand up and squint at the steel ladder that is bolted into the cliffside. 'Come on, Ed! Let's go.'

He rolls onto his side and props his head to the left. 'You're not serious?'

'I am deadly serious.'

'Ooh . . . she's deadly serious. Nice.' Kerry replies from the edge of the pool, where she is making ballerina steps around the water's edge.

'Jen, you wouldn't even jump off the kids' diving board last year and now you want to do a cliff jump?' He laughs. 'Very funny.'

'Fine . . . I'll do it myself, but I don't think jumping off

Lovers' Leap without my lover is going to give us much luck.' I kick off my sliders, pull my green swimsuit out of my bum cheeks and head towards the cliff. The rock surface feels rough and warm beneath my feet as they take me towards the ladder.

'Jennifer! Jen! Wait!'

I smile. I knew he wouldn't be able to resist it. I stop in my tracks and turn towards him, as he pulls his T-shirt over his head and throws it towards the cool box and towels, jogging towards me, running a hand through his hair.

'Are you sure about this?' Ed asks, looking up at the ladder, the fastenings rusting into the slate-grey surface. 'It's quite high.' His Adam's apple bobs up and down as his eyes follow the steps towards the summit, but I focus on the bolts.

The Imaginable Death of Jennifer Jones – #4

Death by Falling Ladder

Fifty years ago, this was a place of fun for the local teens. They would swim in the pool on hot days, skate across it in the winter and climb the cliff on Friday nights, their bodies filled with the daring and optimism of youth. Until one Friday night, Billy Wise, eager to impress his would-be sweetheart, climbed the rock face. Even though Billy knew that the rock was wet from the rain earlier in the day, he could think of nothing other than Eva's lips on his and so he dug in his heels and began to climb. But the rock was more slippery than he had thought and even though he was a good climber, even though his fingers were strong, his boots couldn't find their place and Billy Wise fell to his death. He got the kiss from Eva, but Billy's heart had already stopped beating when her lips met his.

Billy Wise's father – Billy senior – grieved the death of his son acutely. And even though the teenagers talked about poor Billy Wise, it didn't stop them coming to the cliff, Billy's death making the treacherous climb even more of a challenge.

He couldn't bear the thought of another father losing his son and so Billy senior cashed in his life savings and spent months hammering steel into rocks. But when he was almost finished, when he had sold everything he could to pay for the tools he needed, his money ran out. Billy senior begged and pleaded with the community to help pay for the last few rungs of the ladder. And after many cake sales and sponsored walks, he did it. The metal he used to complete the ladder was not as strong as the metal he had used before. But even so, eventually, his ladder was complete.

Jennifer's feet climb, her toes curling against the metal rungs beneath. Around her, the green hills roll and turn their backs, the seagulls call her name in warning, but the sea beyond whispers its encouragement. On she climbs: white knuckles, thumping heart, glistening lip. Jennifer is almost at the top, her foot stepping onto the final parts of the ladder that Billy senior had struggled to build . . . the ladder that years of wind and age had been testing the strength of. As the woman's foot presses down, the rust breaks off, orange dust falling onto the green of her swimsuit as the rung finally pulls away. She watches her fingers holding on to the metal bar, which frees itself. She's free, falling: no longer waiting for the kiss of life.

'Jen!' Ed's voice brings me back as he calls from behind me. 'Hurry up!'

I blink.

I pull myself to the top and walk towards the edge of Lovers' Leap. Beneath me, the pool shimmers with temptation. The sun is beating down and beads of sweat are running along my spine, from the sun as well as the climb up the ladder. The ground scrapes the bottom of my foot as I step back, the jagged edges of the rocks splitting and fracturing, age revealing their scars.

'We have to kiss first,' he says before taking a step forward and peering over the edge. 'It's quite a long way down.' He cranes his neck. Excited voices come from behind us and we move aside to let a pair of teenagers kiss. Laughing and standing on opposite sides of the ledge, they count: 'One, two, three!' Their nimble bodies leap into the air, and their squeals are received by the pool with a splash, just a split second later. Ed takes my hand and we step towards the edge, where the teenagers are swimming towards each other, grinning and smoothing their hair back. They meet, arms around each other's necks; another kiss before swimming to the edge of the pool.

'Are you sure you want to do this?' he asks, his eyebrows meeting as he scans the distance below us.

'Yep. You don't have to if you don't want to do it,' I say, taking in the pallor of his skin and the worry crossing his features.

'What, and let you have all the fun? Not likely.' He grins, with uncertainty resting in the corners of his lips.

We kiss. I taste the salt in our sweat, and the tang of strawberries as we pull apart and stand in our respective positions.

'One, two, three!' I shout. The air around me stills, my ears filled only with the sound of my heart beating as my feet step forward. How easy it is to just step into air. It takes no effort, the same movement that you use when you get out of bed to go to the toilet. I do thousands of these steps every day, and yet none of them have ever made me feel this way. My stomach feels as though it's rising faster than my body is descending, the sensation deliciously different while my eyes glimpse the greens and the blues surrounding me. I am free. Nothing is holding me, keeping me trapped; I can't decide to stop: my action cannot be reclaimed. All too soon, my freedom is taken away from me. I have to tell myself to hold my breath as my body plummets into the water; I have to acknowledge the sensation of feeling cold as the water wraps itself around me; I have to concentrate on kicking my legs hard to bring me back to the surface: I have to choose to live.

I break the surface with a loud gasp, my eyes blinking away the water as Ed swims towards me, laughing. His hands find my waist and he pulls me towards him. I link my arms around his neck as he spins us around.

'That. Was. Amazing!' He laughs again, his forehead meeting mine, our feet treading water, the teenagers sitting on the sides of the pool giving us a round of applause: the old couple behaving like adolescents.

We take the Lovers' Leap jump three more times before we decide to return to our towels. Ed is dozing next to me, his head turned to the side, dark blond hair resting in damp curls across his forehead. I curve my body against his like a comma and try to slow my breathing so that it matches his. This has been fun for him, his shouts and whoops becoming more excited each time we jumped, his legs kicking out like scissors, and I'm glad. But with each jump, my own enjoyment has diminished. With each jump, my enjoyment has been snatched away by the water too soon.

The sounds from day trippers are lessening, the pack of teenagers have long since departed and the pool is becoming deserted. I trace the edges of the rocks, the grooves and ridges, the jagged edges of the smaller ledges that erupt like crystals, until my eyes rest on the edge of a ledge just out of sight. I roll away from Ed, who lets out a small snore, and walk towards the cliff face. The ledge is more visible from beneath Lovers' Leap. It's about another three metres, I'd guess.

'You're not going to do what I think you are . . . are you?' Kerry asks from beneath a wide-brimmed straw hat.

It'll be a longer drop.

'If you want a bigger jump, go somewhere else tomorrow, somewhere safe.'

I won't get a chance tomorrow, I'll have the kids.

I throw a cursory glance at Ed, who is deep in sleep, and then begin climbing the ladder. Once on Lovers' Leap, I follow the ledge around to the right. I hold on to the rock and stretch my leg out, digging my fingers into the grooves of the rock face. It scrapes my hands and knees, but I push myself forward, finding safe footing. Above me hangs the higher ledge. The rock here is strong and there are plenty of footholds for me to be able to scale upwards without much trouble. My throat is dry, my legs are bleeding a little, but the adrenaline is pushing me forward; the need to feel that freedom – even for a few more seconds – is tempting me, calling out my name. I heave myself onto the ledge and roll onto my back. My breath is coming out in short sharp gasps and I lie here for a few minutes, listening to the silence. But the silence is cracked open by Ed's voice and I sit up, frustrated that he has interrupted my moment. I stand up and walk towards the edge; it is higher than I first thought. Ed's hands are waving at either side.

'Come on, Jen . . . enough is enough.' I turn my head and watch as Kerry reaches her hand forward towards me, beckoning me away from the brink.

'You're not here,' I say and turn away from her, my feet stepping into air, giving me my freedom back.

Chapter Eighteen

Ed

I can't believe what I am seeing. She is standing on the edge of the cliff; her head is tilted back and she is smiling. Even from here I can see that she is at peace. I'm trying to decide on a course of action. I know I haven't got time to get to her but that doesn't stop me from looking at the ladder; I know I can't catch her but it doesn't stop me from thinking that I can, and it doesn't stop me from calling her name, even though I know she is going to jump.

My eyes scour the water to where she will land. Sickness rises in my throat as I notice that the blue of the water holds a hidden shadow beneath the surface; the image of the iceberg from *Titanic* pushes into my thoughts. 'Jen!' I shout, but I know it's too late; she is stepping forward. I jump into the water. It's the same action that just an hour ago had felt exhilarating, but this time the water feels heavy and I battle against it, forcing my muscles to work against the gravity and pushing myself to the surface in time to see her body crash into the pool. I don't hear a thud, or a scream, but as my arms begin to slice through the water, I see the blood. And I see Jen floating, arms outstretched, face down.

Her name is caught in my throat as I pound through the water, my fingers grasping at her arm; she begins to kick, her legs sinking below the surface, her head erupting from the water with a huge gasp of air. I pull her into my arms, cupping her legs in my arms the way I hold Hailey when she has fallen asleep and needs to be carried to bed. Jen's arms encircle my neck. I pull her body as close to mine as I can, our chests rising and falling quickly as we each catch our breath.

'Where are you hurt?' I ask frantically, scanning her face, expecting her skin to be pale, expecting to see the fear of death mirroring my own, but instead . . . she has never looked more alive.

'I'm fine,' she answers, smoothing her wet hair back from her head.

'You're bleeding. You're not fine.' I don't mean it to come out the way it does, and I realise that I'm angry with her. I drop her legs and pull away.

'Am I?' And then she laughs, like it's all a joke. But it's not. My anger dissipates as I noticed the red stain running over her shoulder and onto her chest. I run my thumb over the blood and show it to her. She shrugs and turns her head over her shoulder to see the damage. I take her gently by the shoulders and turn her around. Trailing from the top of her shoulder and down to her spine is a cut. It's not deep but it's bleeding profusely. I swallow down the lump in my throat, lean in, move her hair aside and gently kiss the base of her neck. She turns back to me, the vitality of her face changing as our eyes meet.

I swallow hard. 'You've cut your back.'

'Really?' She looks surprised. 'Huh.'

'Huh?' I repeat, my eyebrows rising, my anger returning. She lowers her eyes and sinks beneath the surface, rising with her mouth full of water, which she spits out at me as though we are young lovers splashing at each other in a pool in Ibiza. What does she expect me to do? Splash her playfully? I wipe away the water from my face as her focus goes to something beyond the pool and over my shoulder. I turn but there is nothing there. Blood is creeping back over Jen's shoulder as I return my focus to her.

'We need to stop that bleeding.' My tone is flat.

'It doesn't hurt, stop worrying, it's just a scratch.' Her answer is dismissive and distracted as she scans the rocks again. 'Do you want to have a go?' She's smiling as if I haven't just seen her face down and bleeding.

'No.'

And then I turn and swim to the water's edge, dry off with the towel and watch my wife floating on her back, kicking her legs like she's on the holiday of a lifetime.

I don't often Google stuff about health. I once searched the symptoms of my dodgy knee and ended up being convinced I had a rare type of bone cancer, but I can't help it. The sun is starting to come up; I can't believe I've been on here most of the night. I rub my eyes: they're stinging from sitting here like a dick, scrolling through pages and pages on the internet, trying to work out why my wife is acting all weird.

My hand cups the mouse and hovers over the title which reads: 'What to Do if you Think your Spouse Is Suicidal'. I don't know how my research has led me to this. I started by looking at grief, that led me to mental illness, and then . . . well, this. I left-click and read another piece telling me of the warning signs: loss of interest in daily activities (nope); hopelessness (nope); substance abuse(?). I'm about to exit the screen when a different sentence grabs my attention. Is your loved one making risky decisions, or can you see a dramatic change in their personality? I reach for my cup and drain the last of the cold coffee. My wife isn't suicidal. My wife is just, my wife is just . . . . Jen is—

I turn off the screen and head for the bathroom.

The shower is cold and the jets of water are stinging my skin but it's what I need. I need to wake up. My eyes close against the spray but I open them again quickly; the image of Jen lying face down in the pool won't stop. I wrap the towel around my waist, make two cups of coffee and sit down gently on the edge of the bed. Jen always sleeps on her stomach, same position: head to the side, one arm beneath the pillow, the other at a right angle, her dark hair often covering her face, shielding her from the rising sun. I hook my finger beneath her hair, carefully revealing her face. Her features scrunch up and I can't help but smile: she hates to be disturbed in sleep; her instant reaction is to pout and pull her muscles together. I continue to stroke her hair and her features relax again, just as I knew they would. I let my eyes trail along the edge of the gauze covering the scratch. Old blood has congealed around the edges, marking Jen's pale skin. I blink back the image of the pool again and lean forward to kiss her forehead. The pout returns fleetingly, but then a smile replaces it.

'What time is it?'

'It's early,' I reply. Her eyes open a fraction and she smiles at me, tapping the empty space beside her. I discard the damp towel and climb beneath the sheets as she rolls towards me, entwining her legs with mine.

'We need to talk.' My voice betrays me: it's unsteady.

'I know.' Her eyes are sincere; tears threaten behind them.

I touch her nose with mine.

Sex used to be fun. Sex used to be something that I wanted more of. Sex used to be . . . not this. Not an excuse to silence all the things that need to be said.

Our breathing slows. Jen's head is on my chest as I run my fingers up and down her arm.

'You scared me yesterday.'
'I know.'
'You said you wouldn't do it again.'
'I won't. I promise.'
I want to believe her.
I don't.

Chapter Nineteen

Jennifer

I sit down at my parents' kitchen table, while Dad cuts his homemade flapjacks into neat squares for the kids.

Ed is trying to untangle his watch from Hailey's hair.

'Ouch!' she shouts, fixing him with a vicious glare.

'Sorry,' Ed replies.

'Vladi-vos-tok,' Hailey murmurs under her breath.

Oscar eats a bogey that he has recently examined and then grabs a large piece of flapjack from the plate. Oats sprinkle onto his white school polo shirt.

'Why did Aunty Kerry die?' Oscar asks out of the blue. 'Was she a really bad person?'

'No, she—'

'Did she go to hell because she was naughty?'

'No, Aunty Kerry wasn't naughty,' I explain.

'She was, she let me have sweets before bed when she was the babysitter and I didn't have to brush my teeth.'

'Did she?'

Flapjack-filled faces nod with wide, knowing eyes.

'What else did she do that was naughty?' I ask, glancing over Oscar's shoulder to where Kerry is telling Oscar that he had better not break their pinky promise.

'She let us watch—'

'Oscar!' Hailey warns. My children's eyes meet and hold a

silent conversation, Hailey replying to Oscar with a little shake of the head. He reaches for a glass of milk and takes a large slurp, even though his mouth is still full of flapjack. Kerry ruffles Oscar's hair, pinches a piece of flapjack, jumps up and sits on the kitchen worktop. She begins dissecting her food, fishing out all of the hidden dried apricots that Dad sneaks in because 'they're full of iron'. Oscar's hair remains tidy despite my sister's gesture.

Ed takes a moment, his eyebrows raising with sudden clarity. 'Did she let you watch scary movies?' Oscar begins shaking his head vehemently, causing him to cough flapjack and milk over the kitchen table. Hailey's eyes widen even further and she focuses her attention towards a knot in the wood of the table.

'*Uh-oh . . .*' Kerry smirks. '*Busted.*'

'Did she?' My head swivels away from Kerry towards where Hailey is turning an astonishing shade of red. 'Hailey? Did she let you watch grown-up movies?'

'It was only once.'

'Twice,' Oscar butts in, wiping his mouth with the back of his hand.

'Twice?' Ed folds his arms, his body taking on a 'Strict Dad' pose.

'OK, it was four, but Aunty Kerry said that we were old enough.'

'What movies did you watch?'

'There was the one with the willy . . .'

'Willy?' Dad's face goes pale and Mum has begun to maniacally squirt the draining board with disinfectant.

'Yep . . . it had an eye,' Hailey says quietly.

'Just one,' Oscar adds. 'It was gross.'

'And he was all stiff.'

'But Aunty Kerry said that was normal,' Hailey clarifies.

'Normal?' I squeak.

'Yes. She said that dead people go stiff and that One-Eyed Willy had been dead for a long time.'

'*Oi . . . You guys!*' Kerry admonishes.

'*The Goonies*?' I ask with relief. 'She let you watch *The Goonies*.' My voice is explanatory as I meet Ed's relieved face, while Mum returns the disinfectant to the cupboard under the sink with an audible breath of relief.

Dad joins us at the table.

'So, will she?' Oscar asks again. 'Go to hell?'

'No, love.' Mum puts her hands on Dad's shoulders and kisses his bald spot. 'Your Aunt Kerry will be dancing with the angels in heaven.'

'Aunty Kerry said that there is no heaven and hell and that is what grown-ups say so we behave.' Hailey dips her flapjack into her milk. 'I think Aunty Kerry is a tooth fairy.'

'Why?'

'Because Aunty Kerry was clever and the tooth fairy is way better than an angel.'

'Why?' Oscar asks, his mouth full, the contents exposed.

'Because they're rich, silly.'

I follow insomnia into the kitchen like an awkward friend. Kerry is sitting at the kitchen table, blowing the rim of her cup of Horlicks.

Why are you drinking that? I ask, turning my back on her and filling up the kettle. You hate Horlicks.

'*I hate to break it to you, Jen, but I'm not actually here. Maybe it's you who wants some Horlicks?*' I pause and consider this. Is that what's happening? Are my memories of Kerry mingling with what I want to see and hear? I shake my head. Insomnia laughs at me . . . Do you really think cutting out caffeine is going to stop me? My hand reaches for the tub and spoons some into my cup. My legs take me to the table where I try to sit, quietly massaging my temples.

'Why did you save me, Kerry? Why am I still here?'

I close my eyes, fold my arms on the table and rest my head against them. I'm deep in sleep when my phone rings: red coat, red boots, silver nails, emerald ring. The images begin to fade as I try to order my thoughts, the way I used to before she died. What day is it? It's Thursday. What time is it? Nessa's number blinks on the screen beneath the time, which reads 12:45am. I rotate my neck and lock myself into the downstairs toilet, answering in hushed tones.

'Hello?'

'Aunty Jen?' Erica's voice is quiet and scared.

'Erica, sweetie? What is it, are you OK?'

'I . . . I had a nightmare and I tried to wake up Mummy and she won't wake up.'

Her words are ringing in my ears, its peal drowning out the hammering of my heart. 'Where is Mummy now?' I ask.

'She's in her bed. She's snoring.'

'Try to wake her again, give her a little shake. She must be very tired.' My explanatory tone camouflages my concern. In the background I hear a groan, the muffled sound of Erica explaining that she is talking to Aunty Jen.

'She won't wake up.'

'Stay with Mummy, Erica, I'm coming over. Can you tell me your new address?'

'It's 45 Rosemary Drive, I wrote it in joined up letters on my picture for Daddy.'

'You are a clever girl. Now when I get there, I will knock on the door three times, so you know it's only me. Like a secret password, OK?'

'I can't open the door, Aunty Jen. Daddy says I must never open the door. I will be in trouble and he won't give me my pocket money and I'm saving for the new LOL doll. Can't you use the key?'

'I don't have a key, sweetie.'

'You can use the spare key the gnome has. Mummy hid it, the fishing gnome in the garden has the spare key.'

'Brilliant. Good thinking, I'll get the spare key and then I can make Mummy a nice cup of tea and wake her up.' I'm about to hang up and call for an ambulance when I hear Nessa's voice in the background. 'Is Mummy waking up?' I ask.

'She wants to speak to you.' The sounds from the other end of the phone become muffled and I picture it being passed over.

'What time is it?' Nessa's words run into each other and it takes me a moment to decipher them.

'Almost one in the morning, are you OK?'

'I'm fine. Just had some-wine-that-must-have-been-off. What-time-s-is-it?' Nessa's voice asks again. She's drunk. Very drunk. 'Why are you up?'

The smudged sounds of conversation blur in the background.

'I had a bad dream and you wouldn't wake up. Are you poorly, Mummy?'

'I'm OK, I'm OK. Come and snuggle with me.'

I stay on the line, listening to Nessa comforting her daughter with slurred words until she realises that I'm still on the other end of the phone.

'Thanks, Jen, I'll call you tomorrow.' And with that the line goes dead.

Sleep is far from my grasp.

My promise to Ed rattles my conscience, so I leave him a note in the kitchen explaining that Nessa is poorly and that I've gone to look after Erica. I add that I've got my phone so he can ring me if he needs to.

The dark streets are deserted as I follow the tiny lady trapped inside my phone telling me that my destination will be on the right, I turn off the ignition, step out of the car. Perhaps I should just go home, they're probably sleeping. But losing Kerry has taught me how precious life is. They could both be fast asleep, but then again, something could be wrong.

I lift the rusty latch, releasing the gate, and look at the house, feeling like an intruder. A dog barks further along the street, halting the progress of a black cat along the garden wall which eyes me with suspicion, as well it might. I glance down at my clothes and realise with a snigger that I'm wearing a black-and-white-striped T-shirt and black jeans. I may as well have a bag over my shoulder saying 'Swag'.

Weeds are knotted around the soles of my grey Converse and the knee-high grass makes my progress tricky, so I tread carefully on tiptoes. This is ridiculous. Honestly. I can practically hear the Pink Panther music as I make my way across the garden, my body halting at every noise, every car engine, every squeaking gate.

I give the door a gentle knock and wait, but there is no answer.

'Use the spare key.' The image of Kerry startles me: she has black smudges beneath her eyes, her black-and-white-striped top matching mine, her swag bag clenched in her hands. She had dressed up as a burglar for our Halloween party last year; Nessa was a policewoman.

'There aren't any gnomes in this garden,' I whisper.

None.

A car passes slowly and I find myself forcing my back against the house and standing still. Giggles take over and I have to shove my fist in my mouth to keep myself quiet. Her head leans forward and scans the road, and she then does some weird army movements with her hands which I take to mean we have the all clear. We continue to snoop around the garden when a pair of eyes staring straight at me stop me short. The eyes in question are peering at me from over the fence. They are bespectacled and are resting above a white beard.

'We're in the wrong garden!' Kerry exclaims.

'Shush!'

I eye the gnome warily and tiptoe back out through the gate and into the adjoining garden. Square green lawn. Pots of flowers. And gnomes. Everywhere. This can't be Nessa's house, surely? But then I think about the way that Erica got pretty much whatever she liked: maybe she decided on gnomes for the garden and wouldn't take no for an answer? They all stare at me as I close the gate, tracking my progress along the path, silently judging me beneath their red cone hats. One gnome in particular catches my eye; he is a grumpy gnome holding a sign that says 'Go Away'. I swallow hard and tiptoe past him, launching him a challenging glance over my shoulder. Kerry and I continue to search for the whereabouts of the fishing gnome, giving cursory glances at a gnome leaning against a toadstool, the one dismissively smoking a pipe, taking care to step over the happy gnome couple smiling at each other, until I rest my eyes on the back of the gnome who had peered at me from over the fence.

Kerry does her army moves again. I creep over towards it, turn it slowly around to face me; the effect is like something out of *The Exorcist*.

'Gnome-or-sist.' Kerry sniggers.

The key is hanging from the end of the fishing rod, resting inside a clay fisherman's net. A security light beams from the side of the house. I grab the gnome and crouch behind a rose bush until the light fades, whilst trying not to laugh out loud at the ridiculousness of the situation I have found myself in. The gnome is clearly an expert fisherman and it takes me some time to untangle its silvery haul.

As I catch my breath, I take in the immaculate borders around the garden, the pottery squirrels, the oversized butterflies attached to the brick. This can't be Nessa's house. I check my phone for the address again, as I slow my breathing and realise that I'm right: Nessa's is the house that I had originally gone to, the one with the overgrown garden. I dodge the security light's beam and run through the gate, the gnome watching our retreat with its catch of the day resting firmly in my palm.

I turn the key over and look over to the darkened windows of the house, wondering how to handle this. I can't just go in; it would scare the child to death. I ring Nessa's phone, but there is no answer; I swallow down my annoyance as I follow the overgrown path towards the door. A light flicks on inside the lounge, the yellowy haze framing the curtains, letting in uneven arcs of light. The curtain pulls to the side, framing Erica's face. I wave and smile as if I'm just popping around for a playdate. The key eases into the lock and releases a yellow oblong of light onto the step surrounding Erica's small body.

I bend down and meet her eyes. Gone is the angry expression and taunting face that I last saw; instead here is a very vulnerable little girl. Instinct guides my actions; it doesn't need much thought. I bring her frail body into my embrace.

'It's OK, I'm here,' I whisper.

'Did you bring Oscar?' she asks, sniffing and wiping her nose along her arm.

'No, sweetie, he's in bed.'

'Oh. Mummy is asleep again and I couldn't sleep because she is snoring. Really. Loud. Did you find the gnome? Mummy says nobody would think to look there for the spare key.'

'I did and she's right. Your mummy is a very clever lady.'

She takes my hand and leads me into the kitchen. I try not to notice the half-empty gin bottle without a lid, and the overflowing ash tray that litters the kitchen counter. Tea stains circle sticky patches of sugar which mix with crumbs along the worktop. Erica pulls a chair towards the counter and brings a piece of kitchen towel forward. On top are two Rich Tea biscuits, smeared with watery white icing. Some broken chocolate buttons have been arranged into two wonky, smiling faces.

'I made this for Oscar. To say sorry for biting him.'

I blink back the tears that are stinging my sleep-deprived eyes.

'That's very kind of you,' I say smiling, noticing as I do the red rims around her eyes, the chocolate smudges around her mouth.

'Let's get you a nice drink of milk and you can watch a bit of TV while I go and check on Mummy.' She nods and wanders into the lounge as I head into the kitchen and pour her a glass of milk.

In the bedroom, air – warm and thick – hangs heavily above Nessa, who is, indeed, snoring loudly. The sour, stale smell of cigarettes cringes ashamedly in the corners of the room but alcohol, alcohol is draping itself over the furniture, its decadence proud and eager for attention.

On top of the sheets, Nessa is sprawled, wearing an old violet-coloured T-shirt of Kerry's.

'Nessa?' I shake her shoulder. 'Vanessa?' I raise my voice. She turns towards me, her eyes glassy, confused, and trying to focus.

'Kerry?' She smiles. 'You're late.' Her eyelids flicker and close. I sit down next to her and stroke the hair away from her face; there is almost a smile around her mouth. From downstairs, the sounds of cartoons ricochet into this room filled with sadness and debauchery, and a sob tries to escape my mouth.

'Oh, God,' she groans, sitting up just as she begins to retch. I try to grab the bin but I'm not there in time and Nessa vomits onto the duvet. 'Sorry,' she says. There is a brief pause before she retches again; this time she manages to be sick into the bin.

I wait until she is finished. 'Better?'

She nods, wiping the back of her mouth with her hand. 'Shower,' Nessa instructs, her hand reaching out for the edge of the bed. Her body sways and I link my arm around her waist, guiding the way up.

The shower hangs from the wall and I reach over and turn it on, cool jets of water cascading into the bath as I pour the contents of the bin into the toilet and flush.

Nessa begins to discard her clothes, oblivious to me it seems. Her fingers tear off her T-shirt, but can't negotiate the clasp of her bra. You would think I would feel awkward unfastening another woman's bra, but I don't, it feels like I'm looking after one of my children.

Nessa throws her underwear to the floor and tries to step over the rim of the bath and into the shower, her balance making the movement difficult, and my hand reacts quickly, holding on to her arm as she steps into the water. An unsteady palm lands on the tiles but before long, Nessa is retching again, her stomach empty as she sinks to her knees. Her head is bent, wet hair falling away from her scalp, running over defeated shoulders as she cries. I sit on the side of the bath, stroking the top of her head, watching the droplets of water cascade over the smooth olive skin covering her sharp shoulder blades, drawing trails along her spine.

I open my mouth to offer her some words of comfort, but I find that I don't have any. Kerry is dead. She's not coming back, not to Nessa anyway. Instead, I reach for the plug. The bath begins to fill as I open the shampoo and wash her hair, bringing up her chin and tipping her head back as I would with Oscar. I add conditioner and comb it through, the ends of her black hair resting in a neat line along her back, rinsing it while her eyes stare blankly ahead, conversation knowing its place and staying silent.

After some time, I wrap her body in a towel and lead her into the bedroom. I carefully remove the duvet and replace it with a fleecy throw from the bottom of the bed; Nessa slips on a clean pair of pyjamas, and climbs in.

'*Oh, Ness.*' Kerry has wiped away her black camouflage smudges and is wearing pink pyjamas. She climbs into bed and cocoons the curve of Nessa's back with her body, wrapping her arm around Nessa's waist and closing her eyes.

I reach for one of Nessa's notepads from the desk, ignoring the pages screwed up into balls that litter the carpet, and write her a note, letting her know that I have Erica, that I will take her to school and that I will call her later.

Erica is still awake when I return to the lounge, even though the rest of her body looks like it should be beneath a duvet. She looks up and smiles at me.

'I'm glad you're here.' Her voice is caught in a yawn.

'I have an idea. How would you like to come for a sleepover?' I glance at the clock on the wall. It's just after half-two.

'Yes please! I've never been invited to a sleepover before but—'

'I've asked Mummy, she said it's OK,' I reassure her.

'It's not that . . . will Oscar still be cross with me?'

'Not once he sees those biscuits, now let's grab your uniform, shall we?'

By the time I pull up outside my house, gentle snores are coming from the back seat. I turn off the ignition.

'Can you help her, Jen?' Kerry is still wearing her pyjamas and is sitting in the passenger seat.

I'll try my best.

'Nobody is perfect.' Kerry quotes the closing line from *Some Like it Hot*, her voice fading like the credits on the screen.

Chapter Twenty

Jennifer

Ed is wearing a suit and is standing in the doorway of the kitchen, his expression folded like origami. His skin, originally relaxed and smooth, has creased into confusion, lines forming around his forehead and wrinkling into a frown; his eyes dart from Erica to me and back to her. The tumble dryer tosses Erica's clothes while she sits with freshly showered hair next to Oscar, who is blowing bubbles into his Coco Pops with a straw; Hailey is trying not to laugh. One of Oscar's giant chocolate milk bubbles has just popped all over his face, leaving them all dissolving into laughter.

'Good morning, Daddy,' Hailey announces, her mouth full of cereal and her spoon gesturing at Erica. 'Erica has stayed at our house because her mummy is poorly.'

'Right. Um, Jen?' Ed cocks his head towards the hallway. 'Can I speak to you please?'

I finish putting chocolate spread onto the final piece of toast, pile it on top of the rest of the slices and slide the plate onto the table. Eager hands grab at them before I've barely moved away and into the hall.

'What's going on?' A look of panic crosses Ed's face and I can tell he's trying to keep his emotions in check. 'Please tell me you didn't kidnap Nessa's daughter.'

I burst out laughing. Ed takes a step backwards and

watches me with trepidation. My laughter catches in my throat as I realise he is actually serious.

'What?' I ask him. 'Do you really think—'

The words hang in the air. His expression folds again, and lands somewhere between embarrassment and apology. 'I . . . no but—'

'You thought I'd kidnapped a child, Ed?'

'No, not really.'

'Not really?'

'No. Anyway—' He scratches the back of his head. 'What happened? And how is it she is in our kitchen playing sword fights with a spoon? Look, Jen, there is chocolate milk getting splattered all over the place.'

'It doesn't matter.' I wave my hand dismissively.

Ed takes a step back, his hand thrown melodramatically against his chest. 'It doesn't matter?' he repeats, aghast.

'It's just chocolate milk.'

'Mmmmhmmm? Just chocolate milk?' He leans against the wall and crosses his arms: eyebrows raised, head to one side. 'Since when has "just chocolate milk" being splattered around our kitchen been "just"?'

I shake my head and pull a 'what the hell are you going on about' face. 'Nessa was drunk, Ed. Like, REALLY drunk. I couldn't leave Erica there.'

He pulls himself back up straight. 'And you know this how?'

'I found the key hidden under a gnome in the garden next door and let myself in.' Ed's eyebrows shoot up as he whispers urgently, 'You can't just go around messing with other people's gnomes and letting yourself into houses, Jen!'

'Shush!' I poke my head around the kitchen doorway to see Oscar and Erica drinking the rest of their cereal from the edges of their bowls while Hailey watches them with a look of disgust on her face. 'Everything OK?' I ask, smiling at Hailey's nodding head before returning to mine and Ed's heated debate.

'We didn't just let ourselves in, we—'

'We?'

'Uh-oh. He's on to you.' Kerry takes a bite of toast and crunches closely to Ed's ear.

'I. I didn't just let myself in, Erica rang me and told me where the spare key was.'

'In the middle of the night?'

'Yes.'

'On your own?'

'Yes.'

'When you had no idea who could be hanging around outside Nessa's house? An angry man could have found my incredibly attractive wife messing with his gnomes!'

'You think I'm incredibly attractive?'

'Of course I think you're incredibly attractive, but you're missing the point.'

Kerry rolls her eyes, then grins at me as she makes her way into the kitchen.

'I love it when you say things like that to me.'

'Focus, Jen! Where is Nessa now? Shouldn't she be picking her up and taking her to school?'

'I said I'd take Erica and look . . .' We both peer around the doorframe and then go back to our original positions. 'Look at how well Oscar is getting on with her now. It's good for him.'

'Are you forgetting the mark she left on his arm?'

'No, but . . .' I think of the gin bottle but push the image to one side, screwing the top back on and popping it away in a kitchen cupboard. 'She was just so . . . alone. What else could I do?'

He kisses the top of my head. 'You should have woken me up. You promised, Jen,' he says quietly into my hair.

'I know, but I left you a note and I took the spray you gave me when I went to London with Kerry. I couldn't just leave her on her own, Erica had a nightmare and Ness was sleeping it off.'

'Then Nessa should have got up and made herself a bloody coffee!' Ed's voice rises.

'Shush! Look, I'm fine, and she's clean and fed and Oscar is happy and—'

'Jen?' He steps back and puts his hands on my shoulders, his face concerned and serious. 'Don't you think you've got enough on your plate at the moment without . . .' He sighs. 'This?'

'What would you have had me do, Ed? Tell a five-year-old sorry, no I'm not free? Explain to my dead sister's widow—'

'Wouldn't she be a widower?'

'I don't know, Ed! What would I say to her? Sorry I didn't come and help you with your daughter while you were passed out because I'm too busy sleeping in my Egyptian cotton sheets next to my husband – who is a Viking in the sack by the way—' Ed smirks slightly at this even though his brow remains furrowed, 'so no I can't go around to your house and comfort a five-year-old who is petrified.'

'Fine.' Ed straightens his face. 'But you still should have woken me up.'

'If it happens again I will.'

'Good.'

'Good.'

'So . . .' Ed starts to grin. 'Ragnar Lothbrok, eh?'

'Huh?'

'The Viking?'

'*Oooh, he'd make a good Ragnar.*' Kerry steps back into our hallway just as the tumble dryer beeps the ending of its cycle.

'I'll get the clothes out,' Ed says, passing me into the kitchen.

'He'll figure it out, you know,' she says, examining the last bit of crust before putting it into her mouth.

Figure out what?

'That my sister can see dead people.'

Chapter Twenty-One

Jennifer

Erica and Oscar are singing 'Who stole the cookie from the cookie jar' in the back of the car, while Hailey has slipped on her headphones and is tapping away on her tablet. Oscar and Erica have both been to a birthday party and I offered to stay and bring them back.

'Who are you trying to kid? You offered so you could keep an eye on Nessa.'

I ignore my subconscious and plaster a smile on my face as I pull up outside the house and see that Nessa is half-way through mowing the lawn. Her hair is tied back and she has the beginnings of a tan. Just outside her gate is a couple in their mid-forties who have their faces attached to each other.

'Ugh,' Hailey groans from the back seat. Oscar is giggling. I look into my rear-view mirror and catch Erica's eye.

'I never see my mummy and daddy doing that!' Erica says, giggling.

'My mummy and daddy do that,' Hailey confirms. 'Daddy does it to Mummy in the cupboard under the stairs.'

'No, he doesn't. He tickles Mummy in the cupboard under the stairs because I heard her laughing and then she ate some chocolate.'

'What do you mean, Oscar?' I ask. I know that I should

shove this conversation onto another track, but curiosity is getting the better of me.

'Because you went mmmmmmm, like you do when you eat chocolate.'

'Yes, that's right. I was, um, eating chocolate under the stairs with Daddy.'

'Why were you under the stairs?' asks Erica.

'Erm—'

'They were playing hide and seek,' Hailey butts in, and I'm grateful for her no-nonsense tone.

'And then Daddy hurt his-self cuz he went ugh-ah-ah!'

I swallow down my discomfort. We had thought they were busy watching a film in Hailey's room. I make a mental note to make sure we are more careful.

'You should play Monopoly instead,' Erica interjects, 'and then your daddy wouldn't hurt himself.'

'That's a great idea,' I announce as I look back to where the couple have unlocked their faces and are continuing along the street.

'Or Just Dance, you and Daddy like to play Just Dance on the Wii, don't you?'

'Just Dance?' I ask, as a vague memory of a caravan holiday springs to mind.

'Yes, when we went in the caravan in Wales and it rained the whole time, I woke up because the caravan was rocking and you said it was because you and Daddy were playing Just Dance.'

'Just Dance, yes. Um. Kids, stay in the car while I take Erica in.'

Erica's hand holds tightly to mine as we make our way through the front lawn, which is patchy and yellow, but I'm pleased that Nessa seems to be making some changes. She bends down and hugs Erica, avoiding my gaze, as I stand back and try to hide the concerned expression from my face, hoping that it is buried deep within the contours of my skin, that it isn't there for her to see.

'Daddy's inside,' she announces to Erica, who does an overstated 'Yes!' and runs towards the doorway.

'Pumpkin!' Daniel exclaims, stepping over the threshold: blond hair, long legs, wearing a look of confusion that never seems to go. He is lifting Erica up beneath her armpits and swinging her around as Erica giggles in delight; Nessa rolls her eyes but there is no malice behind them. Daniel and Nessa married when they were young, realised they had made a mistake early on, and split up in a very Gwyneth and Chris kind of way. They are the most abnormally normal exes I've ever met.

'Look, Jen . . . I'm sorry, about the other night,' Nessa says quietly.

'You've already apologised.' Nessa had rung the following morning, her voice cracked, her words broken. 'I'm just glad I could help. How are you?'

'OK.' She smiles. 'You?'

I don't look over to where Kerry is currently cartwheeling across the lawn, her blue summer dress tucked into her knickers. I think back to the beach last year; for any other twenty-five-year-old woman to be cartwheeling would have seemed childlike, but for Kerry, it seemed normal. She just had that way: effortlessly cool, Ed always said.

'I'm fine.' I return her smile with my own. 'I'm OK.'

'Good.' The lies surround us, the 'OK's and 'fine's itching our skin and making us shift our bodies uncomfortably.

'Muuuuuummmmy!!!' Hailey yells from the open car window. 'Hurry up! Oscar has farted and it stinks!'

'Trumped!' I correct. 'I'd better go.' I lean and give Nessa a hug; she holds her breath, her body tense as my arms fold around her. She responds by giving me a gentle pat on the back. As we release each other, the breeze blows her hair in her eyes, blows the hem of my skirt upwards, and I don't look over to where Kerry is giving out a wolf-whistle.

'It's not funny, Ed!' I reply, but I'm trying not to laugh. 'They thought we were playing hide and seek.'

'Well we were, in a manner of speaking.'

I throw the tea towel at him and return to the business of onion-chopping. I'm trying to ignore Kerry sitting on top of the kitchen counter, watching me while I cook.

I continue to ignore her. 'Ed, pass me the garlic press, please.'

He opens the drawer, fishes it out and begins opening and shutting the press with a puzzled look on his face. 'Who do you think invented this thing? I mean, what made this person stop and think, "I know! I'll make something specifically for squashing garlic"?'

'Someone who was sick of having their hands stink, I suppose.' I glance up at the space Kerry had sat in and for a split second, instead of seeing my sister alive and sitting on the kitchen counter, I see her body in the air: red coat, red boots, silver nails, emerald ring.

I catch the tears forming with the back of my hand and continue chopping.

'Are you OK?' Ed asks.

'Mmmmhmmm, the onion is strong. That's all.'

I look up at Kerry. She is wearing an off-the-shoulder black top that we used to call her *Flashdance* top. That top had shrunk in the wash before I even met Ed.

'Jen?' I can hear Ed's voice, but I can't stop looking at Kerry.

Is this what I'm still here for? Is this what you saved me for? To cook dinner and live in this perfect house?

I return my focus to the onions.

'Jen?' Ed's hand is covering mine, pulling the knife from

my hand. He turns me around and runs his thumb under my eyes, wiping away the tears.

I give Ed a watery smile and return to my onions.

But the memory won't go. It takes the breath from my lungs: I feel like I'm suffocating.

'I need to go,' I say to Ed, untying my apron.

'What? Now? What's the matter?'

My fingers are fumbling over the knot, it feels like I'm being trapped, I need to get it off, I need to get this apron off before I'm stuck in it for ever. Ed takes my shaking hands gently away and undoes the strings. I try not to let him see the panic that is tearing away inside me. The strings drop to my sides and I yank the apron over my head, dropping it to the floor.

My fingers grab the car keys from the bowl in the hall. I walk past Ed's concerned face, walk past Hailey as she comes out of the lounge, slam the door behind me, open the car door and reverse out of the drive.

'Where are we going?' Kerry slots her seat belt into the socket.

'Nowhere.'

I put my foot on the accelerator and open the windows so that the car fills with air. 'I can't breathe.'

'Snap!' Kerry laughs and puts a chewing gum into her mouth.

I follow the road until I join the motorway. The sun is setting and I force myself to appreciate the colours, but it's not enough. I indicate and move into the right-hand lane, applying more pressure to the accelerator. The road is fairly quiet; it's after rush hour and a weekday so there are hardly any day trippers.

The needle of the speedometer extends its finger ambitiously, pointing to the numbers saved for emergencies. Normally I hate driving fast; I'm a fifty-mile-an-hour driver, never seeing the point of going beyond that. I sometimes think about the people on the roads who drive over the speed limit, endangering their lives and the lives of others, and what for? If they drive at eighty miles an hour instead of forty, what do they do with that oh-so-important extra time that they have created? Find a cure for cancer? Or do they just turn on the TV, and watch *EastEnders*?

But today is different. As the needle fills with excitement, daring to hit numbers that have previously been forbidden, I feel like I can breathe; the car is filled with air, my heart beating hard inside my ribcage, the suffocation I felt earlier lifting, and I feel the same kind of joy that I had when I stepped off Lovers' Leap . . . but it's not quite there yet. The speedometer continues to rise; with every notch on the dial I feel more alive.

'That's enough, Jen.'

'No . . . it's not. You want me to feel alive, don't you? You want me to live? Well this is living!'

I reach forward and turn on the stereo. Aretha sings out telling me to have a little respect. I risk a glance in Kerry's direction, but she isn't singing along; her eyes are fixed ahead at the road in front, her expression taut.

The playlist continues as the needle ventures forward, my body drinking in this feeling.

I'm alive.

Chapter Twenty-Two

Ed

I don't know what has just happened. One minute we were laughing about our quickie in the cupboard, and the next? The next minute it was like someone had possessed her. Her hands were gripping the knife, the blade was going up and down, up and down, but she wasn't looking at it, chop bloody chop while she was staring into space.

If I hadn't been there, do you know what? If I hadn't been there, I'm not sure that the blade would have stopped moving. I don't even think she would have noticed if the ends of her fingers had been caught by the steel.

And then. Then it was like she was being trapped by her apron strings. I know, right? The connotations of that little episode are not lost on me, I can tell you. I was trying to help her get out, but my fingers were fumbling over the knot, I felt so useless, I mean, I couldn't even undo the damn knot and then, before I knew it, she was gone. Grabbed the car keys, slammed the door and left.

And do you know what is more upsetting? Hailey saw the whole thing. Saw her mum losing the plot and walking out of the house and me standing there, helpless. I mean What. The. Hell. Is going on with my wife? Why can't I help her?

Chapter Twenty-Three

Jennifer

My foot wants to push harder on the pedal, my eyes want to see the needle on the speedometer increase, but I know I need to slow down. As the slip road comes into view, the car reduces its speed and the weight of life pushes down on me. I continue to slow as I approach a roundabout; Aretha's words, that had felt so euphoric moments ago, are now becoming too loud, too intrusive; I reach for the dial – turning it off.

Sense taps me on the shoulder: remember me? I change lanes, sensibly; I check my mirrors, sensibly; I begin to return home along the dual carriageway with tears polluting my vision. Indicators tock as I pull into the hard shoulder and turn off the engine. My whole body racks with pain, my sobbing loud, my muscles contorting, my bones grinding as I try to expel this feeling of worthlessness that has started to take over. Behind my bruised eyelids, words begin to flutter.

I should have died.

The words are swirling around like fog, their meaning running a finger up my spine in a gentle caress. I shake my head, and open my eyes; the words aren't real, just like my sister who is sitting on the bonnet of my car smoking a cigarette isn't real.

I gather myself and step out of the car. The night is

drawing in, side lights are being turned on and cats' eyes begin to blink. I sit next to Kerry and watch the cars pass, listen to the sounds of their speed and the wind as they fly by. Their passengers are unaware of me, unaware of the turmoil inside my body.

'Why did you do it?' I ask, turning towards Kerry, but she has gone, and the pain of her loss punches me. I sit still, I don't know how long for, but there is a pause in the flow of traffic. The road has become empty.

Kerry is tightrope-walking along the feline lights, as they reach forward. I check the empty road and follow her into the centre of the two lanes. This small act of rebellion, of stepping into a place which doesn't normally entertain the pedestrian, ignites inside my body; it tingles beneath the soles of my feet, radiates up through my calves, spreads into my pelvis, warms my stomach and brightens my eyes. My arms stretch outwards; what would it feel like to stand here with the sound of the cars passing? With the knowledge that if my balance was lost, if my balance shifted just a fraction, I could be killed? I close my eyes and picture it: the brush of death passing me by, the nearness of the bumpers, the exhausts, the absolute power of speed.

The image is blocked, like someone has pulled down a projector screen. A picture of my family stares back at me, the beam of the projector displaying them on the screen, dust motes trapped in the tube of light, the three of them, Ed in the middle, my children flanking him: tired eyes, forced smile like they are trying to be a happy family, just the three of them. My eyes flash open. There are the beginnings of car lights, their beam bumping along the slip road joining the carriageway, and I know I have to move. I will. In just another moment. A car from the other side of the barrier lets out a loud horn, the sound colliding against my ear drums, waking me up, smashing sense into me.

'Oi! I'm walking on here!' Kerry sort of quotes from *Midnight Cowboy*, another film I know she has never watched. I look back to where the lights are approaching, my senses heightened, the adrenaline rushing into my veins as they get closer.

I want you to understand that I don't want to die right now. I'm going to move in a second, I'm not going to put the driver in danger, the car won't have to swerve or move out of my way, but that doesn't mean that I don't want to know how it felt for her, how it felt for Kerry in those last seconds of her life.

Just one more minute and I'll move. I promise. Just. One. More. Minute.

Reluctantly, I return to my car. My chest is rising and falling rapidly and as I pull down the visor against the flash from the low-setting sun, my reflection looks alive, but it shouldn't . . . I should have been the one who died.

I throw the keys into the bowl on the desk in the hall. The blue light from the TV is flashing silently through the crack from the lounge door. I take a deep breath and push it open. Ed is sitting in his chair; he looks like he's been crying. I glance over to the small table where a bottle of whisky has been opened and an empty glass sits next to Ed.

'Where have you been?' He sniffs and wipes his eyes as he rises from the chair, striding over, holding my hands, searching my face. 'Are you OK?'

'I went for a drive. I needed to clear my head.' I let go of his hands, walk over and refill the glass, taking a long sip, the heat burning my insides. I like the feeling but can't help but grimace at the taste. I take another gulp regardless.

'Where?'

'Hmmm?' I ask, lost in my own thoughts, the heavy feeling that I had felt when I approached the roundabout returning like lead in my stomach.

'Where? Where did you go?'

'Nowhere.'

'Nowhere? Well next time your children ask where you are at bedtime, I'll tell them that Mummy isn't here because she had to go . . . *nowhere.*'

I drain the glass and refill it; Ed paces the room. 'I just needed some space, I needed to get out of—'

'What, Jen? You needed to get out of what? Out of here? Out of our home?' He throws his hands up into the air, exasperated.

'Yes. No. I—'

'Or is it that you wanted to get away from me?'

'No, of course not . . . Ed—'

He stands up and walks towards me, taking the glass and sliding it onto the dining table before taking my hands again and holding them. 'Tell me what is going on.'

'Nothing is—'

'Don't tell me that nothing is going on!' he yells. I flinch. He takes a breath and repeats, with his voice level, 'Don't tell me nothing is going on. I deserve more credit than that.'

'I can't.'

How can I tell him what I now know? That I should be dead. That Kerry's death was my fault.

'I see.' He drops my hands and leaves the room, hesitating with his hand on the door handle. 'I'll sleep in the spare room tonight. Give you some . . . space.'

I find myself nodding. Why am I nodding? I don't want space from Ed, I need Ed. He makes me feel alive.

'Ed, wait!' I head out of the room and look up to where he has stopped on the stairs, his one hand holding on to the banister. 'I need you, I don't want you to sleep in the spare room, I—'

'This marriage isn't always about what you need, Jen. I think we both need a bit of space.' He gives me a sad smile. 'I'll see you in the morning. Night.'

He takes his hand off the banister as I stand and watch his retreating back.

'I'm sorry,' I whisper.

Kerry sits on the bottom stair and takes off her shoes.

'Doesn't love mean you shouldn't have to say you're sorry?' she asks.

I don't know why my subconscious is thinking about *Love Story* right now, when, right now, my life couldn't be further away from one.

Chapter Twenty-Four

Ed

I bet everything looks OK to everyone else here. Look at me . . . my arms are swinging by my side, both hands clutching my children's as we make our way to the park. I look like the dad that I always wanted to be. The dad that you think about when you find out that you're going to have a kid. Jen was all about the tiny shoes and the soft blankets, but me? I wanted to be Park Dad, Kids-on-my-shoulders Dad, and I bet that is just what I look like. What I bet I don't look like is Wife-is-having-a-nervous-breakdown Dad.

Oscar pulls his hand from my grip and runs towards the open gate. Hailey stops walking and looks up at me. 'Where is Mummy?' The question doesn't bother me, the look in her eyes does.

'She's in bed, having a lie in.'

Obviously, I don't tell my daughter that Jen barely sleeps during the night and that I often hear her mumbling to herself in the early hours of the mornings.

'Will that make her better?'

I turn my back and close the gate behind us. She sucks the end of her plait as we sit down on the bench and Hailey repeats her question.

'Will it?'

'Mummy just misses Aunty Kerry very, very much.' I pull

her under my arm and kiss the top of her head, both of us laughing as Oscar hangs upside down from the monkey bars, his ribcage exposed from beneath his red T-shirt, his pale ribs swinging back and forth.

'Is that why she keeps doing weird stuff?'

My breath catches in the back of my throat. I turn to face her and brush her hair out of her eyes. 'Sometimes when we lose someone close to us, it can make us do silly things. Mummy just needs a bit of time to fix her broken heart.'

'Will it fix mine?'

'No, tickling fixes yours.' I pull her towards me and begin tickling her under her armpits. Just as I knew she would, she squirms and laughs until no noise is coming out. 'There . . . better?'

'A bit.' Hailey scrunches up her nose and pushes her glasses up. 'What about when she is late to pick me up from school. What should I do then?'

'Mummy is late picking you up from school?'

She begins sucking her plait again, avoiding my gaze and focusing on Oscar. 'Sometimes.'

I reach out and wiggle her knee to get her attention back. 'How often is sometimes?'

'Not many, only once, maybe twice?' She frowns and the purple frame of her glasses moves up with the action.

'Maybe Mummy was stuck in traffic. That happens sometimes.'

She nods. 'It hasn't happened since Mrs Woodley talked to her after school.'

My mouth has gone dry. 'Mrs Woodley spoke to Mummy about being late to pick you up?'

She nods. 'Mrs Woodley and Mr Newton.'

'Mr Newton . . . Oscar's teacher?'

She nods again. 'Don't tell Mummy I told you, OK? I didn't mean to break the promise.'

'It's not really breaking a promise if you tell your daddy, we're a promise-free zone,' I say, plastering a fake smile on my face. 'Now, go and see if you can get Oscar to pull himself the right way up, he's starting to look like a blueberry.'

She begins to run off but stops, turns and runs back to me, throwing her arms around my neck. 'Thank you, Daddy, my heart feels a bit less broken now.'

I swallow the lump in my throat as she kisses my cheek, her skinny legs poking out of her denim shorts, ears sticking out and pigtails swinging unevenly.

What I didn't think I would be is Haven't-a-clue-what-is-going-on-with my-kids Dad.

Chapter Twenty-Five

Jennifer

Ed has taken the kids out for the day; the house feels empty and cold despite the sun blazing through the windows.

Kerry is pointing the controller at the TV and flicking through the channels. *Friends* appears. '*Ooh, it's "The One Where Jen Sees Ghosts".*'

I blink.

The screen returns to black, the red stand-by lights glinting in the bottom right corner. Nessa's number flashes on my phone.

'Hello?'

She sniffs. 'It's me. Can you, can you come round? I've done something stupid.'

'What kind of stupid?' My voice sounds urgent and abrupt.

'It's her things, Kerry's *things*, they're just everywhere! Can you just, I can't—' She is crying as I grab my keys.

'It's OK, I'll be there in a minute, just sit tight, I'm coming.'

I turn off the engine and look towards the house where strewn across the front lawn are clothes – Kerry's clothes. As I step out of the car, I avoid one of Kerry's boots, a handbag and a black belt with silver studs on which I remember being part of her eighties fancy-dress outfit. It looks like a tornado has hit.

'Doesn't look like we're in Kansas no more.' Kerry is holding up the black dress she wore to one of the film premieres they went to last year. It was off-the-shoulder with a long split up the thigh.

The gnome, who continues to peek at me from over the fence, is looking undecided about his feelings towards the pink bra that hangs limply from his fishing rod. Kerry's red dressing gown is hunched in the middle of the lawn. The curtain next door twitches, quickly followed by an anxious-looking lady – the gnome collector, I presume.

Nessa's body is crouching down against the front door, her body wracked with sobs.

'Oh, Nessa,' I say. 'Come on, up we get.'

I hold on to her elbow tightly and guide her towards the house, where the front door hangs open.

'One step after the other, that's it,' I say under my breath, ignoring the footsteps along the path behind where I can hear the gossip being launched behind mouths covered with appalled hands.

My sister's widow follows me into the kitchen and folds herself into a chair, bringing her knees up and wrapping her arms around them as I make a coffee. Ed is ringing my phone; I ignore it, turning the phone to silent. The coffee swirls as I add the sugar and pass it towards Nessa's shaking hands.

'I thought I could handle it, sorting out her things. I can't afford to keep them in storage, so . . .' Nessa looks into her cup as she talks. 'But when I started going through her stuff, I just felt so angry with her. She shouldn't be dead.'

'I should be,' I say.

'God, Jen, no, I didn't mean—'

'It's OK. It feels good to be able to say it. I should have died, Ness, it should have been me.'

I should have died.

Every time this phrase enters my head, it seems to get stronger. At first it was just a flutter, the words a faint, soft, slate-grey pencil mark, looping handwriting that I could barely see, almost transparent: a blur; a thought that could be missed, written on a scrap of paper that could be discarded without a second glance. But that faint grey pencil has been sharpened, and these words are finding more definition.

'I know it should have been me, it was me that rang her and suggested we go to the jeweller's that day, it was my decision to stop and look at my phone screen. I should be dead.' The words are like chocolates in my mouth: they melt and soothe; each one has a different taste. I devour them, pass them to Nessa to try. 'Do you picture me dying? Pretend that it was me, not her?'

She hesitates, then nods.

'How do I die?' I ask her, these words exploding like popping candy.

'You get hit, not her.'

I lean forward, eager for more. 'I think about death all the time. I picture how I'm going to die.'

'Me too.' Nessa drains her coffee.

'What am I wearing? When I picture dying, I'm always wearing green.'

She puts the cup on the kitchen table in front of her and turns to meet my eyes. 'You're wearing jeans, your leather jacket and those grey Converse that you're always wearing. I see one of them lying beside the road.'

I grin at this, at this little detail. I'm not going mad. Everyone pictures death one way or another.

'And?' I ask, eager for more.

'Kerry and I come and see you in the chapel of rest and she tells you we're getting married. She looks beautiful when she's in mourning. She wears dark blue, not black, and the sapphire earrings you bought her for Christmas.' Her face collapses inwards when she says this. 'I threw them out of the window!' Her chair scrapes back and she rushes outside.

Nessa shields her eyes from the sun, stepping uncertainly into the garden, muttering 'Jesus Christ' as she bends down and picks up a pair of Kerry's sunglasses.

'They were my bloody favourite, Ness!' Kerry stands next to Nessa with her hands on her hips.

'They were her favourite,' I say.

'I know. I always thought they covered up too much of her face,' Nessa replies.

'Uh-oh.' Kerry pulls her heel backwards, as though she's stretching before a race.

'I'll clear this up.' I ignore Kerry. 'Why don't you get some rest?'

Nessa looks like it's taking all her concentration to keep upright. She gives me a grateful nod and goes back inside.

I begin to retrieve the items of clothing that hang from the bushes and trees like fairy lights at Christmas, apologising to the gnome for his disappointing catch.

'You don't have to look so pleased about picking up my undies, you know.' Kerry is sitting cross-legged in the middle of the lawn, peeling grass into strips. I reach down at the sapphire glinting in the summer sun. I picture Kerry wearing them, wearing blue, telling my coffin that she is about to get married, and smile.

Chapter Twenty-Six

Ed

Jen isn't here.

'Mummy! We're home.'

Even as Oscar shouts the words, I know that Jen isn't here. I throw down my backpack and carry the shopping into the kitchen as the kids put their shoes in the correct shoe boxes, put their sun hats on the pegs in the porch. They're tidy kids, much tidier than I was as a child. I suppose that's Jen's influence on them.

'Where's Mummy?' Hailey asks quietly. 'There isn't any apple juice and something smells in the fridge.'

'I bought orange juice,' I reply, pulling it out of the bag.

'But I don't like orange juice.' Her eyebrows furrow.

'She's probably gone to the shop to get more apple juice.' I smile. My lies are becoming easier; I don't know if this is a good thing or a bad thing. I have no idea where Jen is. 'How about blackcurrant squash instead?'

'OK. Can we have fizzy water in it? Mummy lets us have fizzy water in it.'

'Sure.' I smile and go into the kitchen and open the cupboard which holds the mineral water. Even as I reach for the bottle, I know it's almost empty. This cupboard is never empty of water: Jen always drinks mineral water, always makes the kids drink mineral water. I shake the bottle, as if by doing that it will suddenly become full, but of course it doesn't. Why didn't I buy mineral water? Hailey is staring at the bottle, frowning above her glasses. I bop her on the head with the empty bottle and she giggles. 'Sorry, poppet, no fizzy water, but I'll put some ice in it for you.'

'Can I have a straw?'

'You can. And then I'll make some lunch.'

The kids go out into the garden and I breathe out. The muscles in my neck are tight and I roll it to relieve the tension. OK. This isn't a big deal. I open the cupboards and start putting the shopping away, trying not to stare at the empty spaces where 'things' should be. Where they have always been. Jen is a bulk buyer. We don't run out of things, because she is always one bottle of fabric softener ahead; cereal boxes sit in tidy rows in the garage, waiting to refill the plastic containers. I reach for one and do the shaking thing again. It's still empty, all but for a few dusty Rice Krispies.

Maybe Jen *has* gone to the shop. I dial her number again and leave another message.

'Hi Jen, it's me, Ed, obviously, um again. Just wondering if you're at the shop? We've run out of a few things.' I scratch the back of my head; I sound like a dick. Like I'm ringing her to tell her off that we're out of Rice Krispies. 'Anyway, I've picked up some bits and bobs, but I forgot the apple juice and, well give me a quick ring if you get the chance. I can go to the shop if you're, if you're . . .' What? If she's what exactly? 'Busy,' I finish. Christ, when did speaking to Jen become something I had to concentrate on?

I hang up the phone and drum my fingers on the back of its case. I look at the kitchen again. There are three things that I consider.

1) Jen hasn't been shopping. This is strange, because Jen likes to keep to a routine. Friday is shopping day. It has

always been grocery shopping day. Always. Today is Saturday.

2) There is a washing load sitting in the washing machine. It is sunny. There is a light breeze. Jen would know this. She smiles when she puts the washing out on days like this. Instead, *Lego Batman* pyjamas are staring at me through the washing-machine door; Batman looks pretty depressed about still being inside.
3) The kitchen is in a mess. Don't get me wrong, I couldn't give a monkey's that there is spilt milk on the side, that there is mould growing on the tomatoes in the fridge. I give a monkey's because Jen does. Give a monkey's, I mean.

Why am I talking about monkeys? Who decided to coin the phrase couldn't give a monkey's arse? And why are they thinking about a monkey's arse? Why am I thinking about a monkey's arse? I throw the tomatoes away and wave through the window at the kids, who are drawing chalk faces on the brick barbecue.

In the lounge, I notice three more things:

1) The carpet needs hoovering. Jen loves to hoover; she hoovers every day. She polishes her Hoover like a trophy.
2) There is a distinct lack of cushion-plumping. Not a plump in sight.
3) Dust. Oscar has eczema, only mild but enough to wake him in the night, for him to draw blood on occasion. This is aggravated by dust. There is dust. Everywhere. I would have done it if I'd noticed . . . honestly, I would.

I'm not house-proud, but I am proud of our house, or rather, I'm proud of us in it: of the lines drawn neatly onto the hall wall with the kids' heights, dates, ages written neatly beside them in Jen's handwriting; of the leaf that Hailey had pressed into clay at school and made into a plate that we throw our keys into when we come home; the hat stand that I insisted on buying even though Jen hated it, because it didn't match. I run my hand over it and can feel the grooves that she made as she sanded it down, feel the faint tracks of the paint brush that she had used. Jen loved it when it was finished, it matched the greys and silvers of the hall; I love it because of what it represents, a piece of both of us. I'm proud of the photos of us that gleam from behind glass picture frames that scale the wall along the banister; I love that with every step, I get to see a piece of our lives together. Pieces of our lives that were captured mostly by Kerry: me wiping squirty cream from Jen's lip in a coffee shop; Jen picking a piece of grass from my shoulder; me watching Jen as she threw her head back laughing; me kissing her bump with Hailey hidden inside; the back of us as we walked out of the hospital, both of us with a hand on the car seat. As I carry on up the steps there are the more recent pictures, the number of faces increasing from two, to three, to four, and with the invention of the selfie, five. Kerry always shining brighter than the rest of us.

I stop at the second-to-top stair and lean in at the photo of Jen and Kerry. It's a photo I had taken. Jen had got the giggles; she'd said 'clogged archery' instead of 'clogged artery' and was at the mercy of the type of laughter that you can't stop, no matter how hard you try. When I'd taken the photo, she had already been laughing for a good five minutes and was at the stage where no sound was coming out of her except the occasional gasp for air. Her hands are gripping Kerry's shoulders, and Kerry is laughing back at her. I had taken the photo . . . but it was Kerry that she had been holding on to for help.

Chapter Twenty-Seven

Jennifer

Ed turns off the Hoover as I walk through the door, trying not to smirk because he is wearing my cleaning apron. My cleaning apron is a great source of amusement to my family.

'What. Is. That?' Kerry had asked as I opened the door to her, the year I made it. It was when I tried – and failed – to find a new hobby when the kids were small. I didn't last long at the textiles class, but the fruits of my labour did result in one of my most favourite possessions: my cleaning apron. It has the right-sized pockets to hold: three micro-fibre cloths at the right breast; duster on the left; elastic holsters at the hips (polish at the right, antibacterial spray on the other); bin bags at the tummy, and tealights and a lighter to replenish the wax burners at the belly button. The material was bought from Cath Kidston and is a flurry of flowers on a pink background.

All Ed needs are some hair rollers, a hairnet, and he would fit comfortably in the 'I Want to Break Free' music video by Queen.

'You look . . . busy,' I smile.

'Where have you been?' he asks. I notice his tone has a clipped edge with a hint of annoyance as he gives me a hasty kiss on the cheek; he smells like a mixture of Ed and Pledge.

My shoulders are sunburnt from the June sun while I was picking up Kerry's things and I have the beginnings of a migraine.

'Jesus, Ed, could you let me get in through the door before you give me the Spanish Inquisition?'

'Sorry, I was worried, we're out of Rice Krispies and there is washing in the machine and I—'

'What?' I ask. Kerry is standing behind him, shaking the empty plastic cereal container. 'You were worried because we're out of cereal? You know, Ed, you could go to the shop yourself. You're a big boy, I'm sure you could manage it, and as for the washing machine—'

'I wasn't—'

'There's a silver button, you press it and then the door opens, it's like magic.'

I hate the way I'm speaking to him, but I hate the worried look on his face more. I know this isn't about Rice Krispies – Ed has never been the type of man to expect his dinner on the table, and he always helps around the house even though he knows that I will probably tease him when he doesn't do things right – but the words spew from my mouth regardless. I barge past Kerry, shooting her an angry look; I throw open the door to the garage, where I find a boxful of Rice Krispies sitting neatly in the spare cereal cupboard. I storm into the kitchen, where Ed is gripping on to the draining board and staring out of the window to where the kids are arguing.

'Here are the goddamn Rice Krispies! Did you even bother to look?'

'Jen, calm down.' He turns, and places his hands on my shoulders; they sting and I shrug him off, instead tearing the box open and trying to pull apart the plastic bag inside. 'I just noticed you hadn't been shopping and I didn't know where you were, I—'

'You want Rice Krispies, Ed? Well, here . . .' I pull the bag out of the box as I wrestle with it, 'they . . .' I pinch the top of the bag between my fingers and try to prise it open, 'are—'

The bag rips apart, an explosion of puffed rice hitting almost every surface, every appliance, the hair on Ed's head. Oscar and Hailey run in from the garden, Oscar brandishing a Nerf gun; they both halt in their tracks, a little skidding sound coming from beneath Hailey's jelly sandals; both of their mouths open into an 'o'.

I look at Ed, whose startled expression is being showered with stray puffs of rice, which are being blinked from his eyelashes. The kids look at Ed, they look at each other, they look at me, they look at the Rice Krispies. A giggle rises from my tummy; it clambers through my chest, bubbling up my throat and escaping into the kitchen. Ed catches it, bites his lip and tilts his head; the bubble of laughter floats towards him, his eyes meeting mine, the sound of my laughter popping the tension that had filled the air just moments before. Rice crunches beneath his flip-flops as he makes his way to me. I point at the sound beneath his feet, the bubble of laughter hovering above me as I take in a strangled breath. I jump into the air, my feet exploding the pile of little puffed-rice-shaped bombs, dust flying from my steps. Hailey and Oscar copy my actions, jumping up and down, sending dusty cereal up in puffs of air. Ed slips his hand in mine and pulls me into a waltzing position; I shake my head, releasing a fresh shower of cereal; we begin dancing, Ed twirling me around. The kids' giggles are like background percussion to my laughter, which is achingly relentless. Soon Ed has to release me, because I'm gasping for breath.

Kerry watches the scene in front of her with a smirk; she sits on the kitchen chair, rolling her eyes at me but chuckling to herself. I have a stitch and step towards her, placing my hands on her shoulders as I try to calm the hiccups that have started to take hold.

Ed and I clear away the dusty remains of cereal, the air between us cleared by the gentle way he danced with me, by the humour of the afternoon, by the kids as we watched them jumping up and down as though they were wearing wellies and jumping in muddy puddles: our two beautiful children, our beautiful home, our beautiful life.

'So . . .' Ed scrapes the dust from the pan into the bin, 'what did you get up to this afternoon?' He has his back to me, he is trying to be nonchalant, but I can see by the set of his shoulders that he is tense.

'Nessa's. She's, she's not doing so well, Ed. She was upset, so I went round.'

'I was worried, you said—'

'I know what I said, Ed,' I say quietly, 'but you've got nothing to worry about. I'm OK. Honestly.'

He straightens and turns to me, a forced smile on his face. 'I'm not sure you are, Jen.'

I sigh loudly. 'Can we not do this now? I've had a hell of an afternoon at Nessa's, she'd thrown all of Kerry's stuff out of her window.'

'Thrown it out?' Ed questions, putting the dustpan and brush away and pulling me towards him. I rest my head against his chest, breathing in his smell, a smell that is unique to him, that I can't imagine ever living without.

'She thought she was ready to handle it, going through Kerry's things, but it was too much for her,' I want to tell him, but he's already becoming so . . . suspicious. 'I've spent the afternoon picking up my dead sister's things.'

'I'm sorry. It must have been difficult for you.'

I think about the euphoria I had felt as I picked up every piece of Kerry's clothing, how I was compiling memories like photos in a photograph album, attaching them carefully with cardboard-corner memory holders. I had a wonderful afternoon, but I know I can't tell him that.

Here is what I do know: I can't share these feelings with anyone; I can't tell anyone that my dead sister is currently making herself a cup of tea, yawning and saying goodnight to me. I can't tell anyone that the only time I feel alive is when I put myself in danger.

I can't tell anyone . . . because then they'll know: they'll know that really, I'm falling apart.

Chapter Twenty-Eight

Jennifer

My eyes are hot beneath my eyelids, as I blink; my eyelids strain with the effort; there is no moisture there. Guilt and insomnia are currently best friends and they have ganged up on me, bullying me. Guilt fills my eyes with tears, a cup forever full and cascading over the edge like a waterfall, but then, just when I feel like I have found some relief, insomnia yawns and stretches. It drinks in all of the liquid, all of the fluidity and emotional release, and replaces it with stark, barren inertia.

The kids run into the lounge, filling my arms with suncreamed skin and artificial, strawberry-sweet breath. I breathe in their smell, gulping it down.

Ed throws down his backpack and slumps onto the sofa, in dramatic fashion. 'We have raised monsters! Monsters! I tell you!'

Oscar lets go of my neck and dive-bombs on top of Ed, who winces but lifts a delighted Oscar above his head.

'Daddy let us eat as many sweets as we wanted at the park, because we both jumped in the deep end at the swimming pool,' Hailey says, shifting her weight on my lap: wide, innocent eyes peering over her purple-framed glasses and a smile tugging at the corner of her mouth.

She lowers her voice into a whisper. 'And I had real Coke. Not the diet kind.'

This is demonstrated by her climbing off my knee and jumping up and down on the space beside me. I look over to Ed. The sun has caught his face, red patches of tender skin cover the end of his nose and cheeks. He puts Oscar down onto the floor, throwing up his hands in a 'not my fault' gesture.

'Daddy? Can we go on our tablets now? You promised if we stopped singing "Who stole the cookie from the cookie jar" in the car that we could have a whole hour on them.'

'I did, didn't I?' Ed catches my eye and gives me a wink. 'Hmmm.' He pretends to give this serious consideration; the one side of his mouth curves upwards, with the spark of mischief behind his eyes. The love I feel for him flutters heavily inside my chest, as though it's actually there in physical form: hundreds of moments of our life together hidden in tiny molecules pumping around the inside of my heart; but I can't reach them, can't touch them: they're trapped. 'OK then . . . off you go.'

'Yes!' Oscar punches his fist into the air; Hailey bounces her legs even more enthusiastically, my body riding the aftershocks on the sofa cushion next to her.

'Thanks, Daddy.' She vaults from the sofa, runs over to Ed and gives him a fist bump, following her brother out of the room and up the stairs.

The guilt I feel for being allowed these moments with my family reignites my insides. Kerry will never have one of these moments again . . . because I took her life away from her.

My shoulders sag and fold forward like my lungs have been punctured; I'm left with nothing to extinguish my scorched insides. Ed rushes to me, kneeling in front of my body as I try to breathe, concern stealing the mischief that was there just moments ago and etching worry around his eyes. His hands rub the tops of my legs rhythmically; I grab hold of them, stilling their motion and gripping on to them: holding on to him before I fall somewhere that I may never return from.

'Did I ever tell you about when Kerry tried to help me buy your birthday present?' His voice is calm, a voice trying to anchor me.

I shake my head, even though the smallest of movements steals more of the air from the room.

'I wanted to get you theatre tickets: *The Lion King*. But she talked me out of it, in that way she had of getting her own way.'

Kerry crouches down next to Ed, looking at him with that look of adoration that others often thought was more than sisterly-in-law love. But they didn't understand. She loved him like that because of how much he loves me.

'Jen doesn't want theatre tickets, Ed.'

'Jen doesn't want theatre tickets, Ed.'

The words are spoken at the same time: reality mixing with the unreal.

Ed continues. 'I'd thrown up loads of suggestions – a necklace, earrings, flowers? A picture? But she'd rolled her eyes. I'd started to lose my patience. "Well, you tell me what she wants then!" I'd said . . . and do you know what she replied?'

Kerry tilts her head and smiles at him: *'She wants you, Ed. Always you.'*

'She wants you, Ed. Always you.' Ed repeats Kerry's words. 'And then I knew what to get you.'

My breathing is slowing, the rise and fall of my chest calming until I can find the air to speak.

'You took me on the walk,' I say, a smile ironing out the tightness that is pulling around my mouth.

'I took you on the walk,' he confirms. I close my eyes and feel the heat from his body shift next to me, his arm encircling me. 'We walked to the train station and sat in the seat opposite the door where I first saw you. I gave you a blackcurrant throat sweet because that's what I had in my mouth.'

'We went to the florist's, but I didn't hit you with the door that time.'

The memory is filled with calm, and I feel the light surrounding it, forcing away some of the red-hot vacuum. I picture us walking hand in hand as he led me towards his old address: I'd been wearing a blue-flowered summer dress and he had put his cap on my head backwards because the back of my neck was burning in the midday sun. 'You sat me on the front doorstep of your first house . . .' I lean my head against his shoulder, 'because that's where you'd sat after our first date when you'd got locked out. But it wasn't raining like that day so you squirted water at me from a water bottle.'

'And I took you to the old stone wall by the bus stop because that was where we had our first proper row and that was the moment that I knew I was in love with you but I didn't have chance to tell you because you'd stormed off, jumped on the bus and left me on there.'

'I cried all the way home. I stayed on the bus . . . did the whole round trip but you'd gone when I got back to the wall.'

'I never knew that.' He kisses me gently on the lips. 'Let me help, Jen. Let me help.'

'I don't know how you can. It was my fault, Ed.. . . it was my fault that she died.'

'Oh, Jen . . . listen to me. What happened was an accident. A horrible, cruel accident. You are not to blame for

Kerry's death.' He pulls away from me and grips me by the shoulders. 'Are you listening to me, Jen?' My head wobbles as he shakes me gently. 'Kerry's death is not your fault.'

He pulls me back into his chest and kisses me on the head. 'It wasn't your fault.'

But it was.

Chapter Twenty-Nine

Ed

Is this what they call an existential crisis? I'm sure that's what this is. I close the toilet seat and tap 'existential crisis' into the search bar of my phone as Oscar brushes his teeth.

> People can suffer from an existential crisis for a number of reas—

'Is that two minutes?' Oscar interrupts.

'No, buddy . . . another, um, forty seconds.'

> —ons: guilt over losing a loved one . . .

Ha! Jackpot!

Right. I type in 'how to fix an existential crisis' as Oscar spits. I'll have this sorted in no time . . . I've already diagnosed the problem; I'll have Jen back to her old self by the end of the week.

> There is no quick fix to an existential crisis, but there are a number of things you can do to help. 1. Identify your triggers.

'What's an egg, eggsiss—' Oscar leans over and peers at the screen.

I close the tab and stand. 'Right, what story do you want?'

I distract my son and guide him into his bedroom, ignoring the sounds of Jen crying from behind the bedroom door. I can fix this.

I lean in and kiss Oscar's forehead, closing the door quietly behind me.

'Daddy?' Hailey's voice calls out. I glance at my watch.

'Hey, poppet, what's up?' I smooth down the unicorn's face on her duvet and pinch the end of her nose.

'I can hear Mummy crying.' I turn my head towards the door where Jen's soft sobs can still be heard. 'Is she alright? Is she cross that I drank proper Coke?'

I smile. 'No, no . . . we haven't done anything wrong. Remember how I said that Mummy's heart is a bit broken?'

She nods, her blonde hair bouncing with the action. I tuck it behind her ears and follow the outline of her birthmark with my finger.

'Well, sometimes, to fix it, you need to cry. Just like you did when Chester the hamster died. Do you remember?'

She rubs her eyes, red-rimmed from the chlorine in the swimming pool and the pull of sleep.

'Shall we make her some flapjacks tomorrow?' Her mouth opens wide as she yawns through her words. 'Mummy made me flapjacks when Chester died and then I was OK.'

Hailey's eyes close.

'Sure. Get some sleep now though, OK?'

'Night, Daddy. Love you millions.'

'Love you zillions.'

*

I sit at the end of the bed and watch Jen sleep. I've read all the hints and tips that WikiHow has to offer: spend time outside, talk to people, imagine one of your idols is giving you advice . . . that one is tricky. Kerry was her idol.

Jen is fitful; the duvet has been kicked and punched and twisted. Sweat is clinging to the hair at the back of her neck and she's muttering to herself. Nonsense words, nothing she says makes sense except for when she calls my name.

'I'm here,' I say, but no matter how many times I say it, whatever horrors that are happening behind my wife's closed eyes, my being here isn't enough.

I've got to do more.

Chapter Thirty

Jennifer

I wake with a jolt again: Kerry's body hurtling backwards, feet and arms in front of her, ice-blue eyes staring at a fixed point in the distance: red coat, red boots and the primal scream of brakes; painted silver nails; emerald ring.

I blink.

Ed is asleep next to me; his arm is lying heavily around my waist, securing me to him. My eyes are sore and my throat dry. I ease myself from beneath Ed's arm, dropping a kiss on the top of his hand, and pull on my shorts and vest.

The kids are snoring gently in their rooms: Hailey is lying neatly on her side in a foetal position, her hair wrapped around her index finger, a habit that has stayed with her since her early years. Oscar, in contrast to his sister lying in the next room, is spread out on top of his covers: arms and legs open wide, brown curls sticking up at all angles. I bend down and kiss his forehead and pull the duvet over him.

Outside the kitchen window, the sky is sherbet: pinks, oranges and yellows powder the sky with dawn. I down a glass of water.

Why am I here? I ask Kerry again.

'*Because you have so much.*'

I know.

'I don't think you do,' she replies and re-plaits her hair. *'Come on, Jen, tell me what you have.'*

I was adopted by a wonderful family?

'You were. Tell me something you love about Ed.'

I love that he makes me laugh, that he works so hard every day to make me smile.

'How? How does he make you laugh?'

He . . . A smile tugs around my mouth. He makes heart shapes with tomato ketchup on my plate.

'There you go. How many women would kill for heart-shaped blobs of ketchup?'

The emptiness fills a little but it's not enough . . . my body leans forward, clicking the catch on the window frame, allowing me to inhale the cool stillness of dawn breaking. It's intoxicating, this smell: fresh and pure and clean. I lean my head as close as I can to the window and stare at the horizon. The world has its arms out to me. 'Look at this open space!' it shouts. 'Look at what is around you!' I step back; the confines of my home holding my hands behind my back.

I need to escape, no that's not right, I need to appreciate what I still have. I'll be back before they're even awake.

At first, I'm walking, the air chipping away at the heat inside. Gossamer quietness floats over the housing estate, hushing the ticking of clocks and hum of electricity, but all too soon, my lungs have become accustomed to the cooler air.

I should have died.

But I didn't.

My feet begin to quicken their pace, the molten heat of those words being pushed back by the dry warmth now filling my lungs. I follow my feet, as they stretch into a run, pounding against the tarmac towards the lanes at the back of the estate which lead to the hills. I've walked this route before a hundred times, pushing Hailey in her pushchair, a few years later holding Ed's hand while she clung her arms around his neck, Oscar's head nestled next to my chest in the baby sling, but this path is leading me somewhere else today.

My feet continue to urge my body forward, the dry heat in my lungs gasping for more of the cool air that surrounds me, the exertion forcing them to work harder, my breath becoming deeper, the purity around me filling my body as the path leads towards Hayworth Hill. Muscles in my legs groan and complain and my back is aching, but my lungs want more; I need to give them more. And so, I do. I run faster, the back of my throat burning; my body has been starving for this cleanliness and if I go a little bit faster, I will be satiated.

I don't know how long I have been running, but the sun is rising higher, the last of the sherbet pinks and lemons sinking, the morning blue tearing open the sky. I'm reaching the summit: the houses below turn their backs on me, the sleepers inside kicking off the cover of quiet. The summit arrives too soon. Too soon I see the monument – a tower of decreasing stone circles that children want to climb and parents warn not to.

Reaching the summit of the hill isn't enough.

My fingers grip the stone edges as I pull my knees onto it. I climb onto the next circle until I'm here: the highest point of the county.

But I've got here too soon. Too soon. It's over . . . too soon. My stomach hurts, stitch threading its needle around my insides. My breath feels hot again now that I've stopped.

My head feels light, the view in front of me swaying when it should be still. The burning at the back of my throat tells me I need water, but I have none. My vision blurs, and then my legs buckle beneath me.

The Imaginable Death of Jennifer Jones – #5

Death by Head Injury

Jennifer Jones watches the snow falling heavily over the county.

'I can't remember the last time we had a white Christmas,' she says to her husband as he pulls the sled behind him. Her green bobble hat is adjusted and she walks on, her boots digging into the fresh blanket of snow.

'Come on, Daddy!' their son, Oscar, shouts. 'We're almost at the top!'

'Are you sure it's safe to let them slide down this side of the hill?' Jennifer asks.

Her husband's cheeks are red and he is out of breath. He stops as they crown the crest of the hill and come to a stop. 'It's fine. I did it loads of times when I was a kid. My weight will slow them down and I'll just dig my feet in and stop if I think we're going too fast.'

Her eyebrows furrow beneath the hat.

'What a view eh?' Jennifer exclaims, looking out.

Her husband plods towards her, leaving the kids organising the position of the sled; his wellies leave deep footprints in the snow. His arms wrap around her shoulders as they look out at the snow-topped, Christmas-cake houses.

'It's beautiful,' Jennifer replies.

'Come on, Dad!' their daughter shouts. She is sitting with her legs either side of Oscar, scarlet woollen scarf wrapped around her neck, while Oscar's blue mittens clutch the reins.

'I'm coming!' The husband kisses his wife's cheek. 'Make sure you get a good picture!' he adds over his shoulders, climbing onto the back of the sled.

Jennifer looks up at the monument, straightens the green scarf and steps up, taking out a camera.

'One, two, three!' her husband shouts.

'Wait!' But they have already started moving. Jennifer Jones climbs up to the next level in haste and aims the screen at their whoops of laughter. She sees them in the shot, the trees surrounding them weighed down with heavy snow, the scarlet scarf of her daughter flying behind them, but then the scene tilts, Jennifer's foot slips from beneath her. And she falls, the crack of her head against the stone snapping at the same time as the camera: the aperture capturing the white of the snow, the green of her scarf and the river of blood flowing from Jennifer Jones's temple.

My head hurts when I come to. A dog's wet nose is sniffing in my face, making me recoil. I try to move but a man smelling of expensive aftershave is talking to me. At first, I can't separate his words, the endings and beginnings crashing into each other like surf on the crest of a wave.

'Stay still.' The world around me is soft, like it is outlined in chalk and the artist's fingers have smudged it. My mouth is dry, my body soaked in sweat. The dog licks my face again, but is berated by a voice behind it while an arm is fixed around me, sitting me upright, my back leaning against the base of the statue. 'I think you've fainted, what's your name?'

'Jennifer,' my lips say.

'Right, well, Jennifer, are you hurt anywhere else?'

My head shakes the negative, even though there is a searing pain radiating from my ankle. My cheek is burning too but I'm not sure if that is just because I'm hot.

'Here.' I smooth my hair away from my head, take hold of the can of Coke he is offering me, lifting it to my dry lips and gulping it down. The dog licks my face again and I can't help but smile.

'Are you lost?'

I laugh at this and then check myself. 'You could say that, but no, I'm local.' I pull myself up but take his arm, wincing as I lean on him for a moment.

The man, Richard, helps me home and I chat easily with him. He has an easy-going manner, conversation flows smoothly, my limping is taking us longer to get home than usual and soon I'm talking about Kerry.

'She sounds like an amazing sister.'

'She was. That's why I don't . . .' I pause, rolling around the words in my mouth, chewing them before swallowing. 'I don't understand why.'

'Why she died?' he questions. I nod, looking away. 'And why you didn't?' The words that fall from his lips seem effortless, hinged with an understanding; they pull my gaze back. 'I lost my twin brother to cancer when I was twelve, so I know something of what you're going through.'

'I'm so sorry.' I give his arm a gentle squeeze. 'How did you . . . cope?'

'I didn't. I got into fights, was drinking myself into an early grave by my late twenties . . .' He pulls the lead with his spare hand and the dog looks up at his owner with affection, tongue lolling out of his mouth. 'I made my parents' life an even worse hell than it was already.'

We're almost at my house and so I stop walking. 'So, what happened?'

'I hit rock bottom, almost drowned after throwing myself off Coletown Bridge. I had my stomach pumped and was forced to join AA. I never intended to get sober, but as I was coming out of my first meeting, I met my wife.' A smile breaks out from beneath his skin, the landscape of his face transforming in seconds: the creases between his eyebrows softening; the crow's feet around his eyes deepen. 'She was late for a dance class and her purse fell out of her bag as she ran past.' His smile is infectious. 'I've been sober 2,196 days,' he says with a hint of pride. 'And we're expecting our first child next month.'

'Congratulations,' I say sincerely. 'I'm so pleased for you, for you both. This is me,' I add, looking up at my house.

As his hand raises to knock the door, he pauses. 'Everything happens for a reason, Jennifer. I know that means nothing to you right now.' His eyes meet mine and there is deep understanding in his gaze. 'Fate is an impossible thing to control, but if you can see past the pain . . . you will find reason there. If my brother hadn't died, I might never have met my wife, we wouldn't be having our baby. I'm not saying that one thing is better than the other, but I don't think there was anything I could have done to change my life even if I wanted to.'

Chapter Thirty-One

Ed

Someone is hammering at the door. I reach for the clock: it's only six a.m. The knocking repeats. My leg kicks across to Jen's side of the bed but it's cold; nothing new there.

I pull my boxers from the heap of clothes on the floor, and rush down the stairs. Hailey opens her bedroom door; her cheeks are red and she is rubbing her eyes.

'What's that noise, Daddy?' Fredrick – her teddy – is hanging limply in her hand; his one eye is missing from a fatal incident with one of Oscar's hot wheels.

'It's just the post lady, go back to bed, sweetie, it's early.' I place my hand on her back and return her to her room as another assault on the front door ensues. I know even as I fly down the stairs that something isn't right. If Jen was here the house would smell of the fresh coffee that she can't function without, the radio would be on in the background playing classical music quietly so as not to wake the kids. The house feels cold, and as I slide across the door chain, I realise that the kitchen window is wide open. I'm scared about this as my hand turns the lock on the front door . . . anyone could have climbed through it. Anyone could have got into our house. But that thought is pushed aside as the door opens and hanging on to a tall, well-kept man, who is a complete stranger, is Jen. And she's bleeding.

Again. And again, fear spikes inside my chest.

There is a diagonal cut along her cheek lying parallel to her cheekbone, like some perfectly marred damsel in distress.

'What happened?' I reach for her, taking her out of the arms of the stranger as he ties his dog's lead around the trellis.

'Nothing, I'm fine, I just tripped, that's all.'

'I found her by the monument.' His voice is rich; it suits the clothing and the perfect designer stubble.

'On Hayworth Hill? What were you doing up there at this time in the morning?' I guide her into the lounge. She is leaning her weight on me and limping, there is blood on her white vest and she is wincing every time she puts any weight on her foot.

I position her onto the sofa and thank the stranger.

'It's no problem at all . . . it was a good job that my dog is incontinent, that's all I can say. She was out pretty cold for a few seconds.'

'Out cold?' My voice shoots up a couple of notches. 'What do you mean she was out cold?'

'I'm fine, Ed, I just need a coffee—'

'She's had a can of Coke on the way. My guilty pleasure, I'm afraid, but don't tell the missus.' He winks, laughs and pats me on the back as if we're making small talk at a bar. 'Speaking of which, I'd best be off. She'll be wondering where I am.'

'Thank you, Richard,' Jen interjects, looking up at this stranger as if she doesn't want him to leave. 'For everything.'

'Take care, Jennifer.'

I find myself looking from one to the other and back again like a spectator. I thank the man who seems to have some kind of understanding with my wife, and see him out the door.

I take a deep breath and head into the kitchen, robotically turning on the coffee machine and reaching for the first-aid kit in the top of the cupboard before returning to Jen. My stomach is clenched into a knot. What am I missing? I mean, she's doing everything that WikiHow says she should be doing: time outside, talking to people . . . but I've got to be missing something.

I don't meet her eyes while I wipe her cheek with an antiseptic wipe; she flinches but I still don't look her in the eyes. I don't look because I'm scared of what I'll find there.

'So,' I begin, 'you went for a run?' It sounds like I'm trying to make conversation, like this is normal behaviour, for her to leave the windows wide open while we sleep upstairs, like it's normal for her to go for a run – a pastime that she hasn't practised for years – at what must have been about half-four in the morning.

'I needed to clear my head,' she says, pulling her cheek away as I dab the wound.

'So, what happened?' I discard the bloodied wipe, open another packet with my teeth and continue. There is a fly behind me, I can hear it buzzing and see that Jen is tracking its movements up and down the lounge.

'I think I was probably a bit dehydrated, that's all. It's been a while since I went for a run.'

'It has,' I agree and then take a piece of gauze and tape it over the cut with microporous tape. I'm about to get up when she grabs on to my hand.

'I need to know why, Ed.'

'Why what?' I ask.

She stares over at the sofa as if she's talking to someone else. 'I need to know why.'

'Why what?' I repeat again.

'Why my life was more valuable than hers.'

'None of that matters.' I kneel down in front of her until

she turns her face to me. 'It doesn't matter why you're here, what matters is that you are here.'

'It's not enough.'

She looks off into the distance again, her face twitching and frowning while she thinks it over. It's starting to scare me, this looking off into the distance thing.

'It's not enough?' I say, bringing her focus back to me. 'Me and your kids aren't enough?'

She blinks a tear away. 'It's not that, it's just . . . I feel like part of me died with Kerry, like I've got a hole inside of me . . .' she clenches a fist to her chest, 'and it's filling up with all these questions. Why am I here and Kerry isn't? And . . .' Her face grimaces.

'And?'

'Why was I so lucky? I know I sound crazy, Ed, but the questions just won't stop.'

'So, let's get you some answers.'

'Thank you.'

Chapter Thirty-Two

Jennifer

I'm in the garden before the rest of the world is awake; the sun is pushing its way up from beneath the heaviness of night. Kerry is pegging out clothes on the washing line, shaking one of Ed's pairs of boxers out before hanging them up. I try to rub the sleep deprivation away with the heel of my hand. I'm thinking about what Richard said, about fate. Was Kerry's death unavoidable?

'*Tell me another reason why you should be happy*,' she instructs from the side of her mouth as she holds a peg between her lips.

'My house?'

'*OK . . . so what do you love about it and please don't say your tea-towel drawer . . . nobody should iron their tea towels.*'

I clasp the coffee cup in my hands. 'I know I'm lucky to live in a nice area, that I have everything I need.'

'*That's right, you do, but what makes it special?*'

'The hat stand. Ed wanted it, I didn't, but then . . . we both fixed it up. It's the first and last thing I always notice when I come and go.'

'*Come on, Jen.*' She untangles a pair of socks and reaches for another peg. '*You can do better than that.*'

'That I can imagine myself growing old in it. I can imagine me and Ed babysitting grandchildren.'

'That's better. Grandchildren and growing old . . . aren't you lucky?!'

I nod. I am.

'Jen?'

I blink.

The washing is gone and Ed is standing in the doorway, half-naked and rubbing his hair. I get up, wrap my arms around his waist and lift my chin so he can kiss me. He flinches at my cold hands, and takes them in his, blowing into them and holding them between his own.

'Couldn't sleep?' he asks.

I shake my head.

'We'll mention it at the doctor's. Get you something to help with that.'

'We?'

'Yeah, I thought I'd come with you, I need to pick up my dry-cleaning in town anyway.'

'OK.'

'We can go to that café with the cinnamon buns first if you fancy it?'

'Edward Jones, you always say the right words. You had me at cinnamon buns,' I reply, closing my arms and thinking about all of the things that I should be grateful for.

'Hello, Jennifer, and this must be Mr Jones, do take a seat.' Dr Faulkner re-arranges her ballerina bun and pushes her oversized glasses up her nose. She looks as though she's in her early twenties.

'So . . . how have you been?' she asks, smiling briefly at me over the rim of her glasses before returning her focus to the screen in front of her. 'I see you stopped seeing the grief counsellor after only two sessions?'

I nod.

'Wasn't it helping?'

I shake my head. 'She just kept repeating what I said and following it with "So how does that make you feel?" I just, well, it was hard enough coping without my sister that going to those sessions just felt like something else to add to the things I didn't want to do.'

'OK. And have you been sleeping any better? It's always hard in the early stages of grief, so how is it now?'

'She doesn't sleep,' Ed interjects. 'Well, obviously, she sleeps, but it's always in small amounts. She fidgets all night long, as though she's trying to run a marathon.'

'I'm not that bad.' I roll my eyes at the doctor. 'What is he like?' my face tries to say, but I can feel that I haven't quite pulled it off. From the corner of my eye, Kerry is wandering around the room, leaning into the pictures on the walls, and yawning.

'It's like sleeping on a trampoline some nights.'

I turn to him, my mouth slightly open. I'm about to defend myself, but then I notice the dark circles beneath his eyes.

'How is your mood, Jennifer?'

'My mood? Good thanks, Ed bought me a cinnamon roll in the café before we got here and that's always a good start to the morning, isn't it?' I laugh, then look at her toned arms and skinny thighs. I bet she's been to a spin class this morning and had something green and liquidised for breakfast.

'So, no loss of appetite, no mood swings or anything like that?' I hesitate and ignore Kerry, who is peering over the doctor's shoulder and reading something on the screen and eating a packet of chocolate buttons.

'Nope.' I smile.

'Lack of libido?'

'Definitely not.' I give Ed a sheepish look and the doctor chuckles.

'That all sounds good. So back to the insomnia, have you ever suffered from it before?'

'No. Not really.'

'So, explain to me, if you can, about how it feels when you try to sleep.'

'I start thinking about the accident, and just lately, well, I keep having these thoughts . . . questions really, you know, why I'm here, and my sister isn't, you know that kind of stuff, but that's normal after you've lost someone close, isn't it?'

'Lost? I'm not lost . . . Hellooo? Earth to Jen.' She waves her hands above her head.

I don't let my gaze flicker to Kerry. 'And it's normal to be thinking about them, to be thinking about old memories?'

She pauses, sensing that I haven't finished talking.

'It's just that—' I clear my throat. 'I think about Kerry a lot and I often find myself . . . daydreaming? Replaying good times with her, that kind of thing.'

'Yes, that's all perfectly normal,' the doctor replies. 'I think anyone who has lost someone so close will have those types of questions.'

'Jen has also been . . . acting a little out of character,' Ed butts in, and I try my very best not to scowl at him. I was just being told how normal I am, she was all smiley, and now look, her neat little eyebrows have gone all 'concerned'.

'In what way?'

'Well . . . she's been, um trying new things . . .'

I feel myself redden, thinking about the new position I had insisted we try last night; Ed almost broke his back.

'Like going to theme parks and jumping off cliffs and—'

'It was only a little jump,' I reassure the doctor with a smile. 'It was a place called Lovers' Leap . . . have you ever been?'

'No, no I don't think I have.'

'Oh, you should go, it's beautiful isn't it, Ed?'

He nods, his mouth opening to continue, but I jump in.

'And Ed enjoyed it just as much as me, didn't you?'

'Um, yes, it was great. But then Jen went to the higher ledge and cut herself and—'

'It was just a scratch. He worries too much, that's all.'

'And then she went roller-booting recently . . .'

'I see.' She smiles indulgently at Ed. 'So, these changes are not dramatic?'

'No, but she often stares into space and . . .' His voice trails off as he turns to me, his eyes pleading with me to help him explain things better.

'Right, I think the best thing we can do is to get your insomnia sorted first. It might well be that Jen's moments of lost concentration are a side effect from lack of sleep. I'll prescribe some sleeping tablets and then let's book you in for another appointment in a month to see how you're doing. Does that sound OK? And in the meantime, I'll print off the NHS notes on bereavement for you both to look through. I think that it'll reassure you both that what you are going through is very common. Talking about it and being open is key.' She smiles at us both, hands us the print-out and prescription. 'But, in the meantime, if you have any concerns, please book an earlier appointment.'

We spend that afternoon at Mum and Dad's. Dad at the barbecue, Mum making virgin cocktails for the kids and positively pornographic ones for us.

Kerry and her notebooks are out again; she's judging the kids' efforts with a pen in one hand, notebook in the other. The kids have been making mud pies, marking them out of ten, adding some of Kerry's scribbled-down suggestions: plain flour (not bad but gloopy), shampoo (looks good but a little sloppy), sugar (total disaster, too many wasps), until they found the winner, which was glitter and sand.

Hailey and Oscar soon tire of the fun and games and return to the kids' channels. The sun is packed away by clouds that look like a slate roof, each swollen grey cloud slotting on top of another, while dirty-golden light tries to shine through the gaps, trying to get through, but the darkness is keeping it out. My parents and Ed head into the kitchen to wash up, so I go and sit on the tyre swing that Kerry has just vacated; the edges dig into the back of my thighs as I step backwards on tiptoes, before letting my body swing forward. I feel Kerry's hands push my back, pushing me higher into the air.

'You should have told the doctor more about me, you know, about how much of the time you think about us.'

'I know,' I answer as the force of my movements sends my hair flying backwards. The sky rumbles, the slate roof cracking open, releasing thick rich droplets of warm rain. I continue swinging; Kerry's laughter fills my ears as the rain sticks my cotton summer dress to my legs, plasters my loose hair to my head. I find I am laughing with her, laughing at the way my body is flying higher, laughing because it feels good to be alive, laughing because I know she is dead and yet it's almost as if I can hear her laughter behind me as my body swings forwards and backwards. I can hear hysteria licking the ends of my laughter, because I know, deep down, that spending so much time with my memories is wrong.

Chapter Thirty-Three

Ed

You know that feeling? That feeling when you look at your wife, husband, whoever, someone you know better than yourself but instead of seeing what everyone else sees, you see something else? If you were to look out of this window, this window with blue flowery curtains held back in those tie-back things and see a grown woman swinging on a swing, laughing and smiling, it might even look like something out of, I don't know, *Pride and Preji*-bollocks but without the period clothing, or the tyre swing for that matter, you know what I mean; anyway, what I'm trying to say is that to anyone else it might look OK. It might look almost romantic how she's enjoying herself so much that she hasn't even noticed that it is raining. But. When you've noticed that the woman you love is starting to behave differently, irrationally, this woman swinging and laughing in the rain, wet hair flying behind her looks like something else. She looks . . . wrong.

Brian joins me beside the window. He glances up at his daughter; he watches her actions with unblinking scrutiny, his actions calm.

'Judith, grab a towel will you, Jen is getting soaked.' He throws me a sideward glance: we need to talk about this, we both know what we can see. Brian washes his glass and dries it with a tea towel.

Jen appears at the doorway to the kitchen. Her face is pale, like she's seen a ghost, and she is soon wrapped up in a towel by her mother and guided upstairs to take a shower. Her mother is fussing, and berating her, telling her she should have come in sooner and what was she thinking? Jen avoids my eyes throughout the exchange.

'She's still grieving,' I begin, filling the silence as Brian continues to look at the tyre swing, the last of Jen's momentum hanging on. 'And I think the guilt of Kerry's death is harder for her to cope with than any of us thought. Jen has so many questions: why Kerry died and not her, why Kerry saved her, why she's even here in the first place.'

Judith joins us as I explain about the erratic behaviour, the insomnia, my worries. I look away from their faces. They stay silent, looking at each other with raised eyebrows.

'Maybe now she has something to help her sleep . . .' I can't help but let my gaze slide away from Brian's as I say, 'and if she could, you know, get some answers, she might be able to control it.'

'Control it?' Brian asks sceptically.

'She can't control her grief; she couldn't control Kerry's death . . .' I shrug my shoulders, embarrassed at the psychobabble coming out of my mouth. 'I just think if we can give her some power back, give her something to focus on, then she can start to get better.'

'But she is getting better,' Judith says.

Brian, I notice, looks away from his wife and meets my eyes, understanding clear in his expression.

'She's much better than she was after Kerry died,' my mother-in-law enthuses. 'She didn't talk or get dressed for days and there was that time when she wasn't eating . . . she's much better now.'

'What answers?' Brian pulls the conversation back, just as Jen walks into the room, but I can tell by his expression that he knows what I'm about to say.

'Jen wants to know why she is alive when Kerry is dead . . . why Kerry saved her.'

Chapter Thirty-Four

Jennifer

It's another Monday morning, another normal day where I am here and my sister isn't, but it's been a good morning. Ed brought me breakfast in bed; the sleeping tablets are working, but they make getting up harder than usual. Oscar has showed us how far he can fire a raisin from his nostril – over a metre, which is impressive – and Hailey has given us a squint-worthy rendition of 'A Whole New World' from *Aladdin* on her recorder.

Ed leans in, his lips brushing the skin just below my ear, as the click of the front door latch locks into place behind me. After I've dropped off the kids, I'm going over to Nessa's to see how she is.

His long legs take the steps from the door to the pathway, his grey suit jacket is folded over his arm, his hands run through his blond hair as he unlocks the car doors with a click of the keys.

'Ed—'

Panic fills me. It wasn't there a minute ago. A minute ago, I was putting on my sandals; I was ushering the kids out of the door and into my open car. I hadn't given a thought to Ed's journey to work: I hadn't pictured the other drivers in their metal coffins, half-asleep, half-alive, not paying attention to the way they are driving. What if something happens to him on the way there? What if this is the last time I see him? My feet run down the steps. He turns towards my voice, surprise in his eyes as I throw my arms around his neck, pull him close to me, grip the tops of his shoulder blades as he bends his body down to my height.

'Don't go. Don't go to work.' I pull myself away and meet his eyes. 'Please, Ed, stay here, stay with me, we can keep the kids home, I won't go to Nessa's, we can—' As I speak these words, the laughter and normality I had seen just a short time ago is gone, and the worry, the fear of shattering me is back.

'I can't, Jen. You know I can't, and we can't keep the kids from school.' His voice is level, kind: guarded.

I swallow down the panic; I try to nod, to confirm that of course he should be going to work, of course the kids should be going to school. I want to tell him that I don't want to be alone.

He glances at his watch. 'Look, why don't I drop you off at Nessa's? I can take the kids to school.' He doesn't wait for my reply; instead he beckons the kids over from my car, sitting redundantly on the drive. Hailey is the first to open her door, followed by an excited-looking Oscar.

'Are we going to Muddy Creek again?' his excited voice asks as he arrives by Ed's side, looking up at his dad expectantly.

'No, matey, jump in the back. Mummy is visiting Nessa, so we're going to give her a lift on the way.'

My feet walk around to the passenger side; I open the door and buckle the seat belt around me. It's as though I'm watching these hands complete their actions from the outside. Is it really my brain telling them to do these things?

Oscar's chatter fills the journey with facts about Riley Davies and how every dinner time he eats with his mouth open and it makes him feel sick. I pull down the visor and catch Hailey's reflection: I notice she has put clips in her hair; two small navy bows sit neatly either side of her parting.

'Your hair looks pretty, Hailey,' I say to the freckled face framed in the small rectangle. Her long dark eyelashes flick behind her lenses as she meets my gaze, a hesitant smile lifting her cheeks.

'Thank you. It's the school photographs today.'

'Oh yes, right. Of course it is.'

She pushes her lips together.

'Well, make sure you give your one-hundred-watt smile.'

She nods and turns her attention to the view passing outside the car window.

I turn my head over my shoulder to surreptitiously look at Oscar's appearance and my heart sinks. He has chocolate spread at the corners of his mouth and along the corner of his white polo-shirt collar. His hair is in need of a cut; why hasn't his hair been cut? I take him every six weeks. I close my eyes and try to remember when I last took him. The car stops, my eyes opening, taking in Nessa's house.

'Have a good day, and remember your one-hundred-watt smile, Hailey.' I don't look at her as I say it; I don't want to see the one-hundred-watt roll of her eyes.

Ed's hand grabs mine as I reach for the handle; I turn to look at him.

'I love you,' he says.

'You too,' I reply and walk away from my family towards Nessa's.

'Hi. Jesus, you look like shite,' I greet Nessa.

'I haven't slept . . . you?'

'Like a log . . . it's the tablets. Maybe you should try—'

'I can't. What if Erica needed me and I didn't wake up?'

I follow Nessa into the kitchen. She is wearing a loose

white shirt tied in the middle above denim shorts. I look down at my own jeans: there is a brown stain of something nondescript and the material of my black top is too thick for a day where the sun is shouting so loudly from the sky.

The kitchen is clean. The sun reflects in the silver tap as it spews water into the kettle, the room soon filling with the rattle and groan of the kettle while Nessa spoons coffee into a cafetière. The table is strewn with paper; a laptop perches on top of a notebook surrounded by several half-filled coffee cups. I nod towards the laptop as she passes me the sugar bowl. 'How's it going?'

'Good. At least that's how it felt at three this morning, it might be a different story when I look at it in the harsh light of day, but that's sleep deprivation for you, isn't it?' She adds water, the grains of coffee rising to the top as Nessa adds the lid and plunger.

'Talk to her, Jen. You need to talk to her about how you're feeling.'

Kerry is plunging the coffee down. Her hair is being held in place by a red-and-white-spotted head scarf, like the day she dressed up as a land girl for Hailey's VE Day school fair: a pair of dungarees hang from her frame over a pale blue T-shirt.

I blink.

She is gone: the coffee is still percolating; Nessa is pouring milk into a jug and is arranging cups onto a tray. 'Shall we go into the garden? You like your coffee strong, right? Kerry always plunged the plunger too early, didn't she?'

Kerry sticks her tongue out behind Nessa's back but the image fades, shudders, like the image of another train passing yours.

The sounds of the kitchen are becoming distant: Nessa's voice runs away from me; I try to move towards it but I'm stuck; I'm paused. Nessa continues to move around the kitchen, the minute hand on the clock continues to tock, steam is still billowing from the kettle . . . but I'm still on pause. My eyes try to search the room for Kerry, but they won't move; I need to breathe, but I can't. A fly is bouncing in front of me, its jerky flight path zigzagging in front of my face. Nessa's hand flaps it away, then her eyes meet mine, the panic I'm feeling reflecting in her eyes.

'Jen? Jen!'

Red coat, red boots, emerald ring, car brakes and my name.

'Jen? Oh God, Jen!'

I blink.

The play button has been pushed and I find myself clutching on to Nessa; my body is reaching for her, desperate to hold on; I don't want the pause button to be hit again by mistake.

She holds me, as my body heaves and shakes, the tears salty along my lips as I repeat the words: 'It should have been me.'

I don't know how long I have been crying, how long I have been wrapped in Nessa's arms on her kitchen floor. She hasn't tried to move, hasn't tried to talk; she has just held me.

'We need to get you to a doctor, Jen,' she says softly.

'A doctor won't bring her back.' I pull away from her and wipe my face with my hands as she stands, holding out her hand to me, which I use to stand myself up. I smooth down my hair, suddenly embarrassed by my episode.

'You won't tell Ed, will you? That I'm, well, about . . .' I flap my hands in the direction of where I had just been having a panic attack, 'that?'

'Jen . . . I don't feel comfortable keeping something like this to myself, I—'

'Please Ness, he's worried about me enough. Look, I'll

change, have something to eat and then go home for a lie down . . . OK?'

She chews her bottom lip.

'I promise I'll tell him, just let me find the right time.'

She considers this and then gives me a quick nod.

'Thank you.'

Chapter Thirty-Five

Ed

My phone rings, pulling my attention away from the Facebook analytics for our plastic-free hand sanitiser. I take the call, relieved to have something else to focus on.

'Edward Jones,' I answer.

'Mr Jones?'

'Yes, hello?'

'Hello. It's Mrs Park from Highbrook Junior School. I've tried to contact your wife but there was no answer.'

'Oh, is something wrong?'

'No, well, nothing serious, nothing to panic about.'

OK. Those words should never be uttered when you're getting a call from your kids' school. I'm putting this out there right now.

I panic.

'Oscar has been in a bit of a . . . scuffle on the playground, and—'

'Oscar has been in a fight?'

Right. So, I know that I shouldn't have sounded proud just then. I don't condone fighting, of course I don't, but, well, I've always worried that Oscar might have trouble sticking up for himself and . . . I can't help it, can I, if I'm proud that he's got a bit of fight in him?

'Not a fight as such.'

Oh.

'Oh. So what's happened?'

'He's punched a child on the nose.'

A smile creeps back on my face, but I correct it straight away. I know he shouldn't have done that, but still . . . the smile reappears.

'So he was sticking up for himself then?'

'Not exactly.'

'Oh, right. Sticking up for someone else?'

'It seems that Hailey—'

'Hailey?' I catch my reflection in the computer monitor. Gone is the proud, slightly amused smile and instead my face is creased with concern.

'Some of the children were saying a few unkind words to her. Hailey did the right thing,' she is quick to reassure me. 'She was walking away from the children, who have been spoken to, Mr Jones, so no need to worry there, but it seems that Oscar took it upon himself to hit one of the children.'

'Hold on. How did Oscar hit a child who is older than him on the nose? He wouldn't be able to reach, surely.'

'Oh, the children were his peers.'

'Sorry? Let me get this straight. The kids who were picking on my daughter are Oscar's age?'

'That's right.'

'What were they saying to her?'

'I'm not entirely sure but I'm going to have another chat with Hailey.'

'So how is Hailey now?'

'She's fine. I think she was more concerned that her brother was going to get into trouble. She's in her English lesson with Mrs Woodley. Would it be possible to have a chat about this after school today?'

What do I do here? Jen is so vulnerable right now but on the other hand, the kids need her. I run my fingers through my hair, take a deep breath and reply. 'I'll see if I can get hold of my wife, but if not, I'll be there. I'll pick up the kids today.'

If I fire this advert through and don't hit too much traffic, I can make it.

'That's great. Thanks so much, Mr Jones, I'm sure we'll get this sorted. There are lots of children who are having a tough time at home and who get through it if we address the inappropriate behaviour swiftly.'

I nod. My mouth has lost the ability to speak.

Since when have we been a family having a tough time at home?

I run across the playground, cursing myself for being late. I get a glimpse of Oscar standing beside his teacher by the doors of the empty playground. My heart swells as I catch the look of worry in his eyes; I give him a smile and wave my hand as I jog across the tarmac. Hailey is biting the skin around her thumb – she's looking for Jen, I realise – and seems shocked when she notices it's just me.

I've decided to handle this myself. I rang Jen earlier and told her I wanted to pick up the kids; she sounded tired . . . the sleeping tablets are helping her during the night, but they seem to be making her lethargic during the day too. I make a mental note to mention it to the doctor at our next appointment.

'Hello, Mr Jones, lovely to see you.'

'Sorry I'm late.'

Oscar steps forward and clings to my leg, and I instinctively begin to stroke the hair on his head. Hailey looks straight at me. 'Where's Mum?' she asks.

'She's not feeling well.'

Mrs Park, the headteacher, leads the way. Oscar is still hanging on to my leg like a monkey and I half drag him with each step. 'The children can stay in one of the rainbow rooms while we have a little chat.' She smiles at me as I try to detach Oscar's hands from around my thigh.

The rainbow room is so rainbowy. I hate this kind of place; the bright colours are splattered all over it, like it's telling you that you have to be happy, you have to be rainbowy. If Jen was here, she'd be telling me not to be so grumpy, and give some reasoning for the bright colours having a positive impact. I'd argue that it looks like someone ate too many ice creams with sprinkles on and threw up all over the place. Rainbow room, my foot. But I am the parent and so I smile enthusiastically at my kids and encourage them to have fun. Hailey's face seems to mirror my own thoughts. She doesn't feel rainbowy either, but Oscar is easily swayed by the tub of Lego and so they both leave us.

I follow the headteacher into her office. It smells like air freshener, has pretty boxes containing tissues and word stickers telling me to follow my dreams because 'you never know where they may take you'.

'Take a seat.' She smiles as I lower myself onto the chair, sitting opposite, still smiling.

'So . . .' I begin.

'So.' Mrs Park places her hands on her thighs with a slap.

I jump in response. For a fleeting moment I wonder if the tweed and perfectly shaped chignon are all a bit of an act and for a second, I'm reminded of the first porno I ever watched. There was this secretary and the photocopier was broken, so in came this guy and—

'Mr Jones.' I quickly bring my focus back to the present. 'If I can just start with saying how lovely both of your children are. Hailey is working well above her age-expected level and is always so polite and helpful . . . but Hailey's teacher, Mrs Woodley, has noticed a change in her recently. She is becoming a little withdrawn and seems to be distancing herself from some of her friendship groups, and even though she is still making progress, she seems to be losing concentration often.'

'What do you mean by losing concentration?'

'Mrs Woodley said that she seems to be off in her own little world.'

I think of Jen swinging on the swing in the rain. I blink back the image. 'Well she's a kid, she's probably thinking about, I don't know . . . kid stuff. There is nothing wrong with Hailey.' I sound defensive, I know I do, but she's a kid. Kids daydream, it's what they do.

'Oh, I'm not saying there is something wrong with her, but we just thought we should raise it with you, that we have noticed a change in her behaviour.'

'Her aunty died last year, just before Christmas. It was quite a shock to her. To all of us.'

'We have a member of staff who could talk to Hailey, she is trained in grief counselling, maybe that would help?'

I nod slowly.

'Great, I'll set that up then. Now there is the matter of their attendance.'

Attendance? There is a problem with their attendance? They haven't been off school at all apart from the day at Muddy Creek. I feel sick. Like the whole world knows a secret apart from me.

'Of course, when I say attendance, I do mean the late arrivals. The school day starts at eight fifty-five and although it's only fifteen minutes here and there, Hailey and Oscar are missing a key part of the day.'

I nod as if I know that my kids have been arriving late. 'There have been a lot of road works—' I hate that I'm lying and more to the point, I can see in her face that she knows I'm lying. 'But I'll make sure that they leave earlier in future.'

'That would be great.' She gives me a concerned look.

'When the children arrive late, they are walking into a classroom already set up for the lesson, they may not get to sit with their friends if group work has already started . . . it just gets them off to a bad start.'

'I'll fix it,' I say.

I need to fix it.

'Right then, well let's talk about today, shall we?'

She talks and I listen. I listen as she tells me Hailey is being teased about her ears sticking out by a bunch of kids smaller than her, that they have been calling her Princess Fiona (from *Shrek*, I have concluded). I listen as she tells me that Oscar came 'really rather gallantly' to his sister's defence. I listen as she tells me that Oscar will lose his playtimes for a week and that it would be good if I could have a 'little' chat with him about fighting not solving problems. But all I hear is my own voice.

I need to fix this.

Chapter Thirty-Six

Jennifer

A noise is pulling me from the darkness; it's pinching my skin, shaking my shoulders. My hand reaches out, grasps my phone and brings it to my ear.

'—lo?' my voice says. I try again. 'Hello?' My eyelids are too heavy to open. I heave my head upright from the arm of the sofa and look at my phone screen, but I don't recognise the number. I blink, trying to focus on the digits in front of me. The darkness is calling me, wrapping its warm arms around my body, the warmth spreading into my stomach and chest.

I focus on the digits telling me the time. I panic; the lead in my veins fights against my muscles as I try to push my body further upright. I punch the screen, selecting the school's number; the answerphone picks up. 'Hello!' I shriek as I force my feet into my discarded sandals. 'It's Mrs Jones, Oscar and Hailey's mum.' I spin around, trying to locate my car keys. 'Can you tell them I'm on my way, I'll be right there . . . my car, my car is broke, um, my car is broken . . . down, I'll be there in a few minutes.'

As I step out of my house, rain falls heavily and I'm soaked through by the time I unlock the car and slide into the seat. As I pull the seat belt across my chest, I can see the curve of my breast beneath the green cotton of my shirt; I'm not wearing a bra. I consider going back into the house, but lightning has sliced through the sky and the rumble of thunder vibrates through me.

I reach for the air-con button and turn it on full, trying to wake myself from the fog of sleep which is still beckoning me. I should never have taken a pill in the day, but I was so shaken up after Nessa's that I just wanted to block it out; I only took one and it was still morning when I got home. The anger I'm feeling towards myself brings tears to my eyes. The wipers are hard at work slicing across the screen, right, left, right, left, right, left; the engine purrs encouragement as I slowly back out of the drive.

Traffic is slow; my reactions are slow.

I notice that I'm over an hour late as I pull up outside the school. The roads are clear, because the children have all gone home; all been picked up by their perfect parents. I turn off the ignition and stare at my reflection. My eyes are glassy and swollen, my cheeks blotchy and my hair is hanging in lank tendrils; my hair is wet, of course it looks messy, I try to justify. Nobody will think anything of it – I've just been caught in the rain – but then Kerry butts in. *'It's not rain, it's grease.'*

I snap the visor shut, take a deep breath and climb out of the car.

My feet slip and slide while they try to hang on to the thong of my sandals: they're smooth and gritty all at once, tiny pieces of gravel rubbing their way between my toes.

The school doors loom in front of me. I try to open them, but they don't budge. I press the buzzer; there is no voice on the other end. I buzz again but there is still no answer. I press my face to the glass and pound my fists on the door as another crack of thunder rumbles through the atmosphere. I look up towards the sky as a bolt of lightning flashes across it; my shoulder makes contact with the door and I fall through into the reception area, my knees slamming onto the floor, my hands splayed, starfish-like either side of them. I'm disorientated, the displays in garish colours splattering and swirling all around me.

Warm hands pull me up; Ed's face comes into my view.

Across from us stands Mrs Park and Mr Newton, whose eyes are trained towards my chest. Mr Newton looks flustered: he glances back to my chest, his cheeks turning red as he looks away again. I turn towards Ed, whose eyes are focusing on the same area that seems to be giving Oscar's teacher so much trouble. I look to where I can see my nipples visible through my saturated – now transparent – shirt. I fold my arms over them; shame and humiliation prickle my skin.

Oscar's blue eyes are wide and confused. Hailey's hand grips his tightly but she isn't looking at her brother. She's looking at Ed, a conversation passing between them: it's not one of the roll of the eyes because Mum has said something silly, it's something else – it's a conversation filled with judgement.

'I'm sorry I'm late, the car—' My words are thick and slow.

'Kids, grab your things.' Ed's face is pinched as he takes off his suit jacket and pulls it over my shoulder. His chest rises as he takes a deep breath, runs his hands through his hair as he turns towards our audience. 'Cars, eh? It's about ready for the great garage in the sky, I think.'

Oscar has let go of his sister and slips his hand into mine. I look down at him: his eyes are wide like they are when I'm reading him his favourite story, like he's just seen the page where the monster is hiding. I pull my arm around him and he leans into me, his wide eyes seeking out his sister's. She responds with a barely noticeable shrug.

Ed is talking too fast and shaking Mr Newton's hand,

thanking Mrs Park, laughing too loudly as he talks about the problems we had with my car, listening to the small talk they respond with while his car keys swing from his finger. He asks if they wouldn't mind if we leave my car in their carpark while he runs us home. He'll be back for it in half an hour, he says. Doesn't want to risk it breaking down with us in it while the weather is so bad. It's supposed to carry on all day, he continues, his tone rising by a couple of octaves. I smile over at Hailey, and she returns it with a tilt of her lips before warily looking away.

The silence of all of the words Ed wants to say is camouflaged by a Roald Dahl audiobook: made-up words like 'snozzcumbers' and 'whizzpoppers' rest over Ed's hands as they grip the steering wheel; they try to tickle Hailey under her arms as she stares out of the window; but they don't, they just clamber around the uncomfortable interior of the car, their fizz deflating and popping into the quiet.

Chapter Thirty-Seven

Ed

Please don't let this be what I think it is. Please don't let this be my wife having a breakdown.

This is what I was thinking as I saw Jen, my beautiful wife, my wife who has always kept the plates spinning, has always kept the invisible string that holds our family together taut and tightly knotted, spread, kneeling on all fours in the reception area of our children's school.

That person who was slurring her words, who was wearing a blouse so transparent that we could all see her assets, that person is the shell of the woman I married.

I reached over to help her up, and the look she gave me . . . that look, I've never seen her look at me anything like that. Like she needed saving. Jen has never needed saving; she is the one who saves us.

My wife is standing in front of the kettle, motionless, as she stares out of the window. I look down to where I'm half-way through preparing the sandwiches: a piece of bread half-buttered.

'Jen?' I place my hand on her shoulder and she jumps. 'Could you pop the kettle on while I finish these?' Gently, I turn her to face me. A smile is placed onto her lips. A kiss is placed on my mouth. But the kiss isn't real: her lips don't yield, her shoulders don't relax. I bring her hand towards me, kissing the inside of her palm, trying to breathe some life into her.

'Tea or coffee?' she asks, brightening.

'Coffee, please.'

She turns her back as I continue buttering the other half of the bread and packing the lunchboxes.

'Mummy!'

Her head turns towards Hailey, who is anxiously looking at the clock.

'Remember we are supposed to be in the car in four minutes.' She points towards the timetable we had drawn together the night before, the three of us listing the morning activities while Jen had 'a little lie down'. This is my first attempt at fixing the late arrivals to school.

There are blocks of colour, each one showcasing a morning activity – getting dressed, brushing teeth, putting coats on, putting shoes on; if all of their morning activities are completed on time, they both get a sticker on their chart. Five stickers means a treat, to be selected from the ever-growing treat list: cinema, sweets, park, Muddy Creek, ice cream. Oscar is currently adding making slime to the list.

Everything looks normal.

I can fix this.

Chapter Thirty-Eight

Jennifer

Reflecting from the mirror above the sink is a face I don't recognise. I lean towards the woman staring back at me.

'*Slap yourself.*' Kerry stands over my right shoulder just like she did when she dared me to drink Tia Maria from Nan's cupboard and needed to pretend I was sober. '*You need to get a grip. Slap yourself.*'

I do as she says. But it doesn't help.

'*Really hard, Jen.*'

I stretch my arm out in front of myself, my palm upturned, and bring it full force against my face: the heel hits my jaw, my fingers marking my eyelids, a red imprint clearly visible in the mirror. I smile and repeat the action, waking myself up, making me feel alive.

'Jen?' Ed knocks the bathroom door. I'm red in the face. With a look of panic, I turn to Kerry.

'*Hoooston, we've got a problem,*' Kerry says.

You're telling me.

'*Quick!*' She points to the bathroom cabinet, where inside I know there is a clay face-mask sachet.

'Are you OK?' Ed asks. The handle moves up and down as he tries to open the door.

'I'm, I'm just—'

'*Quick!!*' Kerry points to the cabinet again but has got the giggles and is crossing her legs like she needs a wee. I bite back the humour as I rip open a charcoal mask and begin smearing it all over my face.

'Jen! Open the door!'

'I'm having a poo!' I shout through my lips, which are poised in the same way as Ed's are when he shaves around his mouth as I cover the red marks with black mud. The handle bounces up and down urgently. 'Almost done!' I make an 'Ugh!' noise as though I'm giving birth rather than having a Monday-morning movement. I flush the loo and slide the lock free.

Ed releases a feminine screech and his body jumps backwards, his hand on his chest like a Victorian debutante. The mask is beginning to harden and so I try to keep my face straight even though I want to laugh; I'm aware that beneath the mask, my face may still be red.

'It's just me,' I explain, the words shortened and spoken from that place at the back of our throat which we employ when wearing a face mask. 'Fancy a kiss?' I ask him with the same face-mask-blunted words; I pucker my lips ever so slightly so as not to shed my fake skin. I take a step forward as Ed backs away. My hands form themselves into monster claws, charcoal mask blackening my palms, as I threaten to grab him. Ed looks down at his white shirt and mutters a warning, 'Jen . . .' But I don't care about his white shirt; I care about the way he is looking at me, the relief that is relaxing the muscles between his eyebrows, that he knows that behind this mask is the old me, that the woman in the mirror isn't taking over this body. I advance, small cracks appearing in the mask as I make suggestive eyebrow wiggles in his direction; he retreats down the stairs, glancing over his shoulder at me as I follow his descent.

'Seriously, Jen! I've got a meeting first thing!' But he's laughing, I'm making him happy. I love making him happy;

nobody on this earth has a smile like my husband. It changes his entire face; it turns his already handsome features into a face that you can't take your eyes off: it's enigmatic. I dismiss his protests, knowing that there is a row of neatly ironed white shirts hanging in his wardrobe.

'Stop!' He puts out his hand like a traffic warden, but the smile is there, the love behind his eyes is there. I don't stop; I grab his tie and pull him towards me, kissing him deeply, marking his shirt with my charcoal palms.

'Ugh!! Mummy, you're making a mess of Daddy's face!'

Ed groans beneath my lips, half passion, half disappointment at being interrupted. I give him a nose-to-nose kiss.

'Daddy likes it.' I kiss him on the lips again and turn to Oscar, the monster claws out, as he squeals in delight and runs away upstairs with me in hot pursuit. Hailey is about to step onto the landing but is forced back into her room by her excited brother; she turns her head, tracking his feet as they jump onto her bed, where he begins bouncing up and down.

'Grrr!' I make the claws again and go to tickle Hailey under the arms, but the look she throws me stops me in my tracks.

'I need to get my shoes on or I won't get my sticker.' She pushes her glasses up her nose and barges past me, shaking her head at Ed, who is stepping from the last stair to the landing. His hand stays on the banister as he watches Hailey push past and rush down the stairs.

'I'll—' I move towards him, but he shakes his head.

'Give her a minute. I'll just change my shirt, then I'll speak to her on the way to school.'

I nod.

'Why don't you have a bath and relax?' The look is back behind his eyes, the look that watches my movements like I'm made of glass, like I'm about to crack and splinter into pieces; the look that knows he won't be able to fix me if I shatter.

The bathroom door closes softly behind me. I run warm water into the bath and begin to wash away the mask in the sink. I look up into the mirror.

Half of me stares back.

Chapter Thirty-Nine

Ed

I pull up on the carpark, ignore the messages on my phone that tell me that I'm going to be late for the meeting and instead, slip my hands into the palms of my children and join the snake of suburbia through the school gates. Huh . . . snake of suburbia, I like that. That's what happens when you start reading self-help books in your spare time, you get all . . . wordy. I snap myself back from the self-help books with a knock, knock joke.

'Who's there?' they say in unison.

'Ipe.'

'Ipe who?' questions Oscar, a wry smirk on Hailey's face.

'Ugh,' I say. 'In your school trousers?'

She giggles at Oscar, who is picking his nose thoughtfully. 'Ipe. Who.' He examines his finger and wipes it on his trouser leg.

'I poo,' Hailey explains, catching my eye. 'What is he like?' her face asks.

'Oh!!!' His body folds over in a fit of giggles. I rub the top of his hair, sending it sticking up in all directions before he runs off with a 'Bye Daddy!' towards the school doors, through the playground where his classmates are running around in circles, proclaiming themselves to each be a character from *PJ Masks*. We watch as he skids to a halt, surrounds himself by friends, drawing them near. 'Knock, knock.' His gang lean in closer; he smiles, loving being the centre of attention as he delivers the punch line. The bell is rung; he throws me a quick wave and giggles his way towards the open doors.

'Oscar!' Hailey shouts, chasing after him. He turns and runs back to his sister, who smooths down his hair, rubs the corner of his mouth with her thumb and straightens his collar, her plaits and blue bows swinging, her glasses perched behind her protruding ears.

I've got a lump in my throat as I watch this. Why didn't I do that? It should have been me, us, that makes sure our son is ready for school. Hailey comes back and I have to clear my throat before I can speak to her.

'OK, pudding?' I manage to ask. She grins at me. The summer has brought out freckles across her nose, two of her teeth are missing and her glasses are smeared. I reach over, take them from the bridge of her nose and wipe them with a tissue from my pocket. She takes them from me, stands on tiptoes as I bend down, and kisses me on the cheek.

'Bye, Daddy! Have a good day at work!' She heads past the lower-school building and rounds the corner to the upper school. I follow her around the perimeter; the green crosshatch fence dissects my view, but I watch her. She walks past the clusters of girls gossiping, past the boys reluctantly picking up their football and hanging their bags on their shoulders. She doesn't speak to anyone. And nobody speaks to her. I hook my fingers through the diamonds of green plastic and watch as she disappears through the doors.

Jen's not the only one having a crisis.

Chapter Forty

Jennifer

Ed says we need to talk. Kerry repeats him and stands by his side as he sits next to me on the sofa. He takes my hand.

'This all sounds very serious. You're not dying, are you?' I try to joke. It's not a good joke.

'This isn't a joke,' he confirms, dropping my hand.

I try not to laugh at the joke-less joke, but the fact that I keep thinking of the word joke makes me giggle.

'You need help, Jen.' Again, Kerry and Ed speak in unison, their words echoing each other. This stops my giggling.

'Around the house?'

He takes my hand again, ignoring my attempt at humour. 'Do you remember when we were first together? How we couldn't bear to be apart? How we told each other everything?'

I nod. 'I still can't bear to be apart from you, Ed.' I lean my forehead towards his.

He takes a deep breath and pulls away from me. 'This is . . .' he clears his throat, 'This is part of why we need to talk.'

'I don't understand. Isn't that a good thing? That after all this time I still want to be with you?'

Kerry puts her hand on his shoulder.

'It is, but it's not because of that you didn't want me to go to work the other morning, is it?'

'Oh, that. I just . . . I just had a horrid feeling, you know? Like a premonition, like something was going to happen to you.'

'I get that, but—'

'I just panicked, Ed. It's no big deal.'

'No. That in itself isn't. When Kerry died, I used to feel like that sometimes too, I was scared that something would happen to you, that a car might hit you or the kids, but—'

'There you go then,' I say, as though this concludes the matter.

'It's not just that. Jen, your moods swings are—'

My eyebrows shoot up a couple of notches.

'Hear him out, Jen, you know exactly what he is trying to say.' Just like she did when he tried to convince me that going back to work after Oscar was born was a good thing. I look over at her and roll my eyes. I'm about to reply, but I don't.

Why are you here?

It's a question, not spoken out loud, because she isn't on my sofa. Half of her is buried beneath a headstone, the rest of her released on the crest of a hill that we used to have picnics on when we were kids: nothing but microscopic pieces of ash being carried on the breeze like a bird.

'If I'm a bird, then you're a bird.'

I roll my eyes at her as she misquotes from *The Notebook*.

'That, Jen.' He points his finger at me as if saying you've hit the nail on the head. 'That is what I'm talking about. You keep looking off into space.'

'I'm not looking into space . . . I'm just . . . thinking about when you were trying to convince me to go back to work after I'd had Oscar, do you remember? Kerry told me to hear you out. So, go on, I'll hear you out.' I do my best not to look in the direction of where she was standing when we'd had that conversation.

'Talk to me, Jen.'

'I don't know what to say.' I look at his face and it is as though he is in physical pain.

'Just get it off your chest, Ed, tell me what you think is going on.'

'OK.' His shoulders lift, like his body is filling with all of the things that he needs to say, like the things he needs to say have been hiding inside the cavities of his chest, lurking in the chambers of his heart, skulking about. 'You're not yourself, and I know that you have had a lot to deal with, but Jen, I think it's more than that. Your behaviour is erratic, you're happy one minute, like euphorically happy and I think, you know, she's fine, she's back to normal but then . . .' he clicks his fingers, 'like that and you're on your ass. You don't speak, you don't dress, sometimes I don't think you even know what day it is.'

'It's those tablets from the doctor, they make me feel sleepy and sick, I've stopped them now—'

'I know that, Jen.' He swallows, trying to keep the words inside under control, but I can see they are fighting to get out. 'I've been using that excuse myself, she'll be better once she's slept, she'll get better if I help more with the kids . . .' He doesn't meet me in the eye when he says this. 'But you're not getting better, Jen, you're getting worse. You've stopped obsessing about making the house look nice . . . you haven't lit a Yankee Candle in weeks.' He throws his hands up defensively. 'Don't take that the wrong way, you know I don't give a crap about the state of the house, or Yankee Candles . . . although I do like the smell of the Black Cherry one; anyway, the thing is, you do. Well . . . you did. Being organised, being tidy, is as much a part of you as the colour of your eyes.'

'The colour of my eyes? What are you going on about?'

He drags his hands through his hair agitatedly. 'I'm trying to say that you're different, Jen . . . When was the last time you washed your hair?'

My head is filled with the things he is talking about and I shake it to try and clear the thoughts, the way I try to get water out of my ears when I've been swimming. 'My hair? My eyes? Ed, I don't—'

'You're ill, Jen. You need help.'

'This is ridiculous! You think I'm going mad because I haven't hoovered and washed my hair?'

'Yes!'

'You can't be serious?!'

'That's not what I meant, I—'

'I am not going to listen to this any more.' I get up and go to walk out of the room.

'The kids know, Jen.' His voice is low and serious. It stops my movement. Kerry's hand is on mine, stopping me from pulling down the door handle. I feel Ed's movements coming towards me, I can feel the breath on the back of my neck. 'Do you know what Oscar has just asked me?'

I shake my head. I don't know because I didn't put the kids to bed. What was I doing when it was bedtime? Then I remember I was talking to Kerry in the garden.

'He asked me when you would be happy again.'

I bite my lip, picturing his face, pink from the bath, his *Spider-Man* pyjamas warm from his body, his hair smelling of Matey bubble bath.

'He wanted to know if he could learn more jokes, if he could make you happy again.'

My breath is shallow, my chest rising and dipping with the strain of it. Ed's voice continues even though it cracks in places.

'And Hailey . . . Hailey has changed, Jen. She has no

friends; she worries all the time about Oscar and you. She hardly eats . . . I watched her walking across the playground and not one person spoke to her. Not one, Jen. They need you, they miss you. I miss you.'

I turn to face him. 'I'll do better. I'll go back to the doctor's. I'll fix it.' I kiss the corner of his mouth, stroke the side of his chin, and leave the room.

Chapter Forty-One

Jennifer

'So!' Kerry rubs her hands together and pulls on a pair of rubber gloves. *'Let's get cracking, where shall we start?'*

She's not here. I know she isn't . . . I haven't completely lost my mind. Not yet. My talk with Ed has made me realise this can't go on. I've made an appointment with the doctor. I know I can't tell them the truth, that sometimes I'd rather live in my memories of Kerry than be in the real world: it would hurt them too much. But I can tell them that I feel lost, that I keep losing concentration. That's all it is, isn't it? When I see Kerry, it's just me losing concentration.

I've got up early, just like I used to. I've cleaned the inside of the bin and bleached the sink so far. Just ignoring Kerry for five minutes has let me see how much has changed. I throw the dishcloth away with pinched fingers and open a new packet, pour bleach down the drain, throw open the window, turn on the radio, make a pot of coffee and sing along to the radio as I plug in my phone charger.

The Imaginable Death of Jennifer Jones – #6

Death by Phone Charger

Jennifer Jones is watching the busy café-goers with interest. It is the last rush before the Bank Holiday and there is a feeling of defeat and exhaustion about the room. But it is not the coffee drinkers and the pastry eaters that Jennifer Jones is interested in. She knows her phone battery is almost dead. Towards the back of the café, there is a slow trickle along the wall. Jennifer hasn't yet noticed how the water from the ceiling above is running directly towards the plug socket. She orders an iced latte and makes her way to the back of the room. For a second the lights flicker. But Jennifer Jones is too busy looking around for a free table, to notice. She finds the perfect spot and draws the chair back from beneath the table. From her bag, she unwraps a lead, then crouches down to where the water drips towards the socket and goes about the business of plugging in her phone charger; there is a bang, a flash and then . . .'

I blink and bring myself back into the kitchen. Christ, I hope that's not how I die . . . and just think about the state of my hair.

Oscar bounds into the kitchen. 'Can I have Choco Pillows for breakfast please?'

I kiss him on the cheek, pull back and smile at him, noticing that he has begun to put on a little puppy fat. 'How about Fruit 'n Fibre?'

He scrunches up his nose with a look of disdain.

'I bet I can count more different fruits in my bowl than yours.'

'What do I get if I win?' He folds his arms in front of his rounded tummy and negotiates.

'How about a trip to the park?' He considers this.

'And an ice cream?'

'Deal.' I put my hand out and he shakes it.

Hailey joins us just as Oscar identifies a crescent of coconut in his bowl.

'Hah! Hazelnut!' I gesture to my spoon where half a hazelnut sits swimming in milk. 'That's three all!'

Oscar's head leans in closer to his bowl of cereal, scrutinising the contents.

'Hazelnut isn't a fruit, it's a nut,' Hailey quietly admonishes.

'Three–two!' Oscar beams.

'Good morning, sweetheart.' I smile at her as she pushes her glasses up her nose and tucks her hair behind her ears. 'Do you want Fruit 'n Fibre?'

She shakes her head. 'No thanks, I'll just have an apple. I'm not hungry.' In contrast to Oscar, my daughter has lost weight. The nightie she is wearing is too short, but it is hanging from her shoulders.

'OK. Right.' I clatter my spoon against my cereal bowl and clap my hands. 'Here is the plan. After I beat Oscar at hunt the fruit . . .' I wink in his direction, making him dip his head closer to the bowl, his eyes squinting as he searches the milk, 'we will get dressed, go to the park—'

'Get ice cream,' Oscar interrupts. I roll my eyes at Hailey and the corners of her mouth tilt; it's almost a smile, almost.

'Get ice cream, and then, Hailey, how about we make Daddy's favourite dinner?'

'Ugh, not that horrid canny-whatsit? I hate that, it's all sludgy.'

I ignore Oscar's remarks about my spinach and ricotta cannelloni.

'I agree with squirt . . . it looks like little tubes of grassy poo,' Kerry had said the first time I made it. I blink and push the memory away; I need to stay in the here and now.

'And we can make the white chocolate cheesecake.'

This time, Hailey rewards me with a proper smile, dimples forming, eyes creasing at the sides. 'Can I bash the biscuits?'

'You certainly can.'

Hailey hops onto her chair and peers over Oscar's shoulder, whispering into his ear.

'Banana!' He scoops a spoonful of cereal so eagerly that the contents of his spoon launch the banana and milk over his shoulder towards Ed, who is walking into the kitchen in just his boxer shorts; eyes half-open, bed hair, stubble and a yawn. The banana slice lands with a slap against the wall.

The kids and I dissolve into a fit of giggles at Ed's startled look of confusion.

'Are you coming to the park with us, Daddy?' Hailey asks, biting into her apple.

'The park?' he asks, kissing me on the cheek on the way to the coffee pot.

'Yes. Mummy says we can have ice cream and then she's going to make you a disgusting dinner.'

I watch as Ed's back remains turned toward me. His shoulders are high, tension crawling across his muscles, at odds with his voice, which is enthusiastic and matches his smile as he turns to us.

'Can we have spaghetti and Marmite instead of horrid canny . . . can-lo-ni?'

'OK. Disgusting dinner for just me and Daddy then.'

'Disgusting dinner is my favourite,' Ed replies.

'Higher, Mummy!' Oscar demands from behind the swing. My hands oblige. My eyes are hidden behind my sunglasses as I watch Hailey and Ed. Hailey is climbing her way across some netting towards a red plastic tunnel and they are in deep conversation. Ed occasionally throws a smile in my direction: everything is fine, nothing to see here. My mouth responds appropriately and my hand waves. The day is going well: I haven't looked at Kerry once, even though right now she is hanging upside down from the monkey bars with a lollipop in her mouth.

Oscar jumps from the swing and runs over to join his sister where she and Ed are giving each other high fives. I follow him nonchalantly, trying not to pay attention to the cautious way that my daughter is watching my approach even though she is grinning proudly.

'I did it, Mummy!'

The pride in her eyes melts my insides. She's always been scared to crawl through the tunnel part of the apparatus. Ever since she was little, she's avoided the tunnels in soft-play areas; she's never liked to feel closed in. 'Oh-oh,' Kerry used to say. 'She's coming up to another tunnel of doom.'

'Nice one, Hailey!! You made it through the tunnel of doooooom!' Kerry elongated the ooooh like a ghost. I bat her away as though I'm shooing a bee.

'You did it!' I say, stepping in front of my dead sister as I begin to perform the dance of victory that we made up last year. It involves wiggling our bottoms and doing the two-fingers-across-the-eyes dance, like John Travolta and Uma Thurman in *Pulp Fiction.* But the pride in Hailey's face has fallen away and she looks at me with embarrassment.

'Silly Mummy,' Oscar laughs. 'Can I try?'

I nod and follow him to the beginning of the equipment, helping him up, noticing that the shorts he is wearing are too tight and that his tummy is spilling over the waistband. I glance over to where Ed is kneeling in front of Hailey, rubbing her arms, reassuring her about something. I squint, but I can't make out what they are saying. Hailey nods at him and runs off towards the big slide. Ed walks towards me, pulling his sunglasses from his head over his eyes and throwing his arm around my shoulder.

'Don't you think Oscar is getting a bit chubby?' I say from the corner of my mouth as I clap him for pulling himself up to the next rung.

'He'll grow out of it. But maybe, you should, you know, stop giving him so much chocolate between meals.'

'You're the one who always gives them too much choc—'

Our conversation stops as our youngest tumbles to the floor. Crouched knees, kisses, and sentences ending with the word 'brave'. Oscar rights himself, wipes his snot on his own arm despite me passing him a tissue from the depths of my handbag; quite where all my packets of tissues have disappeared to I don't know. He runs off, climbing up the slide rather than the net, and does the victory dance, his T-shirt riding up.

Ed squeezes my shoulder, whispering into my ear. 'Maybe we should cut back on giving him so many treats . . . do you remember that scene from *The Goonies*?'

I cover my mouth with my hand, trying not to let Oscar see me laughing as I picture 'the truffle shuffle'. Ed plants a kiss on my head as I lean into him.

Chapter Forty-Two

Ed

I look up to Hailey as she crawls through the red plastic tunnel joining the parts of the play equipment together. She used to be scared of being closed in, but she nailed it a few months ago.

I'm feeling good, happy. I'm mean I'm not deluded, don't get me wrong. I didn't expect that Jen would just be better after our tough love chat. Jen is struggling, of that I have no doubt, but walking into the kitchen this morning felt like . . . like I'd been holding my breath without realising it and when I saw them, saw her face, it was like I could exhale, you know? Things feel normal; she seems normal. Take the kitchen, for instance. I know I'd got used to things being different, the coffee not always on like it used to be, the sounds of classical music playing, the smell of the fabric softener coming from the washing machine . . . things that separately don't mean a thing but all together? It smells and feels like home. Our home.

Conversation has stayed on track, and I find myself starting to relax, but Hailey isn't fooled.

'Why is Mummy acting all—'

'All what? It's Saturday, she's in a good mood.'

'I guess.' I reach up and loosen her foot from the netting connecting her way towards the fireman's pole part, the bit that she is always scared to do. So far, I've managed to get her to lean forward and hold it, but she never lets go. 'Do you think she is feeling better?' Hailey sits down and reaches her feet forward, crossing her pink trainers over on the other side of the pole.

'I think so. She's trying really hard, it'll take time but yeah, I think she's feeling a bit better. Now come on . . . you can do it.'

Her hands reach forward as she grips the pole.

'Good. Right, we've got this.' I clap my hands and rub them together. 'Come on, Hales . . . you can do it.'

Her bottom shimmies closer to the edge, her eyes peeking over the top of the frame of her glasses.

'OK. Three, two, one!'

Her eyes screw shut as she pulls her bottom away from the edge and slides down the pole.

'Yeah!' I pick her up and swing her around, plonking her back onto her feet and giving her a high five.

Jen and Oscar arrive by our sides, a smile fixed on Jen's face.

'I did it, Mummy!'

The smile remains and Jen tells her how proud she is. Hailey's face is reddening with pride. 'Well done!' Jen beams. 'You did it, you got through the tunnel.' Then the joy in Hailey's face drops like a stone.

'Silly Mummy!' Oscar giggles and begins swinging Jen's arms forwards and backwards. 'Hailey got through the tunnel ages ago!'

Jen flaps her hand, as though there is a fly.

But as the day goes on, I can see it. I can see that she is acting . . . Jen is just playing a part on a stage.

Chapter Forty-Three

Jennifer

'Harder, sweetheart,' I say, glancing over to Hailey, who is hitting a plastic bag containing ginger-nut biscuits. 'Think of something that makes you really angry. Look.' I take the rolling pin from her hand and begin walloping the bag with gusto, my voice raising so she can hear me above the banging. 'See? I'm thinking about the woman who pushed in front of us at the ice-cream van!'

Hailey giggles, covering her rosebud mouth with her hand, as though she's afraid of letting me see that she's happy.

I pass the pin back to her. 'Got it?'

She nods and begins hammering the bag, biting down on her lip as she does.

'That's it!'

Her eyebrows pull together as she continues. I ignore Kerry, who is licking her finger and turning the pages in the recipe book. I turn away from them and begin breaking up the white chocolate into a pan.

'You're doing it wrong, you're going to burn the chocolate.'

I'm not going to burn the chocolate.

I ignore her. Kerry never baked, she wouldn't have a clue about the best ways of melting chocolate, but she continues to berate me, telling me the gas is on too high, that I should be using a bain-marie.

You don't even know what one of those is!

Kerry wouldn't have known a bain-marie if it bit her on the arse. I grind my teeth, resisting the desperate urge to tell her to fuck off.

Once finished, Kerry has gone and the biscuits inside the bag have been reduced to rubble. 'All done?' I ask, but Hailey has started crying. I take the rolling pin from her while tears stream down her face. 'What's wrong?' I ask.

She doesn't answer but instead runs to Ed, who is standing in the doorway, his face pale. She buries her head in his stomach, wraps her frail arms around him and holds on tightly.

'I think she's caught her finger with the rolling pin.' He nods, concern etched in the lines around his mouth. 'I'll grab an ice pack.'

Chapter Forty-Four

Ed

If someone were to walk in right now, they would see the clean tidy house, they'd see my beautiful wife making a cake with our cute daughter, and they might be envious. They would see my chubby, cupid-like son slurping the last of his spaghetti and putting his bowl into the dishwasher. But what I'm about to do would change that. It would show them the cracks.

I want to pretend that everything is OK, I want to believe that she is getting better, but she isn't. My fingers swipe the screen and I select the video-camera icon. I point my phone in their direction; it doesn't seem weird that I'm filming them, why would it? From the outside it looks like a happy occasion, mother and daughter baking together.

Hailey is bashing the contents of a plastic bag and Jen is smiling at her. She turns her back and begins breaking up chocolate into a pan but as she does it, she takes furtive glances back towards Hailey. And then goose bumps run up my body. She looks into air and shakes her head, her mouth opening and closing. She is having a silent argument with herself, her hand landing on her hip, a gesture of annoyance.

'Just fuck off!'

Hailey has stopped bashing the biscuits and is staring at

her mother. There is fear in her eyes. Jen turns back to Hailey, oblivious to what has just happened.

Jen doesn't know what she has done wrong, that much is clear. Or she's pretending she doesn't know; fussing around fetching an ice pack, consoling Hailey about her hand, making jokes about how strong Hailey is and how hard she must have been bashing the biscuits.

But Hailey's hand isn't hurt. Hailey is hurt. My daughter is hurting because she has seen the same thing as I have filmed on my phone: she has just witnessed her mother acting like she's crazy and shouting 'Fuck off' at the top of her voice. But I let the charade carry on; I let Jen carry on acting and then I take the kids upstairs for their bath. I put them into their swimming gear and empty a packet of Jelly Bath into the water, turning it into green goo while Jen carries on cooking our 'romantic dinner' as though everything is normal. I can hear her now, humming away while the smell of garlic rises up from the kitchen.

Hailey's eyes are red, even though she is giggling as I tip a cup of green slime onto Oscar's head. I stay in the bathroom as long as I can, keeping the kids . . . keeping the kids: keeping the kids away from their mother.

She comes upstairs as they climb into bed and I try to ignore how my body tenses when I hear her feet on the stairs.

'Mummy! I haven't had any pudding!' Oscar folds his arms.

'You had pudding first, remember, you had ice cream then dinner.'

She winks at me and I smile back, but I can tell by the way Jen is looking at me that I haven't quite pulled the smile off.

'You can have some cheesecake tomorrow.' She ruffles his hair, kisses him on the forehead and touches his nose with hers.

I follow her out of the room but put my hand on her

shoulder as she walks towards Hailey's room, turning her towards me. I sniff the air dramatically. 'Is something burning?' I ask.

She sniffs too. 'I don't think so.'

'I'll say goodnight to Hailey, you'd best just check.'

I try the smile again. It's met with uncertainty by Jen, but she nods and goes downstairs.

Hailey's room is filled with the fading pink light of the sunset coming through her pink curtains. She is lying on her side, a book clutched between her hands, a glittering fairy smiling from the cover.

'What-ya reading?' I ask, the bed sinking beneath my weight.

'The purple fairy . . . she is late for ballet class and the wind has blown her tutu out of her fairy house.'

I try not to shake my head. Why can't the bloody fairy be a doctor or an astrophysicist? I smooth her blanket with the palm of my hand. 'I hope she finds her tutu.'

'She will. Books never have a sad ending.'

I open my mouth, about to correct her, but I close it again, letting her believe that all books have a happy ending . . . she'll find out soon enough that they don't.

Chapter Forty-Five

Jennifer

It's so nice to feel normal. I've ignored Kerry all day, well, most of the day. The kids have been good, the house is clean, and I've managed not to burn the dinner. I close the oven door and put the oven glove back into the drawer, noting as I do that I'm almost out of clean tea towels. I'll put a wash on in the morning.

I can hear Ed and Hailey talking as I make my way upstairs; soft voices meet me as I rest my hand against Hailey's bedroom door.

'Listen Hales . . . about Mummy.'

My hand stays against the door, my feet stay still, and I hold my breath in my lungs.

'She was weird, Daddy, AND she swored. She swored a really bad word. Even worse than—'

I lean my ear against the door but miss the end of the sentence.

I swore? When was that?

'You told me to fuck off.' Kerry is sitting at the top of the stairs, licking cheesecake filling from the back of a wooden spoon.

A feeling of unease is climbing up my spine.

'I know, sweetheart.' Ed's voice comes from behind the

door. 'But I'm going to help Mummy, I'm going to help Mummy get better. I promise.'

'Pinky promise?' Hailey asks.

'Pinky promise. I hope she finds her tutu.'

The noise of the bed creaking warns me that Ed is finished and so I hurry back downstairs as quietly as I can, my heart beating hard inside my chest. I reach for the bottle of red wine and fill our glasses, draining half of mine as I hear the click of the bathroom door above me; I refill it.

'It's almost ready,' I announce as Ed walks into the room. I keep my back turned, afraid to see the look of worry that I know is going to be on his face, wanting, instead, to carry on as we were. My hands grip onto the handles of a pair of wooden utensils.

Ed's hands find mine, stilling my salad-tossing. He rests his chin over my shoulder; his warm arm is around my waist. With his other hand, he pushes the salad bowl away and places his phone in its place, his finger tapping on the videos. I hold my breath as I watch the film: Hailey smashing the biscuits, my back turning away. Bile rises in my throat as I see myself talking to Kerry, my mouth working. I'm not watching an old memory, not imagining my sister . . . I'm talking to her. Hailey's face drains of colour as she watches me, her mother gesturing with her hands, mouth opening with a silent conversation, and then the speaker blaring out the words 'Just fuck off!' as my daughter's body visibly jumps. The phone screen tips and stops at this point where Ed must have intervened, taken Hailey in his arms while I prattle on about an ice pack.

The timer beeper from the cooker interrupts the sounds of me breathing. Beep-b-b-b-beep. Beep-b-b-b-beep. Ed leans towards the cooker and stretches his arm, turning it off. The warmth of his arm returns to my waist; his chin is propped back onto my shoulder. He doesn't say a thing: he doesn't need to. The beat of Ed's heart is penetrating between the soft fabric of my blouse, through my shoulder blades, hammering against my own. He begins to explain how I keep looking off into the distance, how he's heard my voice in the garden when there is nobody there.

'I keep seeing her . . . Kerry. I thought I was just replaying memories, but now . . .'

I begin to flit through the past few months: Kerry sitting at the top of the stairs, licking cheesecake off the spoon; the day inside the café when I ran into Nessa, how she had told me Nessa couldn't resist a cookie; her worried face beckoning me back from the ledge at Lovers' Leap . . . those events never happened. I turn to look at her.

'*Surprise,*' she says, blowing me a kiss, a sad apologetic expression on her face. I let my eyes meet hers, acknowledging what, deep down, I have known all along but haven't wanted to admit to. I haven't been replaying memories; I've been hallucinating my dead sister for months.

'She's standing right next to us.'

'Boo!' she says in Ed's ear.

I laugh quietly. 'I'm not crazy, I know she's not really here, but the images keep coming. I've tried to ignore them, her, but—'

'I can't imagine anyone being able to ignore Kerry.' His chin digs into my shoulder as he talks. 'Do you think she's a . . .' he clears his throat, 'a ghost?'

'No.' I want to explain to him how I know, how I have known for months that I'm not well, that something is wrong with me.

'So. What are we going to do about her?'

'Ask her to leave?' I say, licking a salty tear from my lips with the corner of my tongue.

'It's a start.'

'Do you think I'm going mad?' The word 'mad' comes out in a hiccup.

'I think you need help.' I reach for the phone and replay the video, first focusing on my actions but that's not what I'm bothered about, well, not all I'm bothered about. I'm terrified of what I'm doing to my child. To my family.

'I need more than help, Ed.'

'I can help you.' He holds my hands in front of him, pulling them to his mouth, kissing my knuckles and talking into them. 'We can fix this.'

I pull my hands free and try to sort through my thoughts, try to find the words to explain to him what it is that I need to do.

'I need to leave,' I say.

'You don't need to leave, Jen. I can fix this,' he repeats.

'No, Ed. No you can't. I'll go and stay at Mum and Dad's.' I turn and begin to leave the room.

'Jen . . .'

I hesitate, then face him.

Kerry slips her hand into his and leans her head against Ed's shoulder.

'Do you know that right now, I can see my dead sister holding your hand, that she is leaning her head against your shoulder?'

Ed glances down to where his hands are hanging by his sides.

'That it's taking everything in me not to look at her face? You saw how scared Hailey was, Ed. I can't do this to our children, to you.'

'But leaving won't make it better, Jen.' He says the words, but I can tell he knows I'm right.

'No, but I need to protect them until I am. Thank you . . . for showing me the video.'

'What will we tell the kids?' His voice is hoarse, the words strangled.

'We'll tell them Dad is ill or something. I'll go and get my things.'

'Wait.' Ed grabs my hand and pulls me back. 'Go tomorrow. I'll take you, let me explain it to them. Let me help you.'

'Tell him everything, Jen, it's make or break time. After all . . . it's another day tomorrow.'

'What does Kerry say?' he asks, looking towards his shoulder.

I take a deep breath.

'She says I should tell you everything. And then she's just *kind of* quoted Scarlett O'Hara.'

His eyebrows raise in surprise. 'The one about tomorrow being another day?' He ponders briefly. '*Gone with the Wind*? It doesn't sound like one she'd like.'

I nod. 'It's what she does . . . what I do. That's how I know she's not really here. She quotes films that I know she never watched.' I wipe away a tear.

'Well . . . that's a start. So you don't—' a smile crinkles around his eyes, as he quotes from *The Sixth Sense.*

Kerry bats him on the arm.

'That's what Kerry said.'

'Stay the night, Jen. Let's eat dinner, let's talk. Then tomorrow—'

'I'll tell my parents that I can see their dead daughter and that the one they're left with is going crazy?'

'That the daughter they love needs all of our help.'

Chapter Forty-Six

Ed

I wait until I know Jen is in a deep sleep, then move myself from beneath her arm and go downstairs.

I wait for the kettle to boil as Google blinks at me. What did we do without it? Do you remember the days when you would spot an actor and you couldn't place them? I remember me and Jen arguing over this guy, I was sure it was Malcolm McDowell, but Jen was certain it was Terence Stamp. Jen was right and every time a similar conversation came up, she would say, 'Don't make me Terence Stamp you.' There are no Terence Stamp moments now, are there? A quick swipe of the screen and your answers are right there in front of you. Maybe life would be better without it; pre-Terence Stamp I wouldn't be about to read stuff that I know, in my gut, I don't want to know.

I open the fridge; the remains of the cannelloni sit inside a Tupperware tub. I feel like throwing it across the room. Instead, I reach for the milk and go to make a mug of tea, but my fingers are gripping the plastic handle of the carton . . . what would spilt milk achieve? Even so, my hand is shaking as I take out the tea bag and stir in the milk. The spoon clatters onto the work surface, my fingers grip the edge as my head drops to my chest, tears spill unchecked, my chest begins to heave and I have to force my fist into my mouth to stop the sounds of my sobs escaping into our house.

For better or worse. In sickness and in health. I picture her face as I lifted her veil away; the absolute trust in her eyes that she was marrying the right man was there for all to see. Was she wrong? Would another man have been able to help her? I want to be able to protect them; I want to be the one they turn to when they are scared. Jen is my other half. The other half of me. And she's broken. I have to find a way . . . to fix us.

Google is still blinking at me. It's like it's daring me to type the words into the search bar as I sit down.

I rub my temple and lean on the table. My fingers flex and then I type the letters and stare at them as I take a sip of tea.

'My wife is seeing someone who isn't there'. I click the mouse.

The word I don't want to see is the first word I read: 'schizophrenia'.

'Ed?' Jen's voice startles me. I close the laptop and turn to face her.

'Hi. Sorry, did I wake you? I couldn't sleep.'

She gives me an unsure smile. 'Kerry keeping you up?' she says, but she's joking. I think.

'Is she, um, is she here?'

Jen yawns and shakes her head. 'No. Come back to bed?'

I drum my fingers on the top of the laptop. It's warm and for a moment I picture the word 'schizophrenia' burning away beneath my palm. 'I'm just reading through this proposal for the meeting on Friday. I'll need to make sure it's a good one before I ask to reduce my hours for a bit.'

'What will you say to work?'

That my wife is in pieces, I almost say. 'The truth. That my wife is ill and needs some recovery time.'

She exhales loudly. 'Come to bed. It might be the last time we'll be together for a while.'

'Sure. I'll just finish up. Five minutes?'

She nods, chews her bottom lip as if she wants to say something more. 'OK.'

I wait until I hear the click of the bedroom door before I open the laptop. The words blink at me, but I exit the screen. There are going to be plenty of nights alone when I can read through this stuff.

Jen is still asleep when I call my mother-in-law.

'Sorry to call so early, Judith, but I just wanted to let you know what, um, what has happened. It's Jen.'

'What's the matter? Is she hurt?' Her voice rushes from the phone and I curse myself for not starting the call better.

'No. She's fine, nothing like that. But. No, well she's not fine actually. She's—'

'We've noticed she's been . . . different.'

I breathe out a sigh of relief. 'Would she be able to come and stay with you for a while? She needs some space. I'll explain when we get there.'

'Of course. Of course.' The line goes quiet for a moment. 'You've not had an affair have you, Ed? Only Brian told me about the sailor hat and the . . .' she clears her throat, 'handcuffs, and I wondered if you were trying to spice, uh-hem, things up and I thought that there might be problems with things. It's not unusual for a man of your age to have problems with getting a—'

'Please stop. For both our sakes. No, I am not having an affair. Jen is ill, Judith, she—'

Jen's amused voice interrupts. 'Is going round the bend?'

'What did she say?' my mother-in-law asks.

Jen kisses me on the cheek and takes the phone from my hand. 'Hi, Mum. I'm going nuts and need to come and stay. I'll explain later, OK?'

'Nuts?' I hear Judith's panicked voice as Jen moves the phone from her ear.

'Mmmhmmm.' She pauses. 'Pretty nuts, Mum. Pretty nuts. Do you mind if we tell the kids that Dad is poorly? So, if he could pretend to have a bad back or something?'

Jen is talking to, I was going to say to herself, but it's not is it? It's Kerry. I stand in the doorway and watch her as she folds her clothes neatly into her case.

'I know it's the right thing to do, can you see my white bra?' She waits for an answer. 'Thanks,' she says.

You would think I would find this creepy or disturbing and I do but I mostly feel sad. Because, at the moment, she still has Kerry. What happens when we fix this? When the doctor gives her whatever medicine she needs, treats her for schizo— whatever this thing is. What then?

I push the door open. 'Almost done?'

She jumps when she sees me and looks over to the wall beside the window where I presume Kerry is standing. 'Yep!'

She places her bra on the top of the clothes and runs the zip around the case. She arches her back, leans against the bed with her head down. I walk towards her and rub her back the same way as I did through her contractions. A noise leaves her mouth, a strangled cry in a pitch that I've never heard come out her mouth before. I pull her into my arms and try to soothe the sobs that are shaking her body. I don't know what to say, what to do. I just hold her.

'Mummy?' Oscar pushes the door open and rubs the sleep from his eyes. Jen tries to smile at him but turns into my chest instead. I free myself and scoop him up, taking him onto the landing.

'Mummy has had some sad news, Grandpa has fallen over and hurt his back.'

'How?'

'He . . . he was . . . dancing.'

'Dancing?' Hailey looks at me sceptically, joining her brother, her hand resting on her hip. 'Grandpa doesn't dance.'

'Well, he and Grandma, well they started dance lessons.'

'Like *Strickly*?' Oscar asks, pulling his pyjama bottoms from between his bum cheeks.

'Gross,' Hailey states.

'Did he wear sparkly trousers and have a jacket that is too small for him?'

'Of course not!' Hailey rolls her eyes but then hesitates. 'He didn't, did he Daddy? Grandpa didn't wear sparkly trousers and a jacket that doesn't do up?'

Jen joins us on the landing, blowing her nose noisily.

'Mummy? Does Grandpa wear sparkly trousers when he and Grandma do the dancing?'

'Dancing?' Jen asks.

'Um, yeah. I was just explaining that Grandpa has hurt his back when he went dancing with Grandma.' I cringe, but Jen starts to laugh.

'That's right. Silly Grandpa . . . he . . . slipped on a—'

'Glitterball?' I question as she nods.

'That's right.' She smirks. 'Grandpa slipped on a glitterball and hurt his back. So I have to stay with them for a while to help Grandma look after him.'

'Oh.' Hailey looks at me. Her face is confused and understanding all at the same time.

I clap my hands. 'Right, I'll get you two some breakfast and then we'll take Mummy. Let's see if you can get to the bottom of the stairs before I count to ten. 'One, two, three . . .' I plant a kiss on Jen's cheek as I pass her.

'Glitterball?' she asks.

I shrug my shoulders. 'Four, five, six . . .!'

Chapter Forty-Seven

Jennifer

I'm sitting here watching. Watching as Ed tries to explain to my parents what is going on. Watching the way that Ed's hands are gesturing in the same way as they do when he's had a drink. Too much stimulation.

'Adrenaline is what you mean.' Kerry is sitting on the arm of the chair. She is wearing ripped jeans and a He-Man T-shirt.

Whatever.

'Pardon, love?' Dad asks.

'Hmmm?' I turn towards Dad, who is wearing Hailey and Oscar's stage make-up. This consists of thick, drawn-on eyebrows, blue eye-shadow and a smudge of cerise lipstick with a splattering of glitter across the top of his cheeks.

'Nothing,' I reply. Ed opens his palms in a gesture that says 'see what I mean?'.

'I think I'll just go and have a lie down.' I make my excuses and return to the room that I spent my childhood in. There is a *Friends* poster still on the wall. My bottom creases the lemon duvet as I sit down. The familiarity is comforting and disturbing at the same time. I know there is a small burn mark tucked beneath the bottom corner next to the wall, from a piece of ash that landed on it when Kerry and I had been trying to smoke through the window. I look up to where Kerry is blowing out smoke, a roll-up held tightly between her middle and index finger. She's humming 'The Time of My Life' from *Dirty Dancing.*

'So what now?' I ask her. It feels so good to talk to her again, to have her back with me . . . even if I know that she's a result of, well, I don't know exactly what she's a result of. Not yet.

'*You already know*,' she replies.

My door knocks. I turn towards the sound, then back at the empty window and fight the tears.

'Come in.'

'Hey.' Ed ducks beneath the door frame, carrying my suitcase.

'You don't need to knock.' My words come out in a snap.

'I just thought . . .' His face screws up; the fight that was there just seconds ago disintegrates before my eyes. His shoulders drop as defeat sinks into him, forcing tears to escape. His legs don't seem to know what to do with his body: he steps back, steps forward, his head shakes from side to side then hangs towards his chest, his eyes lift towards me, seeking refuge. The case drops to the floor, his body surrendering into my arms. He's hardly making a sound apart from the odd gasp of air. I hold his face in my hands and begin kissing his eyelids, his cheeks, whispering over and over, 'It's not your fault, it's not your fault, shhh, it'll be OK.'

We lie sandwiched together on the single bed, his head resting on my chest. Beneath us, I can hear the kids playing Snakes and Ladders, hear a lawn mower purring along next door's garden, and feel the heat of the sun, warm on my skin.

'Do you remember the day your dad caught us at it in here?' Ed asks, his voice deep and comforting.

I stroke his hair, laughing softly.

'God, I thought I'd never be let back in the house after that.'

'Me neither. Thank God it was winter and the day the heating had broken down . . . we were still almost fully clothed under the duvet.'

'Do you know what he said to me as I was leaving? He said, "Edward . . ." Ed mimics Dad's accent, making him sound like a Peaky Blinder, 'that young girl up there is precious to me. Make sure she's precious to you too.'

'I never knew that.'

'Kerry was their daughter, but you were their daughter too. No matter what happens. Try not to forget that.'

'Do you fancy an under the cover shuffle before you go? For old times' sake?' I whisper.

The kids' footsteps bound up the stairs, answering my question for us. The door flies open and they pile into the room.

'Come on, Daddy!' Oscar shouts. '*Lego Movie* starts in sixty-two hours!'

'Minutes, dummy,' Hailey corrects from behind him.

'OK, OK . . . let's give Mummy a big cuddle.' He pulls himself up, reaching his hand out to pull me up too.

Oscar jumps onto my knee and hugs me briefly, then whispers into my ear, 'Daddy said I can have popcorn AND chocolate, but shush. He said I'm not supposed to tell you.' He propels himself from the bed before turning around, hands on hips, head dipped, serious face and a deep voice announcing, 'I'm Batman.'

I open my arms to Hailey, who steps into my embrace, and hold her tightly, kissing her head. When I pull away, she is looking into my eyes; I can see my reflection in her glasses below her eyebrows, which are raised in concern, worry making her lips wobble. I wipe away the tear that is running down her cheek.

'How long will you be staying here helping *Grandpa*?'

I look over to Ed who looks away, both of us pretending we haven't noticed the tone of Hailey's question.

'I don't know,' I reply honestly. 'As long as it takes for . . . Grandpa to get better.'

'Will the doctors help, um, him?'

I swallow and nod. 'They will and then, once Grandpa has had some time to heal, I'll be able to come home.'

'And will he be fixed? Will he, you know, be normal again?' Her question pulls my body straight, makes my heart speed up. I start to open my mouth, but no sound comes out.

'Grandpa will be better before we know it. Right, we'd better get going or all the good seats will be gone.'

Hailey pushes her glasses up her nose and nods at Ed. Her arms link behind my neck and she gives me a nose-to-nose kiss. 'Bye, Mummy.'

'Bye, pudding.' I kiss her on the head.

Oscar is still in his Batman pose by the door. 'I'm Batman,' he reiterates, then runs from the room.

'Say bye to Mummy!' Ed shouts after him.

'Bye!' His voice chases after him, Hailey following. She gives me a concerned smile and leaves the room. I stand and tuck my hands into my back pockets. Ed rubs the tops of my arms, leaning in and touching his forehead against mine.

'I love you.'

'I know.'

'I'll pick you up tomorrow after I drop the kids off. The doctor's appointment is at ten.' He pulls me towards his chest, pushes a kiss onto my scalp, and leaves the room.

When I wake, I'm disorientated. Red coat, red boots, emerald ring and then, this time, Hailey's face: eyes wide, skin pale.

I should have died.

The words inside are deeper. I close my eyes and picture the capital 'I': it looks more determined than yesterday, more elaborately looped. The sentence is becoming stronger . . . and more beautiful.

I sit up and pull my phone towards me. Outside, the clouds have covered the sun and rain has begun to tap against the window. There are messages from Ed, photos on WhatsApp of him and the kids in the cinema and another of him holding a burnt piece of toast with a confused look on his face. I smile and reply that I miss him.

My parents are in the kitchen. Dad is stirring instant gravy in a glass jug and Mum is setting the table.

'Pie and chips OK, love?' Mum asks.

'I'm not really hungry, I think I might—'

'Sit down, Jennifer.' As usual, Dad's voice is insistent but somehow not confrontational, and I do as he says.

I wait until the dinner is plated before I try to make small talk. 'They say the weather is taking a turn for the worse.' I concentrate on chasing the gravy around the plate with a chip.

'We don't want to talk about the weather,' Mum says calmly. 'We want to talk about you. Now—'

Dad reaches for the salt, which Mum takes from him with a shake of her head; he sighs in response.

'Start from the beginning. When did you first start seeing Kerry?'

I push my plate away and stare at the pattern beneath the track I have made in the gravy. It's blue and depicts a horse and carriage and a woman wearing a bonnet. 'I don't know. At first I thought they were just memories, you know? But then somewhere along the line they stopped being memories and started being . . . Kerry. When she first died, I kept talking to her, I couldn't see her then, but I just wanted to know she was . . . OK. Even though she is dead. Crazy, right?'

'No, love. We've all done that. I asked her to move the curtain.' Mum cuts into her pastry. 'That's what you do when you're grieving.'

'Did she?' I ask. My eyes are focused on the woman in the bonnet but I raise my eyes in time to see the look that passes between them.

'No.'

'I see her move things.' I look up to where Kerry is stealing a chip from my plate and dipping it into the gravy. I watch as the gravy swirls around it; I watch as a drip falls from the end as it disappears into her mouth with a grin.

I blink.

Kerry has gone and a skin has formed inside the gravy boat. Mum reaches her hand towards mine and holds it tightly.

'What is she doing?' Mum's face is full of hope, for a snippet of 'the afterlife'.

'Dipping a chip into the gravy boat.'

Mum grins but Dad's cutlery clatters beside the plate. 'There is nothing to smile about, Judith, what Jen is seeing is a hallucination, she is—'

'But what if Jen isn't sick? What if it really is her? We had the girls baptised, we—'

'Enough.' His tone is serious.

'It's not her, Mum.'

'How do you know? How do you know that she hasn't come back, that she doesn't want to, you know, move on?'

'Because she was vegetarian and would never have dipped her chip into the gravy. She never saw half of the movies that I hear her quoting from. Because she would never have come back and have me talking to thin air and be the cause of me losing my family.'

I push back my chair and scrape the food into the bin and go back to bed.

Ed's fingers land on top of mine and I realise they are tapping nervously on the tops of my thighs. Dr Faulkner leans back, tips her head to one side and pushes her large, fashionable glasses further up her nose.

'What I think we ought not to do is jump to conclusions. Mr Jones, I've no doubt that you've been Googling?' She smiles kindly and Ed nods guiltily. 'The internet is an incredible thing, but it can make hypochondriacs out of us all. I'm guessing the internet threw up some pretty scary diagnoses?' Ed nods.

'He thinks I'm schizophrenic,' I clarify as she gets up and fetches her water bottle, taking a few sips as she sits back down.

'I don't, I'm just saying that is one of the things it could be.'

'Is there any family history of schizophrenia? Mrs Jones?'

'Jen is adopted,' Ed interrupts.

'I see.' She swivels on her seat and taps this information into her computer. 'Have you ever had any hallucinations like this before your sister died?' She spins the seat back to face us.

I shake my head.

'Can you see your sister now?'

My eyes flick over to Kerry, who is sitting on the examination table, raising her hand like she's in school and saying 'Here'. I nod.

'Do you believe your sister is actually there?'

I clear my throat. 'No. I mean . . . I know she's not actually here, but I also know that I can see her, if that makes sense?'

'How do you know she's not really there?'

'Because the top she is wearing is hanging up in my wardrobe at home. She shrank it and gave it to me over a year ago.'

'*Oh yeah!*' Kerry pulls at the black sleeves.

'People with schizophrenia are usually convinced that what they can see is actually there. I'm not saying that it isn't the case here, but . . . I think it is probable that your hallucinations are being caused by something else. Grief is a powerful emotion, Jennifer . . . tell me about how your sister died?'

'She was hit by a car . . . saving me. It should have been me, I should be the one who is dead. It was my fault.'

Her head tilts to the side; her sympathy for me is palpable.

'Jennifer, deep grief can make the most rational of people become irrational and guilt . . .' her head nods towards me, 'guilt can eat you alive if you let it.' She returns her attention to Ed. 'Now before we can go any further with a diagnosis, we need to rule out any medical reasons for your wife's hallucinations.

'Are you taking any drugs?'

Kerry snorts. Ed does the same. '*As if!*' Kerry states.

'What's funny?' the doctor asks.

'Nothing really, it's just that Jen is a bit—'

'*Square?*' Kerry butts in, drawing a square shape with both her hands.

'Square?' I question Ed with a raised eyebrow.

'Sensible,' he corrects, reaching forward and holding my hand.

'Well, we'll do the test anyway, so we can cross it off for your referral to a psychiatrist. I'll book you in for a CT scan too, again to rule out a few other things.'

'Such as?' Ed leans forward.

'Personality changes can be caused by a brain tumour.' I take a sharp breath in. She holds her hands up defensively.

'But again, this is just a precaution so that we can rule it out. I would also like you both to keep a record of your behaviour. We might begin to see a pattern, and again, it can help us rule out certain disorders. Bipolar being one.'

'OK,' Ed and I say in unison.

'Um, how long will it take until Jen sees a . . .' he clears his throat, 'psychiatrist?'

'It can vary . . . I will put an urgent referral through, though, which may help to speed things up. But until then, I would like to see you once a week, Mrs Jones, just so I can see if there are any dramatic changes in your behaviour. Does that sound doable?'

'Sure.'

'In the meantime, I will write you a prescription for antidepressants. Mood and anxiety can affect so many things; after a month or so we can reassess if they have helped.'

'OK.'

'OK,' Ed repeats.

Chapter Forty-Eight

Jennifer

I'm finding the weekdays away from my family and the cacophony of the school run strangely full. Now that Kerry is out in the open, so to speak. The doctor has suggested exercise and so we are currently in the gym on a treadmill. It's been a while since I've power-walked but I have to admit that I'm enjoying it, if I ignore the dry heat in the back of my throat and the strange puffs that are being emitted through my nostrils. I cast a glance in her direction: she has ear buds in and her silver plait is bouncing between her shoulder blades as she runs in her lycra without seeming to break a sweat. I, on the other hand, can feel damp patches beneath my arms and under my boobs, which are bouncing up and down like a pair of helium-filled balloons, my fringe is stuck to my eyebrows and I'm quite sure my face resembles a slightly overripe tomato.

'Do you have to be such a show-off?' I ask between gasps of air as she increases her speed.

She pulls out her ear bud. '*Pardon?*'

'I said . . .' I swallow down another gulp of air, 'do you have to be such a show-off?'

'*I don't know what you mean.*' She grins.

I turn my focus back towards the screen where my mileage is clocking up. 'It's no wonder you are so thin,' I grumble under my breath. 'I mean look at your bum!' I bend my neck slightly to wonder at her perfectly round bum cheeks that are more like apples, whereas mine are more like overripe cantaloupes. And they're as mottled. 'Have you ever been worried about your weight?' I carry on, even though the effort of speaking is making my voice sound strangled. 'No, I don't suppose you have, you're one of those women who are perfectly comfortable with their shape and aren't ashamed to flaunt it in the face of people like me.'

'*Are you trying to get thrown out?*' Kerry's voice makes me jump. She is standing beside my treadmill with a towel around her neck. She unwraps a chewing gum and pops it in her mouth.

I blink.

On the machine next to me, and in Kerry's place, is a lady of more generous proportions than Kerry, or, I should add, myself. A feeling of dread crawls through me as I replay the conversation I have just had with Kerry. My parting line of 'you're one of those women who are perfectly comfortable with their shape and aren't ashamed to flaunt it in the face of people like me' is holding my attention as heat flames into my cheeks. She throws a furious look in my direction; her bottom has more than a touch of the Kardashian and I realise with another flush to my already flaming cheeks that I have just been scrutinising it.

'I, um . . .' I begin as Kerry covers her mouth in embarrassment, 'I wasn't talking to you.' The woman's eyes have a rather feral look about them as she looks me up and down; her perspiring face resembles a colour somewhere between puce and ruby. She continues to pound her lilac trainers along the treadmill deck. 'I have a . . . that is to say I'm not well, I was talking to my sister.'

From beside me, Kerry grabs my earphones and shakes them. '*Tell her you were on the phone!*'

'I was on the phone!' I exclaim, louder than I had intended, making the woman recoil from me. Her head is pulling back, not unlike a horse in the face of an inconsiderate car horn. She alights her machine, ignoring my protests and apologies as she makes her way to the other side of the gym.

Kerry snorts with laughter and then starts choking on her gum. I would pat her on the back, but she's already dead, so what would be the point?

'It's not that funny,' I say as Ed pulls into the cinema car-park for our date night. Mum and Dad are at our house watching TV and having a takeaway while the kids sleep so that Ed and I can have some time together.

'If you say so. So what did she say to you?'

'Nothing . . . she just sort of glowered.'

His laughter is infectious, and I find that by the time we have bought our tickets, I'm laughing again too. He finally controls himself enough to tell me that my arse is nothing like a cantaloupe as we order our snack and take our seats.

'Well that's good to know.'

I haven't told him that Kerry has come on our date too; I didn't think that mentioning my dead sister tagging along on date night would strike the right tone. We're sitting in the middle of the auditorium; there is a space next to me which Kerry hunkers down in along with her tray of nachos. I have a tub of popcorn – salted and buttered – and Ed is hoovering a foot-long hotdog into his mouth; the lights dim and the trailers begin.

A calm settles over me as we begin to watch. It's almost as if everything is normal, as if this is just any other Friday night. On the screen, two lovers are discovering that they can never be together; the heroine is packing her bags while, unaware, the hot Irish male lead sleeps in the room above. I lean my head against Ed's shoulder as the music builds and an accident befalls the hero. This is the type of film I would watch when Ed was away with work. Ed prefers action films or psychological thrillers. I look up to him, to where he is frowning slightly at the screen. This is the type of film that Ed and Kerry would pull apart, the type of film that right now I'm sure he is ripping open plot holes in and inwardly scoffing at the way the hero and heroine keep *almost* getting together but then something gets in their way. My hand flies to my mouth as the hero is told he is going blind and yet he decides to keep the news to himself.

'*Oh please!*' Kerry interrupts the tears forming in my eyes. '*As if he wouldn't just phone her.*' I turn my head to look at her, noisily slurping her drink and scowling at the screen. Ed crunches on his ice cube as I tell Kerry to shush from the corner of my mouth.

'*Oh come on, Jen, it's stupid!*' She chomps on a nacho and shouts at the screen. '*Just call the girl!*'

'You're stupid,' I smirk, and throw a handful of popcorn in her direction, a piece of which she catches and throws into her open mouth.

'You OK?' Ed asks.

'Yes . . . You?' I whisper back. He meets my eyes, the flashes of blue from the sky on the screen flickering as the shot pans to an aeroplane descending, the noise as it touches down on the runway pulling his attention back to the screen.

Kerry sighs as the story moves on from the hero to the heroine opening the door to an old cottage somewhere in the hills. The blonde actress on screen reaches for the phone but decides not to use it.

'*Oh for God's sake! Now she won't ring him!*'

Beside me, Ed unwraps his sweet noisily as I quickly whisper back, my response hidden by the crinkling of his wrapper.

'If she called him, there would be no story. Stop being a grumpy git.' I throw another piece of popcorn.

This is exactly how things used to be and I find myself smiling as I accept one of Ed's packets of sweets, the wrapping crinkling noisily as I tear it open with my teeth.

'Shush!' a man sitting behind us implores.

'Sorry!' Ed throws over his shoulder, rolling his eyes at me as he turns back to the screen.

The film continues, Kerry becoming so keen on her negative dialogue that I have to put my finger in my ear.

A few moments later, a torch beam bounces along the aisle and is pointed at Ed and me. Next to the attendant is a woman with large hair and wild hand gestures. The beam dips as the attendant consults the woman, who is gesturing and pointing maniacally at us. I gulp as she picks out a kernel of popcorn from her hair and glares at me.

'Um . . . Ed?'

'Hmm?' His gaze slides from the screen to the bouncing beam of light and the popcorn-kernelled woman. His eyes widen amongst the flashes from the screen; I'm not sure if it's the colour from the screen or Ed's pallor that has changed to grey.

I look sheepishly up at Kerry, who is standing next to the petite woman. She has her arms arched over the lady's head and is now pointing enthusiastically to the popcorn kernels ensnared within the backcomb and hairspray. I chew the inside of my lip as Kerry starts counting them loudly, laughing as she does.

'*Oh Jen! Jen! Look at that one! It's buried right in there!*' Once she reaches six, Kerry bends over, her laughter so consuming that she has started snorting. In contrast, Ed's face looks anxious. He leans in, speaking into my ear, but I can't hear him, I can only hear the sound of the dramatic music from the screen and Kerry's laughter. I glance up to where my sister – sniggering and looking more and more like she's going to wet herself – narrows her eyes triumphantly as she spots another piece of buttered and salted.

I blink.

Kerry has disappeared.

'Jen?' Ed repeats my name.

'I think I may have thrown popcorn at that lady.' I look up at him with a grimace as his eyes widen in understanding.

The lady in question is now gaining the attention of other cinemagoers. The faces from the flip-down seats flash red as an explosion explodes from the screen. The attendant ushers himself forward along our row.

'I'm afraid I'm going to have to ask you to leave, madam.'

'There has been a mistake,' Ed begins, shifting his body to the edge of the seat, straightening his back. 'My wife is ill and—'

I look up at Ed, tears blurring my vision, the laughter that was bubbling in my chest just moments ago bursting, leaving nothing but a feeling of emptiness as I gather my things and make my way across the empty seats. I try to apologise to the lady waiting at the end of the row, but Ed steers me slightly away, stepping just in front of me, apologising on my behalf, offering to pay for the woman's ticket. Her expression softens as she listens to his words. I can't hear what he is saying; I'm watching the screen instead, wondering if the hero and heroine will finally get their happy ending.

If only mine was as easy as their story.

Chapter Forty-Nine

Ed

A routine has ordered its way into our life over the past few weeks. I get up early, make the kids' lunches, write in their reading journals, iron their uniforms, take them to school, go to work, smile and shake hands, keep my head down, say the right things at the right times, drink coffee, pick up the kids, worry about why Hailey is so quiet, notice that she is becoming quieter with every day that Jen is away, that she has started to get angry and frustrated with simple things that she used to enjoy. I make the dinner – try not to make the chicken nuggets again, try to stop Oscar from helping himself to the biscuits when I'm not looking – bath them, FaceTime Jen so she can read them a bedtime story, say goodnight, blow them kisses as she goes on with her life without us but still with Kerry. I kiss the kids goodnight, clean up, work from home for another couple of hours to make up the time for leaving early for the school run. I call Jen again before bed. Sometimes we watch TV together, her in her bedroom at her parents, me on our bed at home. We say I love you; we say we miss each other.

She says she's getting better, but then tells me what Kerry thinks about the show on TV, laughing about how ridiculous her point of view is. I laugh too, as if this is all normal; I even throw in a few one-liners in response to some jibe

Kerry has apparently said. I don't say how every time she says the words 'Kerry thinks' or 'Kerry says' that it feels like parts of her are falling away from me. I ask if she's taking her medication and she says she is; I tell her she'll be home before she knows it. I run my plans for the weekend with the kids by her: the cinema is now a no go, so last weekend we went to the zoo, which was fine, I mean apart from a whispered over-the-shoulder conversation while we waited for the caterpillar ride and an outraged man who thought Jen was referring to him when she told Kerry that she was 'such a dick'. This weekend we're just having a day at Nessa's because Jen says the tablets are making her ill.

Which brings me to Nessa.

Jen and Nessa, Nessa and Jen.

Jen is spending more and more time with Nessa. Lots more time. Judith seems to think it's a good idea, that Jen has someone to talk to. That is what she said to me. But I'm not so sure; I mean, it's not as if Nessa is in the best place either, is she? It wasn't long ago that Jen was the one looking after her.

'It's good that she's got Nessa to talk to.'

'Why? She's got me to talk to,' I retorted. Even to my own ears I sounded snappy and impatient, but in my defence, I was practising a plait with three pieces of rope tied onto the back of a kitchen chair. The chair stays still and doesn't wriggle around and complain about how I'm hurting its head.

'Oh you know what I mean, Edward, sometimes you just need a girlfriend to talk to. She's not only lost her sister, she lost her best friend too.'

'Daddy. You're hurting my head.'

'Sorry.' I stop the Dutch plait that my fingers have recently learnt to make. Thank the Lord for YouTube. Thanks to the chair and the rope, I've become quite proficient at girls' hairstyles recently. 'Almost done. Pass me the purple bobble.'

'But my swimsuit is green.'

'Oh. Pass me the green one then.'

'We don't have any green bobbles.'

'Yellow?'

'I have banana ones or lemon. Which do you think, Daddy?'

I look over to where Oscar is listening to our conversation, the scrunch of his nose expressing my own confusion. 'They're both yellow. It doesn't matter, does it?' I question as Oscar rummages into the hair bobble pot and holds up the bobbles in question in each hand.

Hailey takes a deep breath and I feel the familiar tug of my heart, the pride that sits on my lips as she explains in layman terms the error of my ways.

'No, Daddy, they aren't the same. The banana ones go with the bright colours and the lemon go with the pale ones.' She pushes her glasses up her nose and points to the banana variety.

'There're pineapple ones too. What about thems?' Oscar drops the lemon and dangles the pineapple variety from his finger.

'Hmmm. What do you think, Daddy?'

'Well, I think that the tone of your swimsuit is of the lime persuasion so I would go with the pineapple, then you've got a tropical theme going on. The banana is a little more pina colada and the pineapple hints at a more refined palate . . . more margarita?'

Girls' outfits are another thing that I'm finding it hard to negotiate with. It took me ten minutes to work out how to do the straps on Hailey's swimsuit. They criss-cross her back and attach themselves onto the suit in some weird clip things. Oscar is wearing swimming shorts. One leg through the hole, the other leg through the other. Simple.

Hailey pulls a face that says my dad is weird, then points to the pineapple bobbles. 'I like the pineapple ones, I think,' she concludes; Oscar pulls back the elastic and catapults it in our direction, then runs into the kitchen laughing.

I bank this conversation, ready to tell Jen. I find myself doing this, storing the good things into one part of my brain like a filing cabinet. 'Things that are OK to tell Jen.' Every night for the past few weeks, Oscar has woken screaming in the middle of the night because he's had a nightmare. At first, he was easily consoled but last night, try as I might, I couldn't. It took Hailey to come into his bedroom and snuggle up to him. She sang 'Somewhere Over the Rainbow' like Jen does and he soon went back to sleep. That goes into the file marked 'Things that are not OK to tell Jen'.

'Can you help me make a volcano, Daddy?'

'Ouch!' The pineapple band twangs against my finger. I twist it back into place at the end of Hailey's plait. 'A volcano?'

'Yeah, for the end-of-term science day.'

'Um . . . OK.'

'It doesn't matter if you don't want to. Rachel Rodriguez always wins anyway.'

'What do you mean?'

'Her daddy is a gineer.'

'A gineer?'

'He makes stuff.'

'Oh! An engineer. There you go.' I release the plait and spin her around to face me so I can check that she doesn't look totally ridiculous.

'That's what I said. A gineer.'

'Well, I got an A in technology so I'm sure we can knock

something up that will give Rachel Rodriguez a run for her money.'

'OK.' Her face tries to not look impressed, or excited, or anything but nonchalant about the whole thing, but I can see a smile tugging at her clamped-down lips.

I make a mental note to Google how to make a volcano. It's going to be the best homemade volcano in the history of homemade volcanoes.

I have to make sure of it if I'm going to keep that smile on my daughter's face.

Chapter Fifty

Jennifer

'Hi, Jennifer? Jenny?'

'Just Jen.' I smile at the psychiatrist.

'I'm Doctor Popescu. Please, sit down.'

Kerry is watching him, her eyes widening as she mimics me flicking my hair, fluttering my eyelashes and mouthing '*Just Jen*'. I try not to laugh. Dr Popescu is gorgeous and clearly my subconscious is only too aware of this fact. He looks Italian – long nose, dark eyes, thick hair – but his accent is more Eastern European, I think.

Dr Popescu smiles. He has a nice smile, not like Ed's or anything – Ed's smile can make me weak at the knees even after all these years – but he's good-looking, in a carefully maintained gym-and-daily-skin-care-routine kind of way.

'So, how are things? Dr Faulkner has passed on your notes and explained a little about your situation. I understand you're taking olanzapine?'

As nothing has changed since taking the antidepressants, my doctor has started to give me some antipsychotic drugs 'to help control the neural transmitters in your brain'. I baulked at the mention of them, and ignored my husband, this man who was sitting next to me and spouting medical terms like he'd swallowed a whole medical dictionary. I mean, I'm seeing a deceased relative, but does that mean I'm psychotic? I check myself. Nobody has said that. *Am* I psychotic?

'And you're living with your parents?' he continues.

I nod. 'Just for a little while, until, well, until . . .' I look over to Kerry, who is mimicking tying a noose around her neck. He tracks my focus and smiles.

'And your sister, Kerry . . . How is she today?'

'*I'm very well thank you,*' Kerry replies, perching herself on the end of the desk and grinning at him. '*Thank you for asking.*'

His question has startled me slightly. 'She's . . . fine, thank you. She's sitting on the edge of your desk.'

He tilts his head and smiles at me. 'You seem pleased that she's here with you?'

I bite my bottom lip and consider the correct response. He seems to instinctively know that I'm being careful of my words. 'It's OK to say you're pleased she's here. If I had the chance to talk to my best friend who died of meningitis eleven years ago, I would be smiling too.' He gets up and gestures to the coffee pot; I nod as he pours me a cup. 'Milk? Sugar?'

'Just milk, please.'

He passes me the cup and sits back down again. 'I'd imagine it must be good to see your sister again after losing her so tragically?'

I nod and take a sip of my coffee.

'Can you tell me how it feels? To be able to talk to her again?'

I take a moment and try to explain how I feel. The fist of anxiety which is knitted inside my chest flexes as I begin to talk.

'When Kerry died . . .'

Kerry is miming: her two hands are careering towards each other, fists colliding, as she fakes her own death by closing her eyes, her tongue lolling out of the corner of her mouth. She looks up and grins before giving me a 'go on' nod of her head.

'. . . all I could think about was the logistics of her death. How her chest wouldn't ever move because her lungs weren't breathing, how her eyelids would never blink, how I would never hear her laugh. I would think about the gap she had created in our lives, how she wouldn't be on the end of the phone after I had a bad day or if I heard something funny. For months after she died, these were the things that I thought about. But eventually, those thoughts started to subside and I felt like I was coming to terms with her death, you know?'

He leans back and takes a sip of his coffee.

'And then I started having these memories of her and they were so vivid that her loss started to feel a little less painful.' I lean forward and put the cup on the desk. 'I'd read this article about healthy grieving and it said that you shouldn't be scared to let yourself remember the good times, so that's what I did. Every time I saw her, it felt like I was getting a bit better, that I was getting on with life. And seeing her makes me . . .'

Kerry grins over at me from where she is straightening a landscape picture that is slightly wonky.

'Happy?' he questions. Tears prickle behind my eyelids as I admit to this stranger what I haven't been able to admit to my husband. Seeing Kerry makes me happy, even though seeing her is tearing my life apart.

'Yes.' The word comes out in a whisper.

'Your sister died in a car crash, yes?'

'Yes.' I clear my throat. 'I mean no . . . she was hit by a car, but we, we were crossing the road. On a zebra crossing. She pushed me out of the way.' I look over to where Kerry has her back turned and is looking out of the window.

'I can't get the image out of my head. Sometimes it's the first thing I see when I wake up.' I close my eyes as I describe it to him. 'Her body flying backwards, her arms and feet in front of her as though she was trying to touch her toes, her blue eyes staring straight ahead, the clothes she was wearing.' I open my eyes and meet his. 'A red coat, red boots and the sound of the brakes screaming.' I wipe away a tear that is rolling down my cheek.

'You know, Jennifer, we have a long road ahead of us. It may be that the tablets aren't the right ones for you, it may be that they take away your hallucinations but replace them with other symptoms. It may be that they don't work at all. We don't have a diagnosis for you yet, it's very early days. But I can tell you that grief is an incredibly powerful emotion, it can affect your mental health in many ways. You've suffered some of these already, sleep deprivation for instance, which then interferes with your ability to think clearly, it can hamper how you make decisions, so problem-solving can become difficult.'

I nod as he reels off these things like a shopping list.

'Have you ever heard of complicated grief?'

'Isn't all grief complicated?' I ask with a sad smile.

He nods. 'It is, but for some, complicated grief can be like clinical depression, it even resembles post-traumatic stress disorder, even though it is neither of these things. Jennifer, it is clear that you are grieving deeply for your sister, for Kerry, but what you are also dealing with is guilt . . . and guilt can be just as hard to eradicate as ghosts.'

'So, what's it like being away from home for so long?'

I reach down to the side of the sun lounger and reach for the sun hat Nessa is passing me – a huge floppy white one, more suited to Audrey Hepburn than me. 'It's . . . quiet. I'm reading a book for the first time in ages.'

She straightens the scarlet cups of her bikini, unravels the hosepipe and begins filling the paddling pool in preparation for the kids' arrival. It's large, half-way between a hot tub and a small swimming pool, and sits in a neat square of lawn. The yellow nozzle coughs and splutters before a surge of water spews from its mouth and pounds against the turquoise plastic of the pool. 'And Ed? How's Ed doing?'

'Fine. I think.'

Nessa steps into the pool.

'I don't know really. I mean, I get the feeling if things were bad, he wouldn't tell me anyway.'

'What do you mean?'

'Oh, I don't know, it's like our conversations are . . . censored? Like I'm trying to protect him and he's trying to protect me so neither of us are really having a conversation at all. It's different because now, when we see each other, we always have the kids . . . we're never really alone any more.'

'And Kerry?'

Kerry is red in the face as she blows up the inflatable Lilo that we took on holiday to Lanzarote.

'Kerry is about to pass out.' I laugh and look in her direction towards the fence where ivy weaves between the wooden slats and honeysuckle leans over from next door. Nessa follows my gaze. 'She's blowing up the pink Lilo that we took on holiday,' I say, explaining.

'When's your brain scan?'

I blink.

Kerry has gone.

'Next week.'

'Have you started taking the tablets yet?'

I nod. 'They make me feel sick.'

'Well, there's bound to be some side effects.'

I don't tell her that every time I take one, they make Kerry sick too.

When we were kids, Kerry would suffer from tonsillitis; every November it would take hold of her. Her temperature would rocket; her skin would be glistening with sweat as her whole body shook. She would get delirious, the world around her becoming distorted and fictional.

A few days after I began to take the tablets, I woke in my old bed in my parents' house with my dead sister lying next to me. Her skin grey and pallid, her body shaking; she actually *looked* dead.

'Yes,' I reply, 'I suppose there are always going to be side effects.' Killing my sister, for the second time, being one. If someone was to ask you the question of whether you could kill your sibling to stay married, to live with your own children, could you do it?

I peer over the top of my sunglasses at Nessa, who is going red across the tops of her shoulders, and offer to put some sun cream on her back. She positions the hose so it stays dropping over the edge of the pool and sits on the lounger next to me. I squirt the lotion directly onto her back.

'That's fucking freezing!' she yelps. 'Your sister was much more forgiving, she always warmed it in her hands first.'

'Are you scared that you'll forget the small things like that?' I ask as my hands rub small circles of lotion onto her shoulder blades.

Nessa pulls her hair across the nape of her neck out of the way of my hands. 'Sometimes . . . but I'm trying not to.'

'I keep remembering things that I haven't thought about for years, like when we were little, she would make little cardboard houses for insects. She'd spend hours decorating them. Dad would get her ripped-off pieces of wallpaper when he went to the DIY shop. Ages she would spend, creating these homes for them.'

'Maybe we could do that with the kids?'

'She would have liked that.' I flick the lid shut on the

bottle as Nessa lies on the sunbed, tummy down, and undoes her strap. 'Maybe I should do more things like that – things that Kerry would have liked – instead of thinking about all the things she can't.'

An alarm plays on my phone, reminding me that I need to take another pill. Kerry drops the Lilo and sits next to Nessa's feet. She watches as I reach into my bag and toss the bottle between my hands. Her chin lifts in defiance: go on then, I know you have to. Her gestures mimic the time Mum caught her sneaking back into the house at half-one in the morning.

'Did you know about this?' Mum had asked me: hands on hips, no-messing-about expression. I'd shaken my head: not me, I know nothing.

'Then who let her in?'

I was beaten; Kerry gave me the look and we were both grounded for two weeks.

I close my eyes behind my sunglasses and Hailey's face hangs on the inside of my eyelids, scared and upset. My eyes flash open and I avert my gaze from Kerry, instead glancing down to the pills in my hand, throwing them to the back of my throat, hitting it like flint, scraping down my insides, cutting away at me. Their capsules separate, the insides spilling out, firing off in different directions, I can feel it . . .

Kerry coughs, covering her mouth with a tissue and bending herself forward.

'I'm sorry,' I say.

'What?' Nessa asks. Her head is turned away from me and she's humming along to the radio. I reach down and pick up my paperback and ignore the fireworks that are exploding in my veins. The sound of the gate creaking open is quickly followed by Oscar's voice clambering towards me; it throws its arms around my neck before his body can follow it.

'Muuuummmmy!'

I lean into him, my arms desperate to be filled with his skin, his hair, his smell. The ridiculous hat falls from my head; my daughter watches it land on the floor.

'Hello, Mummy.' Her voice saunters over to me, ambles and hovers awkwardly.

I reach out my arm towards her. I smile and can feel the red lipstick that I had applied cracking. I never wear this colour, but I wanted to make an effort; I wanted to look my best for him. He isn't looking at my red lips though, he's looking anywhere but at me. I, on the other hand, can't take my eyes off him. His eyes are red-rimmed: he's not sleeping.

'I love your hair, Hales!' My body is desperate to hold her, to inhale her smell, but hesitation sticks to her skin like insect repellent. Instead, I begin to stroke the peculiar plaits that are hanging parallel to her lopsided parting. My heart swells as I imagine her trying to plait her hair by herself.

'Thanks! Daddy has YouTubed.'

'Daddy YouTubes a LOT.'

The knowledge that Ed has tried to plait her hair is like a sparkler in my hands, something new and dazzling, but I know it will burn me if I get too close to it. Oscar runs over to the pool, his chubby legs are less chubby I notice, his shorts a little less snug.

'Does he?' I ask. My lips are smiling at Ed, trying to tell him how proud and how sorry I am all at the same time. I stretch out my hand towards him; he has the same hesitancy around him as my daughter but moves towards me regardless.

'Yep. He YouTubed how to make a dippy egg runny.' Hailey tiptoes across the lawn; she has always walked on her tiptoes, not like with the confidence of a ballerina, more like she's afraid to make a noise, too scared to leave a mark on the ground.

Ed's hand is warm in mine: it feels so familiar, but it

doesn't fit the same way as it used to; his fingers feel too long, my hand too small. His lips brush my cheek, his free hand resting at the back of my head. I wonder if he can feel that my hair is softer; I spent two hours walking around with a conditioning mask on it this morning. Nessa laughed and said I was behaving like a teenager before a first date. Nessa's hands are unsuccessfully trying to fit the two sides of her bikini strap together; I release Ed's hand and help her. It's only for a second but Ed has already left my side and has followed the kids to the paddling pool. The loss of his hand in mine feels different from what I'm used to, like the loss is actually a relief. I open my mouth to speak but close it again; I don't know what to say to him. Conversation that used to fall like rain is barren.

I follow him to the water's edge. 'Have the kids got sun cream on?' I begin. 'Only Hailey burns so easily—'

'Yes. I bought some factor fifty from Boots.' His tone lands somewhere between disappointed and resolved.

'Oh, I thought I told you where the spare sun cream was? In the blue box in the garage?'

He looks away from me, seemingly focused on something much more important.

I try to make light of it. 'Oh. Maybe it was Elvis I told . . . we've been getting on like a house on fire.' It is supposed to be a joke, but his face is telling me a different story . . . it's a split second before he can rearrange his features into mock amusement, but it's there. For that split second . . . he believed me. I place my hand on his arm carefully, 'I'm joking, Ed.' I don't know if I'm trying to reassure him or myself.

'Oh.' Ed looks back at the kids, shielding his eyes from the sun. 'I know, of course you're joking.' He turns his back on me. My hand goes out to reach him – it hovers between his shoulders so close that I can feel the warmth of him through his shirt – but the muscles beneath are tensed and I let my hand drop.

'Besides, if I was going to start talking to dead rock stars,' I prattle on, 'I'd have gone for Jim Morrison, he's more my type.'

He turns to me and gives me a smile that is normally reserved for chatty supermarket cashiers, the ones that want to talk to you rather than get on with the job as quickly as possible. A smile for strangers.

Chapter Fifty-One

Ed

I'm pissed off. I know I'm pissed off, but I also know that I shouldn't be pissed off.

I'm saying pissed off too many times . . . and that's pissing me off too.

We let ourselves in through the back gate where Nessa and Jen were lying on sun loungers listening to music. Nessa was lying on her front, her back bare and shining from the sun cream. That bothered me, because Jen had probably put that on for her . . . all slippery and shiny. And what is Jen wearing? She looks like she's trying to look like Audrey Hepburn. My mood has swung from happy to see my wife to something else. She's wearing red lipstick.

It doesn't suit her.

We're both distracted and looking over to where Nessa is asking Daniel what time he is dropping off Erica.

'Mummy, look! I can hold my head under the water for twenty seconds, count!'

But Jen is walking back to Nessa. Hailey watches her go and starts counting. I try to give the kids my attention, but I hone into the conversation.

'He's on his way. Honestly, I've never known anyone who is always so late . . . he'll be late for his own funeral.' She flinches and catches Jen's eye. 'Too soon?' Jen shakes her head and rolls her eyes.

Oscar erupts from the water at the count of nine. 'Nine,' Hailey says in a bored tone.

'It was not. It was twenty.' Oscar is indignant. 'I counted one-two-three-four-five—'

'You don't count like that, silly. You have to go one Mississippi, two Mississippi.'

'What's a misterzippy?'

She shrugs her shoulder. 'Mrs Park always counts Mississippis when we're getting changed for P.E.'

'Hey, Ed! Why don't you take your gorgeous wife out while I play with the kids for half an hour? Dan will be here in a minute with Erica.'

Jen leans forward and kisses Nessa's cheek.

'Marvellous idea!' I reply; my voice sounds more pleased about it than I feel, for some reason.

I try to ignore the lipstick imprint that Jen has left on the side of Nessa's cheek.

Chapter Fifty-Two

Jennifer

Nessa has suggested Ed and I go for a walk together, giving me a wink that said she knew exactly what my hair treatment and red lips meant I was after. Ed is grumpy: I'm not surprised; I suppose I'd be grumpy if the roles were reversed and he was the one who was psychotic. I Googled it last week: 'Psychosis is a mental health issue that can cause patients to interpret things around them differently from others. This can be through hallucinations or delusions.' See? Psychotic.

I finish the strawberry ice cream that Ed has just bought me, and we walk hand in hand as we approach The Nook. The Nook is a part of the park that is hidden almost, an overgrown archway leading into a small square courtyard. Off to the right, through another barely visible archway, is a hidden garden. The kids think it's magical; we told them it's not even visible to other people and there is some truth in that, you could almost miss it. We duck beneath the ivy that hangs down and almost obscures the small patch of mossy grass. Trees arch over the hidden space protectively, the leaves hanging beneath a pentagram of sky. Fragments of sunlight skittering through, giggling in quiet whispers as they dance and court the silver of the birch tree trunks. We lie back – hand in hand – in the centre of the grass. The ground beneath us is mossy and warm and I feel it yield against me, cushioning my frame. Kerry has left; it's just the two of us. The tablets have relaxed me: my breathing is deep and calm, my skin tingles and fizzes. The Nook is working its magic.

'Is she here?' Ed's breathing is quicker than mine, his body tense, his limbs balancing on the moss rather than sinking into it. I prop myself up on my elbow and look down at him, brushing a stray piece of hair away from his forehead.

'No.'

'Are the tablets working?'

Kerry – shaking and pale – in the bed next to me last night, shimmers, the image just out of reach, like a dream that you try to remember.

'I think so.' I lower my lips and kiss him. His taste and the softness of his lips swallows me; I lower myself into the moment, the magic of The Nook, the fire inside, the fizzing of my skin . . . I wonder if this is what heaven feels like.

'Is this heaven, do you think?' I question against his mouth, my hands slipping beneath his shirt, my leg hooking over his. I feel so alive . . . is that what heaven is, feeling more alive than when you were living?

His hand reaches for mine but holds it firm. 'Stop, Jen. We need to get back to the kids.'

'The kids are fine, they're with—'

'The kids are not fine, Jen.' He looks up at me, concerned. 'Is that what you think?'

His words fire like bullets, each one shattering part of the scene, pulling back the curtain. The ivy loses its luscious greens and instead is ropy and framed by nettles. The moss-like grass feels hard; patches of it are sunburnt yellow and are dry and itchy across the back of my legs.

'I'm getting better, Ed. I promise I will get better, she's hardly here at all any more.' I try to kiss him again. I want that feeling, to be loved and cherished by my husband. I lean over him, letting my hand glide down his body towards his flies.

'Jen, please . . . stop. We can't.'

'Shush, there's nobody around,' I giggle. His hands hold mine firmly, though.

'It's not that. You're not well and I—'

'I feel fine.' I straddle him and go in for another kiss, but his head turns from me. This startles me and I sit back in shock. 'What's going on?'

'Nothing, I just, I . . .'

I lift my legs off his and face him. My skin still holds the fizz, but it's more than the gentle popping of lemonade in a bottle; my skin feels the sting of electric, the burn as it slices through the hairs on my arms.

'You're not well and I'd feel like I'm taking—'

'Advantage of me?' The words tumble from my mouth, the hurt behind them sending my body reeling, The Nook suddenly cold and dark.

'Yes. NO. It's not like that, you, you're, you're acting differently, it would be like I'm being unfaithful.'

'Unfaithful?' My voice is tinged with disbelief. 'To whom? The woman who washes your clothes and cleans your house? The woman who picks out furniture and irons tea towels? That woman? Is that who you're being unfaithful to, Ed? Is that who you're missing?' I can hear the hysteria in my voice as I stand up.

Kerry is leaning back against the tree like she hasn't a care in the world. '*Go easy on him.*'

'You're just as much to blame for this,' I tell her; I don't even try to hide her from Ed.

'He's trying his best.'

'Oh, shut up! You're not even here!'

'The devil convinced the world he didn't exist . . . it was his greatest trick.'

'You've never even watched *The Usual Suspects*,' I reply from under my breath.

I should have died. The words float around my head, but I grab hold of them.

'You should have let me die!' My anger sends the dancing light scurrying away, hiding in the shadows and cooling the air. 'I'm supposed to be dead.' The light ducks its face around the corners of the shadows.

'*What?*' Kerry asks, looking affronted. '*I saved you. I saved you and look at you . . . Look at how you're behaving!*'

A family have found their way into The Nook and are making a hasty retreat back through the archway.

'It's because of you that I'm shouting at thin air!'

'*Stop it, Jen, take a breath*,' Kerry says.

'Stop telling me what to do!' I bend down and rummage into my handbag, pop open the pill bottle, fire two to the back of my throat and swallow.

Kerry holds her stomach and raises an arm to the sky dramatically, falling to the floor like the Wicked Witch of the West. '*I'm mellllltttting!*'

I raise my eyebrows at her and bite my tongue as she sinks. At least I know she's seen *The Wizard of Oz* . . . we loved it when we were little.

She breathes deeply and smiles up at me. My anger dissipates. I know what she's doing, she's goading me into taking the pills just like she would when we were kids and I didn't want to do something. I take a step towards her, an apology on my lips. But Ed is behind me and is pulling my hand back towards him. I look away from Kerry and meet the worry in his eyes. I return my concentration to where Kerry was lying, but she has gone.

'Let's go back home.' Ed avoids my eyes and picks up our things from the floor.

'Home?' I question; my thoughts are becoming muggy, warm and sticky.

'Back to your parents.'

I shake my head. 'No. I want to go back to Nessa's . . . she's the only one who doesn't make me feel like I'm insane.'

'I didn't mean to make you feel like you're insane.'

'I know.' I gulp down the rest of the sentence: you may not have wanted to, Ed, but you did.

'You OK?' Nessa asks.

I flash a glance in Ed's direction and bite my lip. He's apologised over and over on the way back. But I can't seem to forget the way he turned away from me as I tried to kiss him, how he didn't want to 'take advantage'.

Nessa reaches for my hand and gives it a squeeze. I stroke her thumb in thanks, putting on a brave smile, and ask Hailey to help me; I glue the wrapping paper onto the inside of the cardboard box. Nessa, Erica and Hailey are making it into a house for the woodlice that have been collected and deposited into a Chinese takeaway container. I glance over to Ed, who is towelling Oscar down; my son's fingers are pruned and there are grass cuttings sticking to his bare legs. He is completely naked, but Oscar hasn't a care in the world. I try to catch Ed's eye, to communicate without talking the way we always used to. But he doesn't look at me; instead, he averts his eyes. His gaze is fixed to where Nessa and my hands are entwined.

'Did Kerry really like to do this when she was a little girl?' Erica asks as I smile and pass her the glue stick.

'She did.'

'What else did she do when she was a little girl, Mummy?' Hailey waits for Erica to finish gluing her wallpaper.

'Hales, time to go, sweetheart,' Ed interrupts. Erica quickly passes the glue stick to Hailey. My time with them has gone so quickly, and the tug of longing for my old life almost takes my breath away.

'Well . . .' I reach forward and wipe a blob of jam away from Hailey's cheek.

'I liked to blow bubble gum.'

'She liked to blow bubble gum,' I continue, trying to hold on to the last few minutes before Ed takes them home. 'Great big bubbles, not your usual ones. She would try out lots of different types and record them in her notepad. There were pictures of the wrappers and a chart of how big the bubbles were, if they popped on her nose they only scored a five. If they hit her nose, that was a ten, and if they made it all the way to her cheeks, they got fifteen. She even started mixing them – adding quarter of a stick of Juicy Fruit was her winning combination.'

'You never let me have bubble gum, Mummy.'

'Ah . . .' I tap the end of her freckled nose and she wrinkles it, her freckles hiding beneath the creases, 'that's because once . . . just once, she scored a twenty. She blew and blew, but because she was concentrating so hard on blowing her bubble, she couldn't speak and she wanted to show me. Aunty Kerry ran towards me, her cheeks were red and the bubble was bouncing up and down, but she tripped and fell. Her face hit the slabs and the bubble gum was all over her nose and she couldn't breathe. I remember pulling it and pulling it free . . . I was so scared.'

'What did Aunty Kerry do?'

'Well . . .' I pull Hailey onto my knee and stroke her face. 'She was really scared too, and her chin was all grazed and bleeding, but do you know what the first thing she said was?'

'*Did you see? It was a twenty*,' we say in unison.

'Did she get another twenty?'

I shake my head. 'No . . . Grandma wouldn't let us have bubble gum after that. She loved making those lists, there was one about her insect houses, whether her ladybirds preferred purple or pink.'

'Hales!' Ed shouts again, and again disappointment pinches the edges of my smile.

'Right then, poppet. Let's put this somewhere to dry and next weekend we can paint the doors with proper grown-up paint. What colour would you like?'

'Yellow, please.'

'Yellow it is.' I kiss the top of her head as she shimmies off my knee and runs over to her dad. I follow her, passing the cardboard house to Ed, careful not to let it fall into the chasm. I hop over and bend down to give Oscar a nose-to-nose kiss. He smells like summer, like plastic, water and cheap ice lollies.

'Be good for Daddy and I'll speak to you later. Shall I read you the rest of *A Dinosaur Ate My Homework*?'

'No, it's OK. Daddy has read it to me and tonight he's reading me . . .' he cups his mouth and leans into my ear, 'Captain Underpants.' And then he dissolves into a fit of giggles.

I stand, and Ed gives me a brief kiss on the cheek, the type of kiss he would give my mother, both of our feet teetering close to the edge of the rift that slices the ground between us. My skin feels cold where his lips have been.

'I'll see you at the doctor's on Wednesday?' he asks.

'Oh, um I thought we were going for lunch on Tuesday?'

'I can't, Jen. I'm taking too much time off work as it is.'

'Right, yes, of course. What time shall I be ready?'

'Can I meet you at the doctor's?'

'I can go with her if you want?' Nessa offers. 'I've got a screening at eleven but I'm free after then?'

'No.' The abruptness of his tone smashes through the

sounds of summer, through the pop music on the radio, through the wind-up sound of the crocodile who is lopsidedly circling the inside of the pool.

Nessa holds her hands up defensively. 'Oh-kay . . . I was just offering.' She rolls her eyes and after the kids hug goodbye she takes Erica inside to get changed, ready for when Daniel picks her up.

'She was only trying to help,' I say quietly, folding my arms across my chest.

'I know. Sorry, I'm just tired and . . .' I can't see his expression behind his sunglasses. 'Never mind. I'll see you Wednesday.' The cold kiss is applied again as I watch my family walk away from me, pulling a part of me with them.

Nessa's hand lands on my shoulder as the gate closes and I reach up to hold it. Daniel arrives moments later, early for once, and I excuse myself, lock myself in the bathroom and cry. I hear the engine of Daniel's car quieten down the road, blow my nose and return to the garden.

I should have died.

The words float amongst my blurred vision, the end of the sentence becoming hazy, the words becoming weaker, disintegrating and scratching against the inside of my eyelids.

I blink.

'Do you fancy a beer?'

I turn to face her. 'I'm not supposed to drink with the tablets.'

'*One won't hurt!*' Kerry replies. She's sitting in the pool with a cocktail in her hand and pulls her sunglasses down the bridge of her nose as she shouts over.

'Sure,' I say, turning back to Nessa, who has already begun walking back into the house.

A few hours have passed and we've had more than one beer. 'Club Tropicana' is playing on the radio and Nessa and I are sitting either side of the pool. I lean back against the plastic and watch the distorted image of my legs shimmer beneath the water. I begin chuckling as I talk about how Oscar pulled off his shorts and played in the pool earlier completely naked, without a care in the world.

Kerry is carrying a drinks tray towards us. She takes a glass and passes it to me. In my alcohol-fuelled state, my hand reaches out to take it from her.

'Nuts,' I say as I grasp the air.

'Sorry?' Nessa asks, swigging deeply from her bottle. I feel embarrassment heat my cheeks, but I giggle at the ridiculousness of my action nevertheless.

'I've just tried to take a cocktail from Kerry.' I shake my head and let the bottom of my body slide along the pool until my face submerges beneath the water. I hold my breath and watch as pockets of air escape my mouth before I push myself back up.

Nessa watches me with interest and then shakes her bottle. 'Refill?'

'Sure.'

She returns with two bottles, lime wedges trapped inside the neck. I take the bottle from her as she steps into the pool and examine the trapped fruit.

'This is what it feels like when I see her and have to pretend not to,' I say, tilting the bottle towards the light.

'What do you mean?' Nessa reaches over the side of the pool, grabs a packet of cigarettes, inhales deeply and exhales with a rush of warm air.

'Like there is something lodged in my throat.' I watch my finger push the fruit down the neck and into the body. 'It's only when I'm with her that I feel like I can breathe.' I take a long pull on the bottle.

'You know what you need? Rock, paper, scissors.'

'What?'

'Rock, paper, scissors. When I was a kid, my mum used to

play it with me if something was worrying me. Whoever wins says something they love or that makes them happy. Whoever loses says what is worrying them or something that makes them sad.'

'I don't feel like playing a game.'

'It'll help, I promise. I've never played it and ended up feeling worse. Come on, it'll be fun. Kerry and I used to play it.' She gets up on her knees and waddles towards me.

'What did Kerry used to say?'

'Oh, we used to play strip rock, paper, scissors and she could always predict what I was going to do, so, more often than not, I would end up naked.'

'Oh.'

Nessa lets out a throaty laugh. 'Your sister didn't blush that easily.'

'Oh, shush. I've led a very sheltered life.'

'Nonsense, you had friction marks on your knees a few months ago.' She winks and positions her hands into fists. 'Right.' We move towards each other. 'Ready? Rock, paper, scissors!'

Nessa is the paper to my rock.

'Chocolate!' she shouts. Then laughs. 'You're supposed to shout what makes you sad at the same time!'

'Oh. Um, sad films?' I reply.

She rolls her eyes. 'Let's try again. You have to say the first thing that comes into your head or it won't work. But see . . . you watch a sad film but eat chocolate. Problem fixed. Right, fists up. Rock, paper, scissors!'

I snip her paper. 'A tidy house!' I say.

'Losing things!' We both start laughing. 'You see how it works!'

'Let's go again.'

This time my scissors are blunted by her rock. 'Kerry!' we both say. Kerry takes a regal bow and climbs into the pool.

We try again, me shouting the kids, her shouting Erica. At this point we give up and reach for our drinks as 'Spice Up Your Life' begins.

'What were you like when you were a kid? Is Erica like you?' I ask while the Spice Girls go rou-ow-ownd.

'God no. I was a little bugger. Mum said I was always running off, I used to scare her to death.'

'Where were you running off to?'

She shrugs her shoulders. 'I don't know, I just remember not wanting to stand still . . . it kind of made me feel, I don't know how to describe it, itchy? Like unless I ran away I would scratch away my skin. I almost got run over once.'

Red coat, red boots, screeching of brakes.

I blink.

'What about you?' she asks, bringing me back.

'Me? Oh, I was a bit timid, a goody two-shoes. I had to be.'

'Why?'

'Because Kerry would get us into trouble all the time . . . one of us had to be responsible. It's funny, when I was watching Oscar dancing earlier, wiggling his bare little bum without a care in the world . . . I don't think I've ever felt that free . . . even as a kid.'

'What? You never played in the paddling pool in the buff when you were a kid?'

I shake my head. 'At least I don't think I did.'

I look over to Kerry, who is leaning with her arms outstretched along the back of the pool, her sunglasses sitting neatly on her sunburnt nose.

'Don't ask me,' she replies. *'If you don't know then neither do I.'*

I turn back to Nessa, who is untying her bikini.

Kerry pulls down her sunglasses from her nose and peers over the frames. *'Baywatch, eat your heart out,'* she says.

'Um . . . what are you doing?' I ask.

'Taking off my clothes.'

'I see that!' I cover my eyes with my hand.

'Oh, stop being such a prude. Get 'em off.'

'What? No! Absolutely no way.'

'Absolutely no way.' She mimics me with a posh voice. 'My name is Jennifer Jones and I'm far too responsible to have any fun.'

A wet piece of material lands on my face. I pull it off and there in all her glory is Nessa, standing completely naked and downing the rest of her beer.

'Come on. Look, I promise not to make a pass at you.'

My eyebrows shoot up.

'Perfect!' she stretches her arms wide and gestures to the radio which has started playing the 'Macarena'. 'Now strip.' I find that I'm smirking as Ness's boobs start to jiggle with her arm movements. 'How do you ever expect to get better if you don't learn to live a bit?' she shouts at me over her shoulder, jumping up and down and turning to the side.

I laugh and look over to Kerry, but she is nowhere to be seen. Maybe this is the key? Maybe being happy is what I need. Self-consciously I begin unhooking my bikini top and let it drop into the pool and then, covering my breasts with one hand, I pull off my bottoms. Nessa is crossing her chest with her arms in an 'x', then placing her hands onto her hips before 'Heeeeey . . . Macarena'.

'Hurry up, Jen!'

Gingerly, I stand, one arm still across my boobs, the other hand fig-leafed across my lower parts.

'Oh, for goodness' sake!' Nessa takes two steps towards me and pulls my arms apart, dropping them to my sides, then returns to her Macarena, one hand then the other either side of her head, hands crossing onto shoulders.

I reach down, drain the last of my beer and burp loudly before hesitantly joining in. Laughter bubbles up from my stomach as we jump in tandem, splashes of water erupting out of the pool. Nessa winks at me as she swivels her hips. The song finishes and we collapse back into the pool, water sloshing over the edges as we lean back, still laughing. Kerry is still nowhere to be seen. I begin to panic. The laughter gets caught in my throat; the lime in the beer bottle.

Nessa leans forward, laughter sliding into concern. 'What's wrong?'

I stand, my inhibitions lost as I try to see her.

'She's gone! I can't find her!' Panic claws at my insides, scraping and grappling to get out. Oh, God, what have I done? The tablets must be working: I've killed her again.

'Hey! Lady Godiva!'

I turn a full circle at the sound of her voice. Kerry is sitting on the top of Erica's slide, her plait falling across her naked chest, her bare legs crossed at the ankles. My body sags with relief, my legs buckle and I'm kneeling in the water, my heart hammering against my ribs.

I try to control the feelings inside; choked sobs fall from my lips as Nessa slides over to me, arm around my shoulders. 'Hey, shush, what's wrong? What is it?'

I don't know how to answer her, though, because I don't know how to describe how I'm feeling. Am I happy that she's back or not? Should I be? How can I make this decision? Kill my sister, or lose my family? I rest my head on Nessa's shoulder as my naked dead sister slides down the slide. She misquotes from *Top Gun*, asking Goose to talk to her as she smiles, climbing into the pool to join us.

'I don't want to lose you again,' I say.

'I'm not going anywhere,' Nessa replies.

Chapter Fifty-Three

Ed

I'm multitasking. It's not my favourite thing to do. The kids' dinner is cooking, the front door is wide open so I can hear them, and I'm simultaneously contorting my body into a shape that it shouldn't be contorted into while I search for Oscar's snake – Sammy – in the footwell of my car.

'Fuck!' My knuckles have just grazed against something sharp beneath the seat.

'Daaaadddyyyy!!' Hailey is shouting from the doorway and I pull my body back out of the arch it's contorted into, registering as I do that the smoke alarm is going off.

Fishfingers. Burnt fishfingers.

I send Hailey up the stairs with a tea towel and instruct her to flap it beneath the alarm, while Oscar is covering his tear-stained face with his hands as I push past him, pulling open the oven door where smoke pours out. I go to retrieve the oven tray with another tea towel but there are none in the drawer.

'Why are there no tea towels?!' I shout, as I start pulling dusters and dishcloths out of the drawer. 'I mean, is it too much to ask? That when you open the drawer that is supposed to have tea towels in, that there are actual tea towels in there?!' The alarm continues to shriek as I take out the tray with a dishcloth, burning my hand as I do. The tray skitters across the draining board as I curse under my breath. 'Hailey! Shut that damn thing up!' I turn the cold tap on full and wince as it hits the angry red welt that is emerging across my palm. I sigh loudly, my shoulders hunching over the sink as I close my eyes and try to control the confusion inside.

I'm not a man prone to mood swings. I'm the man at work that they send to deal with a difficult client: I don't get rattled; I don't lose my cool. But right now? My cool is well and truly lost.

The alarm stops and Hailey's feet pound down the stairs. A hiccupping sound comes from behind me. I turn my head to where Oscar is crying: he turns to Hailey as she comes into the room, wafting the smoke away with her hand; his face seeks reassurance from her, my daughter's arm wraps around his tiny frame, her eyes meet mine with a look of distrust. It's a look normally saved for Jen.

'I'm sorry,' I say, turning off the tap and kneeling down in front of them, pulling their bodies towards me. 'I'm sorry I lost my temper.' I kiss the tops of their heads, Oscar's body hiccupping from inside his chest. 'I'm sorry,' I say again, kissing harder this time. 'We must have left Sammy at Aunty Nessa's. Let's go and get a McDonald's and then fetch him, OK?'

Oscar sniffs and wipes away his snot with the back of his hand as Hailey watches my face cautiously.

Oscar's head is lying heavily to the right as we pull up outside Nessa's, gentle snores escaping his tomato-sauce-stained face.

'Wait here,' I say to Hailey. 'I'll only be a minute.' I release the belt buckle and jog up to the front door, checking the car over my shoulder as I do. Hailey waves at me. My hand waves back.

There is no answer.

I walk to the side gate where I can hear the radio playing. Pushing open the gate, I step into the garden, where I see two naked women embracing.

This is going to sound odd, but for a moment, I wonder who the women are. It's a moment that stretches and snaps into reality in the time it has taken me to take a breath. By the time that breath has exhaled, I have worked out that the naked woman being held by another naked woman is my wife.

Sammy is lying on the bench. I reach for it, hold it tightly and leave the garden.

Oscar is still sleeping; Hailey is playing on her tablet as I start the engine: inside this car, the world is the same as it was a few moments ago.

But the wife that I'm trying to hold on to is slipping further away. Should I carry on holding on, or just let her go?

Chapter Fifty-Four

Jennifer

I wake in my old bedroom. I have a vague memory of Nessa opening us wine, of climbing out of the pool, of a feeling close to drowning as I started to cry. Nessa brought me home: a taxi ride, a conversation with my parents, Nessa murmuring something about me breaking down, a feeling of drowning and of fear . . . I was so scared of losing Kerry again.

My body is slick with sweat. It's late evening; I can hear birds singing and the rumble of voices beneath me. The panic I felt earlier still sits heavily in my chest.

Kerry is sitting at my old desk, writing in one of her notebooks. *'Hey sleepy head,'* she says, smiling at me.

'Hey.' My voice is hoarse and I reach for the bottle of water beside the bed.

'How are you feeling?'

'How am I feeling? I'm talking to myself after having a breakdown after dancing naked to the 'Macarena' . . . How do you think I am?'

Mum knocks on the door and closes it quietly behind her, sitting down on the bed next to me. 'Would you like a drink?'

I shake my head.

'Something to eat?'

I shake my head again.

She brushes back my hair and cups my face. 'When I first brought you home, I couldn't stop looking at you. You had a scratch down your cheek.' Her finger follows the ghost of the memory, outlining an invisible scar. 'I couldn't believe how lucky I was, that I had been given this perfect little person to look after. I wanted to protect you, I wanted to stop the world from ever harming you again.' She wraps her arm around my shoulders. 'You have to let her go, Jen, you have to let her go.'

'How?'

'I don't know. But her being here is destroying you.'

'Have you told Ed about . . . earlier?'

'We haven't been able to get hold of him, his phone is off.'

'Don't tell him.'

'Jen, you need to let him help you, he—'

'OK, but not yet? Please?' I think of the way he had looked at me at The Nook. I can't bear for him to look that way at me again. 'He thinks I'm getting better, Mum, please, he's got enough to think about looking after the kids.'

'So what are we going to do with you?' She rubs the tops of my arms and tries to smile away the catch in her voice.

'Well, I could start with having a shower and one of your loaded jacket potatoes . . . that might be a start?'

She pulls her body a little straighter, glad to be given a purpose. 'That, I can do.' Mum gets up but hesitates with her hand resting on the door. 'Where is she?'

She turns back to me; I nod towards the desk. Mum takes a step towards it.

'Now you listen to me, Kerry Hargreaves, you need to stop tormenting your sister, do you hear me? Enough is enough.'

I bite down on my lip as I watch Kerry stick her tongue out at Mum in a way she would only ever have dared to do behind Mum's back.

I follow Mum's movements as she straightens her shoulders and clears her throat, and I blink back the tears threatening behind my eyelids.

'Right. I'd best get those jacket potatoes in.' She gives me a smile, wipes a stray tear from her cheek, smooths down the back of her hair and closes the door softly behind her.

Chapter Fifty-Five

Ed

Jen had a bad day. This is what my mother-in-law explained to me last night.

A bad day.

I've been crafting a volcano out of moulding clay for the past two hours with my daughter, who avoids conversations about friends and school like the plague. I've tucked the kids in, read out a story to Oscar in my best Captain Underpants voice, all the time questioning what I saw. Is it possible that she is having an affair with Nessa? Because that's what it looked like. I check in on Hales, who is sleeping soundly, and clear up the detritus that covers the kitchen table. The clay volcano looks somewhat like a giant penis, I can't help but notice with a sigh, and I worry about how I'm going to fix it.

Jen's trying to FaceTime me. I take a deep breath, and sit down in the lounge. Jen's voice is distant and soft around the edges as though it's hard work to open her mouth. Her phone is propped up beside her, hair messy, no make-up on her face. Not exactly the picture of a woman embarking on her first lesbian affair. I don't ask her about what I saw. Instead I ask, 'You OK?' while I watch her swallow down more pills.

'Yeah . . . I've got a bit of a headache. Me and Nessa had a few drinks after you left yesterday.'

'So, you had a few drinks with, um, with Nessa?' I ask oh-so-innocently.

'Yeah, a few.'

'It looks like you had more than a few . . .' My voice is judgemental.

'It's not a hangover, Ed. I've not slept.'

I swallow down the images of them together in tangled sheets, try to stop the words that want to come out of my mouth. I want to ask, but I also want to give her chance to tell me, because if she doesn't, I'm scared that I will never be able to trust her again.

'Kerry is sick, Ed.'

'What do you mean?'

She's not real! I want to scream. I'm real, your children are real, your affair—

I stop this train of thought. I can't talk about this yet.

'The tablets, Ed. They make her ill, she's started waking me at night, she has a fever, Kerry—'

'Well that's good.'

'What?' she asks sleepily, as though I'm speaking another language entirely.

'I mean, maybe that means the tablets are working. Maybe this is the start of her—'

'Dying?' Her voice is a croak, an echo.

'Moving on,' I say softly.

'How are the kids? I'm sorry I missed bedtime.'

'They're good,' I lie. I lie about Hailey becoming more and more impatient with her brother, I lie about Oscar's night terrors, I lie about how I forgot that it was non-uniform day and didn't realise until I picked them up, uniforms amid a flood of jeans. 'Me and Hales are making a volcano.'

She yawns, her eyes unfocused. 'A what?' she asks.

'Never mind, I'll tell you Wednesday.'

'Wednesday?'

'The doctor's.'

'Oh yeah. I've got to go,' she yawns. 'Love you.'

'Love you too.'

Her hand reaches for the screen and she swipes away my face.

I'm being snippy with the kids and I hate it. I used to love coming home to them, hearing about their day and winding them up before bed. I wish I could feel that way again, that they would look at me when I walk through the door like they used to. Instead, they just look at me the same way as when they see an episode of *Go Jetters* that's been on ten times that week already.

'Can I be excused?' Hailey asks with a bored tone.

'Not until you've finished your homework. There are four more questions.'

'Mummy never made me do homework at dinnertime. She let me do it when I came in from school.'

'Well, when Mummy was here, you were home earlier because you didn't go to after-school club.'

'I hate after-school club,' Oscar sulks. 'I have to do the afternoon walk and that means three times around the playground. It hurts my throat.'

'That's because you're fat,' Hailey snaps at him, pulling her book towards her.

'That's enough!' I shout, and both children flinch. I've never really been a shouter but lately, I can't seem to stop myself. 'Say sorry to your brother.'

Oscar is breathing quickly and his lip is quivering.

Hailey scowls and folds her arms. 'No. I was only telling the truth. He is fat, Daddy, everyone says so.'

My voice is dangerously low as I respond. 'You say sorry to your brother right now or—'

'What? You'll ground me? Stop me from seeing my friends, tell my MUM?!' Hailey has tears in her eyes as she stands and pushes her plate away. It slides off the table and crashes onto the floor, peas escaping across the grouting around the floor tiles. Her footsteps reverberate through the staircase as she slams her bedroom door.

'Take no notice of your sister,' I say, putting my arms around Oscar's shoulder and pulling him towards me. 'You're just big-boned. It means you'll be strong when you grow up.'

'She wasn't telling the troof, Daddy, they call me chubster and Mr Newton told me that just means that I'm bubbly and happy. Can I have my pudding now? I ate all my fish fingers even though they are yucky and slimy and grey.'

'Of course, buddy.' I head over to the fruit bowl. 'There's a banana?' I hold it aloft.

Oscar shakes his head. 'It's got brown bits all over the outside.'

'How about a pear?'

He shakes his head again. 'Pears feel like sand in your mouth, they're all stony.'

'Apple?' I turn the apple in question and see that a grub has already made a meal out of it. 'Forget that one.'

'Can I have a chocolate bar?'

I think of the kids teasing him. 'No, buddy. Yoghurt?'

'Does it have bits in?'

'Bits?'

'Mummy always gets me ones without bits.'

I search the contents of the fridge and find it lacking. 'Um . . . cheese slice?'

'Is cheese slice pudding?'

'Yeah. And you get to unwrap it just like a chocolate bar.' I dangle it in front of him like bait.

'Thanks, Daddy!' He snatches it. 'You're the best.' He kisses me on the cheek. 'Except when Mummy's here. Then she's the best and you're just Dad.'

The car is filled with white noise as I drive us to the doctor's. Jen is looking out of the window; her eyes are bloodshot, her hands twisting and knotting her fingers.

'So . . .?'

'Hmmm?'

'What did you and Nessa get up to after your "few drinks"?'

'What? Oh.' I notice the glimmer of a smile as I watch her reaction from the corner of my eye.

'We played rock, paper, scissors.'

My mind flits through my teenage porn collection and tries to link the images in my head with a rock, a paper and some scissors.

'Ed!' Jen's hand reaches for the steering wheel as I almost clip the kerb.

'She's really good at it.'

'At what?' I indicate and pull onto the main road.

'Rock, paper, scissors. She plays by different rules.'

I bet she does.

I reach for the radio and flick through several stations before punching off the dial.

'Ed, is something wrong?' she asks as I pull onto the doctor's carpark.

It's there every time I close my eyes: the curve of her back, her dark wet hair dropping to a point along Nessa's shoulder blade. I park the car and turn off the engine, turning towards her.

'I just didn't sleep very well . . . you?'

'No.' The images are back for a split second. 'Kerry was worse last night. Fevered dreams . . . and I never really sleep well without you at the best of times.' Her hand reaches for mine, which is resting on the gearstick, but I flinch. I don't mean to, but then I'm sure she didn't mean to take her clothes off with another woman. I look away from the hurt on her face and question, as we go into the doctor's office, why I'm the one who is feeling guilty.

The brain scan is clear; the blood tests are clear. I should be happy but instead, I say this. 'So how are you going to fix her?'

I sound like a twat. I know that, but I can't seem to control my twattish behaviour. My leg is bouncing up and down. I need to be at Hailey's science afternoon in half an hour. We've spent most nights this week painting her volcano. She has made tiny trees and a river meanders along the side of the cardboard. The river is made out of paint mixed with PVA glue and glitter; we made a special trip to Hobby Craft for it. I can't miss it. Hailey tried to tell Jen about the science afternoon at the weekend but, well, Jen was having a bad day. Or Kerry was. Even I'm starting to sound mad. And it's beginning to piss me off. You see? I'm a twat. I glance at my watch and the psychiatrist, Dr Popescu, leans backwards into his chair when I say and do these things. He's a good-looking bastard and I've no doubt that he also thinks I'm a twat.

Jen looks at me like I'm something stuck to her shoe.

'It's not as simple as fixing her, Ed.' He leans forward. Even his accent is cool: it's not all full-on romantic like Italian and French; it's more a kind of 'hey look at my accent, it's so sexy but I'm so cool my accent doesn't have to try as hard as those other accents'. Jen's always been a sucker for an accent. I glance in her direction and see that she looks flushed.

Damn it. He even smells good. The fact that this man calls me 'Ed' annoys me. He makes 'Ed' sound sexy; how can he say my name, a name that I have been learning to pronounce since I was a baby, sound better than when I say it? I run my finger around the neck of my shirt.

'It's Edward,' I correct. 'Look, man.' Man? When do I ever call a guy man? His chiselled looks and expensive smell are having an effect on me . . . it's like I'm trying to fit in with the cool kids. 'Could we just cut to the chase?' I snap. My leg continues bouncing up and down in agitation. 'Because I have an important meeting I need to be at.'

'But we've had this appointment date for two weeks, Ed, couldn't you have asked them to change it?'

Sure. I could ask the school to change their science day to another date because my wife is having conversations with her dead sister and considering batting for the other team. I'm sure it would have been no bother at all.

'No, Jen, they can't just change it.'

'But—'

I ignore her. 'Can we just get to the part where my wife stops acting like a—'

'A what, Ed?' she asks.

'I didn't mean . . . I'm just . . . I have to go and we've already been here for twenty minutes and all we've done is talked about stuff we've already told the GP.'

'Edward, I'm afraid this isn't going to just be fixed overnight.' He blinks slowly. Christ, his eyelashes are long . . . I wonder if he has one of those curling things that Jen uses. 'We have to find the root of the problem.'

I try to calm myself down. In through the nose, out through the mouth.

'I see that your GP has changed your prescription from olanzapine to risperidone?'

'Yes, they were making . . . me sick, but these ones . . .'

Jen nods and her eyes track a movement over the corner of Dr Pepper's shoulder. I sigh. Kerry is here.

'And how are you finding them? Have they made any differences to your hallucinations?'

Jen focuses back on the doctor.

'Her dead sister gets ill when she takes them and then Jen feels guilty,' I butt in, glancing at the clock.

Jen's head turns to me slowly and she pushes her lips together. 'It's more complicated than that, Ed.'

'Sorry,' I say. In through the nose, out through the mouth. 'It's just that I've—'

'Got a meeting. Yes, you said. I'll try and be more concise, more cost-effective with my responses. Would that help, Ed?' Jen's words sound angry but her eyes are filling.

My phone vibrates in my pocket. It's the alarm I have set myself so I'm not late. I apologise again and turn the alarm off.

Dr Pepper runs his hands through his hair . . . I bet he conditions. No supermarket shampoo for him. 'How are they affecting Kerry?' He glances down at his notes. I try to place his accent. Eastern European, maybe?

'They're making her ill. When she was little . . .' Jen tracks Kerry around the room. I track the thin air that is causing my life to fall apart. 'She would get tonsillitis, but not, you know, like a bit of a sore throat, she would get these raging temperatures and—'

My alarm buzzes in my pocket. It's the alarm that I titled 'Last chance, dickhead'.

'I'm sorry. I've got to go.' Jen is fighting back tears; she opens and closes her mouth, looking towards the thin air with an expression that says is he for real? I know. Ironic, right?

Dr Pepper begins to rise from his chair and stretches out his hand. I shake it hastily, kiss Jen on the cheek and drive as fast as I can to the school.

Chapter Fifty-Six

Jennifer

Ed's slam of the psychiatrist's door shakes the whole room, myself included. Dr Popescu leans back and points his index fingers together.

'Ed's not normally like that,' I intervene. He doesn't say anything. 'It's tough on him. He's having to look after the kids in the week, juggle the school run and work. He's not normally like that,' I repeat.

'Why don't you tell me about Kerry and her tonsillitis?' he says with a kind smile and so I begin. I tell him how since the day in The Nook I have been trying to take the tablets every day. At first, I thought that because they were making Kerry sick she would start to fade, but she doesn't. I don't tell him how scared I am that she might. She's as real as she ever was but the problem is that now, every time I take a tablet, she wakes me in the night with her fever. In the daytime, she is OK, she just gets cramps every now and then, but the night fevers are stopping me from sleeping and the tablets make me feel tired.

'Do you feel guilty taking the tablets?' he asks.

'Yes.'

'Why?'

'Because I feel like, like . . .' I glance over to where she is tracing the diagram of the brain on the wall with her finger. 'Like I'm killing her. Again.'

'Let me ask you a question, Jennifer; there is no judgement here, that's not my job. My job is to listen and to try and find the right type of therapy that will help you. Do you believe that your sister, that Kerry is standing in this room?' He nods over to the picture of the brain and I realise that I must have given myself away.

'No.'

'Then how can you kill her?' He smiles, rises, fills a small watering can from the tap and tips it into the base of a spider plant. The water that escapes look softer, as though pouring it through the watering can alters it somehow. I think to this morning, when I had tipped water from a cup into the sink. How it had landed with a violent splash, the noise it made like a slap. It's the same water, the same action, but maybe . . . if it's broken up into pieces, it will change into something easier to control.

He gently places the can on the draining board and rejoins me.

'I'm going to ask you a question and I want you to say the first thing that pops into your head.'

I give him a 'really?' look.

'Indulge me,' he replies and puts out his hands as though he's carrying a tray.

'OK.'

'Ready?' I roll my eyes good-naturedly. 'What do you want?'

'To be happy,' I reply. 'Sorry,' I immediately add. 'That's a bit of a rubbish answer, isn't it?'

'Not at all. Some people say "thin", some people say "marriage". Happiness is something I can help you with, fixing up blind dates isn't my area of expertise.' He grins and opens a packet of Rolos, offering me one.

'*Ooh, I wonder if he's going to save you his last one.*' Kerry is bending over in the crab position and her face is turning red.

He catches me looking at her. 'What does Kerry think?'

'She's wondering if you're going to give me your last one.' I gesture to the Rolos with my hand.

'My last one?' he asks, confused.

I shake my head dismissively. 'Never mind.'

'When was the last time you felt truly happy?'

'Before Kerry died.'

He shovels another Rolo in his mouth, chewing thoughtfully. 'Give me a specific day.'

I breathe out of my pursed lips; they vibrate against each other like the sound Oscar makes when he's playing with his toy cars. I close my eyes: memories of birthdays and Christmas mornings, of Ed hitting me with the door in the florist's, of Hailey being passed into my arms for the first time. Big Red Letter days, I suppose, but then another flashback slides into focus. A week before Kerry died, I came home from the supermarket, my bags filled with snacks for the movie we were going to watch later that night; 'Shotgun' by George Ezra was playing on the radio in the kitchen. I landed the bags onto the kitchen floor and followed the sounds of whoops and 'nooos' coming from the lounge. Kerry, Ed and the kids were at the table, playing a game of Snakes and Ladders; Ed was clutching the side of his hair, leaving it sticking out like a pair of horns as Hailey gleefully slithered his counter down a snake. Kerry looked over her shoulder at me and winked.

'Does anyone want a drink?' I asked and took their orders. I returned to the kitchen, singing to George and feeling like someone; I can't remember making the drinks or who won the game, but I remember this feeling of happiness.

I open my eyes again and meet Dr Popescu's, retelling the moment, the way Ed's hair was sticking up and the sounds of laughter as I walked into the house.

'I can't ever imagine feeling that happy again,' I say quietly once I've finished.

He stays silent, turning his focus to the piece of gold foil rolling between his thumb and forefinger.

'I can't imagine never feeling guilty for killing her.'

'Were you driving the car that hit her?'

'No, but—'

He changes the subject. 'Do you think it might be your guilt that is making Kerry ill rather than the tablets themselves?'

'I don't know. I don't think I've really looked at it that way.' My phone vibrates but unlike Ed, I ignore it.

'Do you think you could be that happy again?' he asks.

I look over at Kerry, who is perched on the edge of his desk, helping herself to a Rolo. She winks at me, just as she had that day.

And then I know.

I can't be happy again . . . I won't kill my sister this time.

Our time is up; I gather my things and head towards the door.

'Jen?'

I turn just in time to catch the foil missile heading in my direction.

'Aw . . . he gave you his last Rolo!' Kerry laughs as I smile, thank him and follow her out into the corridor.

Chapter Fifty-Seven

Ed

I've shaken my twattishness on the drive over. And as I step inside the school hall, I'm sure they all see School-science-fair Dad. That is who I need to be right now; that is who Hales needs. Parents and children stand with plastic cups filled with weak tea and cheap squash. Desks are pushed up against the walls, displaying science projects of all shapes and sizes: the volcano seems to be a popular choice, but as I push my way through the crowds, I feel a glow of pride that Hailey's beats these other attempts hands down. I mean. Hands. Down.

I spot her standing awkwardly behind the desk. She is chewing the end of one of her fishtail plaits that I totally rocked this morning. Hailey pulls the plait away from her face, which splits into a wide grin when she sees me. A teacher arrives at the desk at the same time as me and is telling her what a great job she has done. Her cheeks go pink at the praise.

'Thank you,' she replies quietly. 'Daddy helped.'

The teacher turns to me. 'Well you've done a brilliant job, both of you!' He claps me on the back, sips from the plastic cup and goes on to the next table, where what looks like a giant penis is perched precariously. I feel smug that there is no longer even a hint of the phallic about ours.

'Yours looks awesome, Hales . . . way better than the rest.' I look towards where another volcano is belching something that looks like wallpaper paste onto pieces of newspaper; other miscellaneous pieces of debris are sticking to it as it puddles beneath the desk amongst a flurry of teaching staff brandishing blue paper towels.

She giggles and covers her mouth. 'When are you going to set it off?'

The little plastic vial containing vinegar sits neatly inside a papier-mâché rock, waiting for its big moment. 'I was going to wait until Mr Newton comes over.'

She leans forward and whispers, 'I heard that he gives out big chocolate bars to the ones he thinks are the best.'

We fist bump and the room hushes as the headteacher taps the microphone and announces that it's time for the budding scientists to leave their own stations and go and see their fellow scientists' work. Hailey skips from behind her desk and leads me around the room. I notice as we do that her voice is much quieter than at home. Each time a teacher or an adult asks her a question, her shoulders fold inwards, like she's trying to make herself smaller than she already is; her replies are barely audible above the din.

'Holy cow!' I say as we approach a working model of the water cycle. It looks professionally made, stainless steel cogs turning and moving a cloud across a Perspex background. There is no way a kid has made that. 'Whose model is that?' I ask, leaning forward, peering over the mechanics that are moving the river around. There are even sound effects: birds calling, a stream gurgling.

'Oh, that's Rachel Rodriguez's.' Hailey bites the skin around her thumb and gestures towards the pretty Spanish girl across the other side of the room. The other girls are hanging off her like expensive handbags.

'Well, the teachers won't be fooled. It's clear that the kid had no input whatsoever.'

The teachers won't be fooled, right? A knot forms in my stomach. I know I'm being competitive – I can see it in the amused smile Hailey is looking up at me with – but my daughter has spent hours on this project, and right now she needs a win. Just. One. Win.

Chapter Fifty-Eight

Jennifer

My hand is shaking as I fasten my seat belt. I look down at the phone and reread the school text message that I had ignored, alerting me to Hailey's science fair. It rattles around my head, clattering around my thoughts like stones in a sieve. How could I have missed this?

I give the address of the school to the driver. The thought of Hailey not having a parent there makes my heart ache. I have always made sure that there has been someone at all of my children's special days. If Ed or I couldn't make it, it would be Mum or Dad. But I know Ed wouldn't have thought of that. It's not his fault; I always organised that side of things and he's got so much on his plate. As the car banks around a cyclist, I give myself an internal shake. I'll get a diary, a hand-held one like I always used to. I think of the diary that I always had in my handbag, shopping list at the ready, doctor's appointments, hairdressers, play dates, all written down . . . it used to be so easy. As we pull up outside the school and I open my bag, I notice that not only is there no diary, there is no packet of tissues, no mini first-aid kit, no hand sanitiser and travel pack of baby wipes, no power bank in case of emergencies . . . there is just my purse and some Juicy Fruit chewing gum.

Outside the school there are pushchairs parked in cluttered

lines; the deputy head is standing by the door like a bouncer. I garble something about science, and he ushers me through to the hall. I scan the crowd but can't see Hailey, so I follow the cage of displays housing frothing experiments and folded up pieces of cardboard scripted with the names of the children, followed with the letters 'PhD'. All the children are wearing white lab coats and safety goggles hang around their necks.

I spot Hailey's name and feel a lump of pride warm in my chest. It must have taken her ages to make it. My finger traces the grooves running down from the vent, the paintbrush marks where the crater circles the edges of a plastic bottle filled with – if memory serves – bicarbonate of soda.

'This is so cool! Look at all the detail!' Kerry fingers a small tree trunk with gravel circling its base. *'Look inside the boulder!'*

I reach into the lump of papier mâché made to resemble a rock next to the volcano. Nestled inside is a small bottle of something orange; I recognise the bottle, it was part of the perfume tester kit that Ed bought me from Oscar last Mother's Day. I watch Kerry unscrew the lid and peer into the volcano.

'Oh, I've seen this on telly! You pour the vinegar and paint into the bicarb and then it all erupts!'

'I think we should wait until Hailey is here.'

I try to scan the room again but all I can see is the centre of the volcano.

I blink.

Again I try to focus on the crowds, but my vision is drawn to the centre of the volcano, which has begun to bubble. The sound of a gasp from the teacher next to me slaps me. Kerry has gone and I am holding the bottle. The volcano is erupting: running down the clay rivulets is orange foam; the slow trickle is gaining momentum and begins rolling off the edge of the board and onto the floor.

I feel sick.

The teacher next to me disappears for a brief moment, reappearing with a huge roll of blue paper towel. I crouch down and begin wiping the floor. My heart is thumping in my chest, in my ears, in my throat.

I hear my name but it's as though it's dampened, like the treble, the sharpness, has been wrapped up in a damp towel and hidden in the corner of a room, to be dealt with again at a later date.

The room snaps back into focus, the towel unwrapped and shaken, throwing the clarity, sharpening the edges of my name, around the room. Then I see her. I see my daughter, the daughter who would only sleep in my arms when she was a baby, who had my name on her lips if she fell, my name ready to call when she wanted to show me something she was proud of, looking at me; my daughter looking at me as though I'm a stranger.

Chapter Fifty-Nine

Ed

We've almost done the full circuit when we see it. Just as before, blue paper towels are being flapped about; teaching staff are laughing good-naturedly at the trials that come with a job working with children. You know that feeling when, I don't know, like when you've knocked a glass off the table and there is that split second where you know there is no way of stopping it from smashing, but you still try to grab it? That's how I feel right now. Only it's not a glass that is going to be destroyed . . . it's my daughter.

'Never work with animals or children, isn't that what they say?' Mr Newton is laughing. Hailey's hand slips into mine; any embarrassment about doing this in front of her peers has gone and the need, I suppose, to have my reassurance takes precedence as we hurry towards her desk. The crowd of hunched staff begin to stand and step back, Mrs Park looking anxiously around, her eyes resting on Hailey with a sad smile. The crowd and paper towels disperse, leaving a figure on all fours desperately trying to rectify a mistake, trying to tidy the mess of poster paint and bicarbonate of soda. Jen is whispering urgently to the space next to her, her hands scrubbing the floor, the panic in her face making her look even more crazy than usual.

'Jen,' I say. It's not a question, not a greeting, just a

statement. My voice seems to bring her to the here and now; her eyes refocus and land on Hailey's pale face.

'Hailey!' She stands, twisting the blue paper in her hands into knots. 'This is wonderful! Aren't you clever? I'm sorry . . .' She turns back to where the orange food coloured froth is trickling down the side of the volcano. 'I think I put too much vinegar in.'

Hailey steps forward and looks up at her mother. 'It's OK, Mummy.' She wraps her hands around Jen's waist and hugs her, her face turned into Jen's tummy. Thankfully, she misses the giggles from the Spanish girl and her group of accessories on the other side of the room. The girls are wearing lip-gloss even though they're only eight. Hailey doesn't hear the words whispered in ears or see the spiteful fingers pointing over to where orange sludge is already dripping onto the laminate flooring.

Hailey's face looks up to me for guidance, but I don't know what to do. I'm her father, and I can't fix this for her; I can't stop the people in the room from looking in our direction; I can't stop any of it.

This can't go on.

My kids are never going to win if their mum is losing.

Chapter Sixty

Ed

I've been sitting outside Nessa's house like a frigging stalker for the best part of an hour. Raindrops are falling slowly against the windshield as I sit here. No doubt the neighbours will be thinking of calling the police if I don't get my arse into gear and do something.

Come on, you idiot. Get a grip.

Across the road I watch a couple walking hand in hand, their steps quickening as the rain gathers momentum, their walk turning into a skip, a run, laughter following them. I think about the journey back from the science fair as we all sat in silence; even Oscar was quiet. How I guided my wife from the car and into her mother's arms, briefly explaining to Brian in hurried and hushed tones what had happened at the school. How I sat on Hailey's bed reading to her until she finally fell asleep, her eyes puffy from crying behind a locked bathroom door.

I jump as Nessa's hand thumps the passenger window. I reach for the window control, sliding it downwards, letting the sounds and smells of rain on tarmac into the car.

'Do you want to come in?' she shouts above the din. Her hair is covered in one of those plastic covers that my nan used to wear; it looks oddly cool on her head.

'I don't know,' I reply honestly, leaning over the hand brake.

'She's not here.'

'I know.'

'I'm putting the kettle on,' she answers and hurries back into her house, her feet zigzagging along the path and hopping over puddles. I slide the window back up and drum my fingers on the steering wheel. I turn the ignition back on and then off again. If I go in there, if I find out the truth, will I still be able to be the husband my wife needs right now? Does she deserve me to be? I toss the keys between my hands, pull up the collar on my coat and walk into her house.

I sit down at Nessa's kitchen table, and she places a cup of coffee in front of me. I thank her, blowing over the rim, and try to stop myself from shaking. I've never really shaken before a conversation, not even when I asked Jen to marry me, because, I suppose, I already knew she would say yes. I notice the school letter about a trip to a local farm. The return slip is missing; Erica must have taken it back today. I make an exhausted mental note to make sure I fill in Oscar's.

Nessa sits down opposite me. In contrast to Jen, Nessa looks well, made-up, ironed, fresh.

'Do you love her?' I ask. I have no control over these words, and I find my face has arranged itself into something that resembles astonishment or shock. Probably both.

'Ye-es.' The word rolls forward, lilting at the end like a question. Nessa squints at me like I'm mad.

'Because if you love her, you will see that this isn't what she needs right now, she needs stability not, not—'

'Ed, what is this about? Has something happened?'

I take a sip of my coffee, which goes down the wrong way so I spend the next minute coughing and spluttering and waving my hands. Control regained, I continue. 'I saw you both . . . together . . . in the pool. The day you made the cardboard house.'

She tilts her head, her eyes looking upwards as if trying to recollect something. Then realisation dawns and her hand flies to her mouth.

I expected a reaction, but I didn't expect her to try and hide laughter.

'Oh, God.' Both hands fly in front of her eyes now, like the beginnings of a game of peek-a-boo. She's laughing loudly, and I honestly don't know what to do with myself. 'I bet you got a shock!'

'Well . . . yes, I—'

'We'd had a few drinks.'

'I know, but—'

'Naked Macarena, now there's one to tell your grandkids.'

Naked. Macarena. Two words I wasn't expecting to hear today. Nessa stops laughing and looks at me.

'You're not angry, are you? Jen said she had never played naked in a paddling pool and, oh I don't know, it was a good idea at the time. I'm mortified you saw it though! What must you have thought?' She shakes her head in a, I suppose, good-natured way.

'I, um, I didn't see the Macarena.'

'Thank the Lord!'

'I saw you both, you were . . . entwined.'

She seems to register my tone, my face. 'Entwined? Oh, Ed . . . tell me you didn't think? That Jen and I were—'

My face must conclude that 'that' was indeed what I thought.

'But Jen's not gay, Ed!'

'I know, but I thought, I thought, she's not herself, she's—'

'That doesn't mean you suddenly turn gay! Oh, Ed.' She reaches over and holds my hand. 'Don't tell me you've been thinking that Jen and I have been having an affair?'

'No, yes, I don't know. I don't know what to think any more.'

She holds my face in her hands and kisses my cheek. 'You

stupid, beautiful man. Jen has been in love with you ever since you met. Do you know that she spent two hours walking around with a hair repair kit the day before you were coming? That she was pruning and pampering like a teenage girl just because you were coming over?' She kisses my head and gets up. Then she tells me about what happened when Jen couldn't see Kerry, when she thought she had lost her.

'Jen needs you now more than she ever has, Ed. She wants to choose you, but in order to do that . . . she has to choose to kill her sister.'

Chapter Sixty-One

Jennifer

Ed is the type of man who can make it feel like the sun is shining when outside the rain and wind are throwing things around, desperately shouting for your attention. He is the type of man who will step into an argument and calm it . . . pouring oil over troubled waters. He is the type of man who can make you feel loved, safe, worthy even though you know you are acting irrationally because you've only had an hour's sleep, or you have just had one of those days that tarnishes your routine with bad decisions.

My husband is not the type of man to abandon his wife. But he is the type of man who will protect his family. No matter what. That is why, when he is explaining why he never told me about the science fair, I know he is telling the truth.

We are sitting in our lounge. The wallpaper is made of stripes: beige, grey, silver, beige, grey, silver. I stare at the repeating lines: so straight and neat, so tidy and organised. Just like my life was when we chose them. The list of wallpapers that had been narrowed down into a shortlist, my handwriting clear and precise. Lists used to give me pleasure – even my day to day routine was written down in a list – but I don't think I would be capable of even finding a notepad right now.

'Do you understand, Jen? It's just until you get better . . . the kids are seeing too much. We're going to fight this, you and I, but the kids need to be protected.'

He reaches into the backpack that he seems to carry around with him wherever he goes and opens a packet of tissues, handing me one. I will my fingers to reach for them, but they don't move. He leans forward and starts to wipe my face like I'm a child. The texture of the tissue feels rough on my face, like sandpaper. I wish for a moment that it was, that he could rub away this broken layer and reveal smooth new skin, skin that's not warped and brittle.

'I'll tell the kids that you're going on holiday with your parents. I'll tell them they can't go because you have to help with Grandpa's back and I have to work. They'll understand.'

I want to reply but my mouth remains closed.

'I'll come and visit you every day, I'll take you to the doctor's, I'll help you. You're not going to do this alone.'

My hand twitches and reaches for the open packet of tissues on the sofa. And I begin wiping away his tears. I'm not sure he knows that they are running along the curve of his cheeks, that they are glistening on his lips. The room is silent; we stare at each other, trying to wipe away the layer of guilt that is covering us.

'Are we really going to do this, Ed?' I ask. I can see how much this is hurting him; his words are trying to be controlled but instead they come out in a rush.

'We-don't-have-a-choice.'

I glance up at Kerry, who mouths the words, '*I'm sorry.*'

'I'm sorry,' I repeat.

Ed opens his mouth as if he's about to speak but instead pulls me into his chest, where I can feel him shuddering with the sobs he's trying not to let me hear.

*

I don't know how long we've been walking but Kerry and I are sitting on top of Hayworth Hill.

'*You have to do it, Jen,*' Kerry says again, but no matter how many times she says it, I still don't know how I can. '*You have to let me go.*'

'I don't think I'm strong enough,' I reply.

'*You're stronger than you think.*'

'Really? Do I need to remind you of the state of my life right now? Losing you once has cost my family, my sanity . . . my life.'

'*You still have a life; you know you do. You have to let me go. Think about that day, the last day you were happy. You think you can't be that happy again because I won't be there? Right?*'

I nod.

'*But imagine that day without them, Jen. They're here, they're alive, they need you . . . they need you more than I ever have.*'

I close my eyes: the volcano erupts; Hailey and Ed look at me. A sob catches in my chest.

'Will you help me? I can't do it on my own.'

'*Yes, you can. It's going to be tough at first, Jen . . . but you can do it. I know you can. Get stronger tablets in case Dr Popescu is wrong and this isn't just complicated grief.*'

'But they make you so ill.'

'*I can take it. You can do this, Jen,*' she repeats. '*You have to do this.*'

'I know.'

Chapter Sixty-Two

Jennifer

I pull the duvet over my shivering shoulders; the tears won't stop today. I can't stop them. I've lost count of the days I've been here, since I've seen my children. I remember Mum mentioning it was August . . . August used to be my favourite time of year, when I had the kids all to myself. My face hurts, my skin is dry and itchy and my mouth tastes stale.

'Try and take a sip.' Mum is sitting on my bed, holding a straw that has pierced the cardboard carton of the strawberry-flavoured protein shake.

I shake my head angrily.

'Jennifer, take a drink or I'll fetch your father.'

'Come on, Jen. I will if you will.' Kerry looks as bad as I feel as she holds her nose and slurps through the straw, a pinched and soured expression on her face, like the time I made her taste peanut butter.

Kerry stretches and puts the carton onto the bedside cabinet. She rolls onto her side, tucks her knees up, pushes her palms together and rests her cheek against them: the same foetal position that she was in at the beginning of her life, as she heads towards the end of it.

I swallow a few sips of the milkshake to please Mum, even though my stomach cramps. I close my eyes and think back to the volcano, to my trip to the doctor's, where I'd told her that the tablets weren't strong enough.

'Mrs Jones, this isn't an exact science, we don't even know what we're treating you for yet.'

'I want stronger tablets. I would like my sister to leave. No offence.' I flicked a glance towards Kerry: her fingers were re-plaiting her hair, holding her bobble between her straight teeth.

'*None taken.*'

How long ago was that? My eyelids close, Mum leaves, Kerry snores and as I slip into sleep, I see my fingers picking up the capsules, one by one. I see my body shaped in glass, a working sculpture: my heart beating, my lungs expanding, the blood rushing through my veins, through the transparent shell. I watch the fragile glass, fingers reaching for the pills and swallowing them one by one, filling up the inside of the sculpture like a jar: a blue pill, a red one, two white ones, a yellow and black one, a green one. Pill after pill after pill, until there is no room inside the glass for the lungs, and all that is left is a glass body filled with colour.

'Hey, beautiful.'

I open my eyes to see Ed's face peering around the corner of the door.

He closes it quietly behind him. 'Good or bad?'

'Bad.' My voice is a crack, a void, sucking out the daylight.

His shoulders drop a little but a smile forms on his face. 'How are the kids?'

'Good. Oscar has just got his five-metre badge.'

'He's grown five metres?'

'No, he, um, he swam. Five metres.'

'I know, Ed, it was a joke.' I shuffle myself up the bed. 'Let me take a shower and then shall we order a takeaway?' I'm amazed that my voice has the energy to stretch into a higher octave, making it sound like I can't wait to force some food down my gullet.

'Nah. I've already eaten, and I'm knackered, Jen. Why don't we stay in here, eh? I'll go and get us a cup of tea and the biscuit tin . . . What do you fancy watching?'

Kerry is coughing again, a dry hacking that she can't get rid of. I'd suggest Ed runs to the shop and gets some cough medicine for her, but I don't think it would work, what with her being dead and all. I'm struggling to hear what he is talking about.

'Sounds good.'

He kisses the top of my head and leaves the room. As I move myself again, I get a waft of body odour.

'I love the smell of palm oil in the morning.' I roll my eyes at her. Her film quotes are getting more and more predictable and less and less precise. It takes all of my concentration to coordinate my limbs in order to get myself into the shower.

Kerry coughs again. *'I'd offer to help you but . . .'* She mimics a throat-slitting action.

I pull myself from the bed. The floor feels bouncy; the room feels like it is tipped onto its side, a rocket ready to launch inside a child's hand. I reach for the glass of water beside the bed and chuck the water into my face. But it feels warm and doesn't have the desired effect. Kerry laugh-coughs. I order my feet to shuffle me to the bathroom; I step onto the landing, past the stairwell which looms to my left like an orange lozenge sliding downstairs. I can hear my parents' voices, hurried and urgent, and Ed's voice, deep and calming, a never-ending battle like the tides of a sea, pulling and pushing, pulling and pushing. The sea has been doing this since the dawn of time . . . When will it learn that the argument will never be solved?

'She needs more help than we can give her, Edward.' Dad's voice swells and crashes; Ed's pushes it back.

'She just needs more time, let's see how the new prescription helps.'

'My daughter doesn't know what day it is half of the time, and no matter which drugs she's on . . . Kerry doesn't seem to be moving on. She needs more help than we can give her. She needs specialist care, maybe a hospital—'

'You want her sectioned?!'

'We've spoken to the doctor. She's becoming irrational, Ed; if she was admitted into a hospital, she could be monitored. It might be the only way.'

The current takes hold of the conversation, my parents pushing, Ed pulling back as I'm swept away, drowning, no matter how hard I kick.

Chapter Sixty-Three

Ed

I crack open a beer and as Nessa's face appears on my phone, I sigh and ignore it. I'm not in the mood for a deconstruction of her visit to Jen tonight. Hailey's bed creaks above me and I take another sip of my beer. I've taken away the book that she was reading and her tablet as punishment for swearing. I tried to make amends before she went to sleep, but instead she turned her back on me. Oscar was more amenable, enjoying the extra attention he received instead of his sister. We read through his *Lego Batman* comic, talked about his day at summer club, and he told me a secret. Hailey has been in trouble there.

'Two times, Daddy.' He held up his fingers. 'One. Two. Promise you won't tell her I told you?'

'Promise, now snuggle down.' I tucked him in and began to leave the room.

'When is Mummy coming back?' he asked, just as I was switching off the light.

'I told you, while Mummy was helping Grandpa, she ate something that made her really poorly in Greece and she has to stay in a special hospital.'

'But that was ages ago.'

'Well, she's getting better so she'll be back before we know it.'

I go to turn the TV on but can't find the controller. I start lifting cushions but it's nowhere to be seen. I stand and start searching the shelves, moving pictures, bowls of potpourri that have lost their pourri. Anger builds up.

'Fuck's sake!' I shout as my hand catches the frame of a photo of the four of us. Kerry had taken this photo. I hold it in my hand and slump back onto the sofa. I have my arm around Jen's shoulders; her hand rests on my hand in my lap. Oscar is next to me, Hailey next to Jen, looking at each other as if they're the most important thing in the world. My finger follows the outline of us all. Jen happy, sane, content. Hailey the same; all of her milk teeth are still in her mouth, neat and white. Oscar is slimmer; his face is still rounded but his tummy isn't spilling over his shorts. And me. I still look the same. I think. I stand and walk towards the mirror above the fireplace and I'm shocked at what stares back at me. I'm thinner; flecks of grey are starting to emerge around my temples, the curls unruly and in need of a cut; the skin beneath my eyes is sagging.

Has it really been less than a year?

I replace the photo and sit back down, the controller poking my hip from beneath the arm of the sofa. I replay the conversation earlier . . .

She needs more help than we can give her.

Chapter Sixty-Four

Jennifer

'Can we talk?' I turn onto my side and stroke the hair away from Kerry's face.

'*Sure . . . it's not like I'm going anywhere.*' She coughs.

'I know. The tablets aren't working. They want to admit me into a hospital.'

'*I heard.*'

'If I go in, I may never come back out.'

I think about my family: weekends made up of driving to see their sick mother. I picture Hailey's face, telling her friend that she can't go to their birthday party because she has other 'plans'. I think of Oscar, scared and worried at the doors with codes and patients shouting out.

'*You don't know it will be like that. You might only be there a little while.*'

'I might be there for ever.'

I walk towards the window and open it, letting a blast of air blow the hair from my face.

'I don't want Ed and the kids to have to look after me, visit me. I want to let them get on with their lives.'

Kerry sits up and leans on the bed as I say the words. '*What do you mean, Jen?*' There is worry in her voice.

'I mean I have the power to let them be free. I can let them live their lives without this person I have become.'

'No, Jen. I died so you could live.'

I throw up my hands. 'You call this living? Sleeping half the day away, not knowing what day of the week it is? Not being able to live my life with my husband and my children?'

'It won't come to that, Jen. You just need to find the right tablets, the right help.'

'What do you think will happen if they can't find the right combination and I get sectioned? Do you think I'll ever be able to have control over my life again?'

'So what exactly are you saying?'

'You know what I'm saying . . . Maybe they'd be better off without me?' I pull open a notepad, click the pen and begin writing.

'*Um . . . what are you doing?*' Kerry asks, peering over my shoulder.

'What does it look like? I'm writing down how I would, um, you know I mean . . . if I don't get better and I have to—'

'*Overdose? Jen, you're not serious!*'

'No, you're right. What if I'm sick, or worse, what if I shit myself? Not quite the final image I want to leave Ed with. Gosh, there aren't that many choices, are there? Oh! I could always . . .' My blue pen scratches out my suggestion, cutting into the paper.

'Jen, this is completely out of the question.'

'You're right. I want to leave the least amount of bother for Ed when I go, he'll have enough to deal with, you have a point. He'll never get the stains out of the carpet.'

What am I doing? This has got to stop. I turn to Kerry, who is wearing her most superior 'you're acting like a child' look. I sigh, put my hands up in surrender and close the book.

'OK, OK . . . you're right.' I take a deep breath. I need a plan. 'Right. I'm going to stop the tablets so at least I'm in control of my faculties. I'm going to ignore you. I'm going to give my family good memories of me so that if I don't get better . . . those will be the things they will be thinking of, not some woman forcing down protein shakes through a straw and talking to air. I'm going to up my sessions with Dr Popescu; I'm going to need his help even more and he offered twice weekly sessions if I wanted them. But I need your help too. You have to help me. You can't interrupt conversations, you can't shout for my attention, OK? You have to help me make them think I'm better so I can give them what they need. Can you do that?'

'If you stop taking those vile tablets, we have a deal.'

We shake hands and for the first time in months, I don't wake with my dead sister shivering beside me.

'So far so good,' Kerry whispers as we sit at the bottom of our parents' garden. It's been a week without the tablets and I feel more like my old self.

Nessa arrives as I straighten myself and walk into a hug.

'You look good today, new meds?'

'Um yeah. New meds. Dr Popescu thinks we might have cracked it, I see him twice a week now.'

'So he's helping?'

I nod.

'Is she here?'

I shake my head and smile, ignoring the loud crunching sound as Kerry bites into an apple. She stops chewing, her eyes widening and her hand covering her mouth. Kerry swallows a large chunk of apple and mouths 'Sorry' to me.

'Look what your mum found!' We walk towards the bench and I pull up my collar against the sharp breeze. She places another box of Kerry's notebooks beside me and passes one into my hand.

'Kerry Hargreaves 2001 The Bubble Gum Experiment.' The pages are brittle with time but inside, Kerry's writing is perfectly preserved.

'Aw, she was only six. Gosh, she was meticulous, wasn't she?'

'Yep. One obsessive quest to another.' We continue turning pages, returning to the warmth of the kitchen as we go through the next volume.

'Do tulips prefer Atomic Kitten or Pink?'

I turn the pages: *'The Best Assault Course Ever'*. The page was broken into steps. Step one, decide on the number of activities . . . three activities was too easy, ten too many. Then each activity was broken down into effectiveness in terms of excitement, challenge, etc.

'You should do that with the kids,' Mum says, wiping her hands on her pinny as she leans over my shoulder.

'What, an assault course?'

'Why not?' Dad adds, from behind his newspaper. 'You used to love all of that as much as she did. Just make sure you're wearing suitable underwear,' he adds under his breath.

'Did I?'

I turn the page onto *'The Perfect Orange Squash'*, where a list of measurements and a score of 1–5 is listed.

'Do you remember the walking on your hands one?' Mum asks Dad.

They start to giggle. 'That one took days to practise and when you finally got the right momentum, Kerry caught her feet in the washing line and sent the laundry flying!' Dad is grinning. 'We tried to make her go next door and fetch my Y-fronts back, but she refused. Stubborn little monkey. You did it in the end, brought them back into the house dangling from a stick.' He peers over his half-moon glasses at me and winks.

'Is she . . . is she here?' Mum asks. I don't look over to

where I can see her arm stacking plates onto the draining board.

'No. I haven't . . .' I clear my throat. 'I haven't seen her for a few days now.'

Mum breathes out a long sigh and gives a short smile in Dad's direction. 'Well. That's great news, love. Isn't it?'

'It is.' He turns the page of the newspaper. 'It truly is.'

Chapter Sixty-Five

Ed

I want to believe it. I want to believe that she is finally coming back. I'm trying not to let her see how I'm looking for signs of her sister hovering in the background. How every time she laughs, I'm waiting for her to throw a look of shared amusement to thin air. But she hasn't.

The kids are opening their presents from her, both of them wearing brand new uniforms for the beginning of term, shining shoes, new backpacks. Jen is perched on the edge of the sofa next to me. I want to reach out and hold her knee but I'm afraid I could break the spell. The wrapping paper is discarded onto the floor, shining pink for Hailey, glittering blue for Oscar. Oscar's face drops, in complete contrast to the rise on his sister's.

'It's a notebook,' he says as though he's holding a piece of dog poo.

'It's a special notebook. I bought it from a magic shop. A shop so magic that when I went back to get another one for Daddy . . . it had disappeared.' Their eyes widen, but Hailey's quickly adjust to the rationality that seems to take away the magic of childhood and replace it with the realism of adulthood.

'But what are we supposed to do with it?' He turns it over in his hands and flicks through the blank pages.

'I thought we could do some more of our own experiments, like Aunty Kerry did when she was little. She would do the most amazing things and write them down. I thought we could do some of her crazy things.'

It comes from nowhere, the image of Jen jumping from Lovers' Leap, and it takes my breath away.

'What types of things?' I ask. There is caution and fear in my voice, but I don't try to correct myself. Jen has to know that we aren't all out of the woods yet.

'Well . . .' She smiles at me and then each of the kids in turn. 'She wrote down her secret recipe for getting the biggest bubbles. Kerry said adding Juicy Fruit to bubble gum worked the best. So . . .' Jen reaches into her bag again and pulls out two small rectangles in glittering paper. Passes two to me, and two each to the kids, then pulls out her own supply. 'Right, let's write it into your books then. Daddy will help you with yours, Oscar.'

'I don't need help . . . I got my pen licence last week.'

'Pen licence?'

'We get a pen licence at school now when we write neatly. Oscar's is a provisional licence . . . mine is a full one,' Hailey explains.

'Well then. Let's get started.'

Jen shows them Kerry's pages listing the ingredients at the top, the number of chews before blowing commences. We copy it and then tear the Juicy Fruit in half and begin chewing.

My wife's eyes meet mine and for the first time in a long time, I can see a glimmer of light behind them, not a shard of euphoria, but real happiness. I begin blowing my bubble; Hailey is in hot pursuit and Jen follows. Hailey begins making 'uuuuhhhh!' noises, flapping her arms and pointing to the bubble growing bigger; I mimic her actions as Oscar tries and fails to make his gum into a bubble. Instead, his gum flies out of his mouth and smacks onto the TV screen. My bubble pops as I start laughing. Hailey turns her face towards Jen and they both continue blowing, the bubbles getting bigger and bigger. Oscar comes and sits on my knee, chanting 'Hail-ey-Hail-ey!' Jen's eyes widen, as do our daughter's, and then with a defeated pop, Jen's shrinks into a blob of pink covering her nose. Hailey stands and flexes her muscles like she's Rocky, the bubble bobbing up and down in victory.

And for a moment . . . hope flickers inside me like a flame. I'm not a man prone to fanciful talk, but I swear I can feel heat from it; I didn't even know I had been cold.

Chapter Sixty-Six

Jennifer

I wait for them all to leave, running my finger along my bottom lip where I can feel Ed's kiss lingering, the warmth of it, and I know I have made the right decision.

'Jen! Help me with this, will you?'

Mum's pink-slippered feet are standing on the rungs of the ladder. 'I've found another box of Kerry's notebooks.'

I reach up and take the cardboard box from her and carry it downstairs.

'Cuppa?' Dad asks as I land the box onto the pine table.

'Please.' I rip off the tape as Mum joins me, sneezing from the dust in the attic.

'I thought this was another box of Christmas decorations. I thought I'd get them down and give them a bit of a clean, it'll be here before we know it.'

'It's only the beginning of autumn, woman,' Dad says, giving me a wink.

'Oh, shush. You know I like to have everything clean and tidy ready for Christmas.'

My hands grasp a notebook entitled '*Kerry Hargreaves 2006 Top Secret – do not open*'.

'It says top secret for a reason, dearest sister.'

'2006 . . . how old would she have been?' I ask.

'Hmmmm,' Dad thinks. 'Eleven, twelve?'

'Yeah . . . I would have been sixteen.'

The first page reads: *'Things that make Jennifer happy - smile rating 1-5'.*

'How lovely is that?' Mum says, clutching her heart. I flick through the pages: *Giving her my last Rolo (3); Letting her borrow my iPod shuffle (4); Fibbing to Mum about who broke the toilet seat (5)*. There are pages and pages of entries. The book then splits off into *'Chapter Two - Things that make Jen jump - scream rating 1-5'.*

'That little sod!' I say, laughing as I recognise some of the things listed. 'She put that frog in my school bag!'

Dad brings the tea to the table and scans the page. 'You did scream, no wonder you scored a five.' He crunches on a bourbon cream, reaches over and turns the page. *'Dressing up as a ghost and jumping out of wardrobe (5)'.*

Mum clears her throat, trying to ignore the elephant (or in my case the sister) in the room.

'I remember that, she had your shirt on, Dad, and had covered her face in Mum's talcum powder.'

'I don't remember that.'

'No, she made me swear not to say anything or she'd tell you that I pretended to be sick and got the day off school because I hadn't revised for my French exam.'

'Did you? You little swine.' But Mum is smiling.

We spend the evening going through the notebooks, laughing at the things she got up to without us knowing. I miss her so much my heart aches, but I don't look at her once.

Chapter Sixty-Seven

Ed

Jen's coming home. It's been a month with the new meds and I finally have my wife home. She's still not properly back to her old self – I still sometimes see the sad look on her face, she still sometimes stares off into space – but it's different now: she isn't looking at something in the space . . . the space seems as empty to her as it is for me.

Hailey is pulling Jen's case on its wheels through the hall and chatting about how she's a free reader at school. Oscar pulls her hands and drags her into the kitchen, where blue-and-white-striped Greek flags are folded around cocktail sticks and stuck into pieces of pitta bread. He runs to the fridge and pulls out tubs of taramasalata and tzatziki. He has insisted that we prepare a Greek dinner.

'Ta-dah! This pink stuff is trar-ra-ra-slaaaata and this one is tus-in-ki.' His beaming smile looks up at her, eager for praise.

Jen bends and picks him up. 'Oof! You're getting so big!' she exclaims as she pulls him close and kisses his ear, making him wriggle and giggle.

'Me and Daddy made . . .' Hailey looks at me for confirmation as she says, 'moussaka. I helped chop the au-ber-gine.'

'I can't wait to eat it. Aren't you all clever?'

'Wait until you eat before you make your conclusions,'

I whisper into her ear. I kiss her on the cheek and her hand grabs mine, pulling me back to her.

I stand on the threshold of Oscar's room while Jen makes all the right noises for the animals in his favourite story. Hailey appears, smelling of strawberry toothpaste and camomile shampoo.

'Is she fixed?' she asks.

'I think so.'

'But is she properly fixed, like when you bought new legs for the chair Grandpa broke and fixed it with the screws, or is she fixed like when you superglued my unicorn cup together?'

'When was that?'

'The day after Oscar's nose bleeded all over Mummy's bed sheets. You fixed it but I could still see all the cracks. I didn't like it properly.'

'Sorry about that,' I say, thinking of the discarded cup.

'It's OK. It's just that it was never the same after it broke.' She lets go of my hand and pushes her way into Oscar's room, sits on the end of the bed and sucks the ends of her hair.

Jen catches my eyes as Hailey roars like a lion and Oscar dissolves into a fit of giggles. My heart doesn't expand like it's supposed to according to all the romantic audio books that Jen listens to. Her eyes don't twinkle, they don't sparkle or dance . . . but there is a light behind them. I think that's the best way to describe it: there is light, whereas for the past few months they have been dull.

Chapter Sixty-Eight

Jennifer

'Well, that was . . .' I roll off Ed and we both laugh.

'I know.'

Everything is as it should be. This is one of the moments I want him to remember. When we're both flushed with the afterglow of sex, our bodies wet with sweat, our heart-beats racing and in sync. This is the woman I want him to remember.

'God I've missed you,' he whispers into my hair.

'I've missed you too.'

We stay silent for a few minutes, a smile nestled into the corners of my mouth, the rhythmic strokes of his hands up and down my spine.

'Who is your perfect woman?' I ask.

'Is this a trick question?' Another kiss, more strokes up and down my arm. 'You're my perfect woman.'

'Smooth-talker.' I prop myself up on my elbow. 'Seriously . . . like when you were a teenager, who was your perfect woman?'

'I used to have a real thing for Penelope Cruz.'

'Really?' I never knew that. 'So brunettes then?'

He lifts a strand of my hair and twiddles it around his finger. 'I suppose . . . and her accent. Such a sexy accent.'

'Mr Jones . . .' I do a dreadful attempt at a Spanish accent, 'are you saying you would like me to talk like these when we are in ze bedroom?' I straddle him and sit up as he laughs softly. I love Ed's laugh . . . if sounds were food, his laugh would be melted chocolate.

'How about you?'

'Honestly? I always liked blonds.'

'You're just saying that.' He folds his arms behind his head.

'I'm not . . . I always had a thing for Eminem when he was in his Slim Shady era.'

Ed begins rapping, badly, asking me what his name is.

'You rap like a ztar,' I reply, the accent making me snort as he rolls me over onto my back and kisses me deeply.

As we begin again, I'm thinking about how, if something *were* to happen to me, he could find his Penelope Cruz and how happy he would be.

Ed is sound asleep, so I retrieve my notebook and tread quietly down the stairs. Kerry is already sitting at the kitchen table, nursing what looks like whisky.

'All sexed out, are we?' she asks.

I'm about to reply but I bite my tongue.

'Oops. Sorry, I forgot we're not speaking.'

I ignore her and go to make a cup of tea. But then I think about how short life is and instead go into the fridge and pour myself a large glass of white wine.

The pages are smooth beneath my fingertips. I look at my previous entries, still hidden beneath my scribbles. What if . . . what if he works it out? That she's still here? I turn onto a fresh page and begin to doodle again.

~~Driving off a cliff Thelma and Louise style?~~

No. Scrap that.

I wander into the lounge, flick on the TV and turn the

volume down low. There is an old episode of *Friends* and I chuckle to myself as Joey asks, 'How You Doin'?'. My old maths teacher used to look like him . . . we all had inappropriate crushes on him. That was until he threw up into the wastepaper bin in class, poor bloke. He had flu and had been slurping Lemsips noisily beforehand.

Lemsips!

'*Lemsips?*' Kerry asks.

I ignore her.

That would be an OK way to go. I go into the kitchen for a refill and pull out the Lemsip box, scanning the label. Yep. High dosage of paracetamol. But where would I do it? I wouldn't want Ed or the kids finding me here . . . I could check into a B&B? I sit back down on the sofa and pull the notebook towards me. I write the word 'Lemsip' but then cross it out, just as I have with all of the other 'ideas'. Hmmm, I'm not sure about this one. I mean, how many do I have to drink before it's irreversible?

'*What if you started puking it all up? Do you remember that girl at Kira's party?*'

I don't look at Kerry, but I still grimace at the memory. She'd thrown up after she'd necked a bottle of advocaat. It was like something out of a horror movie; it shot out of her mouth like there was a fire hose in her gob. A great long blast of custard-coloured puke. What if that happened? I picture myself, exorcising Lemsip all over the walls of a hotel room, yellow puke dripping from taps and 'Do Not Disturb' signs. No, that won't do at all.

'*Anyway . . . you said you would stop that, Jen.*'

She's right. I'm being ridiculous.

I turn to the birthday section of my book and begin planning Oscar's party instead. It needs to be extra special, one that will make him happy when he remembers it in the years to come. How about a clown? I know most people are afraid of them, but Oscar loves them, loves the ridiculousness of the water-squirting flowers, the falling over, the unicycle rider.

'Jen?'

I blink and turn to Ed, sliding the notepad beneath the cushion as I turn to him.

'What are you doing? It's half-two in the morning.'

'Couldn't sleep,' I reply. 'Want to join me?' I wiggle the wine glass at him.

His eyebrows raise and concern creeps in.

I pass him the glass and he takes a small sip. 'Want one?' I ask again.

'Why not? You only live once.'

We're on to our second bottle and our second game of strip Uno. This isn't a game we've played before, but I'm enjoying it immensely. 'Uno,' I grin as Ed places a red nine onto the pile. I discard my red two with a flourish. 'Off with them!' I clap my hands and stand, doing the victory dance in my knickers and vest. Ed swigs the last of his wine and begins humming a striptease song. He struts across the lounge, wiggling his bum cheeks with every 'da-dum, da-dum', finally ending by jiggling his legs until his boxers hang from his left foot, which he flicks off, landing them on the light fitting. He bows regally and then demands from his victor.

'No more sex for you, Mr Jones!' I laugh, trying to avoid his advances around the table. 'You've got a bad back!' I can hardly get the words out, I'm laughing so hard. He takes advantage of this and almost manages to grab me around the waist, but I manage to escape and make for the stairs. But his hand takes hold of the back of my vest as my feet try to climb. I turn to him, leaning back on the uncomfortable stairs, shushing him, pointing to where above us the kids are sleeping.

'I'll be quiet.' There is so much love in his eyes, so much laughter, that once again I know I'm doing the right thing. His kiss is deep and serious, in contrast to the humour a few moments before. I close my eyes, ignoring Kerry telling me we should get a room as she opens the front door that is locked and walks out of it, slamming it without a sound.

Chapter Sixty-Nine

Ed

Jen is still sleeping as I head downstairs. The kids will be up soon and it looks like we've had a house party. My back is killing me. Sex on the stairs after a bottle of wine is not as good an idea the next morning as it was the night before. I'm not complaining this time though. Nope. I'm definitely not complaining about the sex thing this time because the sex thing now is . . . good. Apart from my bad back. And the friction marks on Jen's.

I smirk as I wash up the glasses, put the wine bottle in the recycling and make a strong cup of coffee. Even with the bad back and a thumping headache, this is the best I have felt for months. I reach for the first-aid box but we're out of painkillers. I turn to the kettle and notice a packet of Lemsips; they'll have to do. I tear open a sachet and make one for Jen too. I open the lounge curtains while I wait for the kettle to boil, and return the cushions to the sofas. Beneath a cushion is one of Jen's notepads. It's open on a page that says 'Oscar's birthday'. It's hard to explain how this can mean so much. To see her neat handwriting listing things that she needs to buy, things she needs to do: 'Book a clown'.

A clown? We normally just do a bog-standard soft play ball-pit-type place. A tug at the pit of my stomach reminds me how hard she is trying, how hard it must be for her to get back to how things used to be. I close the notebook and put it into the kitchen drawer, then head upstairs and wake her with a trail of kisses along her shoulder blade.

'Ugh,' she replies.

'I've made you a Lemsip.'

'Lemsip?' she questions groggily, then laughs.

'What's so funny?' I question.

'It's . . . nothing. I think I'm still a bit drunk.'

'We're out of painkillers,' I say by way of explanation.

She starts laughing again and sighs in a 'you had to be there' way. 'Can I have coffee first?'

'Dadddddyyyyy!' Hailey's voice shrieks up the stairs, making us both flinch. 'Why are your pants hanging from the light?'

Jen throws her arm over her eyes and chuckles.

'I'll go.' I kiss her and run downstairs where Oscar is jumping up and down on the sofa, singing to the tune of 'Twinkle Twinkle Little Star': 'Daddy's pants, Daddy's pants, why I wonder why-they're-on-the-light.'

'That doesn't even rhyme.' Hailey's glasses are removed and cleaned seriously; she returns her gaze to the pants in question.

'There was a spider.' My explanation is lame, agreed, but it's the best I can do after a few hours' sleep, a bad back and a hangover.

'So why didn't you use a towel or something?' Hailey's eyebrows meet as she stares at my boxers.

'I panicked.'

'But you're not scared of spiders.'

I reach up and pull down my underwear. 'We'd been watching a scary movie.'

'Mummy doesn't like scary movies.'

'Who wants pancakes and chocolate spread for breakfast?' Jen grins from the doorway. Oscar punches the air;

Hailey's eyes widen but are then replaced with a wary expression. I think of the last time she cooked with Jen and see that my daughter is thinking the very same.

Jen picks up on this and bends down in front of Hailey, tucking her hair behind her ears, and tracing the 'H' with her finger. 'Do you know that the doctors in Greece think I might have had that nasty bug before I went on holiday? That it was making me act a bit strange?' Hailey pulls at the edges of her dressing gown. 'But I'm all better now, sweetheart, I promise.'

Hailey throws her arms around Jen's neck and kisses her cheek. Jen glances up at me and stares over my shoulder.

My heart doesn't stop but it feels like it does: that look in Jen's eyes is back; it's a second but it's there.

Hailey skips into the kitchen with Oscar in tow. Jen stands, still staring past me, and I want to cry out loud, I can't go back there. She passes me; I turn to watch, even though I'd rather not see her gaze go back to how it used to be.

I'm trying to think of the word that explains how I feel when I notice what she is actually doing: that she isn't looking at her dead sister, she's not acting like the woman who pretended to be my wife for a few months . . . because Jen is reaching up to where, hanging from the corner of the dining-table edge, is her bra. She hooks her fingers through the material and launches it in my direction like a catapult.

'It must have been one hell of a spider,' she whispers, leaning in and kissing the corner of my mouth.

Relief. That's the only word I can think of . . . but it's not the right word. I wonder if there even is a word that can explain how, for a moment, I thought my life was going to be turned upside down, only to realise that it is in fact stable and safe. If I live the rest of my life without a glimmer of anything out of the ordinary, I will die a very happy man.

Chapter Seventy

Jennifer

I sit opposite Dr Popescu and take a deep breath. I'm about to lie to him, tell him that the medication has worked, that Kerry has gone, but before I can, he begins.

'I'd like to talk to you a little bit about some research I've been doing into complicated grief, if I may?'

'Shoot,' I say.

Kerry blows the top off her imaginary gun and holsters it. An *imaginary* imaginary gun: I don't know whether to be impressed by my subconscious or scared by it.

'So, I've found out from my research that there are many reports of "grief hallucinations" in patients who suffer from complicated grief. Some studies have used MRIs to analyse the subjects' brains while they're shown pictures reminding them of the loved ones they've lost. The scans show normal responses in the areas of the brain linked with the hurt of losing someone. But the parts of the brain that show reward are also lit up, which might explain why the brain then begins to make these hallucinations. Does that make sense to you?'

I nod slowly. 'My brain is making me see Kerry to keep me happy?'

'Yes, I think it might be. The studies also showed that people who have some kind of conflict over the death of their loved ones are often more susceptible to these visions.'

'So, someone who feels they are to blame for their sister's death, for example?' I give him a shy smile.

He nods.

'It may feel to you that you have only been struggling with your mental health for these past few months, but if I'm right, you have been battling with complicated grief for almost a year.' He pauses, giving me time to process his thoughts. 'There is a silver lining to this though . . . in most cases, the hallucinations stop after around twelve months of the loved one's death.'

'That soon,' I say, quietly allowing myself to glance in her direction.

Kerry is looking out of the window, not meeting my eye.

'So Kerry will . . . move on?'

'That's what the research would suggest, yes.'

We fall silent for a moment as I process the implications of his diagnosis.

'I've stopped taking the medication.' The words fall from my lips abruptly, the weight of their lie releasing like a sigh.

'Why?' His tone is inquisitive not reproachful.

'Because they weren't working, because they made me and her ill, because . . .' I don't finish. Instead I start crying.

He passes me a tissue. 'If this *is* complicated grief rather than a—'

'Psychotic episode?' I interrupt, smiling from behind my tears as he shrugs his shoulders apologetically.

'Maybe we should consider a different path. If I'm right, if this is complicated grief, then you're going to find losing Kerry again a very anxious time. Let's go back to the antidepressants; I'll see you three times a week for the foreseeable future and we'll reassess in a few months. How does that sound?'

I nod, and blow my nose.

'There is another kind of support you need, Jen . . . your family. Let them help you too.'

Tears start forming again and falling from my eyes, each tiny droplet filled with a different emotion: pain, grief, relief . . . they pour from me.

I imagine ripping up the pages of my notebook and throwing the plans for my own demise through the window. But as I picture the indentations of the blue ink, the peaks and descents of my handwriting, still visible beneath my scribbles, the curled edges of the paper rising and falling as they're carried away by the breeze, I also know that soon . . . I will have to say goodbye to my sister.

'Not long now then?' Kerry says as we sit down next to the river. She blows over the rim of her hot chocolate.

I grip my own cup of coffee and take a sip. My eyes settle on the river, tracking a leaf gliding lazily downstream, while beneath, a furious current is dragging away everything that isn't strong enough to hold on to its place. A couple walk past; they smile good morning at me. Me. Jennifer Jones, who looks like any other woman in her thirties, sitting on a bench, cradling a cup of coffee, her shoulders folding slightly against the chill the November midday sun can't relieve. They don't see the current beneath, pulling away the things that I can't hold on to. I give Kerry a small nod; she's leaving soon, I feel like I should offer her a small amount of acknowledgment.

'So what shall we do?'

What do you want to do?

'Come on, Jen, this is your chance to give me a good send off! Let's make a plan!'

Life is what passes you by while others are too busy making grand plans.

'Ooh, get you and your arty film quotes . . . I would have thought Blow *was a bit too heavy for your tastes.'*

It is, but Johnny Depp looks hot in it. I'm going to miss this . . . talking to you . . . or not talking to you, I suppose.

'I know . . . but you'll be able to get on with your life, Jen, without me holding you back.'

I turn to look at her but she's walking away, swerving past a woman with shopping bags, the top of a box of Christmas cards poking out of the top. I used to be like that: I used to have the Christmas cards already written and ready to go by the end of November, Nativity outfits would be high up on my agenda and the turkey would have already been ordered.

I think back to Christmas when we were kids; how hard Mum and Dad must have worked to make those moments so special. One by one I replay the memories, just like the ones on our home videos, the TV screen blinking into action with the scenes that were never caught: Kerry scratching her head beneath a checked tea towel; a grumpy-faced shepherd; the way we would grin at each when Mum's back turned as we shoved handfuls of Quality Street into our dressing-gown pockets so we could eat them hidden beneath our duvets with our torches and a magazine; Christmas mornings on our parents' bed when we were young; the excitement of Kerry bouncing on my bed shouting, 'He came! He came!'; on to the mornings when we were far too old to have stockings, but still found ourselves on Mum and Dad's bed, legs tucked beneath us as we tore open the presents that Santa had brought: face packs, mascara, nail varnish and always a yo-yo, satsuma and walnuts. Icing-sugar-smeared faces with gapped-toothed grins as we decorated the gingerbread angels that always looked wonky; how we would swap presents behind our backs – a T-shirt, a lipstick – as soon as Dad started clearing away the wrapping paper. Memories that are precious, memories that I will still have even once she has gone.

I find that I'm crying as I look up to see her – my beautiful sister – as she briefly stops walking to stroke a golden labrador. She pulls an 'isn't he cute?' look over her shoulder at me. She always wanted a dog. I close my eyes, trying to fold away the tears behind my eyelids; I try to tidy them, put them away, but before I can, I picture me and Kerry sitting on the sofa watching a Christmas film. We were drinking Baileys and eating a chocolate orange – straight from the fridge – like she always insisted.

'One day, we should all go to Lapland for Christmas . . . I've always wanted to go on a husky ride . . .'

I open my eyes and watch as she blows me a kiss, puts her earphones in and walks along the path.

'We can't afford this, Jen.'

Ed is looking at the e-booking. His mouth is saying all of the responsible things that are going through his mind, but I can tell by the pull of his lips that he's as excited as I am.

'I know . . . but Lapland, Ed. And Dr Popescu said doing something I always wanted to do with Kerry is a good way to say goodbye and celebrate her life at the same time.'

'Is he also going to pay for it?' Ed grumbles.

I ignore him. 'You've only got a few years of the kids being this age, where they can really experience Christmas as it should be. It's on my credit card, not yours, and look at the price! It's a cancellation.'

'It doesn't make a difference whose card it's on. It's our debt.'

'Don't be a spoilsport, I might get hit by a bus before the bill even comes! We can pay it off when the kids are older.' I dismiss his look of shock with a wave of my hand.

Kerry is licking her finger and flicking through the brochure. *'Oh man, you get to go on a husky ride!'*

'Look!' I reach for the brochure, taking it from her dead fingers. 'We get to go on a husky ride!'

'But . . .'

I know I'm bringing Ed round: he's forcing his forehead into a frown, but I can see the laughter lines around his eyes. He turns the page; the lines crack their knuckles, ready to break free as he sees the picture of a little girl who resembles Hailey, in so far as she's a girl and is wearing glasses. I may be stretching the resemblance part a little. The laughter lines relax; here we go. The page turns and there is a full two-page spread of the log cabin, the family of four, the presents beneath the tree. Ed has always been a sucker for Christmas.

'OK.' The laughter lines are released, a full-on massacre across his frown lines.

'Woohooo!' I jump up, pull his hands and make him join in the victory dance.

He glances up at the clock. 'Shit, I'm late. I've got to get to work if I'm going to pay for this!' He grabs his coat.

'Oh, I forgot to check you're OK picking up the kids tomorrow? I've got an appointment with Dr Popescu at three.'

My regular therapy sessions are really helping me; it's good to be able to talk openly. Ed offered to come to the sessions too, but I enjoy the freedom they give me, and there is still the matter of the little white lie that I told him when I stopped the medication. I can be honest-ish with Ed about that now – he knows that my prescription has 'changed' to the antidepressants – but I'd really rather not open up the whole can of worms, not yet. Besides, I get the impression Ed doesn't really like Dr Popescu – I can't imagine why.

'Yep! Got an alarm set on my calendar!' He gives me a hasty kiss. 'Just promise me you're not going to have an affair with him!'

'Promise.'

And off he goes, marching out of the house whistling 'Jingle Bells'.

I love my husband so much sometimes it hurts.

Look at how happy he is!

I resist the urge to wink at Kerry as Nessa knocks at the door.

Are you ready?

'I'm not here, dummy, I could go to the cinema with you both butt-naked and nobody would know. In fact . . .' She begins taking off her shoes.

Don't you dare! I said I would go to a scary film with you because you're about to kick the bucket, I did NOT agree to going with you in your birthday suit.

'Spoilsport.'

I laugh.

'Hey, you ready?' Nessa asks.

'Come in, yeah . . . just let me grab my coat.'

'Are you're sure you want to do this? You do remember that you almost didn't watch *Game of Thrones* because you were scared of the White Walkers, right?'

'I know but, well, YOLO and all that.'

'YOLO?'

'Yeah, you only—'

'I know what it means but you've never really been a . . .' she finger-quotes, '"YOLO" type of woman.'

'Well it's time to change that.'

'OK, then these are the rules.' She begins ticking them off her fingers. 'One: no looking away from the screen. Two: no hiding behind your popcorn. And three: no going to the loo when you think something scary is going to come on.'

'Can I hold your hand?' I ask as I throw my phone into my bag.

'You can, but no getting fresh.' She grins as her phone pings, hailing a message. I watch a slow, deliberate smile cross her face as her fingers flutter across the screen.

Kerry leans over her shoulder, swallowing down a sour piece of orange. Her eyebrows rise.

'Who are you texting?' I ask, pushing my arms into my jacket.

'No-one.'

'Well that no-one is making you smile like a Cheshire cat. What is a Cheshire cat, anyway?'

'It's from *Alice in Wonderland*.'

'But why is it from Cheshire?'

'No idea.' Her fingers finish fluttering and she slips the phone into her back pocket.

'So?'

'So what?'

'You know what . . . Who is making you smile like a cat?'

'Like a cat? That just sounds odd, doesn't it? Maybe Cheshire is a funny place or something?'

'Stop avoiding the question.'

'It's a . . . friend.'

'A friend?' I grin. 'Like a girrrrlllfriend?'

'Oh shush.'

'Oh my God, you're blushing!'

Kerry slams the rest of the orange into the bin, the stainless-steel clang of the lid closing ringing around the room.

'It's . . . look, it's early days yet. She's a writer. We were both working in the pub and got talking. It's no big deal. Right, let's go before we miss the start. I hear that the first five minutes is terrifying.'

'Right. Good. I mean, the scarier the better.'

Nessa walks ahead of me and I stop myself from turning to my dead sister and checking that she's OK, that she is happy that we are all moving on without her.

Chapter Seventy-One

Jennifer

'OK, so . . . our killer playlist,' Kerry begins, sitting next to me on the sofa.

You. Are. Hilarious.

I know.

This is one of the things that Dr Popescu has suggested in preparation for Kerry's . . . departure. We've spoken more and more about complicated grief and the more I hear about it the more I want to believe that this will be the way to get my life back . . . because if Kerry doesn't go, well . . . I push back the image of the page in my notepad, the page with stained carpets and—

'Well, obviously we're going to go with Aretha first . . .'

I add 'Respect' to the playlist, scrunch up my nose and close my eyes, trying to think of songs that remind me of Kerry. Oh, I know!

I add 'Someone Like You' by Adele to the list.

She peers over my shoulder at my phone screen and laughs. We'd played that song over and over the first time we got drunk together. She starts singing, begging not to forget me.

I laugh. Chance would be a fine thing.

'Can you remember the colour of my sick? It was bright orange.' She shudders. *'It was ages until I could stomach another cheese puff after*

that night.' But a smile remains on her face. *'I was only sixteen, it was very irresponsible of you.'*

It's a life skill! That's why I was making you eat plenty of cheese puffs, I say in my defence. I was giving you weak white wine with lemonade, I didn't know you were sneaking into the kitchen and helping yourself to Dad's whisky every time I went to the loo.

'Ooh, how about Olly Murs? You had such a crush on him!'

I still do.

'What was that Bruno Mars song we played in the car the day you passed your driving test and took me to Barmouth?'

'Grenade'?

I add that to the list.

Once we've exhausted our musical memories, finally adding Whitney Houston's 'I Will Always Love You' – a memory of a drunken night at a karaoke bar where I declared my love for Ed in front of a busy pub on New Year's Eve – I sync the speaker, hit shuffle on my phone, and turn up the volume. With elaborate dance moves and enthusiastic smiles on our faces, we start singing along to Olly while he asks if I want to dance with him tonight.

'Ooooh-hooo-oooh-uh-oh-oh-baby!' I warble as Ed and the kids come into the lounge. I take Ed's hands and swing him around as the kids start jumping up and down on the sofa.

'Are we having a party?!' Hailey asks mid-air. Ed spins me around and bends me backwards, a laugh caught in my throat. Kerry is shoving a handful of cheese puffs into her mouth while her head bobs from side to side to the music.

'Kind of!' I shout back as Ed pulls me back up.

'R-E-S-P-E-C-T!' Aretha begins. Oscar stops jumping, his face forming one of concentration while he tries to spell the letters into a word.

'R-E-P-T-T?'

Kerry stops with a puff half-way to her face. *'How does your son not know this song?'* She shakes her head in mock disappointment.

'Respect, dummy!' Hailey tells him mid-bounce.

'Mummy, watch this!' Oscar star-jumps off the sofa. Ed pulls me into a slow dance. Kerry twists the top of a bottle of beer and takes a slug, dancing behind us, with her eyes closed, lost in the moment, swinging the bottle as she does. My head rests on Ed's shoulder as he dances with me. I close my eyes and concentrate on this moment: the feel of Ed in my arms, the grins on the kids' faces as they bounce up and down on the sofa and the image of my sister singing. My eyes open as Ed pulls back from me.

'Why have you got the conga on your playlist?' he asks, humour creasing around his eyes.

'Butlin's.'

'Oh God, the night of the sambuca?'

'And the night I got pregnant with Oscar,' I say quietly.

'I'm amazed I was able to perform.'

'It was conga night . . .'

'It sure was.' He winks and I laugh.

'Come on!'

Kerry stands in front of us, turning her back and gesturing me to put my hands on her shoulders. I wish I could. Instead, I turn my back to Ed and pull his hand to my waist. Ed shouts instructions to the kids to join our conga line as I lead them through the lounge, Ed and I singing loudly and 'Oh-eh-oh-ing' up the stairs, circling the middle of each of the bedrooms before finally snaking back down the stairs into the lounge, where we all slump onto the sofas in a fit of giggles.

The playlist moves on to Bruno Mars. My heart hammers in my chest as Kerry begins singing into her beer bottle, her face changing from amusement to serious intensity as she looks me straight in the eyes, beginning to repeat the lines of the song: she would catch a grenade for me, step in front of a train for me . . . she would die for me, she tells me slowly, putting down her beer bottle onto the mantelpiece.

'Please don't do the same.' Kerry echoes Bruno as the playlist finishes.

Chapter Seventy-Two

Ed

'I don't know why anyone would enjoy it!' Jen says as she double-checks the locks on the front door for the third time. 'I mean, the guy was *normal,* all geekily shy, endearing and then . . .' she shivers, 'you hear his inner dialogue and he's all . . .' She shudders again. Jen has been enjoying a round of horror films since her trip to the cinema with Nessa. She had popped her horror-film cherry and now couldn't get enough – Jen's words, not mine. But we've just watched a box-set on Netflix about a stalker and it has turned her off.

I follow her up the stairs, pulling my dressing gown around me. Yep, I'm Dad-who-wears-a-dressing-gown; he's not quite as cool as Park Dad, but is still infinitely cooler than Dad-who-wears-slippers. I'm freezing, and we haven't even left England yet; God only knows how I'm going to cope with being in Lapland. We fly in a week's time, the anniversary of Kerry's death and two weeks before Christmas. When the tickets came, my heart sank; how was I going to tell Jen? But she already knew, of course she did. She said it was the best way to spend the day, that we'd be so busy travelling and finding our luggage that she wouldn't have time to think about it.

I walk behind Jen into the bathroom; I pee while she brushes her teeth, intermittently continuing the conversation between brushes and spits. 'Can you imagine what must have been going through the writer's mind? I bet she didn't sleep for months.' Jen puts her toothbrush under the running tap as I shake, flush and wash my hands.

She is still chatting about it as we climb into bed. I spoon behind her, pulling the duvet tightly around us and tucking her fleecy-bottomed legs towards me.

'Ed . . . do you think Hailey is too young for us to tell her about stalker types?'

'Yes. Go to sleep, we've got loads to do tomorrow.' I yawn and close my eyes. My lids are heavy, my eyes gritty and sore after a day looking at spreadsheets. But Jen is fidgety and rolls over to face me. I open one eye.

'If . . . if say, something happened to me, you know like I got cancer or something, you'd tell her about stuff like that, wouldn't you? And Oscar too?'

'Yes. Now go to sleep, woman.'

'Did you get the crisp packets out of the oven?'

I groan. 'No . . . I'll get them out tomorrow.'

Our life has become filled with the oddities of Kerry's notebooks. We do a challenge a weekend; this weekend is to shrink various crisp packets to see which ones are the best brand. I'm betting on Walkers, Hailey on Monster Munch, Oscar has gone for Skips and Jen is abstaining as she admits to remembering the winner. Tomorrow we are hole-punching them and adding them to keychains – already ordered from Amazon and waiting patiently inside a jiffy bag.

Working through Kerry's books has often made a normal day into an extraordinary one. If I'm honest, at first I wasn't sure if it was the right thing for Jen, you know, to be so absorbed in Kerry's world, but I couldn't have been more wrong. Dr Pepper came up with a good suggestion that Jen keeps these activities to once a week; I mean I don't like the guy, but it was a good idea. It gives Jen focus, gives her time to absorb the memories of whatever mad obsession Kerry was having that week. Most things we can keep to a weekend, but the Making Daddy Scream one, that lasted for the whole week.

My first was a solid seven (Hailey hiding in the cupboard under the stairs wearing a 'Scream' mask we had from Halloween). The second, I'd give a five . . . clued into their plans, I was on my guard as Jen put two ice cubes into my boxers; the third was a nine, no doubt about it: a bucket of iced water over my head while I dozed on my favourite deckchair in the last of the autumn sun.

Porridge testing was a good week. Double cream and maple syrup won hands down over the salt version preferred by our neighbours in the highlands.

The assault course week was . . . interesting. I did my back in trying to shimmy beneath Brian's old fishing net, Jen got her foot stuck in a plant pot, and Oscar gave Hailey a black eye when he tried to push past her on the slippery slip (a piece of plastic laid down and covered in washing-up liquid).

We're getting to the ends of the notebooks now. I'm not sure how Jen will cope with more of Kerry's absence after we do. So I've planned a few of my own memories of Kerry to help ease the transition . . . like the first time I went to watch her skating with Jen, how she jumped and spun across the ice while I hung on to the edges. I thought we could do that a few times a month; maybe Hailey or Oscar would want to join skating classes. In the meantime, we have the Christmas holiday of a lifetime to ease our way into a life without Kerry.

Today has not been an extraordinary day . . . it's been an ordinary Friday. We've had breakfast, I've been to work, Jen's taken the car for its MOT, picked the kids up, ordered a curry, drunk a bottle of wine, watched an – admittedly – creepy box-set, washed up, locked doors, brushed teeth. Today hasn't been extraordinary, but thinking back to my wife a few months ago . . . for her to have overcome the things she was going through, that is extraordinary.

She sighs and rolls over. A smile fixes itself onto my lips; it broadens as I wait for her to rub her feet together three times before she settles, as she sneezes twice – little cat-like whispers of sound. I wrap my arms around her tightly as we drift into sleep.

Chapter Seventy-Three

Jennifer

I wait until I know Ed is asleep, until his arm around me loosens its grip and I extract myself from the warmth of the bed. Kerry is waiting in the garage as I knew she would be.

It's getting easier not to speak to her, not to react to something funny she says . . . not that she talks much any more. She promised to help me; she loves Ed and the kids; she can see how well they're doing, how well I'm doing. But every night I make my way down here, so we can talk.

'So . . . Lapland.' Kerry pulls her navy-blue fluffy sock-slippers up, wraps her dressing-gown belt tighter around herself.

'Yep!' I run my fingers over the pile of thermal vests that are stacked up on top of the tumble dryer.

'Our last hurrah?' She tilts her head, the question loaded with sadness.

'Our last Christmas together . . . I'll remember this for the rest of my life. My family will remember this for the rest of their lives too.'

As I say these words, anxiety tugs at them, like there is a loose thread. It's been a while since I've felt it, that little nick, that dragging feeling that reminds me that I shouldn't really be here.

'I wish I was really here, that we had done this when I was alive.'

She examines a small gathering of batteries curiously, picking it up for me to explain.

'Torches,' I reply.

I sink down onto the step ladders, still open ready for me to reach up and pull down the cases that I will pack tomorrow, and draw my knees up to my chest. My eyes reach out to the old board games, the broken sledge that we used last year, the old baby swing that would rock a fretful Oscar, kept just in case we had another child, the box marked Easter, filled with plastic eggs to be filled with chocolates, the signposts for the egg hunt, the fake tulips and daffodils that would replace the poinsettia.

Kerry grins and pulls a Christmas jumper over her head: the Grinch's green face is stretched into a grin. Kerry presses a knitted gift-wrapped box stitched into the belly-button area and battery-operated lights begin flashing as a tiny rendition of 'Jingle Bells' begins playing.

I laugh quietly, stand, smooth down the pile of gloves and scarves that await the cases, and turn off the light.

Chapter Seventy-Four

Jennifer

We've been on the sleeper train from Helsinki for a couple of hours. Kerry and I went through an Agatha Christie stage when we were teenagers and always wanted to go on the Orient Express, so this is the next best thing. 'It'll be an adventure!' I'd told Ed. Kerry has been with me the whole time but she's not here right now, not in this cramped compartment; it's a good job because there wouldn't be enough room.

Hailey is asleep with me in the top bunk, Oscar with Ed in the bottom. Sleeping/not sleeping on a train is a surreal experience and so far, me and Ed have spent most of the night talking in whispered tones so's not to wake the kids. It's the best way I could have spent tonight; the idea of seeing Kerry's death from behind my closed lids is something I'm happy to stay away from . . . tonight of all nights. Oscar, we have since discovered, snores louder than a truck driver and fidgets constantly in his sleep, whereas Hailey mumbles, often saying random sentences, making us dissolve into giggles.

'This feels like the first night we spent together, do you remember? We watched *The Rocky Horror Picture Show* and you were too shy to try it on.'

Hailey mumbles something about grainy peacocks as I lie on my back and look at the ceiling. I feel Ed smiling below.

'I wasn't too shy,' he answers quietly. 'I was waiting for you to do it . . . which you did.'

'I did.'

'You did it very well as I recall.'

'You weren't too bad yourself.'

I close my eyes and remember that night, how soft his lips were when I kissed him, how gentle he was . . . as though he didn't want to break me.

'You were so gentle,' I say quietly.

'I'd waited a long time. I'd fantasised about that girl standing on the train platform, one arm raised in a right angle behind her head, eyes looking off at something or someone further up the platform, not at me . . . you only glanced in my direction as the doors closed.'

I hear Ed shifting himself onto his back and rolling Oscar onto his side towards the wall. 'I wonder what you were looking at,' he muses.

'Another man,' I reply, deadpan.

'He was probably more your type too . . . dark hair, brooding eyes—'

'Intelligent, mysterious . . . Nah, I was probably looking for Kerry. She was always late.

'What happened when the doors shut? Did you stare out of the windows like a lost puppy? All sad eyes and palms against the window?'

He laughs quietly. 'No . . . but I do remember hitting that girl with a door.'

'You made me see stars.' I hang my head upside down over the edge of the bed, my hair falling down towards Ed's smirking face.

'How else was I going to make an impression?' He raises his eyebrows.

'Do you ever wonder how different our lives would have

been if you hadn't decided to buy flowers that day?' I ask, returning my head to my pillow.

'Truth?' he asks.

'Truth.'

'I think if it hadn't been that day, it would have been another day. I think it was fate.'

'I love you.' I yawn.

'I know.'

From nowhere, I think back to the day I had gone for a run, when I met Richard – the man from Hayworth Hill – his words from that conversation so long ago replaying in my mind: *'I don't think there was anything I could have done to change my life even if I wanted to,'* he had said.

But what if I don't want to?

What if I don't want to change my life? What if I want to keep my sister and my family?

Chapter Seventy-Five

Ed

It's fucking freezing. I mean cold, like I've never ever felt before. I'm not sure if my fingers and toes are still attached, but I look over to where Jen and the kids are beaming from the sleigh, and I don't care about the fact that beneath my clothes my extremities could very well be perishing. Christ, I hope Jen isn't expecting me to perform later; I doubt she'll be able to find my boy beneath all these layers, and even if she does, I suspect he may be hunkering away, shying from the cold.

'Come on, Daddy!' Hailey shouts, her cheeks red, her eyes bright behind her glasses. Oscar is fidgeting with his scarf and puffing out steam through his nostrils.

'I'm coming!' I jog/stomp my way over to them through the snow. I'm not sure my knees will ever recover from this trip.

I shuffle forward in the snow; soft flakes are falling from the sky again. The sky is blue. That sounds like a simple explanation, but what I mean to say is, it is every shade of blue; above me it is deep blue . . . That's not better, is it? The only way is to describe it by the Crayola crayons that are currently broken in half in the kids' cupboard. If I was to get a fresh new pack and lay out all the shades of blue, they would go from baby blue to periwinkle blue to ruddy blue, to . . .

what colour does Oscar use for Aquaman? Ultramarine – you get the idea – until they end with white . . . next to the horizon, the blue sinks into white.

Snow cushions my footsteps, the sound swallowed, like I've hit mute on the controller. Everything is so quiet here. Well, apart from the sniffs of the huskies, the squeals and creaks of the kids as they sit huddled beneath a fur throw.

My heart swells inside my chest, well, not actually swells because I'm sure that would give me a heart attack and that is the last thing I want to happen here, could you imagine how fucked up that would make my kids? I mean that I never thought being here would be as magical as it looks in the brochures. I felt pretty damn cynical about the whole thing, but as I look at the excitement and joy on their faces . . . no, my heart isn't really swelling but my love for my family is. Just look at them. I reach up onto the sled and stand behind them. Jen is sitting with the kids *Cool Runnings* style, Hailey between her legs, Oscar between hers. My gloves hold on to the driving bow – the arch of wood like a handle.

Ahead of us the snowmobile motor ticks impatiently, ready to clear our path; the snow is falling at a steady pace, but the staff aren't concerned. I'm glad to watch the snowmobile from afar; yesterday Jen persuaded me to let her on one.

In front of the sled the dogs, all eight of them, are impatient to get going.

'OK?' I ask Jen, her face turning and tilting up to me. *Isn't this magical? Isn't this amazing?* it says, and I match her expression. The forest ahead of us is . . . Christ, it *is* amazing; the trees are covered in snow, some of the green patching through the fir, but others are gleaming. When we first got here, I reached up to one of the trees and gave it a gentle tug. I expected the 'snow' to stay still, so convinced was I that this was all fake. The snow on this tree was white – crystal white – like the fake stuff that is already on the pop-up trees from the supermarket. But it fell from the branches, landing with a thud on top of me, a great source of amusement to the kids.

'Ready?' the guide asks. The snowmobile revs its engine and begins and then with a tug the sled starts moving. It's moving fast, like really fast. The kids are squealing, Jen is wooohooo-ing and me? I'm looking down at my family, as we power around bends, following the snowmobile, part of me desperately wanting to enjoy the moment, but as we fly forward, the magic turns into something else: fear. I'm suddenly terrified. What happens if there is a fault with the engine ahead of us? What if it bursts into flames, if we fly into a ball of fire, or swerve, the sled turning on its sides, the fear sending the huskies rabid, my family trapped while being ravaged? The squeals of joy continue as the sled picks up pace. My breath is coming fast, my hands gripping the handle; it seems to go on and on, the paws of the dogs pounding, the rush of the wind in my ears and ice in the air, the snow hanging from the trees; on and on the ride goes.

Eventually, as things do, our journey comes to an end. I step off and, in a few strides, my wife, my daughter and my son are in my arms. They're safe; we're all together; we're all alive.

Chapter Seventy-Six

Jennifer

I can't stop smiling; my cheeks are stuck, but they're not frozen in place – I don't think – I'm just happy. Ed disembarks the sled and pulls me and the kids into his arms; his body is shaking from the adrenaline that I can still feel hammering around my own. The kids are yelping and screeching about how amazing it was and asking if they can stroke the huskies.

'Just a minute,' Ed says into our coats, 'I just want to remember this.' I know exactly how he feels.

'Kids . . . we're going to take a memory picture, OK?' I say.

'A what?' Oscar replies.

'A memory picture, it's where we all take one minute to take a picture, but a picture in our minds.'

'You're weird, Mummy,' Hailey replies, taking off her glasses and rubbing the lenses with her mittens to clear the steam created by Ed's embrace.

'Well, I think Mummy is a genius,' Ed replies. 'You can't smell and listen to a photo, can you?'

'I s'pose. Can we stroke the doggies now?' Oscar is impatient.

'Just a minute, buddy. But first, memory picture. Are you ready? I'll count three, two, one, and then you take the picture with your brains. Remember the smell, the sounds, the feel of your clothes, the . . .'

'Hurry up, Daddy!' Hailey interrupts.

'OK, OK, ready? Three, two, one!' We're all silent for a moment. The guide has pulled out his phone and is taking a snapshot as we all sit there, Ed and I looking into each other's eyes and the kids looking confused but happy, their noses red and their eyes glassy.

'My memory picture is done, Daddy. NOW can we stroke the doggies?!'

'OK, buddy, oof, off we get.' Ed picks up Oscar, and takes hold of Hailey's hand, shooting me a cheeky grin over his shoulder that tells me how lucky we are.

I jump.

Kerry is standing next to me. Her voice is loud in my ear; I can smell the hot chocolate vapour rising from her cup.

'This is why I saved you.'

She leans in and kisses my cheek; the warmth of her lips stays with me for the rest of the day.

Chapter Seventy-Seven

Jennifer

It's Christmas morning. All around the world families have been arranging presents, cooking special meals, meeting up with loved ones, remembering the ones who are no longer here.

I don't really remember last Christmas. I vaguely remember the kids opening presents, the smell of burnt potatoes as Ed tried to cook the dinner, the Queen's speech that sounded so far away, Mum and Dad perched on the sofa. They were wearing brightly coloured paper hats from the Christmas crackers, the colours brash and insulting against their stark faces, both as blank and expressionless as my own.

But today has been different. Today, we've been up since half-five; Santa has been and gone; we're home after our magical trip, tired but happy. The remains of Christmas lunch are lying bloated and tired on the kitchen side – not a sniff of a burnt potato – and we're all slumped on the sofas, Nat King Cole crooning away on the soundbar as the kids retrieve their presents for us. Kerry would always help them choose something for us; Mum and Dad took them on their shopping trip this year.

'Do you like it, Mummy?' My fingers are stroking the calendar. It's a family planner, the months and days dissected into rows and columns, waiting to be filled with the year's activities: the after-school clubs, dentist appointments, birthdays, anniversaries . . . appointments that won't revolve around my sister.

I can't talk.

The air inside my body has gone; the air around me has evaporated. I grip on to the stem of my glass, wine sloshing over the rim. The indulgent smile on Ed's face is falling rapidly as he puts down his own drink and rushes to my side. There is no room; the sofa is piled high with clothes, toys and wrapping paper. He moves Hailey's new keyboard to the floor, sits beside me and rubs my back.

'Mummy?' Hailey's voice is worried.

I force my mouth to open to gulp down the oxygen that must be there; it must be, because look at how my family are still breathing. I drag it in, and release it, I grapple again, again I manage to hold on to it, swallow it, breathe it in.

'Jen?'

I wave my hand, my muscles obeying my instructions, manipulating my features into a smile and somehow, I manage to speak.

'Look at how organised we're all going to be next year!' I cough a few times, take a long sip of my drink, carefully place it onto the coffee table and peel away the cellophane, revealing a navy-blue cover framed by butterflies and flowers. My fingers stroke it, open the first page and extract the pen that is hiding between the wire spirals. January stands tall and proud; I run my fingers along the days that lie ahead until they land on the eleventh.

'Hmm . . . something about that date rings a bell.' I tap my head in mock concentration. 'I wonder if Daddy can remember why that day is special?'

He shakes his head, looking perplexed. 'Nope, no idea why that date should ring a bell.'

'Oh, Daddy, you are silly.' Hailey rolls her eyes at me.

'That's the date you married Mummy, Grandma and Grandpa said it was all smudgy.'

Oscar wrinkles his nose and looks at his sister for an explanation.

'It's when snow has melted and looks all dirty.'

'Sludgy,' Ed corrects, his fingers twirling the bottom of my hair around his fingers. 'It could have been raining cats and dogs and I wouldn't have noticed, because your mummy looked like an angel.'

I shake my head at him, but can already feel that my face is betraying how much I love his words.

'Did you look like an angel too?' Oscar asks Ed, who straightens an imaginary tie.

'No. The bride looks like an angel, the groom looks dapper.'

'What's a dapper?'

'He means that he looked very handsome . . . he would have looked even more handsome if he didn't have a black eye.'

Hailey's eyebrows rise towards her fringe. 'Why did you have a black eye? Robbie in class five had a black eye because Luca in class three punched him. Did you get punched at the church, Daddy? Did the vicar punch you?'

'The vicar?' I laugh. 'No, the vicar didn't punch Daddy, Daddy fainted on his stag do because he had his ear pierced and hit a cupboard door on the way down. His friend from school convinced Daddy that he could do it there and then with a needle and a bottle of . . . what was it, Ed?'

'Tequila.' Ed's face blanches at the thought.

'But he still looked very handsome. Right, I'm going to put this up in the kitchen, then shall we open the Quality Street and watch *Santa Claus the Movie*?'

I take myself into the kitchen, place the calendar onto the counter and grip the edges. I'm still shaky. I put my hand on top of the numbers and feel the days disintegrating beneath. The days I will have without her.

Kerry puts her hand on top of mine. I don't look up; I just watch the silver thumb ring that I never found rubbing across mine.

'You OK?' Ed asks from the doorway.

I look up and wipe away the moisture around my eyes. 'Yeah, I just . . . it's been a busy couple of weeks, and I was just thinking about Kerry, about how it's going to be another year without her.'

He folds me into his chest, his lips kissing the top of my head.

'But you're still here,' he whispers. 'We've still got you.'

'You're welcome!' Kerry kisses Ed on the cheek.

I pull away, unwrap a purple-wrapped chocolate and pop it into his mouth.

'Daddy! The batteries won't fit!'

'Coming!' he replies, giving me a chocolatey kiss and returning to the lounge.

'*You can do it, Jen.*' Kerry picks up the calendar and smiles. '*It's only time . . . it can't hurt you.*'

But I know that it can, it's hurt me before, the seconds, the minutes, the hours without you.

'You can do it. Fill that time with them.' She nods to where laughter is coming from the lounge as the race-car track that Ed insisted the kids would love whirrs into action.

What if I can't?

'You have to.'

My reindeer slippers follow Ed back into the lounge, their antlers nodding with every step as my lips form a smile.

She's right: I have to. Because the alternative will be even harder.

Chapter Seventy-Eight

Ed

'Just give me a hint . . . Where are we going?' Jen asks.

'That will ruin the surprise,' I say. OK, cards on the table, I'm not a romance kind of guy. I mean I'm not completely crap, like I always get roses for her on Valentine's Day, but I felt like after the year we've had that I should step up a bit for our anniversary, you know?

I indicate and pull onto the hotel carpark. We've got the night to ourselves; the kids are at Brian and Judith's.

'Ooh, posh!' The hotel is a castle, an actual castle. I'm not one to brag but as far as weekends away go, I think I've nailed this one.

'Don't worry about the cost,' I intervene. 'I got a Groupon deal.'

She laughs. 'Oh, Ed, ever the romantic.'

'What? You can be romantic and thrifty. Romance isn't about how much money you spend.'

'True. Remember when you gave me your coat when I fell in the sea?'

'I was being gallant, not romantic.'

'Aren't they the same thing?'

'I don't know. But my balls have never been the same after that weekend . . . they were the size of raisins when we got back to the chalet.'

'It was your fault, you suggested we jump over the waves in November.'

'I was trying to impress you by being spontaneous.'

'Well it worked. I think I fell in love with you a little bit more every time your lips turned a deeper shade of blue.'

'I have a sneaking suspicion you're going to love me even more after what I have in store,' I say, winking.

'Ooh, sex swing?'

There was a time in our relationship where Jen's enthusiasm for a sex swing would have been right up there with when Arsenal won the FA Cup.

'No.'

'Oh.' She sighs with a kind of dramatic disappointment. I still can't quite get used to how our sex life has changed. When we first met, it was all the time . . . we were young, everything was fresh, like when I found the faint birthmark on the back of her leg; I felt special, no, not special, I felt privileged. That doesn't work either, does it? What I'm trying to say is when I first saw it, it was as if I'd been allowed to see behind the curtain in *The Wizard of Oz*. It's just a birthmark, he was just a scatty old man, but knowing the truth somehow made that scatty old man something . . . more. That's how it is when you've been married to someone for years: the rest of the world see something different to the person you are allowed to see. But now, it's as if she has other birthmarks that I've never seen before.

'Not a sex swing, but I promise there will be champagne. And sex stuff, if you're lucky,' I add as the tyres crunch into the gravel of the parking bay.

I carry our bags and we climb the steep steps and into the room. It's Tudor in style . . . I think.

'No sex swing but . . .' I pull open the heavy curtain and we look out over the lighted gardens below, the turrets of the castle lit up by soft floodlights. Below us is the courtyard and beyond that is the sea, flat and laid out like a blanket behind the steep green banks that roll onto tall cliff faces.

Jen leans her head against my shoulder. 'I love you.'

'Good, because I'm going out for a bit.'

'Funny.'

'No really . . . I'm going out for a bit.'

'What?' She turns to me laughing.

'Have a bath, and, um, don't look in your case until I tell you.'

'Mr Jones . . . you have got sex stuff planned!'

'Not . . . exactly. Do you trust me?'

'With my life.' The words snag in her throat and for a moment she seems overwhelmed by the year's events. But then she starts coughing. I pat her back as the tears roll down her cheeks as she tries to say the word water through her coughing fit. I pass her the bottle, make sure she's recovered, then grab the bag and leave the room.

Chapter Seventy-Nine

Jennifer

My hand runs along the stone walls inside the en suite . . . although that word doesn't quite fit the small bathroom I'm standing in. My fingers run over the exposed brickwork where the shape of a fireplace remains as the room fills with steam. The bath is claw-footed; a sound escapes my mouth as I sink into the deep water, bubbles shimmering, shifting and nestling against my skin.

I close my eyes, enjoying the luxury. At first, the opulence feels delicate and beautiful as I take in the sensation of my muscles relaxing, of the warmth surrounding me. But the luxury starts to cling to my thoughts, like a cobweb, barely visible until you look closer and see the droplets of morning dew hanging from it like diamonds. The more I begin to enjoy the moment, the more beauty my life begins to fill with, the bigger the web seems to be. I reach out to touch it: the diamonds jangle and chime, the light catching the sun, dazzling in my eyes, hurting my retinas until I have to look away. My fingers are stuck to the web, the diamonds slicing my skin, nipping and cutting as I try to free myself, but I'm caught, I'm trapped by the beauty.

My eyes flash open and I push my body upwards, sloshing some of the water over the edge of the bath.

'That puts death by drowning out.'

Kerry tries to pass me a towel. I ignore her and wipe away the bath suds with my hands. I pinch my eyelids, snapping myself awake. In the bedroom my phone is vibrating. I climb out of the bath, wrap myself in the white bathrobe, sink onto the bed and answer Ed's call. I still feel like the cobweb is sticking to me.

'Hi . . . where are you?'

'I'll be back soon. Did you open your case yet?'

'No, I've just had a bath, like you said.'

'Right, well, open the case and, um put it on.'

'Put IT on? Oh, Ed, no more celebrity masks, I beg of you.'

His voice is soft and rich when he replies. 'No celebrity masks, I promise. I'll be back in about half an hour. Love you.'

'You too.'

I pass my phone between my hands and look towards where my case is standing by the door. Kerry is lying on the bed, unwrapping the chocolate on the pillow.

'Well . . . are you going to see what all the fuss is about?'

The web is disintegrating; it falls from my skin as I open the case and unfold the tissue paper sitting on top of the clothes I had packed. So, this is why Ed had insisted on fetching my bag from upstairs. Sitting inside the tissue paper is an emerald green dress. It straightens itself from the paper as I pull it free, standing up: proud, regal. The material cascades from the hanger; its shape is a fishtail by design, edged with delicate lace. I've never been one for coveting celebrities and fashion, but I can't help but let out a little gasp as I run my fingers along the sweetheart neckline. I lay the dress across the bed; it oozes sex appeal and glamour. I glance back to my case and pull back another piece of tissue; a matching cashmere wrap sits on top of an emerald green underwear set and a pair of kitten-heeled sequinned shoes. They wink at me: hello, well aren't we special? They're like something a flapper girl would wear.

'Oh, Ed.'

The underwear fits perfectly: the bra is not designed for sports and the knickers would be no good for a long day doing the school run, but for a night in a hotel with my husband? They couldn't be more perfect.

I step into the dress, the soft shift gliding over my skin. I face my reflection, turning to the side and following the arc of my waist, the flare of material that smooths over my stomach. Kerry stands next to me smiling, the same pose that we had when I got ready for my first school disco.

'*You look beautiful*,' she smiles.

We both turn towards the knock on the door. The dress hums with each step that I take, the throw warm and comforting around my shoulders. Behind the door stands my husband, dressed in a suit, a darker shade of my dress. He looks shy, uncomfortable but happy. His mouth opens but no sound comes out. Instead, he offers me his arm. 'Shall we?'

I'm following Ed, keeping my eyes closed as instructed. I hear sounds of automatic doors opening, of Ed thanking a man for a favour; no problem, the man says. Smells that are hard to place follow us, as does Kerry. I can't see her but I know she's here; she's walking next to me, holding my hand.

'Almost there.' Ed's voice is nervous, excited like the day he asked me to marry him. His hands rest on my shoulders. 'Wait there, just a second.' I hear him shuffle about and then Nat King Cole's 'The Very Thought of You' begins.

I hear Kerry whisper into my ear, '*I've got to go, but I'll see you later.*' I feel a ghost of her kiss on my cheeks just as Ed's warm hands cover my eyes.

'OK . . . ready?'

'Yes,' I giggle.

'Open your eyes.'

My eyes widen as I take in the scene in front of me. We're

inside a glass tunnel; above us and around us sharks, rays and sea creatures glide.

'Oh . . . Ed.' His name falls from my mouth. The blues and greens shimmer from inside the aquarium, reflecting all around us, as though we're part of it, as though we're at the bottom of the ocean. Bubbles rise; we are surrounded by warm springs while Nat continues to sing about the mere idea of us. Schools of brightly coloured fish seem to giggle past us in flashes of blues, pinks, purples, yellows as larger fish chase them into order like headmasters on a school trip. I grab hold of Ed's arm and point to a shark shimmying past, its backend sashaying from side to side, its majesty commanding attention.

I look down at my dress, look into the water that surrounds us, look into my husband's eyes; he's practically dancing on the spot with excitement, just like the boy I fell in love with, so pleased at his gallant gesture. He points to a giant ray gliding above us, its smile pleased to see us.

In front of us are a table, two chairs, and a fairy-lighted champagne bucket, a small picnic basket resting next to it. My chest rises and falls, my lungs breathing life in and out.

'You once said . . .' he takes my hands in his and faces me, 'that when you were a little girl you wanted to be a mermaid . . . You've made my dreams come true, Jen, I wanted to do the same for you.'

Tears swell, his face blurring through them as they fall over my eyelashes. His thumb wipes one away.

'I don't deserve all of this, Ed. Look at what I've put you through this year; how on earth have I made your dreams come true?'

'You came back to me.'

'May I have this dance?' I ask him.

'It would be my honour.'

Chapter Eighty

Ed

I don't think I have ever been more in love with my wife. Not on the day I first saw her through the doors of that train. Not when she looked up at me and agreed to let me walk her home. Not on our wedding day with her perfect make-up and hair teased into unnatural ringlets around her face. Not when she looked at me and told me she was pregnant, or when she looked down at our new-born daughter. But right now, with the reflection of the artificial blues and greens of the giant fish tank, the bubbles rising behind her head, the stingrays with their goofy smiles passing us by . . . Right now. Her head is thrown back and she is laughing. I take in the gap between the front teeth that I love so much, the smudge of mascara under her eye, the green of her dress, reflecting on her throat like the yellow of the buttercups Hailey thrusts beneath Oscar's chin. Right now, because she has never looked so alive. That look that has been there since Kerry died has gone. Left. Adios, bye-bye. Gone.

They say you never really know what you have until it's gone . . . Do people say that or have I just made it up? Or is it a lyric? It doesn't matter. What matters is that I know what it felt like to lose her. To see her disappear a little bit more as each day passed. And each day, it was like I lost a little bit of myself too.

'Well, husband of mine.' Jen leans forward and kisses me. She tastes of wine and salt. 'You have outdone yourself.' Her head leans to the side and she exhales and looks up at a shark swimming over us.

We're tipsy when we return to our room, kissing outside of the door before I've got the key in the lock. The door opens behind us, and we fall through. I manage to kick it closed before my hands begin to explore the new underwear that is hiding beneath the dress. They are not disappointed.

Our lovemaking starts off with giggles and difficult clasps, with awkward positions and earrings caught in hair, but soon the struggles we have overcome seem to be at the forefront of our minds, as though we can make up for every wrong word we've said to each other with a kiss, every night spent apart while Jen was ill with a touch. Jen sits on top of me, her hips moving rhythmically, her hair falling forward, her eyes filled with love.

I wake up with a start. A door slam? I reach out for Jen, but the bed is empty. Her side is cold.

'Jen?' My voice is hoarse. My hand fumbles around for the light switch and the room fills with it. 'Jen?'

Chapter Eighty-One

Jennifer

'Jen?' I stir and roll over. *'Jen? Wake up.'* I open my eyes to see Kerry sitting beside me on the bed.

I'm tired. Go back to sleep.

'Jen-ni-fer . . . I need to show you something.'

Ed is snoring gently beside me. The green dress is draped languorously over the armchair; you aren't tired, are you, darling? The night is still young, it seems to say. I glance towards my case, to where my jeans and boots are enclosed, but think of the zip and sounds it will make.

'Just put the dress on, we won't be long, I promise.'

I step back into it, watching Ed's back rise and fall, deep in the clutches of sleep, and grab the throw.

Where are we going?

She hops on her foot as she pulls on her boots. *'I just need some fresh air.'*

I slip my fingers into the shoes and leave the room quietly. The hotel is sleeping, the lights are dim, the sounds quieted.

We follow a path down through the gardens to the remains of an outbuilding. The floodlights are low now: dozing. I come to a wall, half-awake, half-asleep. Like me. Peeking over the wall is the sea; it rolls over, tosses and turns, throwing off its cover before pulling it back on. My hands run along the stones of the wall, stopping to watch the turmoil of the water below. I let my fingers follow the grooves around the bricks, the passing of time sewn into each downward pull, each scrape of the trowel.

To the left, there is a path that climbs the steep bank of a cliff, a wooden fence guarding it against the insomniac sea.

'Come on.' Kerry pulls at my hand. *'The view must be immense from up there.'*

I pull my throw tighter around my shoulders and follow her, my hands gliding over the smooth wood. I hesitate as the fence banks inwards, away from the edge of the cliff face, keeping spectators safe from harm.

My thoughts are consumed by Ed; how much better he looks now that I'm 'better'. I hadn't noticed how much I had taken from him since Kerry's death until tonight. Until I watched him talking and laughing. I hadn't realised the emptiness that he'd been hiding from me until I saw how full of life he now is. It's hard to see the volume inside something, isn't it? To calculate how much space there is? But if you tried to fill, say, a cavern with water . . . suddenly, you would have a sense of how empty it was before. That is what it's been like tonight: I could see how full Ed is, full of love for me, for Hailey and Oscar, full of the life we have ahead of us.

As we continue, I notice the fence has a slight wobble, a discrepancy in the integrity of the wood; I stop and look at the spot where I'm standing. The wood has split in several places: tired of its job, lowly paid, long hours. This piece of wood has had enough; it wants to break free, to escape the confines it has been allocated: to feel the power of the water's grip, to be caressed and played with as it swims to far-off lands, places with a new view, new cliffs to stand sentry. I push the wood a little, hear its groan of relief, hear its back crack, shackles falling to the ground as it leaps from the cliff edge. Free. Falling. No longer trapped by duty.

Kerry holds my hands as we watch it hit the water, the waves welcoming it, embracing it, offering to show it the secrets below.

I know why she has brought me here.

'It's time, Jen, it's time for me to go.'

She turns and steps towards the edge of the cliff and faces the water.

Chapter Eighty-Two

Ed

I'm in that moment you're in when it takes your brain a few moments to shuffle your thoughts and organise themselves as my hand taps Jen's side of the bed, my eyes resting on the space beside me. 'Jen?'

Something doesn't feel right. Like that feeling when you wake up after a night out and you know you've acted like a dick, but you can't quite remember what it was that you did.

I get up and push open the door to the bathroom, but it's empty. Even as I call her name again, I know there will be no reply, because Jen isn't here. I glance over to where her dress had been discarded last night: it's missing. My heart is beating hard inside my chest as I call her number, but her phone is beside the bed, my face smiling up from the screen like a joke. Pulling back the curtain, I look down into the castle grounds, but I can't see her down there. Maybe she went to the bar? I'm trying to convince myself that this is a possibility, even though deep down, I know I'm kidding myself. Something in my bones is telling me that this feels wrong.

My clothes are all over the floor and I push my feet into my trouser legs while simultaneously grabbing the room key and reaching for my shirt. Quietly, I descend the steps. The bar is closed; the hotel is so quiet as I make my way out into the grounds.

'Jen?' My voice comes out in a whispered shout; it hurts my throat. I continue calling her name, hurrying through the gardens and narrowing my eyes out towards the sea, towards the cliffs. My breath is hot in my throat as I see it: a flash of green high up on the ridge.

She's there. The image I have tried so hard to fight is back. Jen jumping, lying flat in the water.

Fear courses through my veins, making my feet run, making my voice catch as I call out her name.

I'm breathing hard as I follow the curve of the path. I look up to where I can see her: she's standing next to the edge, her right hand is stretching out like she's holding hands with one of the kids, her dress is bright against the backdrop of dawn breaking, the wind pulling her hair.

'Jen!' I shout again but she doesn't hear me. I'm too far away. I'm too far away to stop her stepping forward.

Chapter Eighty-Three

Jennifer

'Stop!' I take her hand in mine. I look down at the dark water; fear is burning my chest. I didn't think I would be scared. 'You don't have to do this.'

Kerry turns to face me. She is wearing her red boots, red coat, her emerald ring, and is smiling out to where dawn is breaking over the horizon.

'When I was little, if I had a bad dream, I used to sneak into your bed. Do you remember?'

I nod. 'Your feet were always cold.' A tear stings my skin as it rolls down my cheek.

'I always felt safe when I was with you.'

'You were my little sister. It was my job to keep you safe.'

'No, Jen. It wasn't.' She wipes one of my tears away and smiles. *'Me dying wasn't your fault, Jen. It was just an accident.'*

I shake my head, fighting her words. 'It was my fault.'

I take a small step forward, closer to her, closer to the edge. The sea is hungry, snapping its jaws together beneath me. My legs are shaking, my throat tight; the fear of death has a hand on my shoulder and it is trying to pull me back to safety.

'I'm scared.' The words tumble from my mouth as I try to hold on to her hand tightly.

'I wish I could take you with me.' She smiles sadly. *'But—'*

Kerry puts on a croaky voice telling me she'll be right here, pointing to my heart, quoting from *ET*, the film we would always watch if we were sick. Her plait is hanging over her chest in the same position as it was the day she died. '*I have to do this*,' she says.

I nod.

'*It's the best thing for you . . . for them*.'

I swallow hard and peer over the edge again. I close my eyes and try to control the shaking in my legs; I breathe in slowly as my foot takes another step.

Kerry is smiling out towards the ocean, the sunrise catching the glint of green in her ring as she wipes a tear away. She turns her back on the sunrise and squeezes my hands. Her voice is steady and earnest. '*I'm sorry, Jen. I'm sorry for putting you through this. I'm sorry for leaving you alone . . . but you have to go on living, Jen. It's time for me to go.*' Her eyebrows raise as she rests her hands on my shoulders. '*You don't need me any more, Jen*.'

'I know.' The words are caught, they come out as a breath. Kerry takes a step back.

'*Wait!*' Panic stretches my hand out towards her.

The Accidental Death of Jennifer Jones

If a person were asked to describe Jennifer Jones, they would say that she is happy with her life. They would say that she's happily married to Edward, the third man she slept with, who was neither the best nor the worst of her conquests. She is happy with the way her children have turned out, a perfect pair – one of each, Oscar, six and Hailey, nine – who are both well behaved, polite and intelligent. If that person could see her now, they would see a woman dressed in a green dress which whispers with each step she takes, which glimmers in the early morning glow. The wind is playing with her dark hair; it twists and turns in the wind; her blue eyes are bright as she looks down into the water below. She replays the evening, watches herself and her husband laughing beneath a tunnel of ocean, the peace and majesty of the fish as they swam, the light in his eyes as he talked about their children and the year ahead. About old times, about her sister. Jennifer Jones knows that her sister will no longer be there with her. Her hands rest on a fence, high up along a cliff face. The fence has stood here for many years, keeping tourists safe, tolerating the sticky hands of children, as their parents hover closely behind them: not too close now, hold on to my hand, look you can see for miles. But this fence is becoming tired; it no longer has the strength to keep the children safe, to keep their loved ones from harm's way. Jennifer Jones pushes her hand onto the wood until it snaps, cracks and falls. The woman in green leans gently forward and watches it plummet, a sad smile playing on her mouth.

Jennifer Jones knows this is the right thing to do, to say goodbye to her sister, but as Kerry steps towards the edge of the cliff, Jennifer is filled with panic. She doesn't want to let her go. She can't watch her sister die again.

Kerry turns towards the sea. She is ready, at peace, but as Kerry begins to take a step, Jennifer reaches out a hand to stop her. Jennifer knows her husband will come looking for her; she knows he will see the path; he will see the broken fence, he will know at once what has happened. He will ignore the little nagging sensation in the pit of his stomach that tells him that he believed this would happen all along. He will picture how happy his wife has been recently, he will remember the snow and her arm around his neck, the laughter in her throat. He will picture their lovemaking: slow and intense, how blessed he had felt because he could see how much his wife loved him. That nagging in his stomach will be filled with despair at this tragedy; this accident that took away his wife from their children.

The tragic accident that caused the death of Jennifer Jones.

Chapter Eighty-Four

Ed

I've lost sight of Jen as I sprint as fast as I can around the bend of the path. Everything seems harder: it's harder to breathe, it's harder to run, harder to see. I'm repeating her name over and over and over as I picture her body hitting the waves, her body weightlessly sinking beneath the surface, dress floating around her, bubbles escaping her mouth.

But I did everything right, right? She was better, I did everything Wiki told me, everything Google told me, everything Dr Pepper told me. What if I didn't fix her, what if . . .? I can't think of the what ifs. Why aren't I fitter? Faster? I push myself; I run faster than I have in years, Jen's name circling my thoughts of her, my beautiful wife.

Chapter Eighty-Five

Jennifer

'Jesus, Jen!' Kerry grabs hold of my shoulder and shakes me. *'Come on, Jen, enough is enough.'* I look down to where parts of the cliff have begun to tumble into the sea. My feet are dangerously close to the edge.

I blink.

Like a sharp click of fingers in front of me, I picture my family. Ed as he opens his eyes first in the morning, the lazy half focus as he sees my face; Oscar's face looming in front of me as he jumps on top of us, warm and smelling of sleep; Hailey pushing her glasses up her nose and smiling at me as I peer around the corner of her bedroom, telling her just one more page before she sleeps. The images come faster and faster: Oscar sneezing his cereal all over the kitchen table, Hailey bouncing on the trampoline, me and Ed sneaking Christmas presents down from the attic, stifling giggles in case we wake up the kids, the feel of Oscar's hands around my neck as I carry him to bed, the excitement on Hailey's face as she places her tooth beneath the pillow. Faster and faster the images come, Oscar peddling his tricycle – tongue sticking out of the corner of his mouth in concentration – Hailey sliding down a slide – knickers showing as her dress billows around her, Ed fixing a flat tyre – oil smudged across his cheek, Hailey with flushed cheeks, 1st prize sticker on her chest at sports day, Ed shivering and putting his coat around my shoulders, the three of them holding hands while they jump over waves, Oscar chasing Hailey with a frog . . . More and more memories come, until my eyes flash open. My chest is rising and falling heavily, the smile on my face, the hunger to see them making my feet step backwards from the edge.

'You have to let me go.'

I nod.

The love and joy I felt moments ago battles with the loss to come. A flicker of fear runs through me, fear of the visceral pain of grief and guilt that haunted me in the months after she died, that has been burning away inside me for over a year, but with a hiss, the flicker of fear is extinguished: wet fingers pinching a flame. My grief isn't going to start again, this isn't a new death . . . this is just my chance to say goodbye, to start living, for my life to begin again.

'*Goodbye, Jen.*' She kisses the inside of my palm, my hand dropping back towards my side as she takes another step back. '*Tell squirt that adding a blob of PVA glue to his bubble mixture will make it magic, tell Hailey to add a quarter of a Bazooka bubble gum . . . that got me a twenty-five . . . but shush . . .*' She winks. '*Don't tell Mum.*' She steps back a little further. '*And Jen? Be nice to Nessa's new girlfriend . . . she'll want your approval.*' My sister opens her arms and grins at me. '*And . . . give Ed a kiss from me!*'

She winks, and before I can stop her, before I can grab her hand, her body is flying backwards. Her eyes – bright and determined – stay focused on me. Her feet and arms are in front of her, as though she is just trying to touch her toes: red coat, red boots and a flash of green.

The ocean lies beneath her; it throws back the cool, green cover and welcomes her into its embrace.

'Goodbye, Kerry,' I whisper.

I stare at the water below, picturing her body slowly descending, her hair pulled around her like a halo, as she sinks past the blues and greens, the sunrise flickering light through the seaweed, until finally sinking into the dark, her face peaceful and calm.

The sun is coming up; the wind is cold and fresh against the tears on my skin. I take a deep breath – the smell of the sea and the peat of the earth is rich: I feel alive. My skin is covered in goose bumps, my skin tinged purple beneath them, but I'm smiling.

I turn my back on the sea and the cliff, on the grief and guilt that I've been drowning in, and break into a run: my life is about to begin again.

Chapter Eighty-Six

Ed

The path leans around a corner, my calves are burning, why am I even noticing this? I look towards the bend but someone crashes into me, full force. It takes a second to register that it's Jen, that she's in my arms as we slip, our bodies a flash of green and denim as we half roll, half slide down the path.

Jen is on top of me, both of us startled, both of us rubbing our heads . . . and she is laughing. She sits up, kissing every part of my face, as I try to talk, my words swallowed by her lips.

'I thought—' I begin.

'I love you.'

'I thought—' I try again.

'So much—'

'Why were you—'

But the sentence is taken from my mouth with hers, the fear I felt being dismissed by the warmth of her, by the 'aliveness' of her. Is that even a word? Eventually, her kisses stop and I manage to speak as we stand, both of us shivering, both of us dazed.

I pull her towards me and hold her face in my hands. 'What were you thinking?' I ask, searching her face for answers.

'I . . .' She shivers again, and I pull off my jacket and put it around her shoulders. 'I wanted to see the sunrise.'

'Why didn't you wake me?'

'I needed to say goodbye. I needed to say goodbye to Kerry. Properly.'

'Is she back?' I ask; I almost look around.

She shakes her head with a sad smile. 'No . . . she's gone.' Her voice is solid; it doesn't waver, despite her shivers. 'But I'm not.' She leans forward and says this to me as if it's a revelation, her tone the same as it was when she said 'I'm pregnant', when she said 'Yes', when she said 'I do'. An answer beyond dispute, her voice certain and sure.

'I thought you'd, that you were going to—'

She stops, holds my hands in hers, kisses my knuckles and then stares into my eyes.'I know I haven't been myself; I know I've put you through hell, Ed. But I'm getting better, I'm almost there. I can see why now, why I'm still here: Kerry gave me a gift when she died, she gave me the gift of life, and I'm the luckiest woman alive because I get to spend it with you.' She grimaces. 'Christ, that was a cheesy line.'

I grin at her. 'Cheesy lines are my favourite.'

Epilogue

Kerry

The day I was born, it was snowing. It was March, it was unusual, but then again, so was I. A baby born to a couple who thought they were infertile. Two days later and the weather had turned; it was a warm spring day. Mum liked to say that I melted the snow and brought her daffodils.

But I have my own theory.

My sister Jennifer was waiting for me. She looked down into the Moses basket and kissed my forehead.

'Is she mine?' she had asked my parents.

'Yes,' they had answered, smiling indulgently at each other: our family is complete; aren't we lucky?

Jen was there if I had a nightmare, my three-year-old mind conjuring shadows in the dark, somehow knowing before my screams erupted from my mouth, climbing into the bed with me, telling me stories and chasing the demons away.

My sister was there, sat at the table, while I struggled to read the letters that were always jumbled up, backwards, jumping over the page, telling me not to panic, to take my time, that I would get there.

My parents used to say I was their miracle, but I wasn't. Jen was the miracle. Jen could have been given to any family, but she came to ours; she was our gift. When I was with her,

I never felt awkward or out of place because I was 'Jen's sister'. I loved that. Dad always introduced me as 'Jennifer's sister, Kerry' . . . words like sun on sand.

Then the day came when she met Edward. This awkwardly good-looking man that stepped into our house, into our world, as though he had always been there. I had never been there to protect Jen the way that she had protected me, but when he walked into her life, I felt like I had lost my chance, lost my chance to look after her, to give her back the gift that she had always given me.

It's raining and we've come into town for Nessa's engagement ring. I'm wearing my favourite boots, they're red leather and fit like they were made just for me. Jen is talking but I'm distracted: I'm thinking of Nessa and what if she doesn't say yes. We stop at a zebra crossing; the rain is hammering down, there are droplets rolling along the red of my boots, onto the pavement. A car has sped past us, splashing Jen's jeans, but she hasn't noticed, she's describing the way to the jeweller's with her hands – she's always done that, her hands move as much as her lips when she's talking – and her focus is drawn across the road towards her left, which she is gesturing to. The green light flashes; she's still looking in the direction of the jeweller's, still talking as my foot takes a step forward.

But a car is approaching: one wiper is working furiously but the other remains rigid; the car's speed is constant, no hint of slowing down. It's a moment, a split second where my brain processes the pieces of jigsaw that are making the whole, a split second to make the decision . . . but it's not a decision really, it's the way it was always meant to be. My hand punches out and connects with my sister's chest; this movement fills me with euphoria . . . this is it, the thing that has been missing my whole life, the thing that is right.

The car hits, the brakes scream: too late, too late, too late. The pain is like lightning, my body on fire. I'm weightless, the sound of screeching brakes becoming quieter, the raindrops no longer cold on my body, the scream of my sister rolling into an applause as I watch her.

Is this it? My life flashing before my eyes?

Jen's face fills my vision as she watches my feet skating across the ice, my legs jumping, my body spinning, her cheeks pink from the cold, her mouth always smiling and cheering in my direction. As my outfits change and my jumps become higher and more elaborate, so do Jen's shouts and cheers, the gap forming between her front teeth, her face becoming more beautiful with every year that passed. My memories continue as my back hits the pavement: Jen's watchful glances across the playground as I tried to fit in with the popular crowd, always trying that bit too hard, not quite funny enough, not quite pretty enough. As the air leaves my lungs, I see how she looks at Nessa, how she knows as I did that she was the one. I watch Ed and my niece and nephew jumping over waves, the sun shining on their sandy feet and sunburnt shoulders.

The sound of Jen's screams fades away, and the ground beneath my body falls. I'm five years old: Jen's hands are holding mine as we spin around on the ice, our laughter holding us in a bubble as the world around us blurs, only one face holding my focus.

My sister . . . the love of my life.

Acknowledgements

What a journey this book has been on! And before I start to thank all of the wonderful people who have helped form Jen and Ed's story, I would firstly like to thank you. Over the past three years, I have been overwhelmed by the responses to my books. We all lead such busy lives and I can't begin to tell you how grateful I am to the readers who take the time to leave a review, who drop me a message on my social media platforms or recommend my books to friends and family. You are the reason I keep writing on the days when I would rather be eating chocolate and watching Netflix. So thank you, truly, from the bottom of my heart.

Now on to my team. As I always do, I shall start by thanking my agent Amanda Preston, without whom, this book would never have been written. It may surprise you to know that this book started off as a short story for a magazine. I sent it over to Amanda, made a cup of coffee and when I picked up my phone there were three missed calls and an email saying, 'call me now!!' The phone call that followed, and began with, 'It's not a short story. . . this is your next book. I'm a little in love with Jennifer Jones', transformed what had been a short story scribbled in a notebook while Mr Emma sorted out a leaking toilet in our caravan, into the book you have in your hands. To say I would be lost without her is an understatement, she is my rock. Wider thanks go to the whole LBA team, thank you for your advice and votes, you make my decision making a whole lot easier!

To the dream team at Headline. A huge thank you to my editor, Jennifer Doyle. I honestly couldn't have written this novel without your instinct and guidance as well as your constant patience and understanding. You go above and beyond with your endless support, always replying to my emails even when the contents of which can often be an incoherent stream of ideas and questions, thank you for everything. Thank you to Katie Sunley, editor extraordinaire, who is a constant support and works incredibly hard to keep my books on track. I'm in awe of your calm and considered approach. . . I want to be you when I grow up! To Alara Delfosse, I would be lost without your brilliant publicist magic, and box-set recommendations – you are amazing. Thank you to Ellie Morley, champion of *When Harry Met Sally* gifs. I'm so grateful to you for your creativity and support and for answering my 'suggestions' with enthusiasm, even when I need reigning in. . . just a tiny bit.

To Emma Rogers for my breath-taking cover, it will always hold a very special place in my heart, thank you for capturing the essence of Jennifer's story.

To all at ILA who work so hard on my behalf, seeing your book being translated into so many different languages is one of the most wonderful feelings a writer can have, thank you for everything. . . you changed my life.

I have to give a very special mention to my wonderful friend and writing buddy Nicki Smith, who has had her own incredible writing journey culminating with a book out with Oxford University Press this year. Thank you for always being there for me, for your endless generosity and company. Long shall we forget each other's birthdays and continue to have the same topics of conversations – which celebs we currently have a crush on and how much weight we have put on/lost – long into our eighties. I truly would be lost without you.

To the writing community whose unwavering support and companionship keep me sane. A special thanks go to The Fiction Café, The Savvy Writers' Snug and the Chick Lit and Prosecco Facebook groups.

The biggest of squeezes go to the book blogging community. These wonderful people spend hours and hours of their own time, writing reviews and sharing book love. The publishing business would not survive without the generosity of book bloggers and I am hugely grateful to them all. A special mention goes to Anne Cater, Linda Hill, Rachel Gilbey, and Em Digs Books, thank you.

I'm raising a large gin to Josie Silver, Kim Nash, Caroline Hulse, N J Simmonds, Emma Jackson and Claire Ashley who are always there to listen, cheer and support. . . thank you, you all blooming rock.

At the time of writing these acknowledgements, we are currently under lockdown. Never have I missed the hugs of my friends and family so much. I miss you all, I know virtual hugs are not the same but here's one from me anyway.

Lockdown does mean that I have all four of my children and Mr Emma at home. It is probably the only time in my life that I will have you all to myself and for that I am very grateful; you're all my favourites.

REVIEW